NEVER SAY DIE

A list of titles by James Patterson appears at the
back of this book

JAMES PATTERSON
& MIKE LUPICA

NEVER SAY
DIE

C

CENTURY

CENTURY

UK | USA | Canada | Ireland | Australia
India | New Zealand | South Africa

Century is part of the Penguin Random House group of companies
whose addresses can be found at global.penguinrandomhouse.com

Penguin Random House UK,
One Embassy Gardens, 8 Viaduct Gardens, London SW11 7BW

penguin.co.uk
global.penguinrandomhouse.com

Penguin
Random House
UK

First published 2025
002

Printed and bound in Great Britain by Clays Ltd, Elcograf S.p.A.

The authorised representative in the EEA is Penguin Random House Ireland,
Morrison Chambers, 32 Nassau Street, Dublin D02 YH68

A CIP catalogue record for this book is available from the British Library

ISBN: 978–1–529–92239–4 (hardback)
ISBN: 978–1–529–92240–0 (trade paperback)

NEVER SAY
DIE

ONE

JIMMY CUNNIFF AND I are inside the shooting range at the Maidstone Gun Club a little after seven in the morning. For a change, we're shooting at targets and not at people. Even better, the targets aren't shooting back.

As ex-NYPD cops, Jimmy and I have long competed at shooting ranges. With rare exceptions, we've been better shots than the bad guys we've encountered along the way.

Jimmy still feels the need to remind me that he thinks he's better than I am. I now feel almost obligated to remind *him* that in my humble opinion, nobody's better than I am.

"We're still just talking about guns here, right?" he asks.

"Among other things," I say.

I smile sweetly at my partner. And he's not *that* kind of partner, not now and not ever. I'm a criminal defense attorney, he's my investigator and indispensable right-hand man, in addition to being the best friend I've ever had, or maybe anybody has ever had.

Like me, he's also a survivor. At least for now.

It wasn't so terribly long ago that we both survived a late-night shootout that turned the Walking Dunes of Montauk, out near land's end on eastern Long Island, into the OK Corral. One of the shooters somehow managed to get away. The other wasn't quite as lucky.

Jimmy and I aren't here at Maidstone Gun getting ready

for the next time. Neither one of us wants a next time, even though way too many people have been shooting—at both of us—since I began defending a local real estate guy named Rob Jacobson accused of committing his first triple homicide.

Yeah, that's right.

His first.

Of two.

If that sounds like some kind of record, it probably is. People keep telling me I sure can pick 'em. But then no one has ever confused my line of work, or Jimmy's, with church.

The gun club is in Wainscott, about twenty minutes west of where I live. The place has been shuttered for a couple of years because of a beef with the town fathers, mostly from neighbors who got tired of the soundtrack of their lives sounding way too much like an action movie. Now the rifle range and the clubhouse, with its covered porch and big-game trophies inside, looks like some kind of deserted movie set.

Of course Jimmy, who seems to know practically everybody in this part of Long Island, still has a key and the code that got us through the electronic gate on Northwest Harbor Road and past the sign that actually reads: ABSOLUTELY NO ARMOR-PIERCING AMMUNITION. Words to live by, as far as we're concerned.

But I do dearly hate to lose, almost as much as I hate Jimmy's Yankees, being a Mets girl and all. I hate to lose at anything, one of the reasons why they call me Jane Effing Smith.

One of many.

As we get ready to begin today's competition, I am singing the old Aerosmith song "Janie's Got a Gun."

"Janie's got a gun, her whole world's come undone . . ."

"Well, maybe not her whole world," Jimmy adds. "Just this little corner of it."

"You continue to forget something, Cunniff," I say. "I never lose."

"Well, not on the big things."

"You mean like cancer?"

"Yeah, that's exactly what I mean."

"To be determined," I tell him.

"Shut up and shoot," he says.

"Is that your way of telling me to stop singing?"

"Not unless you want me to shoot myself," Jimmy Cunniff says.

We're each using a state-of-the-art gun, a Sig Sauer P320 XCompact. And because this is part of an ongoing competition between two ex-NYPD cops, we're using a clock. Cops use clocks. Ours beeps when we start the timer, telling Jimmy or me it's time to draw our weapon, in what would theoretically be a shootout on the street. Or in an alley. Or even on the Walking Dunes of Montauk.

The clock doesn't stop until after the last shot has been fired.

Jimmy has already set up a rack with a half-dozen steel target plates—six inches in diameter, three-eighths of an inch thick—that he's spray-painted black to more easily determine the location of the hit. The steel is sturdy enough to occasionally withstand a bullet strike without tipping over.

When I leave a target standing, Jimmy usually tells me I shoot like a girl.

"Yeah," I say. "Calamity Jane."

It was what my father the ex-Marine used to call me when he started taking me to the range. I'd say it was right after I stopped playing with dolls. But the only way I would have ever played with dolls is if there had been an Officer Barbie. And probably not even then.

As the leadoff shooter, I step back ten yards from the plates—it doesn't seem like much, but it's the proper distance to test accuracy with even a fancy handgun—and wait for Jimmy to start the clock.

In civilian shooting competitions, missed shots are awarded

zero points. Cops who miss *lose* points, then get smack-talked all the way to the parking lot. Or back to the squad room in the old days.

"When cops miss what they're aiming at," Jimmy says as he sets the timer, "they might hit grandma by mistake."

"Or maybe, say, a client?" I ask him, grinning.

"Don't give me any ideas about that bottom-feeder we're defending," he says, then asks if I'm ready.

I take a big deep breath, let the air out slowly, trying to get my adrenaline under control.

"Armed and ready."

"At least you didn't give me that cheesy line about being born ready."

"No effing way," I say.

I hear the beep and raise the P320 and start firing away.

Six for six.

They all go down.

But even after the last one is down, I want to keep going, reload until I'm out of ammunition and my hand can no longer squeeze the trigger.

I want everything in my life to be this easy. Aim and fire.

I want to stop feeling the way I've felt for the past eight months, that I'm the one with the target on my back.

TWO

JIMMY MATCHES ME WHEN it's his turn, shot for shot, six for six. We're just getting started. I finally edge ahead of him in the fifth round when he misses the last target.

"Oops," I say. "Down goes grandma."

"She had a good life," Jimmy says.

He's smiling. So am I.

"You can't even beat a cancer patient," I say. "Sad."

That wipes the smile off his face, but then this particular subject always does.

"You know I don't like playing that game," he says.

"Trust me," I say. "Neither do I."

Truth is, I had already been having a day, and it isn't even eight o'clock in the morning. Sometimes I get so sick between rounds of chemo that I'm up most of the night. Sometime around four, I drop off to sleep for a couple of hours, only to be awakened by my alarm at six.

Never mind that I almost called Jimmy to cancel. I arrived at the range, trying to act more energetic than the creature that inspired my mother's childhood nickname for me: Hummingbird. He worries enough about me already, telling me every chance he gets that I'm going to get better, and that even if I die, it will be over his own dead body.

He stops reracking the targets and gives me a long look, as if he's getting ready to interview a perp. "Tell me something straight, even if you are a lawyer," he says, as if reading my mind, something he does with annoying frequency. "You sure you got another trial in you?"

"No doubt."

"No bull is what I was hoping for," he says.

"You should know better than anyone that the code never changes with me," I say. "Live to work, work to live."

I don't add, *or die trying.* Frankly, I don't like playing that game, either.

He wins a round, the sixth, when I finally miss. But I come back and beat him one last time, because we both know I'm not leaving on a loss.

"Rematch?" Jimmy asks.

"As much as I would like to beat your butt all the livelong day, I've got to get to the courthouse to meet with my new jury consultant, remember?"

Across an undefeated career in court, I've hardly ever used jury consultants. Certainly not for Rob Jacobson's first trial, where he was acquitted.

Now he's about to stand trial in Nassau County, next one over from Suffolk. Different county, but same charge: the shooting deaths of an entire family — father, teenage daughter, and her mother, whom Jacobson had known back in high school.

This time around, the evidence against him is even worse. Katherine Welsh, the new Nassau County district attorney, is leading the prosecution. Just two days ago, on the eve of jury selection, we were informed of a piece of evidence that had magically, like a baby being left on the estimable Ms. Welsh's doorstep, shown up at her office: a time-stamped photograph of our client leaving the victims' house the night of the murders.

I pleaded with Judge Michael Horton for a continuance, to allow me and Jimmy time to investigate; bless his heart, he gave us two weeks. That same day, I broke down and hired a jury consultant. Just being realistic, this might turn out to be the last big case of my career and to win it, I was going to need all the help I could get.

"So you're still going to meet with Queen Elizabeth?" Jimmy says.

It's what he's taken to calling the consultant, a woman named Norma Banks. Norma admits to being eighty-three, but I think she's dropped a few years the way people drop excess pounds.

"Come on, I know she's old," I tell Jimmy. "But she's not dead."

"Yet," he says. "I was you, I'd drive fast to Mineola, just to be on the safe side."

THREE

IT'S A HIKE TO the courthouse, just under eighty miles. I once mentioned to Jimmy that a trip across Long Island should be measured not in miles, but dog years.

"Don't ever say that in front of Rip," Jimmy said, "on account of how far he is past his sell-by date."

Rip is my dog. I really did think he was a goner when I took him in as a stray and named him "R.I.P." Now, because of tender loving care from the man of my dreams—Dr. Ben Kalinsky, who happens to be the top veterinarian on the South Fork—Rip shows signs of outliving us all.

It's actually kind of funny. Eight months after being told I had a year to live, starting another round of chemo so soon before the start of my next trial, gallows humor has pretty much become my default position.

I promised Norma Banks I would meet her at the Supreme Court building, Nassau County, at eleven o'clock, traffic on the Long Island Expressway and Northern State permitting. She's taking the Long Island Rail Road from New York Penn Station. Her apartment in the West Village is not far from mine, though when she moved in Nixon was president. Or maybe FDR.

The SiriusXM channel devoted to Billy Joel, a good Long Island boy, is now back by popular demand, but I switch to

Doctor Radio, where I keep hoping to hear news of a cure for my cancer, neck and head.

The dream of scooping my oncologist isn't feeling so realistic today, so I tune out the doctors and go back to rock 'n' roll. As shitty as I feel, I'm ready to put this last round of chemo in the rearview mirror, as if I were recovering from a bad breakup, or a midlife crisis. I need my focus to be squarely on the upcoming trial.

Judge Michael Horton—I keep wanting to call him Jordan, because he reminds me of Michael Jordan, and is almost as tall, having been a shooting guard in college himself—knows what I'm dealing with, no reason to keep it a secret from him.

He hasn't told the media that my "situation" was another factor in his decision to delay the trial. And District Attorney Katherine Welsh didn't contest the continuance, to her credit. I'm more than happy to accept their help on this particular matter. Just not their sympathy, theirs or anybody else's.

It's worth mentioning that Katherine, who's both Harvard undergrad and Law, is younger than I am, taller, prettier, and, as far as I know, healthy as a horse.

That bitch.

Only now jury selection is staring me in the face, even as I'm pulling out of a brutal round of chemo—something else I think should be measured in dog years, mostly because it makes me sick as one.

Am I going to be ready to start picking a jury?

Armed and ready.

I'm getting off the Northern State and onto the Meadowbrook when I do decide to tune in to Doctor Radio. Somehow, though, I hit the wrong button and land on a talk show.

And immediately wish I hadn't.

Before I can switch away from it, I hear the voice of

someone who's clearly the host saying, "Rob Jacobson, can that really be you on our caller line?"

Please don't be him.

But the next voice I hear does belong to my client.

Shit shit shit. On a stick.

"The man, the legend," Jacobson says. "Accept no substitutes, Paul."

"Thanks for reaching out," the host says. "So what's on your mind today?"

"Obviously *nothing* is on his freaking mind," I say out loud in the car.

Then I'm pounding my left hand on the horn, causing the car next to me to swerve and nearly sideswipe me.

"Well," Jacobson says, "we could talk about the homeless crisis in New York City, or if this is finally the year for the Knicks, but I thought you might want to talk about my upcoming trial."

Behind the wheel, I am shaking my head and still talking to myself.

"I know you can't hear me, Rob," I say. "But you really are a *raging* fucking asshole."

For the next ten minutes, ten minutes that seem to last longer than both my marriages combined, my client proceeds to do something I specifically ordered him not to do:

Talk about the trial.

Not to the media, not to the members of his family still speaking to him, not to any friends he might have left, not to any of his many girls on the side. Not even to the DoorDash guy bringing him his food in the house he's been renting a couple of miles from mine in Amagansett, while he's under house arrest.

Yet here he is, talking to Paul, whoever the hell Paul is.

Proclaiming his innocence. Telling the listening audience that there's even less of a case against him this time than there was the last time, when in fact the opposite is true. Even saying "Bring it on" when he references Katherine Welsh, the woman who is trying to put him away for life.

"I am so anxious to get my day in court," he says, "I wish it were today."

He pauses, then adds, "What can I tell you, Paul? The witch hunt against me continues. If I didn't know any better, I'd start to think I was a politician."

Somehow my client saves the best for last, after reminding the host that he's once again being defended by the great Jane Smith, whom he calls "The Hamptons Lawyer" and describes as the "undefeated heavyweight champion of the world."

"And let me make it clear that I'm not really talking about her weight," he says. I hear him chuckle. But then he's always cracking himself up, even when under indictment. "If you happen to be listening, Janie," he says. "Love you, babe."

Babe.

I'm banging on the horn again then. This time the driver of the car next to me, a guy, turns and gives me the finger.

I give it right back.

He'll never know it isn't directed at him, or that when I scream out "Asshole!" this time, that isn't directed at him, either.

I drive faster.

FOUR

THE COURTHOUSE HAS OFFERED me the use of an empty conference room for a couple of hours. But I see Norma Banks waiting on a park bench, smoking away.

I cross the street to the small park where she's sitting, looking trim and fit for someone her age, sucking on what my father used to call a heater.

"The little snots wouldn't let me smoke inside the building," she says as her form of greeting.

"The nerve."

I sit, trying to position myself upwind of her on the small bench. She might be a couple of inches over five feet tall, soft white hair that looks as if it sprouted from a cotton tree, accentuated by a pink sweater and blue jeans and running shoes colored both pink and blue.

She knows about my illness—and about my ongoing hope of being a permanent survivor of it. But I have this feeling that if I ask her to stop puffing away, she'll tell me it's a little late for me to be clutching my pearls over secondhand smoke.

Norma Banks just smiles, mostly with eyes the color of the sky.

"Don't tell me. You quit smoking a long time ago."

"I was one of those naïve people who didn't write off the surgeon general as being an alarmist," I say.

"Your loss."

But I smile back at her.

"By the way," I say. "Thanks for agreeing to work with me."

"About time you called me," Norma Banks says. "I was wondering when you were going to wake the fuck up."

I instantly experience her well-known ability to read jurors even after they've been selected—not using technology, only those blue eyes and her fierce intelligence and her instincts.

Neither her age nor her granny looks, however, alter the fact that Norma Banks was—and is—one of the most prominent jury consultants in the country. She's worked with everybody from New York City mob lawyers to big-ticket show-business attorneys in Hollywood. Every time there is a big trial, she hits the talk-show circuit, though after dropping a couple of f-bombs on Court TV, she's learned to watch her language.

Having turned down the chance to work with O. J. Simpson's Dream Team, she memorably commented on-air to CNN: "If the gloves don't fit you must acquit my ass."

Katherine Welsh has enough forensics to make them party favors. She has a murder weapon with Rob Jacobson's prints everywhere except inside the gun barrel. And now—Jimmy Cunniff said this was piling on—she has the photograph of him leaving the house that night.

My client continues to say it was all a setup. As you can imagine, I get a lot of that in my line of work. But he's not the reason I'm skeptical about the State's case against Rob Jacobson. The reason I'm skeptical goes back to something my father told me one time.

"You want to know the only sure thing in this world?" he said. "That there *are* no sure things."

"You know you got lucky with this guy the first time around," Norma Banks tells me now.

She reaches into the ancient leather bag next to her, grabs

a red-and-white Marlboro box. It was my father's brand, too. He was another one who thought that warning on the side of the boxes was for suckers until he dropped dead of a heart attack on a barroom floor.

She lights another cigarette and inhales deeply and then sighs as if she might have briefly glimpsed God.

"With all due respect," I say to her, "I like to think I make my own luck."

"That's a load of bull and you know it," she says.

I am smiling again. I can't help myself.

"Are you under the impression that all of my previous cases somehow won themselves?" I ask her.

"And are *you* under the impression that you've been involved in more murder cases than I have?"

She blows some smoke in my direction. I move my head to the side to avoid it the way you'd slip a punch. At least she's blowing some kind of smoke at me.

"I know you think you're one tough mother," she says. "But it's my job to read people. And what I'm reading with you is that you're scared right out of your designer jeans."

"They're actually Levi's," I say. "But I see your larger point."

In the still air, she leans her head back and blows a perfect smoke ring.

"So we're clear?" Norma Banks says. "I think your client is guilty as balls."

The twinkle in her eyes makes her look much younger than I know she is.

"Is that going to be a problem for you?"

"If it's not for you, it's not for me," she says. "Now let's both of us stop screwing around here and get to work."

We're walking across the street to the courthouse when Jimmy Cunniff calls and without preamble, because there rarely is an ex-cop like him, reports facts he thinks worthy of landmark status. Rob Jacobson is at the family town house in

Manhattan, the place where his father and teenage mistress were shot to death when Jacobson was in high school.

"That's impossible," I say. "He's wearing a goddamn electronic monitoring device."

"Wore it all the way back to daddy's house, apparently."

"What can we do about that, unless they're already on their way to pick him up?"

"What *I'm* going to do is drive to the city and then drag him back out here," Jimmy says. "And not by his ankle, in case you were wondering."

I end the call, for the second time today feeling the urge to kill my own client.

"Don't tell me," Norma Banks says, as almost like a condemned woman, she finishes off one last Marlboro. "Your client did something stupid."

"Guilty," I say.

FIVE

Jimmy

NO MATTER HOW MANY times Jimmy has told Jane that Jacobson isn't worth it, he can't break through. And without confronting her, he can't for the life of him figure why she'd risk whatever time she might have left, because of the fucking cancer, on the likes of this guy, whether he's innocent or not.

Jimmy shouldn't have NYPD plates. But he does. He used to go out with a cute young woman from the Manhattan DMV, and she still takes care of him, this being one of his few relationships with women that didn't end in a dumpster fire. So he parks directly in front of Jacobson's Upper West Side town house and walks up the steps and rings the doorbell, jabbing it hard enough to drive it right through the wall.

A girl in a tight T-shirt lettered TALENTLESS and even tighter black exercise pants answers the door. She's barefoot. It's the middle of the day but the kid has what looks to be a glass of white wine in her hand.

"Can I help you?" she asks.

"Sure," Jimmy says. "We can start with you telling me how old you are."

"How old are you?"

Jimmy nods, ignores the question. "Dalton or Spence?"

Two Manhattan schools for snots like this.

"What are you," she asks, "the truant officer?"

She starts to shut the door. Jimmy holds it open.

"I'll do you one better," Jimmy says, pulling out his wallet and flashing one of his fake badges. "I'm a *police* officer."

"Shit," she says, then whips her head around and yells, "Rob, there's a cop here to see you."

While she's still looking up toward the second floor, Jimmy walks past her and into the foyer. A few seconds later, he sees Rob Jacobson making his way down the stairs as the girl runs past him the other way, spilling some of her wine as she does.

Jacobson is only wearing baggy gym shorts. He's got chicken legs, but surprises Jimmy with what are clearly trainer abs.

"Well, if it isn't fake detective Cunniff," Jacobson says pleasantly, and salutes.

But as soon as he reaches the landing, Jimmy quickly crosses the distance between them, grabs a fistful of the front of the shorts, and gives him a good squeeze.

Rob Jacobson makes a sound like a chew toy.

"I know," Jimmy says, still holding on. "I'm excited to see you, too."

Jimmy nearly knocks Jacobson down as he shoves him ahead and to the left into the living room, one that looks almost as big as the bar Jimmy owns in Sag Harbor, finally shoving him into the first soft piece of furniture they come to.

The bracelet, Jimmy sees, is still attached to Jacobson's ankle. The light on it is blinking, which means it's running out of battery power.

No shit, Jimmy thinks.

"You know being here violates your parole, right?" Jimmy says. "And can land you back in a jail cell for the duration of the trial. You know that, too, don't you?"

Jacobson gives a little shrug to his shoulders, and grins, trying to look as cocky as ever. It continues to make Jimmy Cunniff feel as if his own balls are being squeezed, practically on a daily basis, that he's working for the kind of lowlife he used to happily put away. The only difference with this one is his bank account.

"I just needed to get away for a few hours and blow off some steam," Jacobson says. "Have a little fun."

"With another high school girl?" Jimmy asks him. "She is in high school, isn't she?"

Jacobson grins. "They both are, as a matter of fact," he says. "But, hey, they're both going to graduate with honors."

"Maybe they can finally nail you on nailing underage girls once and for all," Jimmy says.

"They're both eighteen," Jacobson says. He grins again. "Unless they used a fake ID with me."

"What a guy," Jimmy says.

He resists the urge, and not for the first time, to slap the smirk right off his face, and permanently. They both know he won't fire him if he does, or Jane. Jane slapped him one time and she's still here. The reason is simple enough: Rob Jacobson needs both of them, whether he likes it or not. By now, you could write that in the stars.

"How'd you get around the bracelet?" Jimmy asks.

"I know a hacker," Jacobson says.

"Of course you do."

"He's not cheap, I can tell you that," Jacobson says. "But worth every penny. He got into the county system that creates the geofence. What he was doing was only stopgap, but for a day, he could expand my travel area for a hundred miles or so without a notification pinging somewhere."

"What a guy," Jimmy says again.

"The hacker guy?"

"No, you," Jimmy says. "Jane keeps laying it on the line for you, which happens to include even laying her life on the line. She gets you bail when nobody thought that was even remotely possible. And this is the thanks you give her."

"Hey, I love Janie. I even said so on the radio a little while ago."

Jimmy stands. "Go get some clothes on. I'll drive you back out east myself."

"Somehow you seem to keep forgetting that you work for me and not the other way around," Jacobson says.

Jimmy walks over to the couch and leans down, close enough that his nose is practically touching Rob Jacobson's perfect nose.

"Do I have to greet you all over again?" he says in a quiet voice. "Just nod if you're hearing me."

Jacobson nods.

"And before we leave," Jimmy says, still right on top of him, "I need you to do me a favor with those girls upstairs."

"And what might that be?"

"Try not to kill them," Jimmy says.

They're just through the Midtown Tunnel when there's an incoming call on Jimmy's phone. He sees on his dashboard screen that it's from Jane.

But when he answers he hears a woman's voice saying, "This is Norma Banks."

"You're the jury consultant," Jimmy says. "But why are you calling me on Jane's phone?"

"She told me to call you," she says. "We just got to the hospital."

SIX

"YOUR GIRL WAS PISSED at me for calling 911," Norma says to Jimmy, "once she came to, that is."

Jimmy and Norma and Rip the dog and I are in my living room, all of us having finished the burgers and fries Jimmy had picked up for us at Rowdy Hall.

Jimmy and Norma had cold beers with theirs. I drank one of the many bottles of water I've consumed since Norma and I left the hospital.

The emergency room doctor at the NYU Langone Hospital in Mineola ran a battery of tests and concluded that what had happened was almost entirely due to dehydration, something about which I still occasionally get careless, and released me.

"That's bullshit that it was just hydration," Norma says to Jimmy. "It was stress, too."

She has eventually stopped pouting that I won't let her smoke in the house.

"Add some fatigue in there, too," Jimmy says, "from having to keep looking over her shoulder all the time."

"Look who's talking," I say.

On his way to my house, Jimmy dropped Rob Jacobson at his rental with a warning: until the trial starts, if he travels farther than the end of the driveway, Jimmy will call his parole officer himself.

"You'd actually do that?" Rob asked him.

"While wearing a party hat," Jimmy said.

Even though I've already killed two bad guys since taking on Rob Jacobson's defense, Jimmy and I both know there are still too many out there, and very much unaccounted for, and that if I start listing them now, starting with Rob's own son, Eric, it would sound as if I were calling the roll on a dirtbag parade.

I give a shake to my head now and tell myself to stop thinking about them, or the world might once again start spinning on me the way it did at the courthouse.

For the next hour or so, we do manage to talk about the trial and not fainting spells. Well, Norma does most of the talking, turning over an unlit Marlboro in her right hand, while Jimmy and I listen. She's started out by detailing her jury wish list.

"Since none of us has Human Resources to worry about," she says, "let me tell you two that we don't want any blue-collar workers and the whiter the jury the better. And I mean whiter than Wonder Bread."

"Is that even still a thing?" Jimmy asks.

She glares at him and continues. "We want white people in that box, and we want people with money in their pockets. Clarence Darrow once said that most jury trials come down to rich versus poor."

I see Jimmy grinning. Maybe he just wants her to know she doesn't scare him. "I heard you dated him," he says.

He is seated next to her. Norma Banks turns and pinches his bare upper arm enough to turn it red.

"Hey, that hurt," he says.

"No worries, kid," she says. "It just means I like you."

I lean back in my chair, afraid that if I close my eyes, I might fall asleep. It's been a long day, and they're only going to get longer once the trial starts. Jimmy says he'll take Rip out for his last walk of the day. Norma is going to stay the night in my guest room, so we can get up and do work together in the morning.

"One more question about the kind of jury we want," Jimmy says. "Do we want more men or more women deciding about our guy Rob?"

"Women," she says, without any hesitation.

"Even with somebody like him?" Jimmy asks.

"Especially with somebody like him," Norma says.

"He's a very bad boy, Norma," I say.

"That's what I'm talking about," she says, her bright blue eyes practically gleeful.

SEVEN

MARTIN ELIAN LOOKS AROUND his restaurant, Café Martin, every table occupied, the main room noisy but not too noisy, the soundtrack really one of life and fun.

Comme le Seigneur l'a voulu, he thinks.

As the Lord intended.

And Martin knows he should be happy about this, happy about business being good again after he nearly lost everything, first because of COVID, and later because of his gambling, and the mountain of debt both had created.

He promised himself he would stop gambling for good after the very bad men to whom he owed money had threatened to kill him. That was before he saw on the news that his ex-wife, Jane, killed one of those men, even if she hadn't done it for him.

Now the restaurant is back on its feet and so is he.

But for how long?

When he started gambling again, he told himself this time he would only do it in moderation. But Martin Elian is self-aware enough to know that this is an addiction with him the way beautiful women always have been, even when he was still married to Jane Smith.

When he had started betting again, small at first, he had done it legally, with FanDuel and DraftKings, where you could only lose what you put in. He told himself that this was just a way of scratching the itch, and that he would never again put himself into the position of gambling away the restaurant.

But then, after an early hot streak, he started to lose. Not all of his profits from Café Martin. But enough that he started betting with bookies again, thinking it was the best way for him to get even, and fast. Just this one last time. And not with his old bookie on Long Island. A new one in the city.

As much as he hated what he was doing, he knew it was more than just the familiar thrill of the action. There had always been a different kind of thrill for him, when he first started betting on sports, the danger of working with men he knew worked for the mob, making it even more of a guilty pleasure.

But once he got behind, the vicious cycle started up all over again. And then, almost like the natural order of things, he was borrowing from the same people with whom he was placing his bets.

Again.

Now he is more than just behind.

Martin Elian is drowning.

And knows a visit is coming, another part of the natural order of things for people with a problem like his. He just doesn't know when.

FanDuel and DraftKings don't send people around when you start losing with them. The only debt is your own. You're betting your own money, not theirs.

He remembered reading a magazine article by a reporter in Los Angeles who said anyone opening a restaurant wasn't just a chef or a business manager. They were gamblers, too, placing huge bets on themselves.

Toute la vie est un pari.

All of life is a gamble, that is what he keeps telling himself. Only his gambling is controlling him all over again, and not the other way around. He can't shake the image inside his head: taking the kind of money coming in tonight with one hand and with the other handing it over to the men who are essentially his bankers. Just bankers with far more punitive interest rates.

As he surveys the busy main room once again, he sees the man who's kept eyes on Martin since he was seated at one of the window tables.

The man is eating alone, but now he's motioning Martin over.

Now he feels a chill come over him, fearful that this has become a different kind of big night for him at Café Martin.

The man is wearing what Martin, who prides himself on knowing men's fashion, can see is an expensive navy suit, one that fits him so well Martin wonders if it has been made for him. White shirt. Tie the same color as the suit.

He has already finished his dinner, Martin's own signature foie gras appetizer and the most expensive steak on the menu. Now there is only a glass of brandy on the white tablecloth. The man takes a sip, even that simple motion measured with the extreme precision of a surgeon.

Martin has already checked the reservation sheet.

Robby Sassoon is the man's name.

Not Robert.

Robby.

It makes Martin think of the Sassoon Salon on Fifth Avenue where he used to go to have his hair colored. Not dyed. Just colored, to get the combination of black and flecks of gray just right.

Martin reluctantly moves across the room, nodding to some regulars as he does, then extends his hand to Robby Sassoon.

Sassoon smiles warmly as he shakes it, as if greeting an old friend. He has close-cropped dark hair, eyes pale as the color of water, skin that is almost as pale. Martin can't help noticing that Sassoon's nails are polished to a gleam.

"Arrêtez les conneries au travail," Robby Sassoon says.

The accent is flawless, but that is not what makes Martin flinch.

It's the man's choice of words.

Let's cut the shit and get down to business.

"Was there something wrong with your food?" Martin asks defensively.

"Quite the contrary," Sassoon says. "The food was delicious, as I expected it to be. I have to say, Martin, that you're quite an excellent chef, for a dead man."

Martin hears someone call his name from across the room. He turns and manages to wave absently in the general direction, without even seeing where the voice came from, or caring. But he remains frozen in place at Sassoon's table, this man threatening him in two languages, his choice of words as precise, as razor sharp, as everything else about him.

Sassoon is completely still as he keeps his smile fixed on Martin.

"Perhaps we should go downstairs to my office," Martin says, "where we can speak in private."

"Here is fine," Sassoon says.

As he takes another sip of his brandy, Martin sits down across from him, suddenly wanting a drink himself. He keeps his voice low as he says, "Listen, I know why you're here."

"I should have come around sooner," Sassoon says. "We were keeping an eye on you, Martin, even before you came back into the fold, when you were just dipping your toe into those places advertising incessantly on television."

"Wait...how do you know about that?" Martin asks him.

"We know everything about you," he says. "But what you didn't know is that the new people taking your action now are actually *our* people. We just didn't announce the merger to the media."

Martin feels as if he has been cornered in his own restaurant.

"Nothing to say?" Sassoon says. "You're not being a very affable host."

"I just need until the end of next week," Martin Elian says. "A friend is going to loan me the money I need."

Robby Sassoon's voice is barely above a whisper. "Don't lie to me, Martin," he says. "Or I will hurt you much worse than the others ever did."

Sassoon idly picks up the dessert menu before putting it back down next to his glass.

"You called me a dead man," Martin says. "But if I wasn't worth killing before, why now?"

"Just a figure of speech to get your attention," Sassoon says. "I've really come here tonight to let you in on how you can help me help you, if you can believe it."

Sassoon still hasn't raised his voice or changed expression. But there is something more frightening about this man than any of the others sent here before him. And something creepy.

The French word for that is *effrayant.*

"Tell me what you want me to do," he says, "and I'll do it, I swear."

"Well, first I want you to pay up," Sassoon says, "because this is the last warning, unless you want this restaurant, your pride and joy, to become our restaurant. And then I want you to tell any of your friends who like to gamble with the rent money what can happen if *they* don't pay in a prompt manner, just to save me the trouble of telling them myself. Can you do that for me, Martin?"

Somehow the man's voice sounds as if he is purring.

"Yes."

Martin's own voice sounds thick, hoarse.

"Tell them that while they like the dirty pleasure of

gambling with people like us," Sassoon continues, "they need to pay their debts, and promptly."

Sassoon raises his right hand then. Martin can't help himself. He flinches and feels himself redden.

But all Sassoon has done is reach across the table to pat him on top of his head.

"Dinner's on you," he says, then pushes back his chair, pats Martin on the head one more time, and walks out of Café Martin.

EIGHT

NORMA BANKS AND I finish our work by noon. We spend the morning talking more about the dream jury she'd like me to seat, the kind of technology and research she plans for the "whippersnappers" she has working for her, and she reminds me all over again that she doesn't come cheap.

"I'm not in this for the love of the game," she says but then, with the twinkle back in the eyes, adds, "Well, maybe a little bit."

While we're sitting in my car waiting for the Amagansett train to arrive, she says, "I've only been around you for a day, and even I can see you need to take better care of yourself."

"You sound like my mother."

"But one tough mother," she says.

Just like that, another Aerosmith line pops into my head.

"Nine lives," I sing, "feelin' lucky."

"Pretty sure you've gone blowing past nine by now," Norma says.

"But who's counting?" I ask.

She asks when we can next get together. I vaguely tell her in a few days, that I have to go out of town.

"You do know how soon jury selection starts, right?"

"I most certainly do."

"Am I allowed to ask where you're going?"

"No," I say.

She shakes her head. "The tough mother here is you, Hummingbird," she says.

Before she went to bed last night, I told her about my mother's love of hummingbirds, her nickname for me, one Norma has already adopted as her own.

We hear the train then. She gets out of the car. But before she walks up the steps to the platform, she leans through my open window and kisses me on the cheek.

"You take care," she says. "I mean it."

"See there," I say. "You do have a soft side."

"Don't let it get around," she says.

I am telling Dr. Ben Kalinsky all about Norma Banks as we take an early evening walk with Rip.

In this magic time between day and night, the sun has just set over Indian Wells Beach. There's hardly any wind tonight, just the sound of the waves, the whole scene convincing me all over again, not that I need much convincing, that our beaches are the most beautiful in the world. And this one beach, the closest to my house, is my favorite of all of them, making me want to live forever and not just for a few more months. Live happily ever after with this man, and this dog, and in this place.

I know I ought to be exhausted after what was another bad and restless night. But now I am almost hyper, doing even more talking than I usually do in the company of Ben Kalinsky.

"Funny story, by the way," I say as my lead-in on the trip to the emergency room yesterday, something I hadn't shared with him until right now.

"Yeah," he says when I finish. "I mean, who doesn't think a fainting spell isn't a laugh riot?"

Then he adds, "You wait a whole day to tell me about this?"

"I didn't want to worry you."

"It's a little late in the movie for that," he says.

I switch the subject back to Norma, and what an absolute pisser she is, how much I believe she's going to help me at trial.

"I'm telling you," I say. "This old broad is totally rizzed up."

"Rizzed up?"

"Means she has charisma, old-timer."

"And just where did you learn that expression?"

"Netflix, of course," I say.

We keep walking. Rip runs up ahead, occasionally chasing sandpipers, then comes racing back to us. I tell Ben about Rob Jacobson managing to take a day trip to the city without being violated, and how not knowing whether he might have murdered six people was still keeping me up nights, whether I was about to earn him another acquittal or not.

"And that's not even the worst part," I say. "Would you like to know what the worst part is?"

"Shush," he says.

I stop. He stops. Rip goes bounding back down the beach, through the waves, chasing more sandpipers across an open stretch of sand that the water hasn't quite reached.

"What did you just say?"

"I told you to shush," Dr. Ben says. "As in stop talking. As in zip it."

He is smiling at me. That smile worked for him the first time I met him and is still working just fine for him tonight.

"No one has ever shushed me," I say, "at least not as an adult-type person."

"Had to happen eventually," he says. "Somewhat like this."

Then he is suddenly kneeling in the sand and out of nowhere the last of the sun is reflecting off the diamond ring inside the blue velvet box he's just opened.

I don't shush him.

"You're the one with the words, so I'll keep this simple," Ben says. "Jane Smith, will you please effing marry me?"

NINE

ROBBY SASSOON LEANS OVER the roof of his rented car and watches them with his new Pulsar Merger binoculars. They're expensive, but worth it.

So am I, he thinks.

He has followed them here from her neighborhood, just beginning to get the lay of the land out here, learning her personal geography. Then he has waited for them to park and get out of his SUV along with the dog. When they're down on the beach, he parks at the end of the lot closest to the water.

As they walk east, in the direction of what he now knows is the next beach over, the one known as Atlantic, she appears to be doing all the talking, almost nonstop.

Lawyers, Robby thinks. *You have to kill them to shut them up. Fine with me.*

He keeps the binoculars trained on them until he almost can't believe his eyes when they stop, and the guy kneels down, and can only be proposing to her.

Robby Sassoon wonders when the photographer is going to pop out of the dunes and start snapping pictures.

But no one else appears on the beach. It's just the two of them out here right now. Them and the dog.

Maybe when the time comes, I'll do the dog, too.

No extra charge.

He's going to enjoy killing Jane Smith if it comes to that, which it probably will unless things change dramatically, and fast. They have history, he and Jane, even if she doesn't know it. She has a debt to pay, too, just not like her ex-husband's.

Somehow her getting proposed to like this is just going to make it better.

He tells himself to be patient.

Only a matter of time.

They are hugging now in the distance and she seems to be crying. Or maybe they're both crying. Sassoon puts down the binoculars and walks around the car and gets behind the wheel.

He resists the temptation to walk down there and give her a pat on the head.

Plenty of time for that later, too.

TEN

I CAN'T STOP STARING at the ring. A shiny object from which I can't turn away.

Diamonds are supposed to be a girl's best friend. Just not mine. Probably another personality defect.

My second husband, Martin, proposed in the middle of a Central Park carriage ride, presenting a ring with a stone almost as big as this. I eventually ended up giving the ring back to him—throwing it at him like a fastball, to be more precise—after I discovered he'd been cheating on me, on multiple occasions, starting in the first year of our marriage. And then even later, before my miscarriage.

"See if you can regift," I told Martin that night. "If anybody can pull that off with one of your girls on the side, my money's on you."

Only now it's Ben Kalinsky doing the proposing, and I still can't look away from the diamond.

What I can do is start to cry.

It's not just because of the proposal. It's because of Ben Kalinsky, who is every good, kind, honest, and caring thing that Martin never was. Now here he is, kneeling in front of me, asking me to marry him in front of God and Rip the dog. I'm standing on this beach hearing something I never expected— didn't think I even wanted—ever to hear again.

Until he came along.

Until he chose to love me for all the right reasons, even after he learned I was sick.

There are a lot of reasons why I'm fighting so hard for my life. One of them is how much *I* love being a lawyer, and how alive that still makes me feel, even now. But the biggest reason is this man kneeling in front of me.

Now I'm really crying, full out, chest heaving, gasping for air. This isn't the kind of middle-of-the-night crying I do in front of Rip.

This is different.

Much.

Ben smiles up at me, making no move to get up.

"Don't cry," he says.

I can't make myself stop — or start breathing.

"I rehearsed a longer speech," he continues. "I can recite it another time. But for now, I just want you to please say yes."

When I'm able to speak, this is the best I can manage:

"No."

The tears keep rolling down my cheeks. Maybe he thinks it's the emotion of the moment. And it is. Just not entirely the way he thinks.

"No, you don't want to marry me?" he says.

He stands now, and gently wipes the tears off my cheeks with his free hand, the ring box still open in the other.

Somehow he is still smiling.

"Yes, I *do* want to marry you," I say, the words barely making it out of my throat. "But no, I can't... I'm so sorry."

He reaches over again and brushes more tears away. Even now, he wants to take care of me.

I love him, in a way I've never loved anyone. I know he loves me, even though being with me is the reason he'd gotten beaten half to death and then shot. All of that happening to a small-town vet. Yet here we are, and those eyes are just so damn kind, because so is he. As unflappable as he is, there has to be a part of him, big part, embarrassed that the ring is still in the box and not on my finger.

I've always felt he gave me so much more than I gave him. Now it's happening all over again, in the best and most beautiful moment I have had in my so-called life for a long time.

And maybe ever.

I look down and see that Rip is standing next to Ben. He always knows when something is wrong. Suddenly he barks. It briefly makes me smile. Some emotional-support dog he is.

"I want to—but I just can't—" I say. I'm stammering and I know it. "Can you understand that. It's my cancer—the trial—not knowing how long—it's all too much for me right now."

"It's okay," he says in a gentle voice. "Really, it's okay." I can barely hear him over the sound of the waves. "You don't have to apologize, for anything."

I want to tell him to stop being so damned nice for once, it's only making me feel worse.

But I don't, because I feel dizzy then, suddenly afraid I might fall down right in front of him the way I did yesterday in front of Norma Banks.

He seems to sense this, because when I take a slight step back from him, toward the water, and feel one of my feet begin to slip in the sand, his arms are suddenly around me.

"Sometimes it's all just—it's just too damn much—" I say. "I—I can't even find the right words."

"Not even you," he says softly.

"Especially not me," I say.

Some tough mother I am.

He pulls me closer to him and puts his mouth next to my ear and says, "It's all going to be all right."

"I want to believe that so much," I say, as the tears start to come again.

"I promise," he says. "Now let's get you home."

He knows I have an early morning and knows why. He

knows where I'm going. But he keeps one arm firmly around me as we make our way through the sand and up the hill to where we left our sneakers, and where he parked his car, Rip trailing behind us.

"Don't let go," I say.

"I will never let go," he says.

I still feel as if I'm falling.

ELEVEN

AFTER RIP AND I have taken one last, quick walk up and down my street, I tell him he can sleep in my bed tonight, something for which he's always angling.

I've decided to let him sleep there, sand and all.

I've got no strength after what's just happened on the beach. I've already put Rip at the end of the bed, which is where he knows enough to stay, and not push it.

The cleaning people coming tomorrow afternoon can worry about the sand and sheets and blankets and general dog mess. Ben Kalinsky is taking Rip while I'm away, for as long as I'm away.

Back inside, I go into the kitchen and fix myself a small glass of Irish whiskey, even though I'm not supposed to be drinking hard liquor these days.

But what the hell, I tell myself. *You only live once.*

Right?

I take my glass into the bedroom, take a sip of the whiskey, and leave it on the nightstand. After I get under the covers, I see Rip staring at me all over again.

"Don't look at me like that," I say.

He makes a sound like a grunt.

I take another sip of whiskey. It goes down nicely. Probably the time of the night as much as the taste. My father always called it sipping time, when he was the one with a glass of Jameson in his hand.

"I did the right thing, whether you think so or not," I say to my dog. "This isn't the right time, if there even is such a thing for me anymore."

Rip keeps staring. He's almost as good at wordless communication as is Dr. Ben Kalinsky—the man I just hurt, as much as I love him.

"I'm going away in the morning," I say, "even though I've been hiding my suitcase from you; I know how you get when you see a suitcase. And this trip I'm about to take is the only thing I have the strength to deal with right now, not what just happened on the beach."

Dog's giving me nothing. No advice, no sympathy, no encouragement.

Nothing except the hundred-yard stare.

"Okay, I'm going to stop talking," I say.

Rip grunts again.

"But let me leave you with this," I continue. "Weddings are supposed to be happy, and this one would just be too damn sad."

I finish my whiskey. I am even too tired to take my glass back into the kitchen. I just close my eyes as I hear the soothing sound of the whistle from the late train heading west. A few minutes later, sleep comes easily for a change, which is both a surprise and blessing.

In the morning, my sister, Brigid, a cancer patient herself—it runs in the family along with stubbornness—will once again drive me to Kennedy Airport, where I will board a flight to Geneva and the Meier Clinic, where they're going to take what they say is their last, best shot at saving my so-called life.

TWELVE

BRIGID STEPS OUT OF her new SUV and onto the driveway as I carry my bag out from the house. Within seconds, we're both crying. The last time we consistently did this much crying together was when boys started breaking up with us in high school. Me more than her.

Both of us are frankly tired of days like this when one of us is on our way back to Switzerland, once again in search of a magic bullet.

By the way? Our mother died of cancer. We had no way of knowing that cancer would turn out to be the closest we ever came to a family business.

I've always thought of my sister as the pretty one, and the smart one, too, especially when she got into Duke and I didn't. But now that her cancer is in remission, I also think of her as the lucky one.

In her case, it doesn't include lucky in love.

Her husband, Chris, has finally started divorce proceedings. They separated after Brigid testified under oath at Rob Jacobson's first trial that she'd had an affair with Jacobson, once her classmate at Duke. They briefly tried to reconcile, but Chris couldn't get past what had happened. I can't say that I blame him, now knowing my client as well as I do.

On the way to JFK, I ask her about him again.

"For the last time, Rob is back to being a friend *without*

benefits," Brigid says evenly. "Which means that going forward, he remains your problem, not mine."

She smiles, eyes focused on the road, though her expression looks smug.

"Big picture?" she says. "The one who seems incapable of quitting him is you."

Brigid stops the car and steps out onto the sidewalk as I get my bag out of the back.

"I love you so much," Brigid says.

"Trust me on this," I tell her. "I love you more."

She smiles through her tears. "You need to rethink not taking Ben's ring," she says.

I say, "But this girl reserves the right to change her mind if she gets some good news from Dr. Stone Face over there in Switzerland."

It's our mutual nickname for Dr. Ludwig, the German who runs the Meier Clinic, one who in comparison makes all other stoic Germans look like the life of the party.

"In German," Brigid says, "it would be *Dr. Steingesicht*. But I wouldn't call him that to his face."

"See," I say, "you're still the smart one."

Her eyes suddenly fill up again and her face turns bright red, the way it used to when she was upset as a little girl.

"You've always been my hero," Brigid says.

"And you need to set the bar a lot higher than me." I hug her again, tell her one more time that I love her, and then walk into the terminal.

Wishing, not for the first time but especially at times like this, that they called it something else.

THIRTEEN

I'VE BARELY SIGNED MY readmittance papers at Meier when the doctors start poking and prodding and giving me everything except a pregnancy test.

The trip back here happened at the suggestion of my long-time personal physician, Dr. Samantha Wiley, who has been my friend much longer than she's been my doctor, all the way back to the ninth grade when we had adjacent desks.

"There're some new clinical trials, like brand new, that I think we should take a shot at," Sam said.

"You really mean last shot to win the game, don't you?"

"I didn't say that."

"You didn't have to, doc."

"How about you keep playing lawyer, and I play doctor."

"Not the way you played it with Tommy Morgenthau when we were kids," I said.

"Have a nice trip," she said.

They have their own state-of-the-art lab at Meier, which means that new blood work will be back to Dr. Ludwig by tomorrow morning. The Meier Clinic is not much for wasting time, especially not with so many people running *out* of time.

"I don't like to brag," I say to the nurse who speaks the best English. "But I feel like I gave you my top-shelf stuff today."

She stares at me blankly.

"Ja," she says.

Same blank stare.

"Easy for you to say," I tell her, and then head for my room.

I end up with the same one I had on my first visit. Two rooms, actually—like a one-bedroom suite at a five-star hotel—with a lovely view of the grounds and of the mountains in the distance.

After a long plane ride followed by a long car ride and then a morning filled with the poking and prodding, I want to breathe in the incredibly cool, clean mountain air.

And try to feel alive.

It's a walk I know well by now, looping up toward the mountains, around a lake whose name I can't recall, down toward a lush green valley, and finally back toward Meier. I would tell myself that I feel close to heaven up here, but that's a game *I* don't like to play.

A major part of the reality of being a cancer patient is the waiting game, going from one test to another, with hours of waiting overnight for good news.

Or at least not more bad news.

Waiting and wishing and hoping that this is the time when the governor calls, before it's too late, to tell you that your sentence has been commuted.

So I walk into the late afternoon.

I walk and replay the proposal from Dr. Ben inside my head. And immediately start second-guessing myself all over again, wondering, if I really do only have a handful of months left, why I would be more willing to spend them defending Rob Jacobson than with a man who loves me as unconditionally as Ben Kalinsky does.

Not just having Ben as my boyfriend, even though that word sounds sillier than ever to me, but as my husband.

Until death do us part.

After I have walked what must be a couple of miles from the clinic, I'm hit with my usual late-day fatigue or jet lag or both. I turn back and walk toward the sunset, my eyes

45

shielded by my ancient, faded blue Mets cap and sunglasses. I pull the hat down tighter to cut down on the glare and suddenly feel a laugh escape my throat, imagining myself to be in disguise, even this far from civilization.

They'll never find me up here, I tell myself.

They'll never take me alive.

Then I'm laughing uncontrollably, not sure why, unable to stop myself, before I feel more coming on, despite all the beauty around me.

I'm heading up the last hill back to Meier when I see the ghost walking toward me.

FOURTEEN

THE GHOST IS QUITE lovely, speaking to me in a familiar British accent, one I never expected to hear again.

"Fancy meeting you here," Fiona Mills says.

I cover the distance between us so quickly that it must be a tackle she's expecting and not a hug.

"You're not dead!" is the best I can blurt out.

"Funny, that," she says.

I met her on my previous visit to Meier, when the two of us took this same walk together, when she was deathly pale and thin and had lost her hair. The doctors had run out of treatment options, and Fiona Mills was sure that when she left for England, she was going back home to die. The day I said good-bye to her, I was certain it was forever.

But now here she is. In the brief time I've known her, I've found her to be both kind and wise and even brave the way Ben Kalinsky is. I step back then and take a closer look at her. She has put on what looks to be ten much-needed pounds and probably even more than that.

Fiona Mills notices me staring at her hair.

"Want to give Goldilocks' new bob haircut a tug?" she says, pulling on it herself. "I can assure you that it's all mine, even if it's not coming back nearly as fast as I'd like."

"I'll take your word," I say, and then our arms are around each other again.

This makes me believe in miracles.

"How can…how did this happen?" I say when we finally pull back from each other a second time.

"It's all because of the most *brilliant* word in the English language," she says. *"Remission."*

She asks then if I might fancy walking a bit more.

"Brilliant," I say, trying and failing miserably to imitate her lovely accent.

We turn and head back down the trail I'd just climbed, Fiona setting a pretty brisk pace.

As we walk, she tells me that she was preparing for home hospice, honestly feeling as if she were already on her death bed, when Dr. Foyle, her oncologist, paid her a visit unannounced.

Dr. Ludwig had called with news of a brand-new clinical trial.

"Before I'd left Meier, I'd told them no more drugs, they were sucking out of me whatever life I had left and dulling my senses and making me sadder than I already was."

Dr. Foyle explained to Fiona that this trial was not yet approved in England or the US. Then, Fiona said, he asked a hard question—"if I had the strength and the will to make one more trip back here."

"So I finally asked my dear Dr. Foyle if he thought it was worth it. He smiled at me and said, 'What do you have to lose, dear girl?'"

Fiona and her husband flew back here the next afternoon.

"When we arrived they gave me a lot of gobbledygook and gibberish about transductor inhibitors and, let me see if I remember properly, radiometabolic compounds and CAR T-cell therapy," she says. "Oh, and cellular path interruption."

"I mean, who hasn't heard about all that?" I say.

The last rays of the sun are in our faces now. Somehow the wind has shifted and is at our backs, and the sky is suddenly the color of cobalt, and everything seems even more beautiful than it did when I was out walking alone, because now Fiona Mills is here with me.

She pauses in her story, throws her head back, breathes in the mountain air. Then I see her eyes start to tear up. Somehow, though, she is smiling. Brilliantly.

"And somehow it all worked," she says, before quickly making the correction all cancer patients feel the need to make. "Or *is* working. I was here for a few weeks and now I'm back and for now, the gobbledygook and gibberish appears to be in perfect synchronicity, by the grace of God."

"About time She showed up with some of that," I say.

Then Fiona stops suddenly and takes both of my hands in hers as she faces me. "And that will be quite enough about me," she says. "What about you? Are you here for a tune-up, or for gobbledygook of your own?"

"The latter, I'm afraid."

I manage a smile.

"I'll still have what you're having," I say.

FIFTEEN

AS WE BEGIN THE long walk back, I tell her the thought that flashed through my brain just before I spotted her today, that maybe if I was in disguise and on the run, the bad guys wouldn't be able to find me.

"Sometimes I just worry that I'm running *out* of time," I say.

"Rubbish," she says.

"I wish."

"Don't wish," she says. "Believe." She is smiling again. "I didn't die on you and you're not going to die on me."

She gets a few yards ahead, then stops and turns to face me.

"Am I making myself clear, Ms. Jane Effing Smith?" Fiona asks.

I told her that's what my friends called me.

"In the most non-rubbishy way possible," I told her.

I tell her about the upcoming trial then, and about the shootout at the Walking Dunes, and how I shot a man before he could do the same to me.

"And you call me brave," she says.

When she asks me if the nice Dr. Dolittle is still the man in my life, I tell her about Ben's proposal on the beach.

"Congratulations!" she says. "Another reason to keep believing."

"I didn't say yes," I admit to her, almost sheepishly.

"Wait!" she yells. "You turned him down? Now why in the world would *you* do something daft like that, dear girl?"

"I didn't technically turn him down," I say. "I just didn't accept his proposal."

"Now you're the one talking gibberish," Fiona says. "Or just bullshit."

Even bullshit sounds better in her accent, I have to admit. Then I'm laughing again.

"I thought I was seeing a ghost when I saw you walking toward me," I say. "But I was wrong."

"In what way?" she asks.

"You're an angel," I tell her.

On the phone later I tell Ben Kalinsky about running into Fiona, and about her remission, and her saying I'm daft for not accepting his proposal.

"I knew there was something about that woman I liked," he says.

"Just because she happens to agree that I should agree to marry you?"

"Because she went back there to beat cancer and then did exactly that," he says.

Before we end the call, he tells me how much he misses me already, and how much he loves me.

"I know," I say. "I *know.* But for the life of me, I still can't figure out why."

"Well, I know why," Dr. Ben says. "I've clearly always been a sucker for sick puppies."

The next day, as soon as they get the results from yesterday's tests they schedule another new battery of tests for the morning, including even more targeted imaging with another MRI. When they're finished with all that, I am summoned to the office of Dr. Ludwig, for a scheduled Zoom call with Dr. Sam Wylie back in Southampton.

Just the sight of Sam's face on the giant screen across from Ludwig's desk makes me feel homesick and connected to home at the same time, same as my call to Ben had.

"So how's it going, pal?" Sam says.

"Gotta tell you, the fun never stops here," I say. "I've got my aquatics class coming up before lunch, then bingo this afternoon."

I turn to look at Dr. Ludwig. He closes his eyes and gives a sad, dismissive shake to his head. But then he's heard me try to hide my own anxiety behind dumb jokes before. When I look up at the screen, Sam Wylie isn't smiling either. And I know *she* thinks I'm funny.

But there is suddenly a vibe in here I don't like, not even a little bit.

"So what's the good news, guys?" I say finally.

Dr. Ludwig answers for both of them. He's not looking at me. He's looking at Sam's face on the screen, as if he'd rather be talking to her.

"There isn't any good news today, I am afraid," he says.

I'm the one in the room who's afraid.

SIXTEEN

LUDWIG GETS RIGHT TO it, telling me that the chemo hasn't worked the way they'd hoped it would, which means that my prognosis hasn't changed.

The only thing that has changed is the size of the metastasized tumor in my neck.

The pictures they took yesterday show that it's bigger, not smaller.

Not what any of us were looking for, or even close.

I know what Ludwig is really telling me: that barring a Fiona-like miracle, I am still at four months, or thereabouts, and counting. Give or take a few precious days. Or weeks.

My mind wanders back to the old line about how what doesn't kill you makes you stronger.

Unless of course it *does* kill you.

But even in here, even with what Dr. Ludwig has just told me, I'm still crazy enough to be thinking about the upcoming trial, and if I might be able to make it through a fast one.

I haven't told Ludwig about my client being charged with another triple homicide, and the speedy court date that I myself have requested.

I tell the doctor now.

"Out of the question," he says. "The only trials with which you need to be concerning yourself are the ones we will be trying here."

"I'm a multitasker," I say. "I can do both." I shrug. "Just watch me."

He turns back to the screen. "You must be talking her out of this," he says to Sam Wylie.

"I haven't been able to talk her out of anything since she wanted us to sneak cigarettes behind the gym in high school," Sam Wylie says.

"Unless some of what we are about to propose works, and works quickly, she is going to get weaker and sicker," Dr. Ludwig says.

"My body, my choice," I say. "Well, in this case, doc. That concept isn't exactly working the way it used to back in the States."

Neither Ludwig nor Sam says anything right away.

"So what are you proposing, doctor?" I say to Ludwig.

Then the two of them start speaking doctor to each other in a rapid-fire way. About how if they go ahead with their new treatment plan, I need to call off the next round of chemo and start kinase inhibitors, either oral or intravenous, immediately. They go back and forth until they finally settle into agreement about what they call ADC: antibody drug conjugates.

I think I hear them call it "odellamab."

"That sounds like an old Giants wide receiver," I say. "Used to make some amazing one-handed catches."

I sit and listen while they talk more doctor, Ludwig telling Sam about how they will initiate the treatment schedule.

At last, the office is quiet.

Too quiet, I'm thinking.

"Are you telling me you think all of this might save my life?" I ask.

From across the world my best friend says, "We've told you what we think. But in the end, the decision is yours."

Good lawyer that I am—no, great lawyer that I am—I don't hesitate before telling both of them that I'll take the deal.

SEVENTEEN

Jimmy

JIMMY CUNNIFF AND DANNY Esposito, the hotshot state cop who's now become Jimmy's friend, are standing across the street from the Riverhead Correctional Facility as Paul Harrington walks out of the place a free man.

Once Harrington was an honored commander of detectives in the 24th Precinct of the NYPD. Now Jane and Jimmy and Danny Esposito have found him out as the king of the dirty cops, all the way back to the 24th, when everybody thought Paul Harrington was a cop's cop, and on his way to being commissioner someday.

"That sonofabitch," Danny Esposito says.

"You know that's insulting to actual SOBs, right?" Jimmy Cunniff says.

There are a handful of reporters waiting for Harrington on the sidewalk, now that the Suffolk County Sheriff's Office has processed him out, and a couple of TV cameras. Down the block I see trucks from Channel 12, the local cable channel on Long Island, and Channel 4 from the city.

Harrington, big and broad-shouldered and white-haired and still cocky as shit, is smiling like he just won an election, and not just his freedom.

Harrington has been in custody since Esposito, with Jimmy's help, arrested him for—among other charges—sending

55

another dirty cop once in his command, Anthony Licata, to kill Jane and Jimmy that night at the Walking Dunes.

When Harrington thought it was done he placed a call to Licata's phone, not knowing Jane had shot and killed Licata. Jimmy had Licata's phone by then, and took the call, sounding enough like Licata that Harrington asked if it was done. And when Jimmy, still impersonating Licata, asked if that meant he'd killed them, Harrington said of course that's what he meant.

The call was on speaker. Afterward Jane, as an officer of the court, made a sworn statement as to exactly what she had heard.

Jimmy called Esposito, who raced over to Licata's rented home in Montauk and grabbed Licata's laptop. By the time the long night was over, the techs at Esposito's office in East Farmingdale had found audio files on Harrington that Licata had kept as an insurance policy he never got the chance to cash, connecting Harrington to a laundry list of crimes over twenty-five years.

It was plenty enough for Esposito to get an arrest warrant. Attempted murder for starters. Conspiracy. Esposito and Jimmy went to Harrington's home in Water Mill the next morning, and Esposito took great pleasure in reading Harrington his rights, cuffing him, and arresting his ass.

Only now the whole thing has been tossed.

Harrington's lawyer, Gabe Dees, famous on Long Island for representing an ancient and legendary mob boss named Sonny Blum, challenged Jane's version of the phone call as hearsay, saying Harrington denied not only any involvement in the shooting but in ever having sent anybody to the Dunes to commit murder.

As part of the same preliminary hearing, all of the taped phone conversations between Harrington and Licata were also tossed, all because Esposito hadn't obtained a search warrant before removing Licata's laptop from his home.

"The fucking warrant is on me, I have to wear that," Esposito says to Jimmy now. "For one thing, the guy was dead, which meant no expectation of privacy for my partner and me. And I thought they were urgent circumstances, wanting to get a jump on searching Licata's house before Harrington sent somebody over there. But the DA said it didn't matter, it was still fruit of the poisoned tree."

"As much as I hate to admit it," Jimmy says, "Harrington was right that day when we went to his house. We only had what we thought we had. Or wanted to have."

"Now I'd like to shove that poisoned fruit down his goddamn throat," Esposito says. "Or up somewhere else."

"And not only is the guy still in Sonny Blum's pocket," Jimmy says, "Blum's lawyer is the one who gets him sprung."

Blum, they now know because of Licata's taped phone calls, has been running Harrington since way back.

"Harrington's probably been happier in Sonny's pocket than he was in the womb," Esposito says.

"Paid better, too," Jimmy says.

They watch as Harrington finishes with the media. When he does, he sees Jimmy and Esposito and comes walking toward them, swaggering like he's still the boss and the two of them are on the other side of the squad room.

The sonofabitch.

Before he says anything, Jimmy says, "You want me to drop a twenty on the sidewalk, just to get you back in shape?"

"You always were a funny guy, Cunniff," Harrington says.

"Who's trying to be funny?" Jimmy asks.

"But help me out here, Jimmy boy," Harrington says. "Which one of us got banged out of the NYPD for being a very bad boy, me or you?"

Esposito steps forward now. Jimmy puts an arm out to stop him.

"I never got the chance to tell you, Esposito," Harrington says. "Nice collar."

"I hope you told them to keep the cell empty for you," Esposito says. "You'll be back in it soon enough."

Harrington smiles. "You know what I love about you two bindlestiffs? You still don't know how far in over your heads you are."

Jimmy is the one to step forward now.

He and Harrington are very close.

But Harrington doesn't back up, Jimmy has to give him that. He's still got brass balls. Literally.

"You got anything else smart you want to say?" Jimmy says quietly.

"You're the one with the smart mouth," Harrington says, "not me."

Harrington, still full of himself, gives a little roll to the wide shoulders. And grins a shit-eating grin.

"Except if you and your pal here are so smart, why am I out here and not still locked up across the street?"

"You're a disgrace to your badge," Jimmy says.

They're about the same size, and still nose to nose.

"At least I still have my badge," Harrington says.

"I'll make sure they bury you with it," Jimmy says.

"Is that a threat, Detective Cunniff? Or should I say *former* Detective Cunniff?"

Jimmy suddenly shoves him with both hands, hard enough to knock him back, but not down.

"Yeah," Jimmy says. "I guess it is."

Harrington stares at him for a moment, still grinning, then steps around both Jimmy and Esposito and walks away from them down Center Street.

But when he's twenty or so yards away, he stops and turns back around.

"You ever been arrested, Cunniff?"

"Never had the pleasure."

"Always a first time for everything," Harrington says.

He throws back his head then and laughs.

They can still hear him laughing loudly, and for their benefit, as he disappears around the corner, not looking back again.

"I'm gonna nail that bastard if it's the last thing I do," Danny Esposito says.

"Take a ticket," Jimmy Cunniff says.

EIGHTEEN

Jimmy

One Week Later

BRIGID CALLS JIMMY TO give him the heads-up that Jane is coming home from Switzerland a day early, and Jimmy tells her he'll go pick her up at JFK.

"How's she doing?" he asks. "I've been trying to leave her alone while they get her started on the juice."

"So far, so good," Brigid says. "Everybody's very optimistic."

"After just a few days?" Jimmy asks.

"That's what they're saying," Brigid says.

Jimmy says, "You know, you're not nearly as good a liar as your sister is."

"I don't know what you mean by that, Jimmy," Brigid says.

"My ass you don't," he says. "I was born at night, kid. Just not last night."

He's waiting for Jane when she comes walking out of the United terminal. Jimmy has a parking space right out front, having fake-badged the airport cop who'd told him to move along, he couldn't stay there.

Jimmy grins at her before taking her bag.

"You look like shit," he says.

Jane gives a sad shake to her head. "Well, mister, there goes your five-star Uber rating," she says. "I'm going to write off your rudeness to jet lag." She kisses him on the cheek. "Oh, wait. *I'm* the one with jet lag."

Jane does most of the talking as they make their way out of the airport and toward the Belt Parkway, going into detail about Fiona Mills, making it sound as if the two of them had been on some sort of cruise.

"Seeing her," she tells Jimmy, "was better than any medicine they gave me."

Jimmy doesn't respond, focusing the way he usually does on the Belt, the New York version of the Daytona 500. But his hands are tighter than usual on the steering wheel, and he knows it's not just because of the traffic.

"Sounds good," he says finally.

"Sounds good?" she says. "My friend coming back from the dead sounds *good* to you?"

"I don't want to hear more goddamn happy talk about her!" Jimmy snaps. "I want to hear about you."

"Whoa," Jane says. "I know this sounds like a question you should probably be asking me. But are you okay?"

"Are *you?*" he asks.

"All things considered, yeah," she says. "The good news is that because of the drugs I'm taking, I don't have to do another round of chemo. Bottom line? My prognosis is a lot better than when I went over there."

"Is that so?" Jimmy says.

Before Jane can answer, Jimmy yells, "Stop lying to me!"

NINETEEN

"WHOA," I QUIETLY SAY again to Jimmy Cunniff, who sounds more upset, and looks more upset, than he did the day I told him I had been diagnosed with cancer. "Where's this coming from, partner?"

He is suddenly driving way too fast, nearly rear-ending a car in front of us in the passing lane as he hits the accelerator.

Norma Banks once told me that when she's trying to read potential jurors, she studies "micro expressions." But nothing about Jimmy's face is micro, not the obvious signs of strain, most noticeably the red dots that appeared on his cheeks. If I didn't know better—if I didn't know *him* better—I might think he was about to do something I've never seen him do.

Cry.

"You need to slow down," I say softly. "And not just in this car."

He does slow the car now, gets his breathing under control. When he finally speaks again, at least he's stopped shouting.

"We had a deal, okay?" he says to me. "Actually, we have a lot of deals, you and me, none of them written down, all of them understood. But at the head of the list, A No. 1, like they say in the song, is that we do not lie to each other. *Ever.*"

"When did I lie?"

"When you tried to put a smiley face on this shit and make

me think you're getting better," he says, "when we both know you're not."

"*You* don't know that," I say.

"As a matter of fact, I do."

I wait now. I can always tell with him when there's more coming.

There is.

"I stopped to see Sam Wylie on my way to pick you up," he says. "At least I got the truth out of her."

"And what truth might that be, you don't mind me asking?"

"That this is last call for you," Jimmy Cunniff says. "And they're not going to know if these new drugs are working until they do." He pauses and then adds, "If they do."

We ride for a few minutes in a silence so thick it makes me want to open a window.

"Well," I finally say, "so much for my privacy rights."

"When I'm the private detective," he says, "they don't apply."

"Mind if we listen to some music before we change the subject?"

"Yeah, I do mind."

"Okay, be like that," I say, leaning forward a little so that, when he gives me a sideways glance, he can see that I'm smiling.

"Sometimes you forget I'm *only* like that," he says.

There is another long silence until Jimmy says, "Once and for all, you gotta tell your client to find another lawyer."

I lean forward even more, so he can see the big smile that has now crossed my face, just because there's not a thing in the world I can do to stop it.

"There is no other lawyer in his right mind who will take this case," I say.

TWENTY

BY THE EARLY EVENING Jimmy and I have made up enough to be seated at the end of the tavern he owns on Main Street in Sag Harbor.

"I don't want to relitigate the conversation we had in the car," I say to him now.

"Litigate to your heart's content," he says. "You were lying. And I was right about you quitting this case and our asshole client once and for all."

"That's very open-minded of you."

"You're welcome," he says.

I sip some club soda. I'm off real cocktails, because of my drug cocktail, until further notice, even though that makes me feel more out of place here than a vegan.

"I don't want you to start yelling all over again and scare the customers," I say. "But you're not allowed to be more angry about me having cancer than I am. It doesn't work that way."

"Jesus H. Christmas trees," he says. "I know you think you get to make the rules, about just about everything. But what you *don't* get to do is tell me what I'm allowed to feel about your being sick."

"Before I came over, you promised to be nice," I say. "This is nice?"

"Like my mother used to say," Jimmy tells me, "you get what you get and you don't get upset."

"Your mother was full of shit," I say.

I finally get a laugh out of him.

"At least she meant well," Jimmy says.

Both the Mets, my team, and Jimmy's Yankees are off tonight. But there's still baseball on the sets at both ends of the bar. Jimmy Cunniff's theory, one on which I'm totally lined up, is that any baseball is better than none.

"If I promise not to lie to you ever again, will you stop being angry with me?"

"Here's my promise to you," Jimmy says. "I'll stop being angry when you're better."

Then he's looking past me, to the front door.

"You have *got* to be shitting me," Jimmy Cunniff says.

I swivel my stool around and see what he is seeing.

Who he's seeing.

Paul Harrington.

"Of all the gin mills," I say to my partner.

"Mine's the one that suddenly needs to be fumigated," Jimmy says.

We both watch as Harrington walks straight toward us.

"Mind if I pull up a stool?" he says to Jimmy.

"Mind if I shoot you?" Jimmy says.

Harrington casually pulls back the front of his blue blazer to show us the Glock 19 holstered to his belt, probably his old service revolver. I briefly think about challenging the sonofabitch to a shooting contest.

"Only if you get off the first shot," Harrington says to Jimmy.

Then he turns to me.

"Still with us, huh?" Paul Harrington says. "Maybe cancer isn't as tough as it's cracked up to be."

I am tired. Exhausted really, and not just from cancer and jet lag. I am tired of my client, tired of worrying about this new trial, tired from constantly looking over my shoulder because somebody like Harrington might have sent another shooter after me. Or because my own client might have done the same thing.

On top of all that, I am feeling the full effects of the first few days of the ADC drugs. Most of the time I just feel weak.

Just not at this particular moment, with this bum of a disgraced cop standing in front of me, an insult to everything that made me want to be a cop in the first place.

I slide off my stool.

Then with all the strength I have in me, Harrington between me and the rest of the customers in Jimmy's place, I step into the hard, short left hook to the body that Jimmy taught me in Gleason's Gym about a hundred years ago, trying to drive my fist through Harrington's fleshy midsection and all the way out the other side.

I hear the air come out of him as he doubles over.

"Buy you a drink, Lieutenant?" I ask.

TWENTY-ONE

WHEN HE GETS ENOUGH air into him to be able to speak, he actually forces a grin.

"I guess I had that coming," he says.

"Only because neither my partner nor I really think you're worth shooting," I say.

"She didn't mean it about buying you a drink, by the way," Jimmy says. "Now get out of here before I throw you out."

"You sure you want to do that?" Harrington asks.

"Give me a good reason why I shouldn't," Jimmy says.

"Because in our world, yours and mine and hers, information still means power," Harrington says. "And I've got information that the two of you want."

He looks around the room and points to an empty table in the corner, near the big, framed picture of Jimmy, still in uniform and looking very young, posing with Joe DiMaggio at the old Yankee Stadium.

"Why don't we all sit down and I'll buy my own drink and then explain why you need to lay off Eric Jacobson and Edmund McKenzie so that you can both die of natural causes someday," he says. "Her first, of course."

"You want me to hit you again?" I say.

"Do you want to hear what I have to say or not?" Paul Harrington asks.

He does buy his own glass of Jack Daniel's, a double, and

brings it over to the table, and we all sit down. Neither Jimmy nor I knew of a connection between Harrington and Rob Jacobson's son, or with McKenzie, with whom Rob went to high school and who is another aging punk. Both Eric Jacobson and Edmund McKenzie have threatened me recently. I've managed not to shoot them both, though the temptation has been quite strong.

Harrington takes a sip of his drink and sighs contentedly.

"So how do you know those two mutts?" Jimmy asks him.

"I go way back with their fathers. You could say we were all members of the same club."

"In your case," I say, "I'm thinking it's not the University Club."

I take a closer look at Harrington. Jimmy has known him a long time, all the way back to when the whole city thought Paul Harrington really was a hero cop. Now he looks old and overweight and almost as tired as I am, with a red drinker's nose, and spidery capillaries on his cheeks, and eyes that have to see what he's become better than anybody else.

"It's a club as old as the city," Harrington says. "The one where guys like the Jacobsons and the McKenzies get away with shit and guys like me help them do it."

"Your club was supposed to be the NYPD," Jimmy says.

Harrington grins and asks, "How do you think I got membership in theirs?"

I think: Just three ex-cops sitting around a table at Jimmy Cunniff's cop bar. It's just that one of them tried to have the other two killed, by another ex-cop as dirty as the East River.

"Do you really think we're going to let you get away with sending Anthony Licata after us?" I ask.

"We need to move on from that," Harrington says, and takes another sip of bourbon.

"When I'm dead," Jimmy says.

Harrington grins again. He actually seems to be enjoying himself.

"Entirely up to you," he tells Jimmy.

I smile sweetly at Harrington. "How about you stop fucking around and tell us your connection to McKenzie and the Jacobson kid?"

"The connection doesn't matter," he says. "What does matter is that you have now been told they are not to be touched."

"And say we agree to that," Jimmy says. "What do we get in return?"

"I tell you who killed Rob Jacobson's old man," Paul Harrington says.

He looks at Jimmy, and then me, waiting for a reaction.

"Take the deal," Harrington says. "Because it comes off the table once I walk out of here tonight."

"Information being power," I say.

"Damn right," Harrington says.

Jimmy looks at me, and I nod at him.

"Deal," I say to Harrington.

"It involves your client," he says to me.

"You're telling me he's the one who did it?"

"They," Harrington says. "*They* did it."

He pauses.

"Your client killed his old man that day. It was his buddy Eddie McKenzie who shot the girl."

TWENTY-TWO

HARRINGTON DELIVERS THE NEWS as casually as if he's giving us the latest baseball scores.

"If they did it, why'd they do it?" I ask.

"Oh, they did it," Harrington says. "Your client hated his father as much as his own kid hates him now."

"What about McKenzie?" Jimmy asks.

Harrington points at his now empty glass. Jimmy ignores him. Harrington then tries to get the attention of Kenny the bartender, but Kenny turns and walks to the other end of the bar.

Paul Harrington shrugs.

"Both of them have had screws loose for a long time, what can I tell you?" Harrington says. "And McKenzie knew his old man would make it all go away the way he always had before."

"Because his old man had you," Jimmy says. He looks curious now. "Jesus, how many pockets are you in, Harrington?"

"It's a big club, what can I tell you?" he says.

"So you arranged to send your boys over to stage the scene and make it look like a murder-suicide," I say.

"May those boys rest in peace," he says, putting his hands together in prayer.

We were talking about Joe Champi and Anthony Licata, former cops and former NYPD partners until they ended up in Paul Harrington's pocket.

"You just let those two kids get away with murder," I say.

"I looked at it as a practical matter, one that opened up a world of possibilities for me and the boys on my team," Harrington says. "Your client is rich as shit. McKenzie's old man, that old pervert, is even richer. I had other side hustles going before that day. But not like that one."

He touches his glass again. "I'd really like one more drink."

I get up and walk over to Kenny and order another glass of Jack Daniel's and bring it back, just as a way of keeping him talking. From the start, both Jimmy and I thought the murder of Rob Jacobson's father and his young mistress was the beginning of the story, one that included old money and young girls and dirty cops and the mob, a story that kept shape-shifting, almost on a daily basis.

"So what," I say, sliding Harrington's drink across the table, "Eric and McKenzie work for you the way you work for Sonny Blum?"

"Who's Sonny Blum?" Harrington says.

"You ought to know," Jimmy says. "You're his bitch, *bitch*."

Harrington shakes his head.

"If you couldn't make an arrest stick," Harrington says, "you think you can insult me?"

"I'm confused about something," I say now. "If you've been in business with Rob Jacobson as long as you say you have, why would you send somebody to kill us? Me especially. I'm the one who's trying to help him beat another murder rap."

"It wasn't me who sent Licata," Harrington says.

Now Jimmy is the one who looks tired. "We heard you on the phone, remember?"

"I was just the messenger on that," Harrington says.

"Taking orders from Sonny?"

"Who?" Harrington asks again.

"So now you're the messenger again," I say. "Telling us to lay off Eric Jacobson and Eddie McKenzie."

"They still have value to us," he says. "Your client does not."

"Who's 'us'?" I ask.

Harrington stands. "We're done here," he says. "But we have a deal, correct?"

"No," I say. "As a matter of fact, we don't."

"What?" he says.

"No deal."

Then I put up a hand.

"What I meant to say is no deal, you sonofabitch."

"That's not what you said a few minutes ago," Harrington says.

"Well, what can I tell you, Lieutenant? I lied."

I smile at him one last time.

"So shoot me," I say.

TWENTY-THREE

HARRINGTON GETS UP FROM the table and walks out of the bar without looking back at us.

"You believe him?" Jimmy asks.

"Which parts?"

"The murders," he says. "Or should I say, the first ones?"

"Let's say I don't *not* believe him, not to sound too doubly negative."

"But say it's true," Jimmy says. "If it is, we are officially defending somebody who's been murdering people since he was a teenager. And getting away with it."

"Practice makes perfect?" I say.

Jimmy puts his face in his hands and rubs it with his fingers. When he looks back up at me his old cop eyes search my face hard.

"Gun to the head time," he says.

"There must be a better way to put that."

"I'm being serious."

I say, "So am I."

"Do you think he's a killer?"

"No."

"Even after what Harrington just told us?"

"Even then."

"You must have a pretty good reason."

"The best," I say. "I don't want him to be a killer."

Jimmy gets Kenny's attention and mouths "Scotch." Kenny emerges from behind the bar with a glass and a bottle of Dewar's. Jimmy does the pour himself. It's a good one.

"From the time I started working for you," Jimmy says, "you've told me that once you decide to defend somebody standing up on a murder charge, there's one question you never ask: whether or not they did it."

I don't respond right away. It's late and I'm not in the mood to have this conversation right now. And I'm starting to feel slightly nauseous again, which could mean another long, bad night once I get home and get into bed.

But Jimmy always finishes what he starts.

"You told me the reason you didn't ask," he continues, "is because when it came to you putting up the best defense you had in you, it didn't matter one way or the other."

I reach across the table then, cover his hand with mine, and give it a quick, affectionate squeeze.

Then proceed to tell him the exact same thing I told Paul Harrington before he walked out of the bar.

"I lied," I say to Jimmy Cunniff.

TWENTY-FOUR

AS LOUSY AS I feel, I don't go straight home.

I drive to the beach instead, telling myself I would apologize to Rip the dog later for not stopping to pick him up.

They told me before I left Meier that the drugs I am taking affected everybody differently. I assured them that I had learned how to manage chemo and that I would certainly be able to learn what I was calling my ADCs. Antibody drug conjugates. Such a joy and a comfort.

I didn't really start feeling sick until after I returned home. Nausea. Fatigue. Vomiting. So far it's all been no better than chemo, I'm just not hooked up to any machines. But now I am feeling sick just about every damn day.

Being in the presence of Paul Harrington hasn't helped matters much.

I haven't said anything about this to Jimmy or Ben Kalinsky or Dr. Sam Wylie, or even my sister, who understands what I'm experiencing more than any of them. But I'm starting to wonder, every damn day, how I'll be able to get through jury selection if I don't start to feel better. Or more like myself, whatever that means anymore.

Much less a trial.

For now, though, for tonight, I just want to breathe in some clean air, the cleanest air I've ever known, even as close to the sky as I was in the mountains of Switzerland.

My air, near the ocean.

I don't drive to Indian Wells, because even alone out here in the night I know I'll see the scene I've been playing and replaying inside my head: Ben kneeling in the sand and proposing to me all over again. I feel no need to return to what I now think of as the scene of my crime.

I drive the extra mile east to Atlantic Avenue Beach instead, get out of my car, take off my sneakers as soon as I reach the end of the parking lot. I feel the sand underneath my bare feet, am breathing in that air, listening to the waves.

Suddenly I don't feel as sick.

Another miracle drug.

When I'm here, especially at night, alone or with Rip, I can almost convince myself that I'm going to beat this thing.

Almost.

I tell myself that I'm going to find my way to the word that Fiona Mills had called the most beautiful in the English language.

Remission.

I joked with Sam Wylie and Dr. Ludwig that they needed to use all of their technical medical terms in any given sentence.

I just want to use "remission."

Alone on the beach in the night I say, "I'm in remission."

Then I'm shouting it, all the way back to the car, glad I am alone out here in the night.

"I'm in remission!"

It does make me feel a little better.

I tell myself not to think about Rob Jacobson and Edmund McKenzie, and the terrible things they might have done, in Jacobson's own home, thirty years ago. Tell myself not to think about all the people, some of them innocent people, who have died since Jimmy and I took on Rob Jacobson as a client.

I turn and look at the water and then the full moon, and

the kind of big sky full of stars you get out here on clean, moonlit nights like this.

There will, I know, be plenty of time to think about dying, maybe when I am once again wide awake in the middle of the night, and sleep can't find me because the night terrors have gotten to me first.

As soon as I pull into the driveway, I see that all the lights are on in the house.

I see that my front door is wide open.

I shut off the car and lean over to where my bag is on the passenger seat and take out my Glock. Then I am covering the distance between the car and the house, moving along the front of the house, crouching as I move toward the door, keeping myself below the windows.

Invariably, when I drive up to my house, Rip is waiting for me just inside that door, and when he hears the car, somehow knowing it's my car and not someone else's, barks out a greeting, jumping up and trying his best to knock me over as soon as I open the door.

But there is no sound coming from inside the house now.

I press myself against the outside of the doorframe, two hands on the gun now, and yell Rip's name as I wheel around and step inside, immediately seeing that the place has been trashed.

Cushions pulled out of the couch, coffee table turned over. Like that.

Just no barking dog.

TWENTY-FIVE

I CONDUCT A QUICK search of the house and then call Jimmy, who's still at the bar, and tell him what happened.

"You have any idea what they might have been looking for?" he asks. "Or what they might have taken?"

"Just my goddamn dog!" I yell into the phone, before he tells me he's on his way.

All the rooms have been tossed, including the kitchen and the spare bedroom I've turned into an office. My laptop is still on the desk, but its drawers have been pulled out, papers and files strewn across the carpet. In my bedroom I see that the mattress is halfway off the bed frame. More drawers on the floor in there, along with clothes from the closet.

I have no way of knowing if whoever did this *was* looking for something in particular, or if vandalizing the inside of my house was a scare tactic. It meant they know where I live, but absolutely nothing about who I am.

I check the places where I keep my other two handguns. Both are where I left them, one in a bedside table, one in a small bureau in the foyer.

I yell Rip's name again and then whistle. It's a shot in the dark, literally, as he never comes when I whistle. But then he never strays very far.

Nothing.

My house being tossed *doesn't* frighten me, if that really

was their intent. But not being able to find my dog, that's different.

Rip isn't under the bed, it was one of the first places I checked, sometimes he sneaks under there for a nap. He isn't in any of the closets, or in the crawl space underneath the deck, or in the small tool shed in the backyard, whose door he can nose open if he gets the urge.

There have been times when I've accidentally left a door to the house open and he's gotten out. But never once has he gone far, or not come when I called him.

The dog just wants to be where I am. He wanted to be with me even before I took him in.

So where is he now?

I walk out into the backyard and call his name again. All I hear are night sounds. The moon is still high in the sky, no cloud cover at all tonight, so there's no need for me to throw on the floodlights. If he were back here, I'd see him.

But he's not back here.

Was Harrington dumb enough and clumsy enough to send somebody here this soon after he walked out of Jimmy's bar? Or has he done something even dumber than that and come here himself after I blew up the deal he thought he had on Eric Jacobson and Edmund McKenzie?

I plan to find that out eventually.

Just not now.

Now I just need to find Rip.

Jimmy has to be getting close. I walk around the outside of the house and out to the street.

"Rip!"

Yelling my head off now.

I'm probably waking up some of my neighbors. I don't care.

My dog is either lost, or whoever came to my house tonight has taken him just as a way of violating me a little more.

Or that person has done something much worse.

I walk past our mom-and-pop neighborhood fish market tucked on a side street and up to Main Street and then back, a feeling of dread growing, rising up inside me, with every step.

I am walking back toward my house when I see Jimmy pulling up behind my car and getting out of his.

I see he has his own gun in his hand, as the lights over the garage come on automatically.

He starts toward the front door.

"Jimmy," I say.

He sees me coming toward him and puts his gun away.

"Where's Rip?" Jimmy says.

By now it is a well-known fact that he loves Rip as much as I do.

"I still can't find him," I say. "And believe me, I've looked all over."

"We'll find him," Jimmy says.

"Where?" It comes out almost as a wail.

With everything that has happened, it would be too much if the dog is really gone.

Then I hear a bark in the distance.

The sound is coming from the direction of Abraham's Path.

A few seconds later, there he is.

There's an old line I've always loved, the one about how heaven, if you make it there, is every dog you ever loved running to greet you. I don't much like pondering the idea of heaven these days, and whether or not it even exists, for obvious enough reasons. And me the product of a Jesuit education.

But for just this one night the sight of my own dog running for me at full speed, tail wagging like crazy, barking his head off now, will do.

TWENTY-SIX

ROBBY SASSOON HAD PARKED his car at Brent's, the little general store about a mile from her house, and walked back from there.

It's about forty-five minutes, maybe a little more, since he gave the dog a good kick and sent him running out the back door before turning the place upside down.

This was just a warning shot tonight, without her having any idea who was the one firing it.

The kill shot for Ms. Jane Smith would come later, as soon as the boss gave the word.

One for her, one for her partner Cunniff. The ex-cop, and all-around pain in the ass.

Sassoon is standing at the far end of the block, hidden from their view by some high, thick privet in front of one of the other houses, when Cunniff shows up.

A few minutes later, the dog comes running, and then there he is slobbering all over her in the middle of the street.

What the fuck is this, a Disney movie?

Robby Sassoon watches as much of this heart-tugging reunion as he can take before he turns and starts walking back toward the main road, and where he left the car.

He has one more stop to make tonight.

This one will be even more fun.

Robby Sassoon gives a quick look in the back of the car at

his new toy, and then heads west on Route 27, making sure to stay under the speed limit.

Not a night to get pulled over, and have some overzealous local flatfoot want to pop the trunk.

As he is passing through East Hampton, he turns on the radio, hits the button for the Broadway channel on SiriusXM.

Robby Sassoon loves a good show tune.

Let the games begin, he tells himself.

He looks in the rearview mirror and smiles back at himself.

Sometimes he enjoys his work so much he thinks he'd do it for free, even if that thought always passes quickly.

They're playing a song from *Sweeney Todd* now on his radio.

He knows it by heart, it's one of his favorites, even though it doesn't have much of a melody.

"Let the blood start to flow," Robby Sassoon sings. "Come death and murder, those were his trade . . ."

He's feeling a rush tonight. And now a regret.

He should have shot the damn dog.

TWENTY-SEVEN

JIMMY INSISTS ON STAYING the night. There's a brief standoff between us on that, me telling him I'm armed and as dangerous as ever and that whoever did this isn't coming back, at least not tonight.

Eventually, I give in and tell him he can take the couch.

"But just so we're clear," I say, "I let you win this time."

"And just so we're clear on something else," Jimmy says, "I'm not staying because I think he'll come back. I'm staying because I *hope* he does."

Being the good host that I am, I go and get some sheets and a blanket and his pillow and make up the couch for him.

"Do you think Harrington made a call after he left the bar and had this done?" I ask Jimmy.

"Only because I stopped believing in coincidence when I stopped believing in Santa Claus," he says.

"Wait a second. You're telling me there's no Santa Claus!" I say in mock horror.

He nods gravely.

"The Easter Bunny killed him," he says.

After another brief standoff inside my bedroom with Rip, I allow him to sleep on the bed. Then I make sure that both the front and back doors are locked and that the alarm, which I had neglected to set before I left for Jimmy's bar, is fully armed now.

Jimmy and I did some cleaning up before I told him he had to stop, we could finish in the morning.

"I hate clutter even when it's not mine," he says.

"You want to empty the dishwasher, too?" I ask.

In the darkness of the living room I say, "You still awake?"

"Yeah."

I walk over and lean down and kiss him on the forehead and thank him for coming right over when I called.

"I had no choice," he says. "This is where the job was."

Then he adds, "You're still too sick for this."

"Not when I'm pissed off," I say. "And tonight I am royally pissed off."

Before I close the door to my room, knowing from other nights like this that Jimmy Cunniff can snore like a champion, I say, "You gonna go see Harrington in the morning?"

"Way ahead of you on that."

"What does that mean, exactly?"

"It means that that matter will be taken care of shortly."

"Do I want to know how?"

"How about I surprise you in the morning?" he says. "You know how you love surprises."

I say, "I hate surprises."

From the couch he says, "Go to sleep."

"Easy for you to say," I tell him.

My version of white noise tonight is the faint sound of Jimmy's snoring from the other room, and Rip's from the end of my bed.

When I do finally fall asleep, I dream of hummingbirds.

I dream about hummingbirds a lot, but that's probably because I think about them a lot. I take feeding them with the sugar water that I am constantly preparing extremely seriously, like it's a second job. But then these birds have informed my life, have had me loving them all the way back to when my mother loved them the way she did when I was a little girl.

I am a little girl in the dream tonight, but I'm living here, in this house, and it's the fall, and I know the hummingbirds are about to leave, fly back to Mexico until they return in the spring.

Hummingbirds make me want to believe in miracles, just the thought of these tiny birds migrating all that way, those thousands of miles, and then making their way back here.

If that's not a miracle, I don't know what is.

In my dream tonight, I'm standing on the back deck near my feeder, and I'm wearing a dress that my mother bought me when I was ten, before she got sick with her own cancer, when she'd take Brigid and me shopping, when we'd do a lot of things together.

And I start to cry in this dream, because the ten-year-old me already has cancer. My mother's fine but I'm the one who's sick, and I'm afraid I'll never see the hummingbirds ever again, because I won't be here when they come back.

When I awaken in the darkness, I can feel the tears on my cheeks and, for once, I don't want to go back to sleep, because I'm afraid of how the dream might end.

TWENTY-EIGHT

THERE IS A SECURITY camera at either end of the quiet street. Sassoon uses a suppressor and casually shoots out both of them.

He has parked the car a couple of blocks over, taken his new Knight Armament SR-15 Mod 2 out of its case, the thing looking sleek and beautiful, chambered in 5.56 NATO, the rimless bottlenecked cartridge family, but compatible with a .223 Remington.

"You get what you pay for," the guy who'd sold him the semiautomatic had said after Robby had been the one laying out $4,000 for the gun, "including versatility with ammo."

Then the guy had said, "You hunt?" and Robby had told him, "With great versatility," already thinking about getting off forty-five rounds a minute the first chance he got.

Like right here and right now.

He's tired of amateurs giving killing guns like this a bad name. Assholes. Guns like this one, like pieces of art, really did belong in the hands of professionals.

He is whistling softly to himself as he walks along the side of the street, the gun pressed to his right leg, just in case a car might happen by. But he quickens his step as he gets closer to the house, wanting to get on with it now, knowing he won't have a lot of time once he opens fire and begins waking the whole neighborhood the fuck up.

But first he's going to wake the owner of the house the fuck up.

Just one light on upstairs. One lit over the front door.

Sassoon already knows the master bedroom is in the back of the house, second floor.

He is still whistling softly as he raises the gun and starts shooting, strafing the windows of the bottom floor first, shattering the windows, lingering just long enough on the front door to splinter five or six holes in it, top to bottom.

"Yeah," he says to himself. *"Yeah."*

The speed and power of the Knight Armament are as advertised, Robby Sassoon feeling the surge of adrenaline as he keeps the gun on the house before raising it and now blowing out the windows upstairs, the glass raining down from there. When he's finished, he trains the gun on the weather vane at the top of the house and blows it to bits, like the thing just explodes.

How long has it all taken?

A minute?

Maybe less than that.

He sees the light upstairs go out now. So he didn't hit him with a stray bullet. But he didn't come here to hit him. Robby Sassoon has come here to shoot up the man's house and let him know that there's a target on him, too.

He wonders what it must have sounded like inside once he started shooting.

Sassoon hears shouting now from the other end of the street, sees lights coming on in one house after another, inside and out. But he's already on the move, running around the house and through the backyard, the escape route he gamed out the other day.

By the time he reaches the car, he hears the first sirens in the distance.

More music to his ears.

Almost like a show tune.

TWENTY-NINE

STATE COP DANNY ESPOSITO is surprised to see the two black SUV's, SOUTHAMPTON TOWN POLICE written in huge letters on the side, parked out in front of the house, lights flashing.

What are they doing here?

Esposito slams on his brakes, pulls right up onto the lawn, jumps out of his own car, shows his State Police badge to the first cop trying to stop him.

When he looks past the cop, he sees what's left of the front of the house.

"What the hell happened here?" Esposito says.

"What *happened*?" the kid from Southampton Police asks. "What happened is that somebody turned this guy's house into a fucking rifle range."

"Anybody inside get shot up?" Esposito asks.

The cop shakes his head.

"Nope."

"Shit," Esposito says. "I was afraid of that."

"You wanted somebody to get hit?" the cop says.

"A guy can dream," Esposito says.

Every window in the house has been blown out. There are bullet holes in the door, top to bottom, and between the first- and second-floor windows. The flashing lights from the patrol cars show the glass in the front yard glistening like a hailstorm just blew through.

"Gotta be some kind of AR-15, right?" Danny Esposito says.

"Hell, yeah," the kid says. "One of them *sport* rifles."

He puts air quotes around *sport*.

Esposito points toward the BMW in the driveway.

"*Is* the homeowner here?" he asks. "Or did he miss all the fun?"

"Was here, and is," the kid says. "He must be one lucky bastard."

"You don't know the half of it," Danny Esposito says.

They both see the blown-out front door open then. And there, standing in the entrance, wearing a bathrobe with the belt hanging down behind it, what appears to be a glass of whiskey in his meaty hand, is former Commander of Detectives Paul Harrington.

Esposito heads straight for him.

"Looks like somebody tried to send you a message," Esposito says to him.

Harrington throws down some of his drink.

"Next time they should just send a text," he says, and walks back inside.

THIRTY

JURY SELECTION BEGINS AT the courthouse in Mineola tomorrow morning. Katherine Welsh will be in one corner and I'll be in the other even if I'm somewhat under my normal fighting weight. Judge Michael Horton will be presiding over it all.

I am hoping that the familiar excitement of that, the rush of a new season starting, will somehow mitigate how truly lousy I have been feeling on a daily basis ever since Switzerland. At least when the college hockey season was starting up, I could start hitting people.

"I have to start feeling better," I say now to Sam Wylie at the Candy Kitchen.

It's always a good place for us to meet for coffee, this diner in Bridgehampton that is pretty much halfway between Southampton, where Sam lives and works, and where I live in Amagansett.

"You're going to start feeling better," she says. "The drugs just need more time."

"I don't have time!" I snap, loudly enough to scare a couple of farmers I recognize who are seated at the counter.

"Hey," Sam says softly. "Hey now, girl."

"Sorry," I say. I manage a grin. "It must be the drugs talking."

"I know you don't want to hear this from me," she says. "But it was your choice to go ahead with this trial."

"You sound like a lawyer correcting the record," I say.

She smiles. "Don't be hurtful."

I get up from our table suddenly, nearly knocking over my coffee cup, telling her I'll be right back.

"If you need to make a call, you can make it in front of me," she says.

"I need to go be sick," I tell her.

I'm on my way home, feeling slightly better—as low a bar as that is these days—when Rob Jacobson calls and asks if I can stop by his rented house, there's somebody he wants me to meet.

"A drum majorette you met while you were dog walking?" I ask him.

"You're the one with the dog," he says.

"No, actually you're the dog," I say, then tell him I'm in the car headed that way and will be there in ten minutes.

If there's a girl in the house when I arrive, she's nowhere to be seen. Maybe she's sleeping upstairs. After all, I know how teenaged girls love their sleep.

But there is a man—much too tanned and skinny as a steak knife—in the living room with my client. The Maserati in the driveway surely belongs to him.

He has black hair flecked with silver brushed straight back and worn long, skinny jeans that are too young for him the way his long hair is, a pink polo shirt with the collar turned up, and white Stan Smith sneakers that look fresh out of the box. The whole presentation comes from somebody obviously trying way too hard, somebody who's too done, in just about every way.

"This is Thomas McGoey," Jacobson says.

"I recognize Mr. McGoey," I say. "Isn't his face on the ads with his 800 number?"

I pronounce it Mc-*gooey*.

"It actually rhymes with go," he says.

"Be my guest," I say.

I am just inside the door and make no move to get any closer to either one of them.

I know McGoey only by reputation. He's a big-city criminal defense attorney—same as I am—full-time publicity hound and cable TV whore generally regarded as being every bit as sleazy as most of his clients. I sometimes think the only mob guys he hasn't represented are in the movies.

I ignore him and turn back to Rob Jacobson.

"Why is he here?" I ask, as if McGoey isn't.

"I've hired him to be your second chair," Jacobson says.

THIRTY-ONE

IT'S A RARE MOMENT in my life when I am actually speechless. But not for long.

"You are," I say to Jacobson, "a made-in-America, one-of-a-kind, world-class scumbag."

McGoey says, "And here I thought that was me."

When I turn to him, I see the shark smile on his face.

"Fuck off," I say to Thomas McGoey.

McGoey stood up when I came into the room. Now he puts up his hands in surrender and sits back down on the couch.

"I can explain," Rob Jacobson says.

"No," I say. "You can't. Maybe to your new buddy here. But not to me."

"Can I just say one thing?" McGoey says.

I try to glare him back into silence. But I've seen him enough on television and on courthouse steps to know that to really get him to stop talking, I'll need to hit him with one of my old hockey sticks.

He and Rob Jacobson will get along swell, as long as neither one of them wants the other guy to actually listen.

"Listen, if you quote me on this, I'll have to kill you," McGoey says.

"Have one of your clients do it," I say. "They all seem to know how."

He lets that one go.

"As I was about to say," he continues, "I know you're the best. Everybody in our business knows you're the best. Half of us actually come right out and admit it. The other half just lie about it."

"Are we going anywhere with this?" I ask. "Because I just remembered I have to be somewhere, which means anywhere except here."

"I've read the transcript from the first trial at least half a dozen times, and that was before Rob called me," McGoey says. "And I swear, I felt like I did in the old days watching Michael Jordan play ball. A freaking master class in trial lawyering, no bullshit."

"Not from you," I say. "No, sir."

He ignores that, too.

"I don't know how you pulled it off, but you did," McGoey says. "Listen, false modesty isn't in my tool kit. But it would be an honor for me to work with you."

"You're not working with me."

"Janie," Rob Jacobson says. "Everybody on the planet says this case against me is stronger than the first one, even if I am still innocent."

"Of course you are," I say.

"I just happen to think that the only thing better than one top gun is two," Jacobson says. "So why don't all of us sit down and talk this out. Thomas and I were talking about the trial before you got here, and he has some very good ideas."

"Here's my best idea," I say. "I quit."

Rob Jacobson starts to say something and I put a finger to my lips.

"You're done," I say. "And we're done."

As I walk toward my car, having left the door open behind me, I suddenly feel as if a huge weight has been lifted off my shoulders.

From the looks of my client, I'm guessing it's one hundred and seventy-five pounds, or thereabouts.

THIRTY-TWO

HE'S HALFWAY DOWN THE front walk, shouting that I need to wait up, we're not done here, as I'm about to get into the car.

I lean over the roof and put up a hand to stop him.

"And don't try coming after me," I say, "unless that hacker friend of yours can do another get-around on your bracelet."

"We need to talk this through," he says.

"You know, it's funny, Rob," I say. "I can't hear a word you're saying, because the shit you keep pulling like this just keeps shouting at me."

I shake my head.

"I keep asking myself why I'm still with you," I say. "Everybody I know keeps asking me why I'm still with you. And I am now officially tired of trying to come up with any kind of answer that makes sense."

"Like I said," he says. "I'm innocent."

"Are you?" I say.

As I pull out from behind McGoey's Maserati, I can see him at the end of the driveway, waving frantically for me to come back.

Still talking.

I drive around for a few minutes, first up to Atlantic Beach, then back to Indian Wells.

Then back into the driveway behind the Maserati, back into the house.

Rob Jacobson and McGoey are where I left them when I walk back through the front door without knocking. They both look genuinely surprised to see me, but they ought to, since I sold my exit like I was Meryl Streep.

"I was just fucking with you, Rob," I say. "And my second chair here. You both ought to know I don't quit, even when I'm the one defending a world-class scumbag. It's just one more thing that makes me the best."

"I knew you'd come to your senses," Jacobson says. "It's like I've told you from the start. We're a team, Janie."

I sigh. "How many times do I have to tell you not to call me that?" I ask. "Only people I like get to call me that."

"You and I *are* going to make a great team," McGoey adds.

"What do you think this is, Mc-gooey," I say to him, "a dating app?"

Then I turn my attention back to my once and future client.

"You know *why* I'm not quitting?" I tell him. "Because I want to be there in the courtroom, standing right next to you, when you go down for murder this time."

"But you never lose," Rob Jacobson says.

"First time for everything," I say.

THIRTY-THREE

NORMA BANKS AND I are standing outside the court-house in Mineola, the first wave of juror interviews for Katherine Welsh and I set to begin in less than half an hour in front of Judge Michael Horton, who, from what I've seen so far, seems to think he might be the son of God.

Norma has dressed up for the occasion, or at least her personal version of dressing up, in a pretty blue maxi dress and blue sneakers almost the same pale shade as the dress. She may have had her hair done, there seem to be a few more curls today, but I can't be certain of that and am afraid to ask. She has lit a new cigarette off the one she'd just finished.

"You're sucking on those things like you think the judge is going to send you to the chair," I say.

"The world was a better place when smoking indoors wasn't treated like a crime against humanity," she says.

"Yes," I tell her, "those certainly were the days."

She narrows her eyes. "You sure you're ready for this?" she asks. "Don't take this the wrong way, but you look like shit."

I mention to her that I've been getting a lot of that lately, and why would anyone possibly take a comment like that the wrong way?

"It's like the universe is trying to tell me I'm sick or something," I say.

"For the last time, kiddo," she says, "you do not have to do this."

"Actually, I do."

"It's not worth it," she says, "and your client is certainly not worth it."

"I know that," I say. "But I finish what I start."

"Even if it kills you?" Norma drops her cigarette and stubs it out on the sidewalk.

I smile at her. "Is that the entire pep talk? Or is there more?"

She smiles back at me and gives me a playful shrug in the direction of the front doors.

"Let's get this party started," she says.

As soon as I sit down, a serious case of DA envy once again sweeps over me.

It's as if Katherine Welsh is the one seated at the cool kids' table. She is dressed in a to-die-for navy suit that not only is made for her but really looks as if someone *did* make it for her. Somehow she seems to have even more long auburn hair than usual, is wearing heels that make her nearly six feet tall. As far as I can see, she is in absolutely no danger whatsoever of anybody suggesting that she looks like shit today.

Norma Banks sees the way I'm looking at my opponent and gives me a sharp elbow to the ribs.

"Just remember something," she says quietly, nodding in the direction of Katherine Welsh. "Somewhere somebody's tired of her."

Welsh puts down her briefcase next to her chair and walks over to our table. She's smiling, as if she's not just ready for her close-up, she was born for it.

I stand and shake her outstretched hand, hoping she doesn't notice me rising up on my toes as I do.

"So," Welsh says, "we're really gonna do this."

"There's still time to switch sides," I say. "I frankly like yours better."

She leans closer to me. "Is it true that Thomas McGoey is going to be your second chair?"

"Word travels fast."

"You know how it works with social media," she says. "Gossip is halfway around the world before I even get my new shoes on."

I look down at her shoes when she says that, I can't help myself.

"Oh, shit," I say. "Those are Manolos, aren't they?"

"Guilty," Katherine Welsh says, then says in a throaty voice, "God, how I love that word."

Then she quickly says, "How are you feeling, Jane? Really."

I make myself taller again and say, "Just barely strong enough to kick your ass."

As if I've suddenly confirmed to her what she's probably thought about me all along, Katherine Welsh shakes her head.

"Jane Effing Smith," she says.

"For the defense."

THIRTY-FOUR

THOMAS MCGOEY ARRIVES A few minutes later, acting as if he's out of breath but clearly wanting to make an entrance, dressed as if he's on his way to the Wise Guys Prom after he leaves court:

Black pinstriped suit with extremely wide stripes, blood-red tie whose brand I can never remember with a knot as big as his fist, and a pocket handkerchief to match. He's splashed on a bit too much cologne this morning for my taste, but then I've always considered any cologne at all on a man pretty much a deal-breaker.

McGoey nods at Katherine Welsh. She nods back, almost imperceptibly, without changing expression before turning her back on him and saying something to Reid Burke, her assistant DA and second chair.

I introduce McGoey to Norma.

"I've heard a lot about you," McGoey tells her.

"Sadly," she says, "I'm forced to say the same about you."

McGoey grins. "Don't worry, I'll grow on you."

"Yeah," Norma says as we watch the first group of jurors filing into the box. "Somewhat like mold."

McGoey focuses on me now, real excitement on his face, rubbing his palms together like a kid about to have an ice cream sundae set down in front of him.

"Okay," he says, "let's do this, counselor."

I angle my chair just slightly, so I'm facing him directly.

"Thomas," I say. "Look at me."

He does.

"Don't talk," I say.

"Listen," he says, "you've made it abundantly clear that you don't want me here."

"And I've tried to hide it *so* well," I say.

"But I *am* a pretty damn good lawyer," he says, "and I can help if you'll just let me."

"And when I do need your help," I say, "you'll practically be the first to know."

We all hear "All rise" then as Judge Horton has just walked in.

"I used to date lawyers," Norma says to Thomas McGoey. "But I've been clean for a long time."

THIRTY-FIVE

THE STANDARD FOR POTENTIAL jurors, no matter where the case is being tried and no matter how serious the charges, is always supposed to be the same:

Any potential juror who admits that he or she or they can't put aside their personal feelings and biases and apply the law impartially is summarily dismissed, no parting gifts, thanks for showing up and at least trying to do your civic duty, good-bye, drive home safely.

"If they do promise to be impartial," Norma Banks has told me, "then it becomes our job to decide which ones are trying too hard to get into the box and which ones are trying too hard to run the hell away from it."

Some, I know from my own experience, are just pissed they got called, don't want to be bothered, are more than willing to do everything except direct-message the judge to tell him or her or them that there's no way they can be impartial, just because sitting through a long trial seems to them like doing hard time of their own.

Through it all, though, the charge from the law for Katherine Welsh and me is the same, despite the fact that we have our own, and wildly opposite, agendas, and view the other side as the dark side:

To somehow seat a competent and hopefully diverse jury

that properly represents the community and will give the defendant a fair trial and the state an equally fair hearing.

Now, that sounds good and even high-minded. But all trial lawyers, either side of the aisle, know it's all complete BS. Both Katherine Welsh, repping the state, and me, defending a client who reminds me of every single bad choice I've ever made with men in my life, want the same thing in the end.

We want the jury to love us.

We have both been looking for love as we have grinded our way out of the morning and through the lunch recess and into the afternoon. Both Katherine and I have already gone through a handful of peremptory challenges when unable to agree on a candidate, for a whole laundry list of reasons.

I stand now, wearily, and begin questioning a woman from Westbury who runs her own small public relations firm in that town. She appears to be in her late thirties or perhaps early forties, well dressed, smart. Her answers to basic questions have been fine and occasionally ironic, first with Katherine Welsh, now with me.

Time for me to get to the money question.

"Just knowing what you know about the case, do you think you'll be able to give a fair hearing to the facts as they're presented to you?"

She gives a quick shake of her head.

"Probably not," she says evenly.

"Would you mind telling the court why?"

"Well, Ms. Smith, it's probably because the summer before last, your client failed to get me into bed despite relentless efforts, and an even more relentless refusal to take no for an answer," she says, still not changing the tone of her voice. Smiling now, rather wickedly, I think. "And then when he couldn't fuck me, he tried to do the same with my eighteen-year-old daughter."

"Okay then," I say. "Excused."

As I begin walking back to my table, I am well aware of the slow murmur running through the other potential jurors in the box.

But this one isn't quite finished.

"Don't turn your back on me," she snaps.

I wheel back around.

"You've already been excused," I say.

"Not until I get my money's worth," she says. "The good news, or maybe it's bad news for you, Ms. Smith, is that my daughter and I are still alive, which perhaps cheated you out of the chance to defend the sonofabitch on a couple of more murder raps."

Judge Horton is banging his gavel now. *"Step down, please,"* he says.

Finally, the woman does stand up from the witness chair, and begins walking across the courtroom, the sound of her clicking heels suddenly very loud. As she passes my table she slows only long enough to hiss, "Tell him that Missy Werner hopes he rots in hell after he rots in prison."

I watch her as she keeps going, *click-click-click*ing her way toward the courtroom's double doors before she is through them, and gone.

Norma Banks has followed her exit right along with me.

"Good talk," Norma says.

THIRTY-SIX

WE STAY AT IT for another couple of hours, with no further dramatics.

I am tired enough as we approach the end of the afternoon that I allow McGoey to start interviewing candidates. But as concerned as I am that he will, at worst, embarrass me, and at the very least try to make the whole thing about him, he does a solid and professional job. He mostly asks the same questions I would have asked and generally does nothing that will make that second chair of his empty by tomorrow morning.

Norma Banks has a yellow legal pad in front of her, and different-colored Magic Markers. She has been taking notes all afternoon when she isn't in my ear making snarky and occasionally profane comments about the ones upon which Katherine Welsh and I have agreed, and the ones we've both rejected.

Sometimes I would look over and see this, in red:

"FULL OF CRAP."

Or this in green:

"Dumb ass."

Or this one, in black:

"Shut up and get out asshole."

That one makes it impossible for me to stifle a laugh, even as McGoey is questioning a retired insurance agent from New Hyde Park, male, who looks old enough to have gone to college with Norma Banks.

"Something you find amusing, Ms. Smith?" Judge Horton says.

"Fighting a cold, Your Honor."

"Fight harder," he says.

It is a little before five o'clock when the last prospective juror of the long day sits down. He appears to be around my age, good-looking, dark suit, open-necked white shirt, mostly gray hair. Edward Oslin is his name. Retired venture capitalist, he says. Living now in Brookville, a place I know isn't for cheapies.

McGoey begins to stand. I stop him with a hand on his forearm.

"I'll take the cute guy," I whisper.

"*Tutto bene,*" McGoey whispers back, then grins. "It's an expression some of my other clients often use."

I start out making small talk with Edward Oslin, almost as if we'd met at a bar, and he goes right along with it, at one point saying he's enjoying himself more than he thought he would, at which point I see Katherine Welsh roll her eyes.

But we're almost up against Judge Horton's five o'clock deadline. And I really am tired as hell, so it's time for me to get to it.

"If seated, would you be prepared to stay both present and engaged across what might be a lengthy trial?" I ask him.

"Got nothing but time these days," he says. "I've discovered you can only play so much golf. Though I do have a very nice boat."

Another roll of the eyes from the district attorney, followed by an audible sigh.

"How much do you know about the facts of this case?" I ask Oslin.

"Only what I've read in the papers, and online," he answers. "And to be honest, I'm aware of the previous trial involving Mr. Jacobson."

"Any opinions about that one?"

"I actually followed it pretty closely. And to be honest

again, you turned out to be even better than I'd heard you were, because it frankly shocked the shit out of me that you managed to win him an acquittal."

He immediately turns to Judge Horton. "Sorry, about the language, Your Honor."

Horton shrugs. "We've already had somebody sitting where you're sitting drop the f-bomb today. I'm past having my delicate sensibilities be offended by language, even if it is getting late."

"One last question, Mr. Oslin," I say. "Do you have any other opinions you'd care to share about the events that have brought us all here today?"

I'm standing right in front of him when he shrugs, and smiles.

"Just one, I guess," he says. "Just off what I know already, I think he probably killed these people, too."

And, I think, *there it is.*

What a perfect way to end my day.

"Excused," I say.

"I object, Your Honor!"

I know immediately that the voice belongs to Norma Banks, even before I turn around to see her standing, with her hand raised toward Judge Horton like a kid in school, until Horton grins and explains to her that she's not allowed to object.

Norma apologizes. But even before she sits down, she is furiously waving me back to our table. When I get there, she grabs my arm and jerks me down close to her with surprising strength.

"Just what exactly do you think you're doing?" I whisper to her.

"It's the dumb ones we throw back," she whispers back. "This guy we keep."

"Why, because you think he's cute, too?" I ask her.

"No, you dumb-ass," she says. "I like him because he thinks you are."

THIRTY-SEVEN

NORMA TELLS ME THAT McGoey has offered to give her a ride to the train station.

"Does this mean you're warming up to him?" I ask.

"No," she says, "it means I never rode in a Maserati."

When they're gone, it's just Katherine Welsh and me alone in the courtroom. I'm still in my chair, mostly because I don't have the strength to even start thinking about the long ride home.

Welsh comes over.

"Well, to use that last guy's own words," she says, "that certainly shocked the shit out of *me*."

"Because I accepted him, you mean?"

She raises her perfect eyebrows and nods.

"He did say he thought your guy did it, did he not?" Katherine Welsh says. "As a matter of fact, it sounded like he thinks Mr. Jacobson has left a longer trail of victims than John Wick."

"I have great confidence in my powers of persuasion," I tell her, "what can I tell you?"

"I thought about using a challenge just because Norma was so fired up to have you seat him," she says. "But I decided to roll with it."

"And the good news is we get to do it all again tomorrow!" I say with completely false enthusiasm.

She remains standing over my table, still looking like a million bucks after a long day of legal grunt work.

"I really only know you by reputation," she says. "And I know what you said before about being all set to kick my ass. But are you absolutely certain you're going to be able to see this thing through?"

"Hundred percent," I say, without any hesitation.

"Well," she says, "I just wanted to say that."

"Noted for the record."

I can't tell whether she's trying to be sincere, or just trying to soften me up. When you have been at this kind of work as long as I have, with the scars to prove it even after one win after another, grading high on cynicism and sometimes even paranoia becomes part of your genetic code.

On the other hand, maybe she is being sincere, and isn't looking for an edge the way I always am.

Most of the time I like being Jane Effing.

Just not always.

"See you in the morning," I say.

She's still putting papers into her briefcase when I turn at the door.

"Katherine?" I say.

She swivels her head around.

"Thanks for asking," I say.

"You're welcome."

"By the way? I don't have any choice but to see this through."

My words sound surprisingly loud in the empty room.

"Because you're sick, you mean?"

"Because I owe it to my client," I say. I pause then and say, "Because even dead I'm a better lawyer than McGoey is."

Rip is waiting for me when I've unlocked my front door and deactivated the alarm.

"Oh, you think I don't know what that face means?" I say to him. "So you think I look like shit, too."

He just stands there, tail wagging, until he comes over to me and rubs up against my leg and lets me scratch him behind his ears. It's as if he knows how truly lousy I feel at the moment, in addition to how lousy I must look, my rescue dog rescuing me all over again.

"You try living on death row," I tell him, "and see how you like it."

He barks suddenly.

"Oh, wait," I say. "You already did that."

THIRTY-EIGHT

Jimmy

JIMMY GETS A CALL from a former criminal informant of his, a weasel he hasn't heard from in years and, until tonight, one Jimmy thinks might be dead by now, just going off the laws of probability for snitches like him.

But it turns out he's still among the living, still going by just one name, Blue.

"Remember me?" Blue asks.

"How'd you get this number?" Jimmy asks him back.

"That's how you greet a long-lost friend?"

"Lost, maybe. Never a friend."

"But still a giver," Blue says. "So do you want to know what really happened to Bobby Salvatore or not?"

Salvatore was a longtime bookie for Sonny Blum, and someone who kept wandering in and out of the Rob Jacobson case until somebody blew up his boat.

"How'd you know that I'm interested in Salvatore at all?" Jimmy asks.

"Because," Blue says, "even if my hearing isn't what it used to be, I do still manage to hear things now and then."

"So what have you heard and what is it going to cost me?"

"This one is on the house," Blue says. There's a brief hesitation at his end before he adds, "until maybe I need to call in a favor down the road."

Then he gives Jimmy what he has and who he has, which

is why the next afternoon Jimmy Cunniff is at Café Luxembourg, 70th and Amsterdam, always one of his favorite lunch spots in Manhattan, seated across a table from a slick young guy named Jeb Bernstein.

According to Blue, Bernstein has taken over Salvatore's book, despite the fact that Bernstein has been denying that fact up and down since he and Jimmy *sat* down.

"If you're not with Sonny," Jimmy says, "and not in the dirtbag line of succession due to Bobby's untimely passing, then please explain something to me, kid: Why are you here?"

There is a brief flicker of amusement in Bernstein's eyes, as if they're both in on the same joke. But Jimmy sees wariness in the eyes, too. He knows this look, having sat just like this across from a lot of smart guys deciding how much they want to tell him, or maybe just how much they think he'll believe.

"Why am I here?" Bernstein says, leaning back and staring at the ceiling. "Boy, who hasn't asked themselves an existential question like that at some point in their lives?"

"That an answer?"

"That a serious question, Jimmy?"

Bernstein doesn't look like someone who belongs in Bobby Salvatore's former line of work. He frankly looks like what he's told Jimmy he is, a former MBA from NYU who went to work in the National Football League office not long after getting his master's. Spent a few years after that working at the sports book at Caesars in Las Vegas. Then a year at Bally's Atlantic City.

"And now," he says, "I have worked my way back to the big, bad city."

Bernstein is slowly working on a Virgin Mary that has a lot going on in it, huge celery stalk and olives and even a jalapeño, salt and pepper around the rim of the glass. Jimmy is sipping black coffee.

"Why *did* you agree to meet with me?" Jimmy asks him.

"I like famous people," he says. "And, boy, are you and Jane Smith famous now. When you reached out to me, I thought, 'Wow, a chance to sit down with a real celebrity.'"

"Cut the shit," Jimmy says.

"You first," Jeb Bernstein says.

Jimmy looks around the room. It's a good New York room. He remembers seeing the actor Liam Neeson here a couple of times. Back in the old days, somebody'd told him, Neeson had a place in the neighborhood.

"I have a source," Jimmy says, "and a pretty good one, who swears that despite your denials, you are now moving up fast in Sonny Blum's organization."

"Who's Sonny Blum?" Bernstein asks innocently.

Jimmy nods. "The last guy who tried to fade me with a line like that ended up getting his house shot up like it was the toll booth in *The Godfather*." Jimmy grins at him. "Since we are speaking of godfather types."

"You need better sources, Jimmy."

There's something about the way he says his name that makes Jimmy want to reach across the table and give him a good smack.

"I'm in real estate," Bernstein says.

"For what," Jimmy says, "burial plots?"

"Yours or mine?" Bernstein asks, not missing a beat.

"I wasn't aware that Sonny Blum's interests ranged to real estate," Jimmy says.

"That sounds like something you should take up with Mr. Blum."

"I would," Jimmy says. "But he's a hard man to get a hold of."

"You seem to know more about him, and his interests, than I do," Bernstein says.

"Maybe you should google him," Jimmy says.

"I'm sorry I couldn't be of more help, or if I've wasted your time," Bernstein says. "But it sounds as if you should really be talking to Mr. Blum, and not me."

"I will eventually," Jimmy says.

"You sure about that?" Bernstein asks.

"Very."

Jimmy stands.

"Wait," Bernstein says. "You're not staying for lunch? I hear the cheeseburger here is practically, well, to die for."

Jimmy leans down now, both palms flat on the table, his face close to Bernstein's. He can hear and feel the area around them suddenly get much quieter, as if someone in Café Luxembourg has hit a mute button.

"Kid," Jimmy says, "you're not going to last a year with Sonny Blum."

Bernstein doesn't lean back, or flinch even slightly, just keeps his eyes (almost more black than blue) locked on Jimmy's.

"Wanna bet?" Bernstein says.

THIRTY-NINE

ROBBY SASSOON AND JEB Bernstein are walking north in the 60s on the East River Greenway, between the FDR and the water, moving up on New York Hospital. It is understood between the two men, though they've never come right out and discussed it, that Bernstein is in his current position with Sonny Blum because Robby was the one who blew up Bobby Salvatore's boat with him on it.

Robby spared Anthony Licata that day by telling him to get off the boat once it was out on the water because the hit was coming. By then Robby knew that Licata, who had stopped being useful to Sonny Blum, had about the same life expectancy as a container of milk left out in the sun. What he didn't know is that it would be the lawyer who got it done with Licata in Montauk. That was the night when Robby realized what a worthy adversary Jane Smith was and why, when the time came, he wanted her to know that he was the one getting it done with her.

Unless her cancer became even more aggressive and spoiled all his fun.

As always, Robby is dressed in business formal, even on a long outdoor walk like this. Dark suit, one of many that look exactly like this, white shirt with just the right amount of starch, dark tie. The only concession he has made to being on the path used for walking and biking and jogging is his pair of black Cole Haan oxfords, with the air soles that make them feel as soft as sneakers while still looking very sharp. But in almost all matters, Robby Sassoon is a practical man.

The kid Bernstein looks as if he's just come from his one o'clock class. But Robby knows, just off the time he's spent with Jeb Bernstein and the research he's done on him, that the kid is a natural for this world, and the kind of work he's doing, and the man for whom he's doing it. Bernstein, just by the way he dresses, is far more concerned with appearances than a thug like Salvatore was. But every bit as much of a killer.

"What did you think of Cunniff?" Robby asks.

"He'd bother me more if I knew he was going to be around longer than he actually is," Bernstein says.

In the distance, Robby can make out the RFK Bridge, even if he still refuses to call it that, one of those who won't give up calling it the Triboro, the way New Yorkers won't give in and call the 59th Street Bridge the Ed Koch. The renaming of the bridges is one more thing in the modern world that offends Robby Sassoon's sense of order. Soon they'd be coming for the Brooklyn Bridge, too, wait and see.

"Trust me," Robby says. "Cunniff isn't to be underestimated any more than the lawyer is."

He hears Bernstein chuckle. "Nor are we, of course."

Like we're a team, Robby thinks. *Like we're Jane Smith and Jimmy Cunniff.*

Until we're not.

Traffic on the FDR is backed up both ways. It is another reason why Robby Sassoon does as much walking as he does when he's in the city, always giving himself time to get from one place to another. Or one job to another. He doesn't need the stress of Midtown traffic, the unpredictability of it, the jarring sound of car horns. All he wants is order in his life, and in his work.

"I've been meaning to ask," Bernstein says finally. "How did your meeting with Martin Elian go?"

Robby smiles to himself as he recalls the look on Elian's face that night at his restaurant. He looked so scared when he realized who Robby was and who had sent him that it was as if Robby had picked up a steak knife and put it to his throat.

"We now have his full attention in regard to his payment responsibilities," Robby says, "and, more importantly, his payment schedule."

They walk a few yards in silence before Robby asks, "I'm genuinely curious: Why do people continue to avail themselves of your services when they have all those legal options now?"

"That's a very good question," Bernstein says. "For one thing, and unless you fuck around the way somebody like Martin Elian has, bets with us are settled on a weekly basis, or monthly, or whatever we've worked out. For another, you don't have to navigate those systems advertised incessantly on TV that seem to grow more complicated by the hour. And finally, we, as bookmakers, believe we offer a better and far less taxed product, at the same time we allow our customers to float debt." He chuckles again. "Until they abuse that privilege, or think we've somehow forgotten them."

"I'm told that the big juice for the online places is crazy," Robby says.

"It is," Bernstein says. "But you want to know what's really the best part, at least on our end? We've now got the same cops and even judges who used to try to bust our chops laying down action with us left and right. If you can't lick 'em, join 'em."

"Some world," Robby says.

"Isn't it, though," Bernstein says. "And you're talking to a guy who used to work at a place, the NFL, that used to try to act like gambling was the devil."

"You ready to head back?" Robby says.

"Sure," Bernstein says, and then tells Robby why he wanted to take this walk. He has a new job for him, a request from Mr. Blum that they both know isn't a request at all.

"You know why we understand each other?" Robby says. "It's because we're both gentlemen. Bobby Salvatore was a lowlife and a scumbag, one who refused to keep up with the times."

"So you can take care of this matter with her?" Bernstein says.

"I might even buy flowers first."

"How soon?"

"Today."

"Seriously?" Jeb Bernstein asks.

"Why put off until tomorrow when you can kill today?" Robby Sassoon says.

Bernstein probably thinks it is a gesture of camaraderie, or even friendship, when Robby reaches over and pats him on the head. He has no idea that it's Robby's calling card, but then no one does, until it's too late.

FORTY

HE WAITS UNTIL HE sees her hang the CLOSED sign in the window a little after six thirty.

The Uncommon Florist is tucked into a far corner at Bridgehampton Commons, directly across from Staples and down the row from Dunkin' and Barnes & Noble and The Gap. Most of the other places in this part of the big outdoor mall, with the exception of the huge King Kullen grocery store, are already closed.

Robby Sassoon has parked his car a few hundred yards away on the far side of the parking lot and walked to the flower shop from there.

He has listened to the entire cast recording of *Les Misérables* on the way out from Manhattan.

"Look down, look down," he sings softly to himself as he makes the long walk from where he's left the car in front of TJ Maxx. "You're standing in your own grave."

It's fitting that she'll be surrounded by flowers, he tells himself.

By now he knows when she likes to close up for the day and, better yet, knows how easy it will be for him to pick the lock on the back door without being heard and simply walk into the store from there.

He has done his due diligence on the owner, Beth Lassiter, knows that she was once a softball pitcher at the University of

Florida, and that she moved up here after a divorce five years ago and started her own small business.

But there is more to her story than that. Much more.

Beth has a secret.

She has a gambling problem. An even bigger problem is that she likes to bet on baseball, which Jeb Bernstein says is even riskier than betting on other pro sports, just because to be successful—which few are, he says—you have to follow the sport even more closely than all the bean counters who pretty much run baseball teams now. It means, Jeb says, that even the savviest baseball bettors don't know nearly as much about the sport as they think they do. Or need to.

Sadly, Beth Lassiter isn't smart or savvy about who she's betting on or how much she's betting, which is why the adorable little place where she sells her flowers and plants is about to go under, and why she is planning to disappear, something else Robby has learned in researching the pathetic state of her life.

Beth Lassiter just plans to close up one night and leave Long Island for good, having already told the owner of the house she's been renting in Sag Harbor that she won't be renewing her lease.

Details, Robby thinks.

The devil is always in the details.

The devil in this case being me.

Beth isn't about to run from the back rent she owes on the Uncommon Florist, although that would be bad enough. She's also about to run out on the $200,000 she owes to Jeb Bernstein, which means the big money she owes to Sonny Blum.

Robby walks around behind the grocery store and quietly lets himself in the back door she hasn't even had time to lock yet. Beth Lassiter never hears him as he walks up to where she's standing at her counter, her back to him, and puts his hand over her mouth.

"Hush," he says softly into her ear.

★ ★ ★

He wants to feel badly for her, he really does, all the beauty around her, the roses and lilies and bouquets she's already arranged in vases; and all the orchids, purple and white, big and small, on the long table that stretches along one of the walls in the front room.

But he doesn't feel badly for her.

She did this to herself.

They all do, none of them ever considering that actions will have consequences.

Robby has tied her to a chair in the back room, knowing he will untie her later and leave her on the floor in the front room, as if this is some kind of smash-and-grab robbery gone wrong, the cops will never know how little cash there actually was in her register.

His Beretta is in his hand now.

There is tape over her mouth, but at least she has finally stopped struggling.

Beth Lassiter is just crying now, her red, terrified eyes fixed on him, as if she's afraid to look away.

He has pulled up a chair and is sitting close to her.

"I will remove the tape so that we can have a civilized conversation," Robby says. "But I want you to know that if you scream, I will shoot you right now. Nod if you understand what I'm saying to you."

When Beth Lassiter nods, vigorously, eyes focused on the gun, he reaches over and removes the tape, trying not to hurt her as he pulls it off her.

As soon as he does, she says, "I can have the money by the end of the week. I told Jeb that."

Robby sighs. "But that was a lie, wasn't it, Beth?"

"*No,*" she says. "My sister...in San Francisco...her husband is rich."

Robby is sadly shaking his head. "There is no sister," he says. "There is no money, apart from all that you lost because you were dumb enough to bet on baseball in the first place, and then keep doing it once you were in the hole."

She starts to sob now, chest rising and falling, almost unable to breathe.

"Beth, Beth, Beth," Robby says, patting her knee. "You should know as well as anyone that there's no crying in baseball."

"I . . . just a little more time," she says, barely able to get the words out.

"And if it were my decision to make," Robby says, "I would give you that time. But my employer has decided to make an example out of you."

"But if I'm dead, you'll never get the money," she says.

"Unfortunately, my employer sees no reasonable expectation to get it with you alive, even if he takes everything you own," he says. "Which, frankly, and without being too hurtful, isn't much at this point, is it?"

The last thing she sees before he shoots her are the flowers, as if she's somehow done the arrangements for her own funeral.

After he's staged the robbery scene to his satisfaction, he lets himself out the back door and begins walking back across the parking lot to his car. As he does, one of his favorite songs from *Les Mis* is back inside his head.

"Lovely ladies, ready for the call," he sings. "Standing up or lying down."

As always, Robby tells himself, *you never really can go wrong with a show tune.*

FORTY-ONE

DR. BEN KALINSKY AND I had scheduled a stay-at-home date for tonight.

"What doesn't kill you makes you stronger," I said after informing him that I would be doing all of the cooking.

"Isn't that supposed to be your line?" he said. "And just for the record, counselor? I *like* your cooking, something I've pointed out on multiple occasions."

"Okay, it's official," I said. "You really do love me."

But a few minutes ago he called to tell me he's going to be late: he's stopped to check out some police activity at Bridgehampton Commons on his way from Southampton; he couldn't help himself.

"You poor thing," I said. "I've gone and turned you into a crime junkie."

"Next I'm getting one of those police streamers."

"Scanners," I correct him. "And what kind of activity is going on, if you don't mind me asking?"

"You know that little flower shop in the Commons?"

"Sadly, I do not."

"Well, it's where, about a month ago, I picked up that orchid you like," he says. "Woman named Beth owns it. Or did."

"Uh-oh. Past tense?"

"Apparently somebody broke in to the place and shot her," Ben says. "Cops say it looks like a robbery."

"At a *florist?*"

"Just reporting the facts, ma'am."

"How many times do I have to tell you not to 'ma'am' me?"

Ben finally arrives right before eight. Pasta tonight for us, my homemade marinara sauce, big turkey meatballs because small meatballs make me crazy, and a salad chock full of veggies I picked up at Balsam Farms. I'm even feeling well enough that I am going to allow myself a glass of Quilt, one of Ben's favorite cabernets and one of mine.

Jimmy is in the city. I asked him why and he said, "A fool's errand, most likely."

"No one better for work like that than you," I said, before he told me to do something totally inappropriate, at least for a lady.

I pointed that out to him.

"What lady?" he said.

Jury selection is well concluded by now. Opening statements will be on Monday. I am in the early stages of writing the first draft of mine. I explain to Ben over dinner that I've decided to make it shorter than what have occasionally turned into epic poems in the past.

"So as not to lose their attention by going on too long?" he asks.

"So as to keep from falling over if I go on too long."

He smiles. "Marry me," he says.

"No!" I say, quickly and emphatically enough that he laughs.

I drink some wine. It's going down without incident. So far, so good.

"You look beautiful tonight," Ben says.

"The witness is reminded that he is still under oath."

"When it comes to you," he says, "I only tell the truth, the whole truth, and nothing but. Or something along those lines."

"But those lines can blur, as you know."

"Because love is blind?" he asks, still smiling.

"Obviously!" I say, and then lean across the table and kiss him, the force of it surprising both of us.

"Be careful," Ben says, "or we might not be able to eat in this restaurant ever again."

"Who gives a shit?" I say. "The food here sucks."

We're in bed later, Rip having been banished to the living room, but with a bone, as I'm not a monster. The windows are open. In the distance, more than a mile from the water, I can hear the faint and familiar sound of the waves, even over the traffic on Route 27.

If I do make it to heaven—and being the lawyer I am, I'm confident I'll be able to talk my way right past Saint Peter—I still want to be near the ocean.

"Are you absolutely certain you're ready for this trial?" Ben asks now.

"Even the district attorney is asking me that now," I say. "Pretty soon the checkout woman at the IGA is going to want to know."

I turn slightly. "Do *you* think I'm not ready for this?"

We lit one of my favorite candles before the festivities in here, a wood sage scent from Jo Malone, so I can see him smile again in the flickering light.

"I'm just worried that while the spirit is clearly willing, the flesh might be a tad weak."

I smile back at him. "Well, I think I just disproved that, didn't I?"

He kisses me. It doesn't feel anything at all like a good-night kiss, and we both know it.

"Mine's not weak," he says.

Our faces are very close, our eyes wide.

"Really?" I ask. "Round two?"

"You only live once," Ben says, and I have just enough time to tell him that one really is supposed to be my line.

FORTY-TWO

Jimmy

ROB JACOBSON STILL REFERS to the Manhattan town house where his father and his father's teenaged mistress were murdered—back when Rob was a teenager himself, and where, if Paul Harrington is to be believed, Jacobson himself murdered his own father—as his home away from home.

"Is that what guys like you call a fuck pad these days?" Jimmy asks when he stops by Jacobson's rented house in Amagansett after lunch.

"You can use it if you want," Jacobson says, "provided you ever get laid again."

"I'd rather just search it," Jimmy tells him.

"For what?"

"Something," Jimmy says, "or anything that might actually convince me you didn't do it and might help Jane convince a jury. Again."

"See there," Jacobson says. "I knew that deep down you really cared."

"Gonna need a key."

"Mi casa es su casa," Jacobson says.

"Just get the fucking key," Jimmy says.

Jacobson goes upstairs and returns with a key and hands it over.

"Knock yourself out," he says. "I'll call and tell my house-guests that you're going to show up."

"Don't tell me," Jimmy says. "More debutantes?"

"Would you expect anything less?"

"Definitely not anything more," Jimmy says, and leaves, happy to be away from Jacobson, the way he always is. By now there isn't a day that goes by when Jimmy Cunniff doesn't find himself wondering whose side he is really on here.

Other than his own.

Jane, in her heart of hearts, is still holding out hope that Jacobson might be innocent of killing the Carson family, same as she held out hope, even after his acquittal, that he hadn't murdered the Gateses.

Jimmy wants him to go down.

It would be the first loss of Jane's career if he does go down, and maybe her last. But it's different for Jimmy, in his own heart of hearts. If things do play out that way, if the asshole does get convicted, Jimmy will put this one into the win column.

Hundred percent.

FORTY-THREE

Jimmy

ONE OF THE GIRLS answers the door.

Jimmy can't help himself. When they're as young as this one clearly is, he thinks of them as girls. If that makes him feel older than he really is, screw it.

"Rob told me you might show up," she says after Jimmy introduces himself. "I'm Kellye. With another *e* at the end."

"Can't ever have enough," Jimmy says.

She steps aside and Jimmy enters the ornate foyer, with its marble floor and what he's sure are expensive paintings on the walls. He's been here before, and is always more impressed with the marble he's standing on than the art. He finds himself imagining all over again what the walls of this place, even the ones down here, could say if they could talk, about all the messed-up shit they've seen here, all the way back to the days when Rob Jacobson's old man was the master of the house and head pervert.

Like father, like son.

"How old are you, Kellye with an *e*?" Jimmy asks.

She grins. "Rob told me you were his chief investigator, not from the Census Bureau," she says.

Smart, Jimmy thinks.

It makes him want to like her.

But if she's got any kind of relationship with Jacobson going, he'll be able to fight the urge with absolutely no problem.

"How come he's letting you live here?" Jimmy asks now.

"Other than me being as fun as I am?"

"Define fun."

"Are you asking if we're fucking?" Kellye says. "Because we're not."

"So then what benefits does he get out of letting you live in his house?"

She shrugs. "Like, he doesn't have to pay a housekeeper?"

"But there's somebody else living here, too, am I right?" Jimmy says.

"Paula."

"Is Paula hooking up with him, either when he sneaks into the city or out there?"

"Every chance they get," Kellye says.

"Is Paula here right now?"

"If you drove in, you probably passed her on the LIE," she says. "Today is a booty call day out on eastern Long Island, pretty sure."

"What does Paula do?"

She grins again. "For Rob, or in general?"

"In general."

"I think she's majoring in being famous at NYU," Kellye says. "Hence doing it with Rob."

"What about you?"

"I'm an actress."

Jimmy nods. "Aren't you all," he says, and proceeds to ask her if she has any problem with him searching her room along with every other one in the place. She tells him she's got nothing to hide and is on her way to an audition for a TV commercial.

"Looking to bundle your car insurance?" she says in a perky way, but Jimmy is already on his way up the steps.

When he gets to the top of the ornate staircase, he turns and looks down at her.

"Does it bother you that he might have killed those people?" Jimmy asks.

"I've got an even better question," she says back to him. "Does it bother you?"

Jimmy methodically goes room to room, starting on the top floor. At least Jimmy feels like a cop today.

Focus on that, he tells himself.

There are rooms here that look as if they belong in a museum, but he knew that before showing up today. Five bedrooms in all, so many bathrooms he's lost count. The smallest bedroom, on the third floor, must have been the maid's quarters at some point. There is a small home theater on the second floor.

But no family pictures on any of the walls, on any of the floors. Not a single one. Maybe Jacobson had them taken down at some point. Or maybe they were never here at all. All Jimmy knows about Jacobson's mother is that she died young. Cancer, he thinks he read somewhere when he and Jane first took the case. But no pictures of her, no pictures of her husband, no pictures of their son, as a baby or young man or anywhere in between.

The second-floor study is where the bodies of Robinson Jacobson and the girl—Carey Watson—were found, on the floor in front of the huge antique desk. But the drawers of the desk are all empty, as if they had been cleaned out, maybe years ago.

Jimmy takes out his phone and takes some pictures of the room, anyway, just to have a visual later of where the story really started for Rob Jacobson, whether or not he did his old man and whether or not his buddy Edmund McKenzie, another son of a rich man, another mutt, helped him.

Jimmy stands in the middle of the room and looks around and wonders if living here ever gives these two girls the creeps.

By now he has spent a couple of hours in the town house and marked it a total waste of time. He'll tell Jane all about it on the ride home, maybe after making a quick stop at the original P. J. Clarke's for a cheeseburger, something else that will surely bring back memories, and good ones, of his cop days, back when he was trying to put bad guys away, not save their sorry asses.

He lets himself out, locks the door behind him, does stop at Clarke's for a burger and a beer, and is walking to where he parked his car on East 55th Street, the lights of the city on all around him, when he reaches for his phone and realizes he must have left it on Robinson Jacobson's desk.

Pissed at himself, he drives back over to the West Side, finds a spot at a hydrant in front of the building, and impatiently fumbles with the key for a minute, cursing, before he gets it to work and lets himself in.

Kellye is standing in the middle of the foyer, pointing a gun at him as he steps inside.

"Hey," Jimmy says, putting his hands up. *"Hey."*

She points the barrel at the marble floor when she sees who it is.

"You could have rung the bell," she says.

"I was in a hurry," he says. "And I do have a key."

"You're lucky I didn't shoot you," she says.

Jimmy is the one pointing now, at the gun.

"Where did you get that thing?"

"I found it," she says.

"Where did you find it?" Jimmy asks her.

"Where Robby must've hid it."

FORTY-FOUR

Jimmy

THEY ARE SEATED AT a corner table at Jimmy's bar late, the place still fairly crowded on a Friday night. Jimmy called the meeting on his way back from the city.

His whole life Jimmy Cunniff has never called it Manhattan or thought of it that way. Always the city. If you grew up in the outer boroughs like he did, you were always going to the city. Or coming back from it. Even if all you ever wanted, even as a kid, was the NYPD, the city was the goal.

He called both Jane and Danny Esposito once he had his phone back and told them what he had—or might have—and that they couldn't wait until tomorrow to decide what to do with it.

"How did you know I might not be on a date?" Jane asks.

"You already had your date night for the week."

"Am I really that predictable?" she says.

"We both know the answer to that," Jimmy says.

The gun he took from Kellye is on the table in front of them. He had the girl put it in the baggie that he held open for her, even knowing that the only usable prints on the thing were likely going to be hers.

"So you think this could be the gun Rob used on the Carsons?" Esposito says.

"I think you meant to say that *someone* might have used on the Carsons," Jane says.

132

Jimmy sees a cocky grin from the guy. By now Jimmy is well aware what a cocky bastard Danny Esposito is. But he has to admit Esposito wears it well, like the leather jacket, and the long hair, and the shades that he at least manages to take off when he's indoors, sometimes only as a last resort, the sunglasses being one more piece to help him stay in character.

"Whatever could have gotten into me?" Esposito says to Jane, and drinks some beer. "Occasionally I forget I'm a dedicated public servant." He toasts her with his mug. "My apologies."

"Accepted," Jane says, "even though we both know you're not really sorry."

"But as you are a dedicated public servant," Jimmy says to Esposito, "and a sneaky shit when you need to be, you are going to test-fire this thing tomorrow—or have somebody test-fire it for you—as a way of looking at the lands and the groove measurements of the rounds they recovered at the scene and in a couple of the bodies."

"And if the gun turns out to be the murder weapon," Danny says to Jane, "then you, being a dedicated officer of the court, will be duty bound to turn it over to Katherine Welsh, correct?"

"*Shit,*" Jane says. "I was afraid of that."

Esposito makes eye contact with a good-looking blonde at the far end of the bar and gives her the nod.

"Stay with us," Jimmy tells him.

"Guy can look," Esposito says.

"And dream," Jane says, looking across the room at the blonde.

Now Esposito says, "Has it occurred to either one of you that somebody besides Jacobson might have hid that gun at his place?"

Kellye showed Jimmy where in the town house she'd found it, in a closet in the master bedroom, top shelf, underneath more cashmere sweaters than you'd find in the men's department at Bloomingdale's.

"What was this Kellye girl doing in there, by the way?" Jane asks.

"She says she searches the place from time to time, hoping she might find cash he might have stashed and forgotten," Jimmy says. "Like his rainy-day fund."

"Sounds like a sweet kid," Esposito says.

"Daddy's little girl," Jimmy says.

"Well, sugar daddy maybe," Jane says.

Jane takes a sip of red wine. Jimmy was surprised when she ordered it, but doesn't say anything. Maybe she's feeling better tonight.

"Or maybe the gun really does belong to Jacobson and he *wanted* her to find it," Esposito says.

"Or wanted me to find it when he agreed to let me search the place," Jimmy says.

"But you didn't. She did. And why plant his own murder weapon, if that's what it is?" Jane says.

"To mess with us?" Jimmy muses. "Wouldn't be the first time, right? And it's a long-established fact that the guy obviously thinks he can get away with anything."

"Maybe he wanted to see if you'd actually turn it over if you did find it?" Esposito says.

"The asshole does love playing games," Jimmy says. "And not just sex games."

"Does he own this particular gun?" Jane asks Jimmy. "I know you've already checked."

"If he does own it," Jimmy says, "he didn't buy it legally, because I did make a couple of calls on my way out."

"Means shit," Esposito says. "You know who can get a gun these days? Everybody. You know where? Anywhere."

"But let's say, for the sake of conversation, that it was used on the Carsons that night," Jane says. "Why keep it instead of tossing it into the ocean, or one of the many other bodies of water available to him?"

Jimmy drinks some of his beer. "Because he's batshit crazy?" he says.

"Or because he's just hot-messing around with the two of you all over again," Danny Esposito says.

"But if it isn't Jacobson who wanted the gun found," Jimmy says, "who did?"

Quietly Jane says, "Maybe somebody who wants Rob to look guiltier than he already does. And who knows even he isn't batshit crazy enough to keep the murder weapon around like a keepsake."

No one says anything until Jimmy suddenly slaps the table hard with the palm of his hand, making the mugs and Jane's wineglass jump.

"*Fuck!*" he yells, causing heads to turn in their direction from the bar.

"What's wrong?" Jane asks him.

"What's wrong," he says, "is that I'm suddenly not nearly as sure as I'd like to be that our guy did it."

He drains his beer and holds up his empty mug so that Kenny the bartender can see it.

"Sonofabitch," Jimmy says, lowering his voice now. "Did those words really just come out of my mouth?"

He sees Jane smiling at him, as she reaches over to pat his hand.

"You're the one who sounds sick," she says.

FORTY-FIVE

EVEN BEN DOESN'T KNOW this, but I've taken to washing my hair only in the bathroom sink, as a way of making sure it's still not falling out.

I was one of the lucky ones who *didn't* go bald during chemo, and maybe I'm due for something that passes for good luck across the same hideous journey as any other cancer patient. My sister, Brigid, was not as lucky, which is why she ended up buying various wigs of various lengths as a way of making herself look natural.

I may be done with chemo, but a girl can't be too sure about something as important as her hair.

Dr. Sam Wylie keeps reassuring me that it's rare for someone to have a delayed reaction with hair loss.

"How rare?" I asked her earlier today on the phone.

"Extremely."

"Give me some numbers."

"There's no point," she says. "You know you've never been any good at keeping numbers straight in your head, all the way back to high school."

"I'm more concerned about what's happening on top of my head, doc," I tell her, and Sam tells me to trust her, there's a better chance of me losing my sense of humor than my hair.

But I am testing very high on paranoia these days—any cancer patient who says they don't is lying—and that is why

I continue to do a wellness check on my hair every time I wash it. Even after I'm done and dried, I pull on it, as if trying to determine whether or not it's real.

Tonight I wash it again, as a way of distracting myself from the nausea I was feeling after just one glass of red, and not even the whole glass, over at Jimmy's bar.

No hair around the drain when I'd finished my shampoo.

No harm, I tell myself, no foul.

But this has still become one of those nights when I can't even remember what it was like for me before I routinely felt sick to my stomach, and so weak in the middle of the day I had to lie down; when I wasn't experiencing the mood swings that came with the medication they pumped into me in Switzerland, the chemically induced hot flashes and night sweats.

When I finally cool down enough to fall asleep, my mind still racing with the possibility that we may be in possession of the murder weapon—and that I may have to turn it over to the district attorney—I don't dream of hummingbirds tonight, or my mother, who loved hummingbirds even more than I do.

Tonight I dream as if I'm the one flying, before diving straight toward the water like a gull and then disappearing into the darkness below.

Then I'm wide awake suddenly, sweating more than ever, out of breath, panting the way my dog is at his end of the bed.

When I'm fully awake, I call Rob Jacobson and tell him about the gun Jimmy took off his friend Kellye at the town house.

"Not my gun," he says, trying to sound innocent, not exactly a role he was born to play. "The last gun I knew about in that house was the one my father used on his girl-friend, before he turned it on himself." He pauses. "By the way, Janie? You ever think how appropriate it was, him getting one more piece like that before he rested in peace?"

"You're not funny," I say.

"Little bit?" he asks.

"You know, Paul Harrington says you were the one who shot your father that day," I say.

"You need to stop talking to dirty cops as much as you do, Janie. Starting with the one who works for you."

"You should try saying that to Jimmy's face," I say. "Now *that* would be funny."

"Janie," he says again, knowing how much I hate him calling me that, "how many times do I have to tell you I've never killed anybody?"

Then he tells me he has to cook up some eggs for someone named Paula, whoever the hell she is.

I take Rip for a long walk on Indian Wells Beach. On our way home, I decide to stop at Jack's on Main Street for coffee. I've never really been a coffee nerd, but I like the coffee here as much as I do from the Jack's near my apartment in the West Village.

As I'm standing in line, Rip waiting for me in the car, I hear a male voice behind me say, "Excuse me, but aren't you Jane Smith?"

I turn to see a tall man, nice tan, open-necked white shirt. Not bad looking.

"Tragically, I am."

"Your trial starts soon, right?"

"Day after tomorrow, as a matter of fact."

I'm grateful that I've now moved to the head of the line, having already exhausted my capacity for small talk with a stranger, even a good-looking one.

"Well, good luck with it," the man says.

Then he does something odd, startling me as he reaches over and lightly pats me on the head.

FORTY-SIX

WHILE I WAIT TO hear from Danny Esposito about the gun, I spend Saturday morning at home, once again going over my opening statement, doing what I always do, writing and then rewriting the first draft longhand.

So it's me and my legal pad and my cursive Catholic school penmanship, the floor around my desk filling with crumpled-up yellow paper as I try to get it down right, occasionally stopping to read out loud before crumpling up more paper. I don't even think about writing the ending yet—ending to a beginning—because I know there's no point until I find out from Danny what happened when he test-fired the gun the girl found at Rob Jacobson's town house, and then ran the ballistics on it.

At the bar last night, Jimmy told me that he only felt good about having done some real cop work in the city, even though the gun had basically fallen into his lap, along with a lot of potential problems for us.

"Real cop work as opposed to what?" I asked.

"Aiding and abetting."

"You still feel as if that's what we're doing with our client?"

"You said it, not me," Jimmy replied before walking me out to my car.

Aiding and abetting.

Is that the way I might be going out?

Thomas McGoey shows up at noon for our planned trial prep, having picked up sandwiches for us at Goldberg's on his way from his place in Quogue. My lunch order is a corned beef Reuben, even knowing my stomach will probably pay a heavy price for that later. McGoey is having an Italian sub that when he takes it out of the bag looks to be as long as his arm.

"A hero from a place called Goldberg's?" I ask. "Isn't that some kind of mixed message?"

"I pride myself on embracing all cultures and ethnicities."

"Italian especially, from your client list."

He grins. "Always remember something," he says. "It's not personal, Jane. Just business."

"Please don't do The Godfather," I say, "I'm begging you."

"Are you joking? With my aforementioned client list, those movies are like finishing school."

We eat and talk about the gun, McGoey trying to convince me that we actually might be able to use it to our advantage if it does turn out to be the one that fired the bullets found at the murder scene.

"But if it does belong to Rob and he did plant it at his own house, I mean, what the fuck?" McGoey says.

"Maybe at this point he's convinced himself that he really is bullet*proof*."

It's odd seeing McGoey not wearing what I think of as his shark suit. White polo shirt today, slightly wrinkled, jeans faded to nearly the color of the shirt, beat-up topsiders, no socks. By now he's devoured his sub. I've eaten about half of my sandwich, giving the rest of the pastrami to Rip, who, when it comes to food, absolutely does embrace all cultures and ethnicities.

But sitting across from McGoey at the kitchen table, it occurs to me how comfortable I am talking lawyer with him, even with what Jimmy calls his goombah résumé.

"I assume you still plan to come in hot on Hank Carson's gambling," he says.

"Hank will be just one of the dead guys I plan to put on trial."

"Who's the other?"

"Bobby Salvatore."

McGoey nods. "Nothing like prosecuting those no longer with us to defend themselves."

"While keeping in mind that Carson is the victim, and it is going to be our theory that it was his gambling that got his wife and daughter killed."

We move out to the back porch after we've cleaned up the kitchen. When we're outside, McGoey begins throwing one of Rip's disgusting tennis balls for him to fetch. Clearly a dog guy.

"You know the drill," I say. "Do whatever it takes."

"And then you *really* get serious after that."

I smile now. "I have a special practice these days," I say. "I only handle one client."

"Wait, you get to do The Godfather and I don't?"

"You're still only second chair."

We sit there for a while as Rip keeps chasing the ball.

"Your dog likes me," McGoey says.

"He likes you because your arm hasn't fallen off yet."

McGoey turns to face me. "How about you? Do you like me?"

"TBD," I say. "At least for as long as I'm still around."

"You're too hard to kill," he says.

"Something else that's TBD."

We go over our witness list.

"I see Sonny Blum isn't on here."

"Not yet."

"But how can you call him if you can't find him?"

"I've got Jimmy Cunniff looking for him, is how."

"Still not going to be easy," he says, "not even for Jimmy."

"My father always told me that the easy jobs don't pay very well."

"So you're sure you can serve him?"

"Yes, she lied," I tell Thomas McGoey.

"Music to my ears."

"I've only spoken to Jimmy about this," I say. "But the real reason I want to get old Sonny on the stand is because he's the one I really plan to put on trial for the murder of the Carson family. Bobby Salvatore worked for him. Hank Carson was in the hole to *him*. And, on a slightly more personal note, it's his goons who have tried to kill me on more than one occasion."

I smile at him again. "So at the very least, I owe him a good beating."

"You know how dangerous he is."

"Almost as dangerous as I am," I say.

McGoey is on his way back to Quogue, and I tell myself I'm going to work on the opening statement for a couple more hours. But I'm suddenly so tired that I turn on a baseball game from a past postseason that does include my Mets, lie down on the couch, and promptly fall asleep. The ball game ends up watching me.

I am awakened by my phone.

When I grab it off the coffee table I see ESPOSITO on the screen.

"I got the results," he says.

"Talk to me."

"You want the good news first, or the bad news?"

"Surprise me."

"Actually," Danny Esposito says, "there is no good news."

FORTY-SEVEN

ROB JACOBSON'S RENTAL HOME is, as we like to say on the South Fork, on the south side of the highway. It means he's living closer to the ocean than where I am, on my own side of the highway.

Jacobson's lady friend, at least of the moment, is just leaving when I show up unannounced following my phone conversation with Danny Esposito.

"Jane," my client says amiably, "this is Paula. Paula is about to walk to the Jitney stop."

The Jitney is the luxury bus that shuttles people between the Hamptons and Manhattan.

"Don't talk to strangers," I say to the girl, who looks just like all the rest of them. Tall, young, blond, so skinny I really want to recommend a hot meal as soon as she gets to Manhattan, jeans so tight I find myself wondering how long it takes for her to get into them. Getting out of them apparently isn't an issue.

After Paula kisses Rob good-bye, I say to her, "Does it ever bother you, being in bed with this guy?"

"Hey, I'm a lot cheaper than you are," she says, and then adds, "Adios," as she gives me a wave of the hand, theatrically shaking what I have to admit is an almost perfect butt as she walks away.

"No dumb blonde that one," Jacobson says.

"Define dumb," I say.

When we're both seated in the living room and after I've declined to join him in a glass of wine, he says, "Is this a business call, or social?"

"I am all business today, Rob."

"Damn, I was afraid of that," he says. "So what's up?"

"The gun your other squatter found in the town house is the one used on the Carson family," I say. "Bullets are a match."

"Wait...*what?*"

"You heard me."

"Janie," he says, "my answer on that gun hasn't changed. I have no goddamn idea how it got there."

"Don't lie to me!"

I surprise myself with how hot the words come out. Sometimes I'm able to resist the urge to yell at him this way. Not today. Fuck him.

He gives me what I now think of as The Smirk, a smile that is smug and arrogant and almost breathtakingly annoying, sometimes all at the same time.

"You want me to stop lying to you *now?*" he says. "What would be the fun in that?"

He reaches into the ice bucket on the coffee table, pours himself some white wine, takes a healthy swallow of it, and smiles approvingly.

"I'm sure I've mentioned before what a scumbag I think you are," I say.

"Repeatedly."

"With cause."

He's still smirking then as he says, "Hey, I've got an idea: Want to go upstairs and fool around a little bit? Paula won't be back until next weekend."

I stare at him. I've long since lost the ability to be shocked by anything he says, or anything I find out he's done. But then he acts like a pig, or sounds like one, all over again.

"Now that I think of it," I say, "'scumbag' might actually be insulting to all the other scumbags in the world. So I take that back."

He shrugs.

"Well, it was worth a shot," he says. "I was just thinking that if you're going to talk bad to me, it would be much more fun for me if we were in bed while you did."

FORTY-EIGHT

Jimmy

THE THROUGH LINE BETWEEN Sonny Blum and so many elements of Rob Jacobson's case has grown so long that Jimmy now has Jane as fixed on Blum as he is. He's promised not only to locate Blum but also to find a way to serve him so that she can call him as a witness.

When she asks how he plans to do that, he says, "They found bin Laden, didn't they?"

"It took them years, which we don't have."

"Maybe if they'd asked me, they would have found him sooner."

"Please promise me you won't get shot while you're looking for Blum."

"Okay," Jimmy says. "But only because you said please."

He really does feel as if he keeps hearing Blum's name get called every time he turns around. Hank Carson was in deep to Bobby Salvatore. Sonny's guy. Now both of them are dead. Paul Harrington was in Sonny's pocket a long time, which meant Harrington's two top foot soldiers, Joe Champi and Anthony Licata, cops every bit as dirty as Harrington, were in there with them.

Now both Champi and Licata are dead, thanks to Janie.

And it was Champi, about a hundred years ago, who turned up at Robinson Jacobson's town house right after Jacobson and his girlfriend, Carey Watson, ended up good and dead. As far as Jimmy is concerned, that's practically the same as putting Sonny in the room with them.

Jimmy is at the end of his bar on Saturday night, remembering the night when another one of Blum's guys, Len Greene, came in and told him that as long as Jane and Jimmy backed off they'd be left alone.

Except now Jane is not only refusing to back off, she is dead set on calling Blum as a witness and putting *him* on trial for murder, starting first thing Monday morning, putting him on trial every bit as much as Katherine Welsh was about to do the same with Rob Jacobson.

What a freaking mess.

Jimmy drinks some beer and thinks:

I'm right back to where we started. Hoping somebody doesn't kill my girl before cancer does.

He turns to look at the room. Still a decent crowd tonight, even late. Good for business. But Jimmy has known from the start that this bar is more than just business with him. It's every good cop bar in which he ever drank when he was still on the job, and even after he wasn't.

That's really the best part for him, he knows in his heart.

The way this place takes him back.

He is considering having one more for the road when he hears the ping that means a text coming in to his phone. He grabs the phone off the bar and checks who the sender is, but the ID is blank.

And when he opens the first text, he feels as if he's back in the boxing ring, breathless after taking a body shot to the rib cage.

It's a picture of the woman he knows right away is Beth Lassiter, the Bridgehampton florist who was shot to death a couple of days ago, the one whose face has been plastered all over the front page of *The East Hampton Star.*

Beth Lassiter is on her back, eyes wide open in death, one bullet hole in the center of her forehead, one in her chest, flowers strewn all around her on the floor, as if the shooter had arranged them.

No cop that Jimmy knows would be sending along a photograph like this; it can have only come from the shooter.

The fuck.

Jimmy clicks on the second text.

Your boss needs to keep my boss's name out of her mouth.

Unless she wants to be laid out like this.

Jimmy makes a call as he's running out to where he's parked his car in its usual spot in the back lot.

Then he decides to take a drive.

The fuck, he thinks again.

One in particular this time.

FORTY-NINE

THERE IS NO GATE at the end of the driveway on Bay Road, no lights on in the house.

But the Maserati is parked in front of the garage.

It takes Thomas McGoey a long time to answer the door after Jimmy insistently keeps ringing the bell.

"Do you realize what time it is?" he says, vigorously rubbing sleep out of his eyes.

Jimmy promptly gives him a two-handed shove, knocking him back about ten feet, nearly putting McGoey down before he steadies himself.

McGoey's eyes get even bigger as Jimmy closes the distance between them.

"What the hell do you think you're doing, coming in here like this?" McGoey says.

"Who did you tell?" Jimmy says, keeping his voice low.

"Who did I tell *what*?" McGoey says.

He's wearing long pajama bottoms, but no shirt of any kind, or Jimmy would have grabbed him by the front of it and lifted his ass right off the ground.

"Who did you tell that Jane plans to call Sonny Blum?" Jimmy says.

"I didn't tell anybody," McGoey says.

"You tell one of your goombah buddies?" Jimmy says, ignoring him. "Is that how it went down?"

"Will you take it easy, please?" McGoey says.

He's not looking Jimmy in the eye, even with Jimmy right on top of him. He's focused on Jimmy's hands instead, as if they're not going to be at his sides for long.

"And though we both know what a hot-shit lawyer you are, Tommy," Jimmy says, "I would strongly advise you not to lie to me."

There is just barely enough room between them for McGoey to slowly put his own hands out in front of him, making sure the gesture is completely nonthreatening.

"Can we sit down and talk about this?" he says. "Or do you just want to continue to act like a tough guy?"

"You think I can't do both, tough guy?" Jimmy asks him.

McGoey sidesteps Jimmy now and walks into the spacious living room. He sits down on the leather couch and gestures to one of the chairs across from it.

"I'll stand," Jimmy says.

"Suit yourself."

"You worked with Jane today," Jimmy says. "I know this because I just got off the phone with her. She says the only two people she's talked to about adding Sonny Blum to her witness list are me—and you. She hasn't mentioned it to Norma Banks yet, or her boyfriend, or her fucking dog. But she knows I don't talk, Tommy. Which leaves only you."

"Listen," McGoey says, "if I've learned one thing with the people I have chosen to represent, it's to not go outside the family."

It's interesting, Jimmy tells himself, watching McGoey gather himself, almost like the guy is shaking off a punch Jimmy never threw.

"You can believe me or not," McGoey continues. "But if there's one thing my clients know, it's that I don't talk either. It's one of the many reasons why I live as well as I do. The operative word being *live*."

Jimmy starts to say something, but McGoey isn't quite finished.

"I am well aware that people in Sonny Blum's world, even if they're competitors, occasionally share information when they see it as being mutually beneficial, it would be naïve of me not to think that way," he says. "But I'm not one of those people, Cunniff. And while you may not believe me on this, I actually like Jane. And wouldn't do anything like you're suggesting to jam her up."

Jimmy walks over and sits down next to him, and shows him the photograph of Beth Lassiter, and the accompanying text.

"Jesus," McGoey says softly.

"And Mary, and Joseph, too," Jimmy says.

He takes his phone back and stuffs it in the side pocket of his jacket.

"For the last time," Jimmy says. "You're sure you didn't talk about Sonny with anybody?"

He sees McGoey's eyes get big again, just like that, but not because he's afraid he's about to be hit.

"Wait, there is just one," he says. "But I just assumed he already knew."

FIFTY

I AM SITTING ON a bench in Amagansett Square with Rob Jacobson on Sunday morning, the day before the trial.

Technically, Amagansett Square is outside the perimeter allowed by his ankle bracelet, though tomorrow that perimeter will be expanded to include the courthouse in Mineola.

The dispensation I've gotten from his probation officer includes my promise — one officer of the court to another — to shoot my client if on the walk into town he tries to make a run for it.

"I assume you're joking," I was told by the probation officer.

"Ammmmm I?" I'd said in a singsong way.

Jacobson and I have both gotten iced coffees from Jack's. I set mine down now in the grass in front of the bench.

"I've asked you on a number of occasions if you know Sonny Blum by something other than his truly shitty reputation," I say. "And you have told me, every single time, that you do not."

I get The Smirk now.

"Does anybody really know anybody else?" he asks.

"Rob," I say, "here's some free legal advice for a change: Please don't fuck with me today."

"No chance," he says, "not after the way you turned me down yesterday."

"Sigh," I say.

"Come on, that was funny."

I ignore him.

"McGoey told you that I plan to go after Blum," I say. "And a few hours later, one of Blum's people sends me a death threat through Jimmy."

"Wait, listen to me—"

"No, *you* listen," I say, cutting him off. "The only way Blum knows is if you went and told him. Which means you've been lying to me about him all along."

"I didn't tell him personally, *okay?*" he says. "I just spoke to someone who can get a message to him."

"And why would you even consider doing something like that?"

"Because we've had a deal, for a long time," he says. "Sonny and me. And the deal is that when I come across something that could hurt him, I tell him. It's that simple."

"Who's the person you told?"

"It doesn't matter," he says. "All the way back to when my father was the one dealing with him, Sonny has wanted to be informed if I learn that his interests might be... compromised."

"He owned a piece of your father, is that what you're telling me?"

"Yes," he says, staring across the wide expanse of lawn.

"But let's bring it back to you," I say.

"About time," he says.

I close my eyes and give a quick shake to my head.

"Tell me exactly what you told whoever this intermediary was," I say.

"Just that you plan to call Sonny as a witness, if you can find a way to get a subpoena handed to him."

"And what was the response?"

"That it can't happen," he says. "That because you work for me, I can't *allow* it to happen."

"And just when exactly did you plan to pass this information along to me?"

"I was told that I didn't need to," he says. "That someone else would deliver the message."

A couple of pretty young women walk by. The right age to be right in what Rob Jacobson considers to be his wheelhouse. Tight bodies, swinging everything they have just enough as they pass us by. Both of them giving Rob the eye. Neither one of them seeming to have a care in the world.

As if they're both going to live forever.

As they walk away, I watch them as wistfully as my client does.

Then I take out my phone and show him the picture of Beth Lassiter that Jimmy forwarded to me.

Jacobson doesn't act shocked, or surprised, or even mildly upset.

"She owed Sonny a lot of money," he says.

"So he has this done?"

"Sonny considers these object lessons."

He shakes his head.

"Trust me on this, Jane," he says. "You have to find another way to defend me and leave Sonny out of it."

"And you trust *me* on this," I say. "There is no other way."

"Find one."

"Why, so he won't have us both killed before this trial ever gets near a jury?" I ask him.

We sit in silence for what feels like a minute.

"Only you," he says finally. "For the time being, Sonny Blum has apparently made the determination that I'm still worth more to him alive than dead." He pauses and then says, "But that could change. Things are transactional with Sonny, and always have been, with my father and now me."

"So I might not be worth more to him alive," I say.

"Pretty much."

Rob Jacobson turns to me now on the bench, his face

serious, The Smirk wiped completely away, and gently takes both my hands in his.

"You need to understand something, Jane," he says. "McGoey's not just here to be second chair. He's here to be a backup plan."

"A backup plan?"

"Do I have to spell it out for you?"

"Please do," I say.

"In case you don't live to the end of the trial," he says.

FIFTY-ONE

I MAKE WHAT FEELS like a thousand-mile journey to Mineola, where I am meeting Katherine Welsh.

I haven't told her I've found the murder weapon—only that I have a present for her.

"And it's not even my birthday," she says.

"It's going to feel that way," I say.

We meet in Katherine Welsh's office, not far from the courthouse, on Old Country Road in Mineola.

She's dressed casually on what is supposed to be her day off: cotton pullover and sleeveless vest and black jeans and a pair of well-worn Dr. Martens boots. Even dressed down, she looks annoyingly well put together.

"I could have met you halfway and saved you some driving," she says.

"I've found you can make really good time when you're taking the high road," I say.

She frowns.

"That sounds mysterious," she says.

"Not for long."

The gun is in my purse. There are two guns in there, actually. One is my Glock 27, since with Rob Jacobson in my life I never go anywhere without it. The other is the bagged Glock 19, 15-round mag, that fired the bullets that killed the family for which Katherine Welsh is now trying my client.

She asks if I'd like water or coffee.

"I'm fine," I tell her.

"Why do I get the idea you're not fine?"

I force a smile. "I'm not answering another question without my lawyer present," I tell her.

She smiles back at me. "I want to say something, before we get to whatever we're getting to here," she says. "I have this feeling that the two of us would be friends if we were meeting under different circumstances."

"I'm a bitch," I say.

"Same!" she says.

We both laugh at that.

Then there's a silence between us, as if this is some sort of awkward first lawyer date, until she says, "So what *is* all the mystery?"

I've dropped my bag next to my chair. I reach down now and remove the plastic bag and place the bagged gun on her desk.

"This is your present," I say.

She looks down at the gun and then up at me.

"Is that what I think it is?"

"Yes."

"May I ask how it ended up in your possession?" she asks.

"Yes, Katherine, you may," I say, and then force another smile as I add, "If it would please the court."

I proceed to tell her about Rob Jacobson's houseguest and Jimmy's visit to the Upper West Side town house and the girl pulling a gun on Jimmy when she thought he was an intruder, and then Danny Esposito having tested and retested the gun yesterday.

Katherine Welsh gives out a long, low whistle.

"Goddamn," she says. "The missing murder weapon, at long last."

She pauses. "In his own goddamn house."

"It wasn't exactly as if the girl found a buried treasure," I say.

"You have your treasures," Welsh says, "and I have mine. Even when the treasure finds me."

"Prints are useless," I say. "The girl's were on it. And Jimmy's, he grabbed it before he realized what she might be handing over. But that's all the staties could pull."

I sit back down in my chair.

"Of course," I say, "this doesn't prove anything."

"As a matter of fact," she says, "it does."

"Not that he did it."

"No," Welsh says. "It proves that *you* did the right thing, Jane." She nods to herself. "It's funny you brought up the high road before. A friend of mine gave me a T-shirt once that has 'The high road sucks' on the front. And on the back it says, 'But you have to take it.'"

"There are times when it sucks way more than others," I say. "But in the end, we're the same in one other way: We're both officers of the court."

"Not everybody in your shoes would have done what you just did," Welsh says.

"No need to rub it in."

She stands now. I stand. We both know there's nothing more to say, at least not this morning. She walks me to the door then, but before I walk out of her office, she puts a hand on my shoulder.

"Please don't thank me again," I say. "I can only take so much gratitude."

She smiles again.

"Wasn't going to," she says. "Just wanted to remind you that I'm going to kick your ass with or without a murder weapon."

"Bitch," I say.

FIFTY-TWO

THE DRIVE TIME DURING Rob Jacobson's first trial in Riverhead was about half what I'm facing now. Both Jimmy and Ben have tried to convince me to rent an Airbnb in Mineola— to spare me the daily, three-hour round-trip drive.

I have consistently refused, just as they've refused my insistence that I *like* being in the car. Mostly I like being *alone* in the car.

"To quote my sainted father," I said the last time Ben brought it up, "go pound sand."

He smiled. This was at dinner on Sunday night, just the two of us. And the dog, of course.

Then I told him again what I'd assumed both he and Jimmy already knew: the double shot of alone time in the car got me ready for each day in court and also gave me a chance to review the day's proceedings. Nothing against either one of them, the two great loves of my life along with Rip, who only occasionally tries talking me into doing things I don't want to do.

Dr. Sam Wylie emails me Sunday night to inform me that she wants to see me in her office for one last pretrial check of my vitals. So I leave my house at six thirty on Monday morning and make a stop in Southampton.

"Body temp, pulse rate, rate of breathing, blood pressure," she tells me now as I sit down.

No receptionist at this hour. Just the two of us, meeting

the way we used to meet before class in high school, about a hundred years ago, when we were the hot chicks who thought we were going to live forever.

"You may think of them as vitals," I tell her. "Me? I think of them as the Four Horsemen of the Apocalypse. And by the way, I looked it up, and blood pressure isn't technically considered a vital sign, you just measure it along with those other bad boys. Or girls, as the case may be."

"I thought I was the one who did the homework for both of us when we had a first-period quiz," she says.

It turns out my blood pressure has risen over its normal numbers.

"We'll just write that off to where you're headed after leaving here," she says.

"You realize my brain needs all the blood it can get today, right?"

"Look at it this way," she says, offering a crooked grin. "Lack of the proper amount never seems to have slowed you down before."

"I've probably mentioned this before, doc," I say, "but you're never going to make it as a stand-up comic."

"Wait," she says, "check this one out: A lawyer walks into a doctor's office..."

"You know what's funny about doctor's offices?" I tell her. "Not a single goddamn thing."

Just like that, the funny goes out of her.

"You can do this," she says quietly.

"Just about everybody who says they love me keeps suggesting that I *can't* do this," I say. "And they all seem to know me pretty well."

"I've known you longer."

I've seen her cry before when we've been seated across from each other like this. Every time she has, I've pointed out, and quite correctly, that it's the patient who's supposed to be doing the crying.

I'm afraid she's about to restart the waterworks, her eyes having turned a telltale shade of pink.

"The last time you cried in front of me," I say, trying to cut her off at the pass, "I think you even ruined *my* mascara."

Then I add, "They all think the trial is going to kill me," before I add, "in more ways than one."

"I simply won't allow it," Sam says.

She stands. I stand. She comes around her desk and we fall into a hug and then she is crying. But I stand strong. No way I'm doing my face all over again.

"You got this," she says finally.

"Hold the thought," I say. "But you need to let go of me now."

She does.

"I've never asked you this before," Sam Wylie says, "and whatever you tell me won't leave this room. But do you think he killed that family?"

"Which family?" I ask her.

"You know which family."

I don't hesitate.

"No," I say.

FIFTY-THREE

AS LOUSY AS I feel most mornings, I arrive in Mineola to an important reminder that there is still a ritual of which I never tire:

The walk I am taking toward the courthouse; my dear friends in the media waiting for me outside; the few minutes of back-and-forth I will spend with them; then through the doors and through the metal detectors before eventually making my way into the courtroom for one more murder trial—maybe my last—the kind that Jimmy Cunniff calls boxing without blood.

"Oh, there's blood, all right," I tell him.

"Not yours," he says.

I do keep things short with the media today, knowing that once the trial has started, I'll be out here, before and after court, spinning like I'm one of those pixie figure skaters in the Olympics.

"Jane," says a reporter I recognize from CNN, "don't you ever get tired of defending this guy?"

"Don't you ever get tired of *watching* me defend this guy?" I shoot back.

"*Yes!*" she shouts.

"If you're going to cover this thing," I say, "do what I do."

"And what's that?"

"Fake it till you make it."

It gets a decent laugh. But I'm not wasting my A material on opening day.

"Jane," Lisa Rubin of MSNBC says, "all joking aside, you have to admit that the evidence against your client seems pretty overwhelming."

"Wait a second, Rubin," I say. "Are you and the district attorney thinking about opening a bar together?"

"Is that an answer?"

"Here's my answer: The evidence against Rob Jacobson this time around is actually *under*whelming. The facts of this case, the ones that will bring Rob another acquittal, are more stubborn than I am."

Then I say, "Okay, gotta go to work."

They're still shouting questions as I head inside. I'm aware that Rob Jacobson is waiting for me in a conference room. So are Thomas McGoey and Norma Banks, who's going to be with me every day of this trial, closely studying the jury when I'm not.

But before I head for the conference room, I make a pit stop in the nearest ladies' room, one I discover is blessedly empty. I go to a stall, close the door, sit down, grab the can of Red Bull in my bag, and drink it down as if I won't make it across the desert unless I do.

I know that Red Bull is probably about as good for my perpetually sensitive stomach as battery acid. But I need a boost from the sugar, and an even bigger boost from what is essentially a caffeine bomb.

When I come out of the stall I toss the can in the garbage, then splash just enough cold water on my cheeks to refresh me without ruining my makeup.

Then I do what I always do right before the main event is about to begin.

I lightly slap both cheeks and say, "Showtime."

But today I hesitate, staring at the woman staring back at me. It's as if I'm looking into the eyes of my mother.

FIFTY-FOUR

NORMA BANKS AND I make a bet as to how long Katherine Welsh will go with her own opening statement. Welsh, of course, is going first, the way prosecutors always do, since it is the state's burden to prove that my guy did the deed of which he's been charged.

I've established thirty minutes as our over-under number, like this is one of the dumb, prop bets popular in Jimmy's bar, where people guess the total number of combined points they think will be scored in a pro football game, among other things.

Norma bets the under.

"Wait and see, she won't even come close to half an hour," Norma whispers to me as Katherine Welsh confers one final time with her own team on the other side of the aisle. "She's already kicked our ass just by showing up."

I have Norma with me at my table. I would never mention this to her, but I see it as a way of making me look younger.

She's to my left. McGoey is to my right and Rob Jacobson is to his right. They've both just asked why they aren't in on the bet.

"Because men don't have equal rights at this table," I explain. "That's why."

Katherine Welsh is wearing a black pantsuit that on her looks like formal attire. I know it's a Cucinelli because I passed on buying the same suit at the Cucinelli store in East Hampton, having decided it was too pricey, at least for me. In comparison the charcoal blazer and matching skirt I'm wearing, purchased a couple of weeks ago at Rag + Bone, looks downmarket.

This is only Day One, and I'm probably the only one keeping score on this, but she's already taken a big early lead in the runway competition.

As she walks to the middle of the room, Norma Banks is whispering to me again.

"She looks like Lawyer Barbie," she says.

I can't help myself. I laugh, and as soon as I do all eyes in the courtroom, including Judge Horton's, are suddenly on me.

"Care to let us in on the joke, Ms. Smith?" Horton says.

I may be amused. He's clearly not.

Before I can respond, Norma Banks says, "Blame me, Michael. I made an inappropriate comment."

"What's inappropriate, Ms. Banks, is referring to me as anything other than Your Honor in this courtroom," he says. "Is that clear?"

I see her fighting a smile.

"Yes, Mich—yes, *Your Honor,*" she says.

Then Judge Michael Horton addresses Norma and me as if addressing two misbehaving girls in the back of the classroom.

"Don't make me separate the two of you," he says. "Now please proceed, Ms. Welsh, with the court's apologies."

"No apology necessary," she says. "Opposing counsel is probably only laughing now to keep from crying later after the State has presented its case."

Over the next twenty-five minutes—I occasionally check my watch—Katherine Welsh proceeds to kill it, laying out her case like a surgeon carefully laying out instruments in an OR. She speaks at length about DNA evidence which, as she happily points out, only ended up in the system once the defendant was being tried in the murder of the Gates family. This DNA evidence, she says, was sprinkled "like pixie dust" around the Carson home in Garden City.

"The defendant didn't know it when he murdered these three innocent people, having always considered himself to be above the law," she says, "but it was as if he were leaving a trail of crumbs that would take him all the way to this courtroom, and this trial." She pauses before adding, "And this reckoning."

She talks about the witnesses the State will call, all the people who will testify to having seen Rob Jacobson in the company of his old high school friend, Lily Carson, and her daughter, whom Welsh describes "as the kind of underaged young girl the defendant has sexually abused in a serial way."

Welsh pauses again at this point.

"Another mother, another daughter," she says, and now turns to face Rob Jacobson. "What *are* the odds?"

Then she turns back and is once again speaking directly to the jury.

"Fool us once, and by 'us' I mean the state, shame on him," she says. "You know the rest of it, ladies and gentlemen of the jury. If this particular defendant is allowed to fool us again, the everlasting shame will be on us all."

Another theatrical pause.

Woman knows how to work the room—I have to give her that.

"A shame that will last the rest of our lives," she says. "Or until he kills again."

As she heads back to her table, she only slows long enough to give me a look that's like the stare-down I used to get in college hockey after being run into the boards.

Right before she sits back down, she says, "Oh, and one more thing."

Wait for it.

Katherine Welsh then walks right back out there and tells the jury about the gun.

Maybe we would be friends if we'd ever met outside this room and this case, I think. *Because I would have played it just the way she just played it, saving the murder weapon until the very end.*

Now that Welsh is back in her seat, Judge Horton says, "Ms. Smith."

Norma Banks gives my hand a quick squeeze. I take a last sip of water, take in some air, get to my feet.

Showtime for real.

I'm the one walking to center stage now.

"Thank you, Your Honor," I say.

Then I'm the one speaking directly to the ladies and gentlemen of the jury.

"Well, of course he did it," is the way I begin.

FIFTY-FIVE

I HAVEN'T PLANNED TO begin this way. But now that Katherine Welsh has taken her shot at me, I decide to go with it.

Maybe it's the cocktail of Red Bull and adrenaline and being further hot-wired with nerves that pushes me even further. I give her table a quick pat with my hand as I walk past her.

"Of course he did it," I say to the jury. Then I follow it up with this:

"Because the guy did it before, right? Stands to reason."

My tone is conversational as I begin to walk back and forth in front of them, making eye contact with as many of the men and women staring back at me as I can manage, as if this is the start of story time.

Which it is.

"Come on," I say. "You know what you're all thinking, even if the only way you'd admit it is if I gave you truth serum. He killed that other family and got away with it, and now it turns out he'd already done the exact same thing with another father and mother and daughter who'd only committed the capital crime of being in the wrong place at the wrong time."

I lean on the banister now, right in front of the woman who is Juror No. 7, a high school teacher from Williston Park.

"C'mon, you can tell me," I say, lowering my voice and trying to sound conspiratorial. "I promise to keep it between the two of us."

She smiles at me. In that moment, I have her on my side, whether she'd ever admit *that* without truth serum or not.

I turn and walk back to the middle of the room. I always like to stay in motion as a way of holding their attention.

And I'm certain that I have their attention now.

"My esteemed opponent wants you all to believe that my client's guilt is a foregone conclusion," I say. "She expects you to simply follow her wherever she wants to lead you. Some people would say she wants you to follow her like sheep, except that sheep are highly intelligent animals, despite the popular misconception about them. Somewhat like the misconception about my client's guilt in this case."

I briefly turn to Katherine Welsh now and give her the same dead-eye look she'd just given me. Only I hold mine a beat longer.

I know she thinks she's tough.

I'm tougher.

"But if they do follow you down a dead end, that will be the real crying shame, won't it, Ms. Welsh?" I say, speaking directly to her.

You're not supposed to call out the other side in an opening statement.

But she started it.

I walk back toward the jury.

"The real and lasting shame of convicting Rob Jacobson for crimes he did not commit is that it will do nothing to bring justice to these three victims," I say. "Because convicting an innocent man never does that."

Just like that, I feel as if I'm rolling with material which by now I know by heart. I tell them that by the time I'm back in front of them for my summation — "Trust me," I say, "you're definitely going to want to stick around for that" — they will have done everything with the DA's alleged DNA evidence except fold it into a paper airplane.

There's no such thing, by the way, as "alleged" DNA evidence. It either is or it isn't, but they don't need to know that.

"Rob Jacobson wasn't anywhere near the Carson home the night three people were tragically murdered," I continue. "We'll prove that, too, when we show why that photograph of him leaving that home on the night in question is as fake as the most fake thing you'll find on social media today." I grin. "Unless you still believe that Bitcoin is safer for you than real money."

I turn back to my new buddy, Juror No. 7.

"Please tell me you don't believe that," I tell her.

She doesn't just smile back at me, she shakes her head vigorously, no no no, and laughs.

"You know what hype really is, ladies and gentlemen?" I say. "It's short for hyperbole. It's an exaggeration whose intent is to persuade you, usually of something that's not true. And what is not true today and won't be true over all the days to follow inside this room and will never be true, is that Rob Jacobson is guilty."

There is more I've planned to say. I know I haven't gone as long as Katherine Welsh did. But I feel my legs starting to go, and it's not as if I can call a time-out and wait to get them back.

I'm back in the middle of the room now, my back to Judge Horton, squarely facing the jury for the last time this morning, trying not to let them see that I'm running out of gas.

"I'm not about to tell you my client is a Boy Scout," I say. "If he ever even read the Scout Oath, which I sincerely doubt, he likely skipped the last part about being morally straight. Because he's not. Never has been, never will be, that's *not* in his DNA. When it comes to women both young and old, he's acted like a pig so many times in his life even he's lost count."

I give him a quick look over my shoulder and see him

trying to glare me all the way back to law school before I once again turn back to the jurors.

"He has been a sonofabitch with women for most of his life," I tell them. "But what he doesn't do to women is kill them, or a husband and father, even though someone has gone to great lengths to make it look as if that's exactly what he's done. You know what we're really talking about here? A well-planned and brilliantly staged setup, including that gun Ms. Welsh talked about." I pause. "*Especially* that gun, which so conveniently turned up at my client's town house in a place where it's amazing the housekeeper didn't find it."

One more pause.

Finish strong.

"When something's too good to be true, ladies and gentlemen, it usually is," I say. "*That* is the authentic truth of this case. And whether opposing counsel likes it or not, and whether all of you particularly like my client or not, the truth in the end is going to set my sonofabitch of a client free."

I sit down then before I fall down.

FIFTY-SIX

I'M BACK IN THE conference room with Rob Jacobson and Norma Banks and McGoey after Judge Horton has announced that he's decided to adjourn for today, and that Katherine Welsh can begin calling witnesses first thing tomorrow morning.

I want to run across the room and give him a big kiss.

"I don't appreciate being called a pig by my own lawyer," Rob Jacobson says to me now.

"Get over it," I tell him.

"Don't do it again," he says.

"Rob," I say wearily, just wanting to be out of this room and on my way to the car, "please stop talking now."

"And let's face it, kid," Norma Banks says, "if it oinks like a pig."

"I have to take shit from her, grandma," he says, wheeling on her. "Not from you."

She gives him her Mrs. Claus smile and says cheerily, "Wanna bet?"

"You might not be in any mood to hear this right now, Rob," McGoey says. "But Jane was great out there."

"I thought her job was to draw blood from that bitch DA," Jacobson says, "not me."

Norma says, "You didn't see it, because you wouldn't. But it was a way for Jane to get the jury on her side."

I say to Jacobson, "What she said."

Then I stand.

"We're not done here," Jacobson says.

"Yeah," I say, "we are."

He's hired a car and driver to bring him to court and then back to Amagansett. Norma Banks has, in fact, rented an Airbnb for the length of the trial, so as to avoid hours of daily train travel between here and the city.

McGoey has offered to drop her at the house in his Maserati. When she asked if she could drive, he said no.

"Because I'm old?" she asked.

"Yes," he said.

I answer a handful of questions from the media waiting outside. Basic stuff, as if both the questions and answers were rehearsed. The last one is about how I thought I did today.

"You were in there, right?" I say to the reporter.

"I was," he says.

I grin.

"Dude," I say. "You still have to ask?"

When I get to my car, I see Rob Jacobson's son, Eric, leaning casually against the front left fender.

If he was in court, I didn't notice him, and his father didn't mention that he was there. Maybe he slipped into the back.

There's a smirk on his face that he's either learned from his father or is just part of their messed-up genetic code.

"Pretty sure I recall telling you the last time I was in your presence that if you ever came near me again, I'd shoot you," I say.

I reach into my bag.

"Is that any way to greet family?" he says.

I sigh.

"You've probably heard this plenty of times," I tell him. "But please step away from the vehicle."

He doesn't move. But does flinch slightly when my hand

comes out of the bag, before he sees I'm just pointing my key fob at him.

"Ask you something?" he says.

"When you get off my car."

He doesn't.

"How can you live with yourself?" he says. "Really. I'm curious about that. You know he did it. You know he did them all. Do you just not give a shit because you're dying?"

He cocks his head to the side, as if suddenly curious about something else.

"You think you'll even be alive to see the end of this trial?" he adds.

I remember his father basically saying the same thing to me when we were talking about Sonny Blum, the day he talked about Thomas McGoey being a backup plan.

But there's nothing for me in talking about that with Jacobson's deadbeat son. So I open the driver's side door and get behind the wheel and then I suddenly have the car in motion and the door, still open, knocks him down as I drive past.

I look in the rearview mirror and see myself smiling.

Jane Effing Smith.

Maybe I won't make it to the end of the trial.

But I ain't dead yet.

FIFTY-SEVEN

IT'S ALREADY BEEN ARRANGED that Jimmy is coming for dinner. When he arrives, he offers to take Rip to the beach for a quick run. I give them both my blessing.

"It occurs to me that I'm turning into a professional dog walker," he says when they return. "Or runner, in this case."

"But just think how much Rip *wuvs* his Uncle Jimmy," I say.

"Don't push it," he says.

He's brought steaks from Schiavoni's Market in Sag Harbor. I tell him, almost as an apology now that he's gone to the trouble, that I'm really not that hungry. He says, "I don't give a shit, you need to eat." Then he tells me I can sit on the terrace and learn from the master while he grills.

"Do you ever worry at all about my cholesterol?" I ask.

"I'll get to that when I'm no longer worrying about the other *c* thing," he says.

When we're outside and he's working his magic on the grill, I tell him all about my encounter with Eric Jacobson, almost word for word. Jimmy agrees I should have just shot the kid and called it self-defense.

"You would have been making the world a better place," Jimmy says. "And a safer one, especially for girls."

"I did nearly run him over," I say.

"*My* girl," Jimmy says.

When he announces that the meat is five minutes away from perfection, I go inside and slice up a tomato and some mozzarella and splash on some balsamic dressing.

Once we're at the kitchen table, Jimmy keeps feeding Rip steak under the table even after being admonished not to.

"Dog doesn't have to worry about cholesterol," Jimmy says.

"Maybe he should."

"Are you serious?" Jimmy says. "This is the first damn *dog* with nine lives."

He's drinking beer. I'm sticking with sparkling water tonight, taking no chances. With the first day of witnesses tomorrow, the last thing I need is my stomach giving me a middle-of-the-night wake-up call.

Jimmy takes a sip of beer and notices me smiling at him. "What?" he asks.

"Does it ever occur to you how much we sound like an old married couple?"

"Only because we are," he says. "And the reason we've lasted this long is because we never ruined things with all the other—"

"Are you referring to sex, detective?"

"Hey," he says, "can't you see I'm eating here?"

When we finish, and I've eaten more than I expected to, he says that I should go sit down in the living room, he'll clean up. When he joins me, he's made himself a cup of coffee.

"You know what I think about sometimes?" I say. "A lot of the time, actually."

"What's that?"

"That I can't go on winning forever."

"Says who?"

Rip has settled in next to Jimmy, who's absently reaching down and scratching him behind an ear.

"I talked to Norma," he says. "She says you did good today, laying bricks on how the whole thing is a setup."

"I'm hoping like hell that I did," I say. "Because it's pretty much all I got."

I lean back and stare up at the ceiling.

"Who hates Rob Jacobson enough to kill three people as a way of setting him up, or maybe even six?" I ask.

"I've seen a lot of elaborate frames in my life," he says. "But this one would win the blue ribbon."

"Should we start our list of suspects with friends, or family?"

"Wait, I got one. How about Sonny Blum, the great and powerful Oz?"

"Rob says that Sonny still wants him alive," I say.

"Does that mean alive and a free man, or locked up for the rest of his miserable life?"

"Maybe," I add, "this whole case is just about Sonny getting tired of waiting for Hank Carson to pay what he owed, and having him popped?"

"And popping his whole family at the same time?"

"But then why set up Rob, and why wait this long to plant the gun?" I ask him.

I put my head back again and close my eyes.

"Goddamn them all," I say softly. "And goddamn this case."

Jimmy asks if I need him to walk Rip one last time. I tell him thanks, but I'll do it, I could use the air.

"You sure you're not too tired?" he asks.

"Stop treating me like an invalid."

He grins. "I only do it because Uncle Jimmy *wuvs* you, too," he says.

FIFTY-EIGHT

I GRAB RIP'S HARNESS and leash and stick my Glock into the side pocket of the adorable new Faherty vest I bought at their store in Amagansett. Rip and I walk toward Abraham's Path, cutting through the Sportime tennis club. Brigid and I used to play tennis on these courts, before she got sick, and before I got sick.

We stretch out the walk, eventually making our way over to Town Lane, then back up to Abraham's Path and past the train tracks alongside which, on a gentle, good night like this, I once was involved in a shoot-out with Joe Champi.

Rip and I have moved farther away from the ocean by now. So the night has grown more quiet, which is perhaps why I'm then certain I hear footsteps behind me.

As does Rip, who lets out a low growl.

I shorten his leash as I turn, taking the Glock out of my pocket in the same motion.

No one there.

At least no one I can see.

Only some of the club's lights are on at night. I can't remember when they close down the place for the winter months, but on this October night I am pretty sure it is soon. I search the area behind us one last time, the courts and the gravel paths between them and the small clubhouse area, and still see nothing.

Hear nothing.

But Rip and I walk more quickly now, back across the club's large front parking lot, back toward Abraham's Path, more lights here and also across the street, where there's a softball field and a court where kids play volleyball in the summer.

When we're out on the sidewalk, I come to a stop, sure I hear the faint crunch of gravel from somewhere behind us.

"Who's back there?" I yell.

Nothing.

I take one last look behind, gun still in my hand, and then Rip and I are jogging toward my street. Even *with* a gun in my hand, I feel like a scared little girl suddenly.

I hate feeling like a scared little girl.

But right before we make the left, I stop maybe on instinct, spin around, then see someone running across Abraham's Path and toward the train tracks.

Not just running.

Sprinting.

And even though I know better, Rip and I now sprint in the same direction.

When we get to the tracks, I see a figure disappearing down the tracks in the distance, to the east.

I stop then and surprise myself by firing a shot into the sky.

"Hey, God!" I yell. *"Duck!"*

Then I fire again.

In the high heat of the moment I'm really surprised at how good that feels, my finger on the trigger and the brief explosion of noise, even as Rip starts barking his head off.

"What," I tell him, crouching down to pat his back, "a girl's not allowed to have a little fun?"

We continue walking back home. I feel a little less scared than I did a few minutes ago, thinking the long day and night is over, and that it's time to at least try to sleep.

But it's not.

Because when we get back to the house, Brigid is sitting on the front porch. When I get near her, I see that she's been crying.

"I couldn't find the damn key you gave me!" she says.

When I take a closer look in the porch light, I notice the darkening bruise on her left cheek.

"Who did this to you?" I ask.

She doesn't answer at first.

Finally, almost inaudibly, she says, "Rob."

"Rob *hit* you?"

She looks up at me then, ashamed, like a little girl caught doing something naughty.

"It's not his fault," my sister says. "I asked for it."

FIFTY-NINE

I INSIST THAT BRIGID spend the night, then try to get her to talk about what just happened between them, promising I'm not looking to judge her.

"It's my fault," she says, over and over again.

"A man taking a hand to a woman is never her fault," I say.

Brigid, eyes shining, shakes her head. "I know you think you know me so well, Jane. But you don't know me nearly as well as you think you do."

"Noted for the record," I say. "But what I do know is that you can't be with this particular man."

"The problem is, I can't *not* be with him," she says, and then says she's tired of talking, tired period, and is going to bed.

She's already gone when I'm awake at five thirty, wanting to take Rip to the beach for an early walk before I have to leave for court. No note from my sister. She's just gone. Before Rip and I do drive over to Indian Wells, I text Rob, not knowing if he's awake or not, and tell him I need to see him at court about a half-hour early.

It turns out he is awake, against all odds.

What up?

I text him back.

Trial stuff. Important.

Will explain when I see you.

Three hours later, I am seated across from him in the courthouse conference room, trying to play against type, which means I am forcing myself to remain calm instead of doing what I so desperately want to do, almost need to do, which is bounce him off the closest wall.

"What's so important?" he asks.

"My sister came to see me last night after she left your house," I say. "She was pretty upset."

I stare at him across the table and find myself wondering all over again what my sister still sees in him. Not the good looks of an aging frat boy. I'm thinking more about the rats crawling around inside him, the ones you discover are there the more you get to know him. And my poor sister has known him since they were at Duke together.

"That's between Brigid and me," he says.

"Not today it's not."

"What did she tell you?"

"You mean after I saw where you hit her in the face?"

"Yeah," he says. "After that."

"She actually tried to defend you, by telling me that she wanted it."

And then he gives me his patented smirk-smile.

"Can't lie to you, Janie," he says. "At least not on this one. She *did* want it."

I have my hands in my lap, and suddenly realize that if I squeeze them any harder I am going to feel small bones in them starting to break, one by one. Losing it with him, even now, does me no good, and I know it. I can't change my sister, and I certainly can't change him.

"I'm asking you for the last time to stay away from her," I say.

His expression doesn't change.

"You should have figured out by now that she can't stay away from me," he says.

"She's sick," I say.

"You said it, not me."

He's baiting me and I know it. He wants to get a rise out of me, and I'm not going to give him the satisfaction. At least I can be one woman who doesn't give him what he wants when he wants it.

"If you ever lay a hand on her ever again, you have my word that I will walk away from you, and walk away from this trial," I say. "And then you can see how having Thomas McGoey as your first chair works out for both of you."

"You've quit before," Jacobson says.

I'm thinking about McGoey now, and the conversation we had about *The Godfather*.

"But it isn't business this time, Rob," I say, eyes locked on his. "It's *extremely* personal. She's my sister."

"There's nothing wrong with a little rough sex once in a while," he says, keeping his eyes on me.

"You can tell that to your future cellmate if I walk out this door," I tell him.

"So that's your offer?"

"A take-it-or-leave-it offer."

He leans back in his chair and folds his arms in front of him, looking up at the ceiling now as if deciding.

"So you're basically making me choose between you and your sister," he says. And smiles again. "Not exactly the way I had this particular fantasy playing out."

I stand.

"That's it, we're done here," I say, walking around the table and toward the door.

"You're bluffing," he says. "Winning means way too much to you. That's why you won't quit."

"Watch me."

"What would you do without me in your life?"

I say, "Die in peace."

My hand is on the doorknob when he says, "Okay. *Okay.* I'll stop seeing her."

"What if she doesn't want you to break it off?"

"Trust me on this, Janie," he says. "I know how to cut them loose."

There's more I want to say to him. I don't. So I just open the door and am nearly into the hallway when I hear him say, "Hey?"

I turn back around.

"In case you were wondering?" Rob Jacobson says. "The Carson girls liked it rough, too."

SIXTY

THAT SAME MORNING, AROUND the same time, Robby Sassoon is standing in Allen Reese's kitchen when Reese comes walking in there from his backyard.

The view of the ocean, Robby thinks, *even from here is something, well, to die for.*

"What the fuck is this?" Reese snaps when he sees Robby standing there.

Reese is tall, wide, bald, tanned, and clearly scared shitless at this intruder in an otherwise empty house, even if the intruder is dressed as impeccably as Robby is and, Reese has to see, is as good-looking as he is, the sunlight streaming through nearly a wall of kitchen windows glinting off Robby's earring. Robby has even added a little extra bronzer today, though his color isn't nearly as deep or brown as Reese's.

"A powerful real estate mogul like yourself should have a better alarm system, Allen," Robby says.

Robby watches Reese's attitude change now, can see it even in a setting like this, Reese still desperate to come across as a big guy. It's something they all fall back on, that pose, even when they're scared little boys.

"Okay, I'll bite," Reese says. "Who are you and what are you doing in my fucking house?"

"Well, if you put some thought to it, Allen, you can

185

probably figure out what I'm doing here, even if who I am is irrelevant to that particular discussion."

And, just like that, Robby can see some of the rope go out of Allen Reese, along with some air, almost like exhaust. He's wearing a faded blue Giants T-shirt and cargo shorts. He seems to be in pretty good shape, all in all. The stubble of his beard is white, making him likely older than he looks at first glance. The face, Robby sees as he studies it more closely, is too unlined. Either filler or Botox.

Or both.

"Sonny sent you," Reese says.

"You've been a bad boy," Robby says.

"I was just surprised because you don't look..."

"You mean, look the part?" Robby chuckles. "Quite the contrary. This is a part I was born to play."

Robby takes another look around. The kitchen is big enough to serve as a three-car garage, the morning sun really like a spotlight in here. Or like high beams fixed squarely on Allen Reese, real estate agent to the rich and the famous.

"Listen, maybe you know this and maybe you don't," Reese says. "But Bobby Salvatore and I had an understanding, because he knew that in the end I was always good for the money, even when I was a little late."

"Until, sad to say, Bobby was the one who was a bad boy," Robby says. "May he now rest in God's heavenly embrace."

"Hold on," Reese says nervously. "It was Sonny who had that done?"

"That's another discussion for another day," Robby says. "And besides, I'm not here to talk about Mr. Salvatore. I'm here to talk about money you owe to Mr. Blum that is long past due."

"I know you don't want to hear this and Sonny probably doesn't either," Reese says. "But it was a slower summer than usual out here. On top of that, I'm still digging myself out from a divorce. And on top of *that,* I had a very bad first month of the pro football season. And *that* you probably do know."

"Fascinating," Robby says. "But where's our money?"

Before Reese can answer, Robby moves quickly across the kitchen until they're on opposite sides of a granite-topped counter. The huge stove is to Reese's left. He must have been preparing to make himself breakfast before he went outside. There's a frying pan on the stove, the eggs are out, a container of milk. Cooking spray. Salt and pepper shakers. American cheese. Even an onion. Doing it up big himself. Man of the people.

Reese is wary now that Robby has closed the distance between them, his senses suddenly on high alert.

"You're obviously aware of the sum of money that has brought me here today," Robby says.

"Million," Reese mumbles.

"Actually, Allen, that was last week's number," Robby says. "Now it's two."

"What...*no!*" Reese says, as if in pain.

"It's like they say in the commercials," Robby says. "Late fees do apply in this case."

"Sonny just up and *doubled* it without telling me?"

"Cost of doing business," Robby says. "This isn't Draft-Kings. And so you know? I'm the one telling you."

"Just give me a couple more days, and I'll have it," Reese says.

"End of *this* day," Robby says. "Or the number will double again." Robby's shoulders casually rise and fall. "Funny world, right?"

"When you're gone I'll start making some calls," Reese says.

"You've got a bad habit, Allen," Robby says, almost soothingly, "to go along with a big ego and a big mouth. That is a very difficult combination, in Mr. Blum's eyes."

Reese tries to laugh, but the sound that comes out of his throat makes it sound as if he's choking.

"Sonny's not going to kill me," he says. "You don't kill a golden goose."

"Or a bronzed one, in your case," Robby says.

"Whatever."

"Think of it another way," Robby says. "He won't kill you *yet.*"

Then before Allen Reese can move, Robby grabs the frying pan and smashes it down violently on Reese's left hand.

Reese screams in pain, shocked at what's just happened to him, but before he can move back, Robby holds down his arm and smashes the hand again.

Then Robby calmly places the pan back on the stove as Reese stares down at his hand, shaking there on the counter.

"I mean, Allen, who the hell is betting on the fucking Giants this season?" Robby asks.

Reese, still staring at his hand, somehow responds as if Robby has just asked a serious question.

"The points were just too good to pass up . . ."

Robby puts a finger to his lips.

"Stop talking now, before I break your other hand," Robby says.

Then he reaches over, pats Allen Reese on his bald head, and leaves.

SIXTY-ONE

I AM WELL AWARE of the change Welsh has made with her opening witness. The original plan was to call the first detective to arrive at the Carson home the night of the murders.

The call Katherine Welsh made last night—after Brigid fell asleep in my guest room and I was still very much eyes-wide-open awake—was a courtesy on her part, nothing more, Welsh knowing before she made the call that there would be no grounds for me to object to the change she was about to make.

"I've gone back and forth on this," Welsh told me on the phone. "But I finally decided this was the best way to handle things. Put it out there, first thing, so to speak."

"Do what you have to do," I said, and told her I'd see her in court.

So to speak.

But even knowing what's coming, it's still jarring when I hear her stand and say, "The people call Jimmy Cunniff."

"What the—" I hear Norma Banks say from my left, and I give her a look that stops her right there.

Jimmy walks through the gate and makes his way toward the witness stand, wearing his one good suit, white shirt, navy tie. He's even shaved and, I see, shined his shoes for the occasion, trying not to look like what we both know he is, which is a grumpy witness, if not a hostile one.

He's testified plenty of times, in his life as a New York City cop. Has sat in that chair so many times he's lost count.

Just not like this.

As Jimmy takes his seat, Rob Jacobson, face clenched like a balled fist, leans past Thomas McGoey and motions me to come closer to him.

"You couldn't give me a heads-up on this?" he hisses.

I feel a big smile cross my face. I can't help myself.

"Not as much fun when you're the one getting smacked in the face, is it?" I whisper to him.

SIXTY-TWO

KATHERINE WELSH WALKS JIMMY through the pre-liminaries as quickly as she can manage, starting with his job description with me, his background as a former NYPD detective. Jimmy answers politely, on his best behavior because he's promised me he would be.

Welsh is on her own best behavior, steering clear of asking Jimmy about the way his career with the NYPD ended, which means when he was asked, and not politely, to leave.

He is, after all, her witness on this day.

Before he's all mine.

Welsh gets to it now, walking over to the clerk's table and picking up the bagged gun that the jury probably hasn't even noticed until now.

"Let the record show," she says, holding up the gun, "that this is very much Exhibit 1."

"Yeah, like you think you're number one, Barbie," Norma Banks whispers.

This time I give her a kick under the table.

"Do you recognize this gun, Mr. Cunniff?" Welsh asks.

"Yes, I do."

"And could you please tell this court why you recognize it?"

"Because I was the one who presented it to Ms. Smith once it was in my possession," Jimmy says.

"And how did it come to *be* in your possession?"

Jimmy then explains, almost in cop shorthand, why he went to Rob Jacobson's town house on Friday, and how he first saw the gun in the hand of one of Jacobson's houseguests.

"That houseguest is an extremely young woman, correct?"

"I'm not sure what 'extremely' means," Jimmy says. "All women her age look extremely young to me. But I'd guess in her twenties."

"One of two women that age currently living at Mr. Jacobson's town house, isn't that also correct?"

I'm up then.

"Objection, Your Honor," I say. "I'm not sure the age or the gender of the houseguests is relevant to this weapon ending up in this courtroom, unless Ms. Welsh wants to check their IDs."

"Now I object," Welsh says.

"Wait," I say, grinning at her. "I was first."

"Sustained and sustained," Judge Horton says, going to his gavel for the first time today, before telling Katherine Welsh, "Please proceed."

Welsh then walks Jimmy, whom she's already preinterviewed earlier this morning, through how and where Kellye found the gun in Jacobson's closet and how once she handed it over to him, he then drove back out to Long Island and handed it over to the State Police for testing.

"So to be clear," Welsh says, "it turns out that the murder weapon was in the defendant's possession all along."

"Objection," I say, on my feet again. "This gun being discovered at a place that is no longer my client's primary residence is hardly the same as possession."

"Sustained."

"Let me rephrase, Mr. Cunniff," Welsh says. "What you're telling the court is that the murder weapon was found, hidden among some clothes, in the defendant's closet?"

"According to the young woman, yes, it was," Jimmy says.

"No further questions at this time," Welsh says.

But as she walks back to her table she turns to the jurors and says, "To use the same expression I used in my opening statement...what *are* the odds?"

SIXTY-THREE

BEFORE I AM OUT of my chair and walking over to question Jimmy Cunniff under oath for the first time, Rob Jacobson once again motions me to come closer.

Then he whispers, "Clean this up."

I then lean behind Thomas McGoey, whisper in my client's ear that he can go fuck himself.

"Good morning, Jimmy," I say brightly when I'm standing in front of Jimmy Cunniff.

"Good morning, Ms. Smith."

"I think at this point in our relationship, we can both be on a first-name basis," I say.

"You're the boss," Jimmy says, and I hear some chuckling from the jury box. A good thing. I want them to feel as if they're eavesdropping on a conversation between a couple of old pals.

Which, in essence, they are.

I go through some preliminaries of my own, asking him how long he was with the NYPD. He tells me. I ask how he progressed through the ranks to detective, and he tells me that, too.

"In the course of your career, you ever see a murder weapon planted?" I ask.

"On multiple occasions."

"And did the people doing the planting go down for that?" I ask.

Jimmy shrugs. "Sometimes it was the plant*er* who went down, sometimes the plant*ee*. And sometimes none of the above."

"And how often were you able to catch the people who planted a weapon as a way of framing someone for a crime he, or she, didn't commit?"

"Objection," Katherine Welsh says. "Ms. Smith is clearly leading this witness. Your Honor, I'm sure Ms. Smith and Mr. Cunniff are often in the habit of finishing each other's thoughts. Unfortunately, it's completely inappropriate in these circumstances."

"Sustained," Judge Horton says.

"Let *me* rephrase," I say. "If someone *were* trying to frame someone for murder, wouldn't it be easy for them to hide a weapon as a way of making it look as if the person being framed had been the one hiding it?"

"All you'd need," Jimmy says, "is access to the weapon, and access to the hiding place."

I nod, and grin. "And how many people would you guess might have access to our client's town house?"

"At this point in time?" Jimmy says. "A shorter list might be people who *don't* have access."

"Objection! Calls for speculation."

"Sustained," Horton says. He then focuses a withering glance at Jimmy. "I understand that you are a bar owner, Mr. Cunniff, isn't that right?"

"Yes, Your Honor, it is."

"Well, you're not seated at the end of the bar this morning," Horton continues.

To me the judge says, "Proceed."

"Jimmy," I say, "you've often told me that jails aren't filled with smart people, isn't that correct?"

"It's an expression cops use quite a lot."

"But smart people, even if they're guilty, often find a way to stay *out* of jail, isn't that also correct?"

"Unfortunately, it is."

"And if they're *really* smart, they can frame someone for a murder they didn't commit," I say, not even attempting to make a question out of it.

"Objection!" Katherine Welsh says, shouting this time.

But I'm already walking back to my table.

"Withdrawn," I say. "Nothing further."

SIXTY-FOUR

I SIT BACK DOWN, suddenly exhausted, feeling a little sick and a little dizzy at the same time, as if my condition had once again chased me down from behind, and tried to knock me down, as jazzed as I'd felt questioning Jimmy, and finishing up the way I had.

I drink some water and feel Norma Banks's eyes on me.

She touches my shoulder and mouths, *You okay?*

I nod.

Hey, I'm not the one under oath.

From my right I hear Katherine Welsh say, "Redirect please, Your Honor."

Jimmy must have expected this because I see that he hasn't moved.

"I've done my research on you, Mr. Cunniff," she says. "And what that research tells me is that you weren't just a good cop, you were considered, at least at your best, a great cop."

Well, I think, *until he wasn't.*

"I like to think that I was," he says. He grins. "Though some of my superior officers thought otherwise from time to time."

Welsh lets that settle. But she has my attention now, just because I have no idea where she is going with a line of questioning that hasn't really started with a question.

"It was your job as a great cop to arrest the guilty," she says, "and then hope that they were brought to justice."

Still not a question.

"That was the goal, yes."

"And what that really means is that you had a sense of right and wrong," she says. "Which is why you brought that gun to Ms. Smith when you could have thrown it into the Hudson River. Because it was the right thing to do, isn't that right?"

"I thought it was."

Even Jimmy seems curious now.

"So does the cop in you believe that this defendant, whether he's your client or not, hid that gun because he continues to think he's above the law?"

I yell "Objection" as Jimmy is saying, "I never said . . ."

And before Judge Michael Horton can respond, Katherine Welsh is plowing right ahead, saying to Jimmy, "Doesn't the cop in you really believe this defendant is guilty as charged, Mr. Cunniff?"

Horton's voice is the one rising now as he says, *"Sustained!"*

Then Katherine Welsh is the one saying, "Withdrawn."

The courtroom goes silent before Horton calls for a brief adjournment.

We all rise as the judge heads for his chambers. When he's gone, Rob Jacobson says to me, "What just happened here?"

I keep my voice low, too tired to raise it.

"What just happened," I say to him, "is that she just did to me what she said she was going to do."

"What's that?"

"Kicked my ass," I say.

Then I add, "And yours, too, for what it's worth."

Fifteen minutes later, Norma Banks finds me on the floor of the ladies' room.

SIXTY-FIVE

NORMA TELLS ME TO stay where I am, nearly sprints toward the door, comes back with a bottle of water.

She orders me to drink the whole thing, watching while I do.

Then she sits down next to me.

"Did you faint?" she asks.

Another woman comes through the door, sees us next to each other on the floor, promptly leaves.

"I don't think I lost consciousness," I say. "I just got dizzy and managed to sit down before I fell down."

Norma Banks reaches over and pinches my arm, making me wince.

"Don't lie to me, missy."

"Okay," I say. "Maybe I did close my eyes for a second. But I'm fine now."

"My ass," the old woman says.

After a few minutes she slowly helps me to my feet, takes me by the arm, and walks us out of the room and up the hallway.

"I can walk on my own, thank you," I say. "And I do *not* need to be looked at, if that's where you're going with this."

I knew there was a nurse's office somewhere in the courthouse, there had been since COVID.

"Not going there," she says, "even though you probably do need your damn head examined."

I'm still feeling groggy enough and unsteady enough on my feet, even though I'm not going to admit that to her, to offer much resistance.

"I just need to sit down for a second," I say.

"Got just the place," she says.

Then before I realize where she's taking me, she's knocking on the door to the judge's chambers and walking us right in without waiting for permission to enter.

Judge Michael Horton, still in his robe, looks up from his desk, clearly surprised at unannounced visitors, even with Norma Banks leading the way.

"We need a moment, Michael," she says. "And we're not in court right now, so please don't give me any of that Your Honor shit."

A few minutes later Katherine Welsh has joined us, along with Jimmy Cunniff.

"Norma is overreacting," I say to Judge Horton.

"Hard to believe a thing like that could ever happen," he says drily.

"I just had a bit of a sinking spell in the ladies' room," I explain.

"Jane needs to take the rest of the day off," Norma Banks says, "even if she doesn't think she needs to, Your Honor."

That gets a smile out of the judge. "Now you cut the Your Honor shit, Norma," he says to her.

"I'm fine," I say again. "Really."

"She fainted," Norma says. "People don't faint for no reason."

I look over at Jimmy. "Help me out here," I say. "I've got this."

"What you've got, pal," he says in a quiet voice, "is cancer."

"Be that as it may, I'm well enough to continue," I say, turning back to Judge Horton.

"Overruled," Horton says. "We will resume at nine in the

morning if you're up to it. If not, we'll resume at nine on Wednesday."

He nods at Katherine Welsh. "I assume that's acceptable to you, counselor?"

"You know something, Your Honor," she says, "I feel a touch of the stomach flu coming on, and I'm the one who needs to take the rest of the day, something of which I'm sure you can inform the jury, right before I inform the media."

"You don't have to do that," I tell her.

"I know I don't," she says. "But I just did."

She is the first one to head toward the door. Before she leaves, I say, "Quit trying to make me like you."

She stops, turns around.

"I'm a cancer survivor, too," she says, and leaves.

SIXTY-SIX

JIMMY REFUSES TO LEAVE me alone in the house, meaning alone with only Rip the therapy dog as company, and stays until Dr. Ben arrives from his office.

Jimmy reluctantly gave Norma the keys to his own car for the short trip to her Airbnb, then drove us in my car back to Amagansett. Along the way, and over my objections, he placed a call to Dr. Sam Wylie to tell her what had happened.

When Sam was on speaker, she asked if I'd eaten anything before court. I told her I'd had an energy bar. So she asks what I had to drink and I tell her two cups of coffee and a Red Bull, does that count?

"Oh good," she says. "The breakfast of champions."

Then she says, "You know you've gotten weak like this before when you got yourself to the brink of dehydration."

Jimmy says, "Her boyfriend's an animal doctor. Is there a way for him to stick an IV needle in her ass to get her attention?"

"Just make her drink about a gallon or so of water when she's back at the house, get her to bed as soon as you can, and call me in the morning," Sam says, before adding, "Idiot."

"That's not a nice thing to say to Jimmy," I tell her.

"We all know who I meant," Sam says.

When we're in my living room Jimmy sits next to me on the couch and watches as I put away two plastic bottles of water, making me promise that I'll eat something after Ben arrives. I promise.

When Ben does walk through the front door, Jimmy puts his arm around me, kisses my hair, and says, "I love you."

"Hey," Ben says. "Hands off my girl."

Jimmy stands. "Fine," he says. "You can have her."

Ben takes Jimmy's place next to me on the couch. Rip is at our feet. Then Ben pulls me close to him.

"Hey," he says. "You okay now?"

"No," I say.

I start to cry. It all comes out of me in a rush, the kind of crying I usually try to keep to myself. But tonight I can't stop myself.

Ben doesn't say anything. Neither do I. We stay where we are, barely moving, for what feels like a long time, as I just let it go.

When I do finally try to say something, he gently puts a finger to my lips.

"Hard as this might be to process," he says, "sometimes the best thing for you is to *not* talk."

I look up at him, only imagining how awful my eyes must look, along with my face in general. "Where the hell have you been all my life?" I ask.

"I'm here now," he says, smiling at me. "Take the win."

And I do.

SIXTY-SEVEN

JED BERNSTEIN'S OFFICE IS located on the second floor of his small brownstone on West 68th Street. He is still there when Robby Sassoon buzzes him from outside.

Robby has called ahead to tell Bernstein he's coming, on his way back from Southampton and the visit he paid to Allen Reese.

Bernstein, Robby sees, has a spreadsheet in front of him. Next to it, he's taking notes on a white legal pad, with a No. 2 pencil. Old school.

"Making a list?" Robby asks as he sits down across the desk from Bernstein.

"And checking it twice," Bernstein says.

Robby enjoys working with Jed Bernstein, even knowing he may have to kill him down the road. He just doesn't know yet how far down the road.

It has lately become clear to them both that Sonny Blum has been methodically tying up loose ends—apart from the ones he's had Robby eliminate entirely—in his business.

No one in Sonny's orbit has come right out and said it, and certainly not Sonny himself, but Robby feels as if the old man is dying. And, if that's really the case, he's clearly made the determination that he's not going to leave this world being owed money. By anyone.

This, Robby knows, is not his immediate concern, because

what he is more concerned with presently is a much bigger picture:

Being the one to take over the business when Blum is gone.

Blum has no children. His two brothers are long since dead. There was a time when the people around Sonny thought that he treated Bobby Salvatore like a son, until Salvatore was viewed as a loose end, and then eliminated.

Robby feels himself smiling now, with a panoramic view of the big picture inside his head.

Why not me?

It's something he's been thinking more and more frequently.

Why not now?

To Robby, the entire drama, the way it's playing out, reminds him at least a little bit of *King Lear*. Robby just doesn't see it as a tragedy in the end, certainly not from his point of view, not if he plays things right.

"What's on that list?" he asks. "Or should I say, who?"

Bernstein puts down his pencil. Robby really does like the way Jed Bernstein takes pride in his appearance, the way he presents himself, even if Bernstein is far too prepped out for Robby's tastes, cashmere sweater and white shirt underneath. There's even a faint whiff of cologne between them in the office. If Robby doesn't miss his guess, and he's rarely wrong about these things, it's Frédéric Malle. One of his own favorites. Over three hundred a bottle.

Another thing over which they can bond.

Just not for long.

"What I have here in front of me," Bernstein says, "are Bobby Salvatore's debtors." He makes a *tsk tsk* sound, clicking his tongue against the roof of his mouth in disapproval. "Having taken a deep dive into Bobby's finances, it appears as if Mr. Salvatore was as late collecting as many of his clients were paying up."

"Unless they had paid in a timely fashion," Robby says, "and it wasn't reflected in Bobby's bookkeeping."

He smiles. "Perhaps 'skimming' should have been listed as his cause of death."

Bernstein gets up now, walks over to his liquor cabinet, picks up a bottle of Hennessy Paradis, and pours them both a glass.

They clink glasses.

"To the good life," Jed says.

"Or death," Robby says, "as the case may be."

When Bernstein sits back down, he asks, "How did it go with Reese?"

Robby flicks an imaginary piece of lint off the lapel of his black suit.

"I may have gotten a little overemotional," he says.

Bernstein grins. "How overemotional?"

"Well," Robby says, "in the short run it's a good thing that Allen isn't left-handed."

Bernstein toasts him with his glass. "I'm just messing with you. I'm aware of what happened and so is Mr. Blum. Reese actually called and told me what you did to his hand. And by the way? I respect a man who takes pride in his work." He pauses. "These people need to pay their debts."

They drink to that and sit in silence for a few moments. Somewhere, maybe from the floor below, Robby can make out classical music playing.

"Do you ever think about what happens to this operation when Sonny is gone?" Bernstein asks finally.

"Often."

"Do you think our employer has a successor in mind?" Bernstein asks. "Or does he want to just keep it all when he dies?"

"Good question," Robby says, trying to sound as noncommittal as possible. "Sonny's current circumstances remind me of *King Lear*."

"You're not going to believe this, but I saw Glenda Jackson of all people play the part at the Cort Theater a few years ago," Bernstein says.

"Then I don't have to tell you that Lear's daughters didn't get along too well."

"Greedy bitches," Bernstein says. Then grins. "But you and I get along extremely well."

"Maybe it's because we know where all the bodies are buried," Robby Sassoon says.

Bernstein makes a small snorting noise. "You've buried enough of them."

When their glasses are empty, Bernstein gets up, brings the bottle over, refills them.

"You ever wonder why Mr. Blum hasn't just taken out Rob Jacobson?" he asks.

"Often," Robby says again.

"He still acts as if he needs Jacobson, for some bizarre reason," Bernstein says. "Or maybe even owes him. I've never had the balls to ask why."

"Fortunately, I don't owe Jacobson a thing," Robby says.

"Nor do I," Bernstein says.

Jed Bernstein throws down the last of his drink and stands.

"It's going to be good being king," he says.

For me, Robby thinks.

SIXTY-EIGHT

BEN ASKS WHAT HE can do to make me feel better, somehow find a way to end a shitty day on a positive note.

"Cure world hunger and cancer?" I say. "Not in that order, of course."

"Absent that."

"Then take me for ice cream," I say.

"Where?"

"Carvel," I say.

We both know the closest Carvel is in Bridgehampton. Ben says we could stop on the way and grab dinner at Bobby Van's, then go to Carvel for dessert. I inform him that Carvel *is* going to be dinner.

"So ice cream is the cure for what's ailing you, at least tonight?"

"For crying," I say. "Ever since I was a little girl."

Ben orders a black-and-white shake when we get there. I order two scoops of soft-serve chocolate ice cream with hot fudge. He knows how much I like to wait out the fudge until it settles on the bottom.

He turns to me at the counter. "You want sprinkles?"

I shake my head. "You don't mess with perfection," I say. "No sprinkles, no nuts, no whipped cream. Chocolate on chocolate. Bring it on."

We go back to the car and he actually seems happier watching me savor my sundae than he is drinking his own milkshake. I tell him I feel as if I have time-traveled my way back to high school and had him along for the ride.

"I wish I'd known you then," Ben says.

"Be careful what you wish for. I was a handful, and not just of sprinkles."

"Ohhhhh," Ben says. "*That's* when you were a handful. Good to know."

He leans over and kisses me. "Ah," he says. "Cold lips, warm heart."

And just like that, I feel as if I want to start crying again. Even after we've gone for ice cream.

I don't. Instead I swallow hard, choking back the tears, and say, "I'm tired of being tough."

"I'll bet."

"Even when I was a kid, I had to learn how to be tough once my mom got sick. Then my sister got sick. And now I'm sick." I take a deep breath. "I'm even more tired of being sick than I am of being tough."

Ben says, "You don't have to be tough when you're with me."

"Sometimes I forget that."

"Don't," he says. "Or I'm not marrying you."

"You're *not* marrying me."

"We'll see about that," he says. "You may have noticed, I'm still playing the long game."

"Then you should start looking around for somebody who actually is capable of playing a long game herself," I say.

He lets that one go, and then we're heading east on 27. But when we get to the Founders Monument at the traffic light at the end of Main Street, he makes a sudden right on Ocean Road.

I ask where we're going.

I see him smiling.

"When was the last time you made out in a parked car at the beach?" he asks.

Now I smile.

"High school," I say.

SIXTY-NINE

I SIT OUT CROSS-EXAMINING Katherine Welsh's first witness the next morning, as chipper as I'm feeling, in addition to being extremely well hydrated.

The witness is Karina Morales. She was the Carson family's housekeeper for the ten years preceding their deaths and had cleaned the house the day of the murders. Jimmy Cunniff and I have both known this for weeks, because of his own investigation. I still consider Karina Morales nothing more than a soft target.

I know what Welsh is doing here, laying bricks in preparation for her second witness of the morning, the man who collected DNA samples from the Carson house after the bodies were discovered.

Welsh wants the jury to know how squeaky clean Ms. Morales left the place, not knowing she was making it practically pristine for the DNA goodies the bad man would leave behind later.

Or so Katherine Welsh wants the jury to believe.

Karina had scrubbed that day, oh, God, had the woman scrubbed. She vacuumed. She polished. She did the laundry. Then scrubbed even more. Welsh successfully creates the impression that had Karina Morales failed to remove any unwelcome spots or hard-to-clean stains she would have considered taking her own life.

"Girl loves her work," Norma Banks says, getting close to my ear.

"If they made a mess when they got home later," I say, "maybe she killed them."

The next witness is Steve Salzman, a young, earnest, bald second responder. "I'm very passionate about how work like mine can bring criminals to justice," he says. He talks about DNA evidence as if he's talking about porn.

By way of introduction to the jury, Welsh has Salzman state his official title: Crime Scene Evidence Technician. It has become common practice for nonpolice personnel, usually hired by district attorneys, to do jobs like Salzman's.

He points out that he was hired by Katherine Welsh's predecessor, Gregg McCall—the man who hired Jimmy and me to investigate the Carson murders, before McCall disappeared from the face of the earth, his body never found. We assumed he had been killed by the late Joe Champi, the dirty ex-cop I'd removed from the face of the earth before he could do the same to me.

Now that Karina Morales has stepped down from the stand, Welsh demonstrates her own brand of housekeeping as she starts to make her case to the jurors that the trace evidence is so damning and irrefutable that the rest of the trial will seem like a mere formality.

The defendant did it.

And how do we know he did it, boys and girls?

All together now.

"The DNA!"

Welsh allows Salzman to conduct a tutorial about how DNA is collected and where he'd collected it *from:* bedside table in the main bedroom, sheets on the daughter's bed, underneath daughter's fingernails, mother's sweater, the living room rug near where the cops had found Hank Carson's body. Touch DNA. Hair follicles. A single drop of blood on the bedside table. Somehow Salzman does all of this without making it sound as if he's speaking in code.

He finally loses me when he gets around to polymerase chain reactions, and how useful that can be to target specific areas for forensic testing.

"Am I going on too long?" Salzman asks after finally coming up for air.

"You're doing fine, Mr. Salzman," Welsh says.

"Objection," I say wearily, more out of a growing sense of boredom than anything else. "The witness is here to talk about the evidence, not sound as if he's hosting his own show on TruTV."

"Overruled," Judge Horton says. "I'll allow it."

"But, Your Honor…"

"Butt down, Ms. Smith," he says. "And let's face it, your heart wasn't really in the objection, anyway."

Well, he has me there.

Salzman then goes on to explain why it took as long as it did to identify the DNA he did collect that day, that they didn't find a match until one of the original detectives working the case suggested they go into the state database looking for a match after Rob Jacobson was tried later for a remarkably similar triple homicide.

"The detective said it was common sense," Salzman says, "because it looked as if Mr. Jacobson had committed the same crime twice."

Butt out of chair again.

"Objection," I say. "Witness is offering commentary again. And flawed commentary at that."

Horton sighs.

"Sustained," he says. Now he's the one who sounds weary. "Ms. Welsh, I see that the detective in question is on your witness list. You will have ample opportunity to have him explain why he thought it was a good idea to link the science when he's the one sitting in that chair."

"You're absolutely right, Your Honor," Welsh says. "I beg the court's forgiveness."

Now she turns back to the witness she does have in the chair.

"You're certain that none of the evidence you did collect was cross-contaminated in any way, correct?" she asks.

"It was not."

Welsh turns to Judge Horton. "If it would please the court, we can put slides up on the screen showing that the DNA Mr. Salzman found and the DNA from the defendant are a match," she says.

"Not necessary," I say from behind her. "We get the picture, counselor. Literally."

It goes on like this for several more minutes. I let Welsh run with the guy, until she's clearly winding down, saying, "Just a couple of more questions, starting with this one: Mr. Salzman, in a world where we've been conditioned to people constantly manipulating the truth, DNA doesn't lie, does it?"

"Not in my experience, no, ma'am."

If it bothers Katherine Welsh being "ma'am"ed, she hides it extremely well.

"And in your thorough forensic examination of the crime scene, did you recover any other evidence for which you found a match in the database?"

"No, I did not."

Welsh gives me a look, then turns to the jury.

"So that the jury gets this picture—literally—we have the defendant's DNA found where police found the three bodies. We have the murder weapon found at the *defendant's* home in New York City. And, just to make the total picture even more damning, we have a time-stamped photograph of the defendant in the immediate vicinity of the Carson home."

"Objection," I say. "I'm sorry, did I miss a question there for the witness?"

"Sustained," Judge Horton says. "I was hopeful that it was

the beginning of a question, Ms. Welsh, until it turned into what I unfortunately have to describe as speechifying."

"Understood," Welsh says. "Here is my last question for you, Mr. Salzman. Is there any doubt in your mind, in light of evidence that you yourself collected, that the defendant was the last person to see Hank Carson, and his wife, and his teenage daughter alive on the night in question?"

"I'm a scientist," Salzman says. "Scientists deal in evidence, then test the evidence. It's not our job to prove things. All we can do is report our conclusions."

It's not an answer, but clearly Katherine Welsh doesn't give a rip whether it is or not.

"And all of us in this courtroom know what the conclusion is, don't we?" she says.

She's not looking at him. She's looking at the jury again.

Then she sits down.

Rob Jacobson, face red and angry all over again, leans past Thomas McGoey and whispers to me, "Why the hell did you just let her leave it like that?"

"Because now I get a turn," I say.

SEVENTY

"HAVE YOU EVER TESTIFIED at a murder trial before, Mr. Salzman?" I begin by asking.

"No, ma'am."

I turn to the jury and open my eyes wide. "*Ma'am?* I heard you call Ms. Welsh that. You can't possibly think I'm as old as she is, can you?"

I see some of the women in the box laugh.

I'm here all week.

And just getting started.

Now I'm facing Steve Salzman again.

"I am going to make the assumption that in preparation for your testimony here, you studied the use of DNA as it has applied to other murder trials," I say. "Am I correct about that?"

"As a matter of fact, you are."

"And in those studies, in what was effectively your own trial prep, did you find a single case where DNA was the *single* determining result or conclusion or fact in proving a defendant's guilt beyond a reasonable doubt?"

He hesitates.

"I'm not sure what you're asking," he says.

"Let me see if I can make it clearer for you," I say. "Wouldn't even a cursory Google check tell you that often the opposite is true, that DNA—sometimes years after the

216

fact—has often been used to prove the innocence of someone falsely convicted of murder by noble lawyers from places
like the Innocence Project?"

"Objection," Welsh says, jumping to her feet. "Now who's
giving speeches, Your Honor?"

"Overruled," Judge Horton says. "But Ms. Smith, let's
move on from you sounding like an unpaid spokesperson for
the Innocence Project."

"My pleasure, Your Honor."

I walk toward the witness stand now, stopping only a few
feet away. Jimmy Cunniff has always said that in moments
like these I remind him of a boxer cutting off the ring. Even
a girl boxer.

"Can a person's DNA be harvested?" I ask Salzman.

"Harvested?"

"You see, Mr. Salzman, I did some forensic trial prep of
my own. So what I'm asking is if someone who knew what
he, or she, was doing, could they recover DNA off someone's toothbrush, for example, and then—again, knowing
what they were doing—preserve that DNA along with a few
drops of water in a test tube for future use?"

"I guess that would be possible, yes."

"*Objection!*" Katherine Welsh says, much louder than
before. "Your Honor, it's also possible that Ms. Smith could
become an astronaut if she trained for it. But as far as I know,
she hasn't."

I've never been able to help myself in moments like these,
no matter how many times I've been warned by judges.

"I'm starting to feel a little weightless right now, to tell you
the truth," I say.

"The objection is overruled," Horton says. But then to me
he says, "Ms. Smith, please let it be noted for the record that
you're not as amusing as you clearly think you are."

Am too, I think.

But what I say is this: "If it pleases the court, what I'm

trying to establish with this witness, in a scientific way I'm hopeful he will appreciate, is that there are a lot of ways why and how my client's DNA could have ended up in that house, and near those victims, without him being the one to leave it there. So what I'm really asking the witness is if he thinks it's entirely possible that someone other than my client committed these crimes?"

"It would be extremely difficult to plant that much evidence," he says, "even for someone who did know what they were doing."

I grin at him. "But possible," I say, before adding, "like becoming an astronaut."

"Yes," he says. "Possible."

"And on the subject of hair follicles," I continue, "isn't it true that someone whose intention *is* an elaborate and creative frame-up would only need access to someone's hat, or even hairbrush?"

"Objection," Welsh says. "Your Honor, that isn't a serious question. It's just more of Ms. Smith's fever dream about this murder being a setup."

"Sustained," Horton says.

"Your Honor," I say, "I'm just attempting to make the jury aware that this trial isn't over just because of DNA samples that Mr. Salzman collected at the murder scene, but is rather just beginning."

"We can all see what you're attempting to do," Judge Horton says. "You're telling a story. And I'm telling you that this story needs to come to an end now."

"Understood," I say.

I know I can call Salzman back to the stand later if I think I need him. But I don't think that I will—once I've got my own expert on the stand.

"Mr. Salzman, let's approach this from another direction. Is there any way for the science you're here talking about to know how long DNA has been present, whether on a hard surface or any article of clothing or on a rug?"

"No," he says, "there's not."

"One more question: Is it possible that DNA, even belonging to the same person, can alter slightly over time, so that while it's still clearly a match, it's not an exact match?"

"Yes," he answers, "it is possible, but it would require a longer explanation."

"One I'm sure you could give this court, in both chapter and verse," I say. "But for now, a simple yes or no will do."

"Yes," he says. "It can alter."

"No further questions," I say, "at least not at this time."

Katherine Welsh is back on her feet before I'm back in my chair.

"Redirect please, Your Honor," she says.

"To be clear, Mr. Salzman," she says, "the defendant's DNA was only found in close proximity to the three bodies, when it wasn't in fact *on* the bodies, right?"

"That's right."

"What a coincidence."

"It would be some coincidence."

Welsh says, "And there was that one drop of blood on the nightstand in the main bedroom, right?"

"Yes," Salzman answers.

"And we both know that the Carsons' housekeeper has testified that she took a scrub brush to all the hard surfaces in that house on the day in question, don't we?"

"I heard the same testimony you did, Ms. Welsh."

"So sometime after Ms. Morales thoroughly cleaned that house and before you arrived at the house, somehow a drop of Rob Jacobson's blood ended up on that table," Welsh says. "Not something from a test tube, or a toothbrush, or a hairbrush, or a ball cap. Mr. Jacobson's own blood."

"Yes."

"And with blood, you can tell that it's fresh, can't you?"

"Without a doubt."

"Without a reasonable doubt," Welsh says.

Not a question, not intended to be.

"No further questions," she says.

In that moment, I do feel a little bit like a boxer.

One who just got cut.

SEVENTY-ONE

Jimmy

JIMMY IS BACK AT his bar after having left court early, tracking Rob Jacobson's car as Jacobson makes his way east. When he sees that Jacobson is approaching downtown East Hampton, Jimmy tells Kenny, who's working a double shift behind the bar today, that he might see him later and not to steal too much while he's gone.

"Too late," Kenny says.

He hasn't called ahead because he wants to surprise Jacobson, have him be at least a little bit off balance when Jimmy asks him what he wants to ask him, once and for all.

He is slowly pulling up Jacobson's street when he sees the girl up ahead, making her way up the front walk to the rental house and then walking right through the door without knocking or ringing the bell, barely breaking stride.

Jimmy keeps driving, passing the house, almost not believing his eyes.

But only almost.

It isn't Halloween yet, but the girl walking toward the house looks as if she's come directly from cheerleading practice.

SEVENTY-TWO

JIMMY TURNS THE CAR around and comes back, stopping two driveways up from Jacobson's.

There he waits.

When he finally does walk in, also without announcing himself, he sees they haven't made it upstairs yet, but they are getting after it, all over each other on the couch. Jacobson must have opened the wine bottle on his coffee table before she arrived.

He's already managed to get her sweater off.

It's then that the girl notices Jimmy standing there.

"Hey!" she yells, and immediately wriggles away from Jacobson, trying to cover up as she does, nearly knocking over the wine bottle.

Jacobson tries to play it cool, as if Jimmy showing up this way is somehow just part of the scene.

"Sorry, Cunniff," he says casually. "Threesomes aren't Shauna's thing." He exaggerates a wink at the girl. "At least not yet."

It isn't the first time Jimmy has imagined himself putting a bullet in this guy, put everybody out of their misery in the process.

"Your probation officer would be so pleased," Jimmy says.

"Whatever," Jacobson says. "Thanks for stopping by. Now get the hell out of my house."

Jimmy walks over to the girl's maroon sweater with EHHS on the front, casually picks it up off the floor, and tosses it at her. The skirt, he notices, is gray. Maroon and gray. The East Hampton High School colors. School spirit. Rah rah rah.

"I stay," Jimmy says. "But she goes."

Jimmy turns to the girl and says, "You're the one who needs to get the hell out of his house."

Shauna is frozen in place, as if unsure what to do, wearing just a bra from the waist up, with the sweater now sitting there on her lap.

Jimmy takes out his phone, points it at the two of them, and says, "Smile."

"Shauna," Jacobson says, "you stay right where you are."

"Fine with me," Jimmy says. "But the kid ought to know that it will take me about twenty minutes, tops, to find out who she is, who her parents are, what their contact information is. After that I text them this picture of their little girl."

The color drains from the girl's face, just like that. She stands up and pulls the sweater over her long brown hair and, without saying another word or looking back, grabs her purse and heads for the door.

"Call me?" Jacobson calls after her.

The girl turns around.

"Not happening," she says. "This is too weird even for me."

When she's gone, Jimmy says to Jacobson, "You're welcome."

"For what? Pissing on the only good part of my day?"

"For maybe saving your life, you stupid shit."

"You know, Cunniff," Rob Jacobson says, "I still need to remind you from time to time that you work for me."

"Keep telling yourself that."

"Get out," Jacobson says.

"Not until we talk."

"Talk about what?" Jacobson says. "By the way? She's seventeen, in case you were wondering. The age of consent in this state."

Jimmy's phone is still in his hand. He holds it back up for Jacobson to see. "I'm sure that will be a great comfort to her father once he gets a look at his baby girl starting to undress for you."

Jacobson calmly reaches for his glass and drinks some wine.

"I *get* the picture," he says. "Okay? I get it. Now what's so important that you felt the need to barge in on me like this."

"I never asked you this straight up, but I'm asking you now," Jimmy says. "Simple question, but needs to be asked: Did you kill those people?"

"Which people?" Jacobson says.

Jimmy shakes his head. He can't believe he ever went to work for this guy without getting his shots first.

"There's nothing me or anybody else can do about the Gates family, you already got tried and acquitted on that one," Jimmy says. "You know I'm talking about the Carsons."

Jacobson shakes his head in disbelief.

"No shit," he says. "You're asking me that *now*?"

"Like I said. Just you and me. Straight up."

"And if I say yes, what, you drive over to Jane's house and tell her what I said and she quits me once and for all?" Jacobson says. "I know her by now. Not as well as you. But I know her, which means I know that whatever she might say, the reason she's still around is that she doesn't believe I did it. Or at least can't make herself believe that I did."

"This isn't about her," Jimmy says. "This is me asking you."

Jacobson grins his snarky grin, as if he can't help himself from always falling back into the wise-ass pose.

"I refuse to answer on the grounds that it may tend to incriminate me," he says.

Jimmy quickly crosses the room and lifts him up off the couch, then jerks Jacobson closer until they're nose to nose.

"For once in your miserable life," Jimmy says quietly, "look me in the eyes and tell me the truth."

He grabs the guy's sweater a little tighter.

"Did. You. Do. It?"

Jimmy's not sure if what he's seeing in Jacobson's eyes now is fear. But it might be. Maybe Jimmy in this moment has finally made him feel cornered like the sewer rat that he is.

"I didn't do it," he says.

Jimmy lets him go, then shoves him back down into the couch.

"Then who did?" he asks.

"You want to know the truth?"

"Yeah," Jimmy says, "surprise me."

"I think Eddie McKenzie killed them all," he says.

SEVENTY-THREE

JIMMY DRIVES BACK TO the bar, not ready to go home yet, having nowhere to go except there.

On the way to Sag Harbor he's thinking that a guy who's been accused of killing six people is involved with more women — of all ages — than Jimmy is these days.

He's looking ahead to one more night when he's not ready to go back to the empty house. He keeps telling himself that he might finally be ready to have someone in his life again, for the first time in a long time, when all of this is over.

But only if it's ever over.

Jimmy takes his usual seat at the end of the bar. There's a football game on the television set closest to him. This time of year, there always seems to be some kind of football on. Jimmy's old enough to remember when college football was Saturday afternoons and the pros were Sunday afternoons and Monday nights.

Stop it.

Thinking about the old days was just another way of making you even older than you already are.

He turns his thoughts back to Edmund (Eddie) McKenzie.

Another rich man's son with the morals of a sewer rat.

But the one who had it in for Jacobson since high school.

The one who may or may not have been at Jacobson's town house the day Jacobson's father was shot to death, along with

226

a girl about the same age as the one Jimmy just encountered in Amagansett.

McKenzie is the one who may or may not have done one of the killings himself at the town house that day, if you could believe another sewer rat like former Commander of Detectives Paul Harrington.

Eddie McKenzie: another sick, spoiled boy who never grew up. But does that make him sick enough to have done everything that Jacobson has been accused of doing?

McKenzie is also the one who was accused of rape when he and Rob Jacobson really were still boys, a rape he swears up and down that Jacobson committed and then stood by and watched as McKenzie took the weight on it.

Maybe McKenzie did wait all this time to get even.

Could he have known enough about blood and hair and DNA to plant it near the bodies? Why the hell not? You can learn just about anything these days on the internet, including how to build your own bomb.

Maybe Jacobson is right about him, and somehow McKenzie is the one who killed both families, and it just turns out he did a much better job of planting the evidence at the Carson house than he did later when he killed Mitch Gates and his wife and his daughter.

Or, it suddenly occurs to Jimmy, another way of looking at things, there are two killers instead of just one.

"*Goddamn it!*" Jimmy says, and slaps the bar in front of him.

"You okay, boss?" Kenny asks.

"Do I look okay?"

"Trick question?" Kenny asks, grinning.

"I'm too old for this shit," Jimmy says.

"Who isn't?" Kenny says. "Want another beer while we ponder that and other deep questions?"

Jimmy shakes his head, stands, leaves a too-big tip next to his glass.

"You don't have to tip me," Kenny says. "You're already paying my salary, remember?"

"Excellent point," Jimmy says, and picks up the twenty and replaces it with a fifty and leaves.

When he's approaching his house, he sees the downstairs lights are on. Jimmy is sure he didn't leave them that way. He's always been a bit of a wing nut on conserving electricity, his parents having drummed that into him when he was growing up and there was barely enough money for his father to put food on the table in their small apartment in the Bronx.

Jimmy keeps going, past the house, slowly drives to the end of the street and parks there, shutting off the car and removing his gun from the glove compartment before he gets out.

He cuts across his next-door neighbor's lawn and makes his way along the front of his house, ducking down as he passes the living room window.

Then he's at the door, hand on the doorknob as he gives it a slow, gentle turn.

Unlocked.

He's also sure he left it locked. He never forgets to do that.

Jimmy turns the handle, then he's opening the door, stepping into the house, gun out in front of him.

The man is sitting there on his couch.

He looks at the gun in Jimmy's hand, barely changing expression.

"You use that, better make sure you kill me with the first shot," he says.

Then the man says, "You know who I am?"

"I do," Jimmy says, lowering his weapon.

"We need to talk," Sonny Blum says.

SEVENTY-FOUR

BLUM WEARS A TAN windbreaker that might have fit him at some point, but is now at least two sizes or more too big. Baggy khaki pants spotted with visible stains above the knees. Sneakers, more gray than white, with Velcro flaps designed so that men Sonny Blum's age don't have to tie them.

Jimmy's unsure of Sonny Blum's actual age, but sitting here in Jimmy's living room, he looks older than the earth.

Wispy white hair, what little there is of it, sprays out in all directions. His skin is the color of dust. His hands, there in his lap almost as an afterthought, seem to be the oldest part of him. Signs of living as long as he has can be hidden—all but the hands.

"There was no car out front," Jimmy says, taking a seat in the armchair across from him. "And I'm assuming you didn't walk. So how did you get here, some kind of wiseguy Uber deal?"

"The guy I sent to your bar that time, Len Greene? Snappy little dude? He dropped me and then said he'd take the car to the next block over."

"So I wouldn't call the cops and have them run the plates as a professional courtesy?"

Blum shrugs. "Let an old man have some fun. I was just fucking around."

"Len pick my lock?"

"He's like one of those Swiss Army knives," Blum says. "Got a lot of uses."

"I'll bet," Jimmy says.

"You gonna put the gun away?"

"I'd tell you not to make any sudden moves," Jimmy says, keeping his Glock 9 leveled at Blum, "but I'm guessing that ship has sailed."

"I heard you were a funny guy," Blum says.

It seems to take a lot of effort for him to get the words out. Jimmy is already leaning forward to hear him better. Blum's eyelids look puffy, and there's a yellow tint to his eyes.

"You don't quit, I gotta hand it to you," Blum says.

"Neither do you," Jimmy says. "You still fucking with people by wandering around in a robe?"

"Too old, too tired," Blum says. "And that old goombah, Gigante, his brother was a priest? He was more convincing than me." He nods at Jimmy with his chin. "You didn't buy that I was crazy?"

"Only like a fox."

"Yeah, I still got it."

"So to what do I owe the honor?" Jimmy asks.

"I came here to tell you, man to man, that you got me all wrong."

Jimmy says, "Somehow I doubt that."

"What I'm here to tell you is, I had nothing to do with those three people dying."

"I'm told that Hank Carson owed you a lot of money," Jimmy tells him.

"He did."

"Just out of curiosity," Jimmy says, "how much did the late Mr. Carson owe you?"

"A million, give or take a few thousand," Blum says.

"Lot of money."

"He's lucky something unfortunate didn't happen to him sooner," Blum says. "Lucky for him he finally paid."

Now he's got Jimmy's attention.

"You're saying he wasn't still to the bad with you when he died?"

"Paid up in full, to Bobby Salvatore, couple of days before he *did* die," Blum says. "Maybe you're not as much of a hot shit investigator as I heard you were."

Blum shakes his head. Even that seems to require most of the strength he has in him. When he stops, his head falls a little to the side.

"It was supposed to be last call for the guy," Blum says. "I sent Bobby thinking he was going to have to clip him. But Carson shocked the shit out of Bobby and shocked the shit out of me and paid in full." He nearly smiles. "Still no problem in this world that a bag full of money can't solve."

The old man's lips look cracked and dry. He licks them now.

"Carson told Bobby he didn't want to die because of what he owed," Blum says. "Then he pays up and dies anyway. Funny world, right?"

"Tell me again why you're here," Jimmy says.

"Your girl needs to keep my name out of her mouth at this trial," he says, "before something happens to her."

"In case you haven't figured it out already, she scares about as easily as I do," Jimmy says. "And she wants you to testify."

Blum laughs, which then turns into a coughing fit.

"Something funny?" Jimmy asks.

"Yeah," Blum says. "You thinking I give a rat's ass what she wants."

"I'll pass your message along, though I'm not sure it will do any good."

"I don't want to have to kill her," Blum says.

"Good to know."

"I want her alive, because I don't want the kid to go down for this."

"Kid," Jimmy says. "You're referring to Jacobson?"

Blum nods.

"Why is that?" Jimmy asks.

"I got my reasons."

"You own a piece of him?"

"A piece?" Blum starts laughing again, and then the coughing is worse than before, the sound even more harsh this time around.

"I own him," Sonny Blum says, "the way I owned his old man."

He leans back into the couch, as if all this talking really has exhausted him. Jimmy takes a closer look at him.

People have feared this man for fifty years, maybe more than that. Still fear him.

And he can't even catch his breath.

Without being asked, Jimmy goes into the kitchen and comes back with a glass of water. Blum drinks some of it and hands him back the glass.

"Taking out a whole family, like that, was never my style," Blum says. "People know that if you don't pay what you owe me, you end up paying a different way. That's how it works. How it's *always* worked. But even if Carson hadn't paid, I wouldn't have touched the wife and the daughter." Another little nod with the chin. "You may not believe me, but even I have rules."

"A lot of people tied to that family are dead," Jimmy says, "starting with the district attorney, McCall, who hired Jane and me to look into the murders in the first place."

"I don't kill cops and I sure as shit don't kill DAs," he says. "Like I told you, you can believe what you want to believe. But I do have a code."

They sit in silence until finally Jimmy says, "Sonny, what the hell are you doing here, really?"

"Somebody went to a lot of trouble to set the kid up and have him go down for this," Blum says. "But I don't want that to happen and neither do you. It means we're on the same side of this thing, whether you like it or not. And might even be able to help each other out."

Jimmy feels another grin come over him.

"So that's really why you came here?" Jimmy asks.

"Why I came here," Sonny Blum says, "is because I want to hire you."

SEVENTY-FIVE

JIMMY CALLS ME AT five thirty in the morning, not apologizing, telling me he knew I would be awake.

It's still dark outside, but I'm already dressed in sweats and a hoodie and about to take Rip to the beach for a run after I feed the beast. But I'm not telling Jimmy Cunniff that.

"How did you know this wasn't going to be the one morning when I wasn't up this early?" I ask.

"You're always up," he says.

"Carpe diem," I say.

"Seize this," he says.

"So what's up, since we both clearly are?"

He says he needs to tell me about a visitor he had the night before.

"Okay, I'll bite."

"Sonny Blum," Jimmy says.

"Good one."

"I'm telling you, Sonny Blum paid me a visit."

"Did he have Elvis with him?"

"Jane, I'm serious."

"Sonny Blum, at your house."

"In the flesh, though I have to say it's pretty saggy flesh at this point."

"And you're just getting around to telling me this now?"

"It was late after he left and I didn't want to wake you, on the outside chance you were sleeping for once," he says.

I tell him then that Rip and I are practically on our way to Indian Wells and to get his ass over there.

"Sonny Fucking Blum," I say, but he's already ended the call.

The wind is coming hard and loud off the water, hard enough to keep blowing Jimmy and Rip and me sideways as we head in the direction of Atlantic Beach, though I'm doubtful we will make it all the way there.

I know I have to leave for court early this morning, because I need to make a stop at Sam Wylie's office. It's because of another stop I made on my way back from Mineola yesterday afternoon, one only Sam and my oncologist, Mike Gellis, knew about. Now that I'm back from Switzerland, they're my own personal medical dream team, the firm of Wylie and Gellis.

Jimmy is telling me on the beach, without commercial interruption, about everything Blum said after Jimmy walked in and found him on the living room couch.

Including that he wants to hire Jimmy.

I say, "Okay, now what's the punch line?"

"No punch line."

"He tells you he wants to hire you and you both somehow manage to keep a straight face?"

"He did," Jimmy says. "And we did."

"And how did he take it when you turned him down?"

"Well, see, that's the thing. I didn't."

Then he adds, "Per se."

I stop walking. Jimmy and Rip keep going until they realize they've left me behind. Then they both turn around and come back.

"Let me see if I have this straight," I say. "You're considering a side job with a known killer?"

He grins. "You did."

He moves out of range before I can kick him. "Just kidding," he says. "We're currently only working for an *alleged* killer."

"Cunniff," I say, "you tell me right now that you're messing with me and you really did turn him down."

"Relax," he says. "I did. But I might also have mentioned that I wouldn't be averse, going forward, to sharing information with him if it gets us both to where we want to go."

"Aren't you the guy," I ask him, "who keeps saying that everything in this case, even before it *was* our case, seems to run through him?"

"I still think it does," Jimmy says. "But maybe not the murders."

He raises his voice again, but maybe not just to be heard over the wind and the waves.

"*I need to know who did it!*" he says.

"And we, you and me, need to win this case," I say. "Please keep in mind that's still job one."

"I want it all," Jimmy says, "and so do you."

"Did it occur to you that he might be playing you?"

Jimmy winks at me. Or at least tries. It always looks more to me like an eye tic. "What if I'm the one playing him?" he asks.

Rip has run toward the dunes and come back with a stick in his mouth. Jimmy throws it back in that direction, the wind getting him a good carry.

"I've got a better what-if," I tell him. "What if you end up crossing your new friend and it gets us killed?"

"You're not dying," Jimmy says.

"Really."

"I won't allow it," he says.

I tell him that remains to be seen, and then tell him about the stop I need to make in Southampton, and why I need to make it.

"I'm going with you," he says. "And don't tell me not to."

I smile at my partner.

"One more thing you won't allow," I say.

SEVENTY-SIX

Jimmy

JIMMY AND JANE DRIVE in separate cars to Southampton.

"You really don't have to go with me," Jane says to Jimmy.

"Yeah, I kind of do," he says.

Jane calls Sam from *her* car and then calls Jimmy as they are passing through Water Mill, telling him that the results expected first thing still haven't come in. Jane says she wants to be in the room when Sam gives her the news. She plans to wait as long as she has to, short of making herself late for court.

He waits in his car, parked next to Jane's, in the small parking lot outside Dr. Sam Wylie's office. Jimmy has done this before, in this same lot. And can't remember a time, not a single one, when Jane has come out of that office with good news.

It's always the same feeling out here, like he's about to get hit.

All he knows today is what she told him before they left the beach, that she had undergone her latest CT scan on the tumor in her neck late yesterday afternoon, when Sam Wylie and Jane's oncologist, Dr. Gellis, put in a fix at Southampton Hospital, and allowed her to be hooked up to the machine much later in the day than was usually allowed for computed tomography which, Jane explained to Jimmy, is where the "CT" comes from.

She then tried to tell Jimmy about what the machine actually does. He stopped her when she got to IV contrast agents and dyes. Actually begged her to stop.

"As long as you understand it, kid," he said.

Her next CT scan was scheduled for two weeks down the road. But she decided just like that, being Jane, that she wasn't going to wait, that she wanted the new pictures right freaking now.

Sam has fast-tracked the results, too, ahead of the usual twenty-four hours. No surprise that these two have been friends since high school. They both want what they want when they want it.

Jane has already caught one break—the trial is starting an hour late today, at eleven instead of ten. The court clerk called her last night to tell her that Judge Horton has a long-scheduled doctor's appointment of his own.

It is an established fact that Jimmy is better at waiting than Jane is, even if she'd also been a cop, where being as good at waiting as shooting a gun was part of the job description.

But he can't imagine what the waiting must be like with cancer, going from one test to another.

Jimmy doesn't listen to the radio while he waits. He doesn't drive up to the CVS on Main Street and buy a newspaper, as much as he still likes having the paper in his hands. He just sits in the quiet of the front seat and remembers something he read in the *Times* the other day about manifesting, and how if you believe in something hard enough and well enough that you can allow it to come into form.

Jimmy sits here and manifests Jane getting some good news today for a change, manifests like that's the most important thing he'll do all day.

Eight o'clock now.

She needs to get on the road soon.

They both do.

The dashboard clock says 8:06 when she comes walking out the door and straight for Jimmy's car.

He can see right away that she's crying.

Now Jimmy is the one who can't wait any longer, gets out of the car, walks toward her.

When he's right in front of her, he stops and says, "Whatever it is, I'm here."

She's crying hard enough, making a complete mess out of her makeup, that she can't get any words out right away. The tears just keep coming, her chest keeps rising and falling.

So it turns out Jimmy does have to wait a few seconds more.

"It's bad?" he says.

She gets some air into her.

At last, she shakes her head.

Finally, she says, "It shrunk."

SEVENTY-SEVEN

I'VE NEVER BEEN ONE of those women who carries a small cosmetics department in my purse. But I know I have enough to get the job done between when I arrive in Mineola and before Katherine Welsh calls her first witness of the morning, a high school friend of Morgan Carson's.

Norma Banks has just pulled up in her Uber when I'm getting out of my own car.

"What happened?" she says, the bright blue eyes locked on me. "Something bad happened, didn't it?"

"No, something good," I say, adding that I'll tell her when I'm inside, right before the two of us blow past the media rope lines, me only offering a wave of the hand as I tell them all to have a blessed day.

From behind me I hear one of the male reporters call out, "*Blessed* day? Who *are* you?"

When it's just Norma and me in the ladies' room, I tell her about the tumor shrinking and why that matters, how the best I've done before this, since the day Sam Wylie sat in the same office and gave me the news about my cancer, was the tumor not getting any bigger.

"Fuckin' ay," Norma says.

"You know there's no victory laps in this game, right?" I ask.

I'm leaning over the sink getting myself as close to the

mirror as possible, doing the best I can with what I've got to work with, like I'm in training to be a makeup artist.

Behind me I see Norma smiling.

"So the shit they gave you in Switzerland that's been making you feel this shitty since you got back is actually working," she says. "Is that what you're telling me?"

"I'll ignore your language and just say so far, so good."

"*Very* damn good, if you ask me."

"We can't get crazy with this."

"Shut up," Norma Banks says, "and take the win."

"That's what my boyfriend says to me sometimes."

She pats me on the shoulder.

"Of course he does," she says. "One of the keys to success in this world is hanging around with people smarter than you."

I smile into the mirror as I put the finishing touches on my face, then step back to admire my handiwork.

"So you're saying that's what I'm doing?"

"Fuckin' ay," she says.

SEVENTY-EIGHT

THE YOUNG WOMAN'S NAME is Brooke Milligan, and she is currently a freshman at Hofstra, and at Garden City High she was Morgan Carson's closest friend.

She has been on Katherine Welsh's witness list from the start, so I asked Jimmy to do a deep dive on her. On the condition that I never again use the expression "deep dive," he agreed and he'd done good.

That's how I know Ms. Milligan is here today and under oath trying to kill our client dead with her knowledge of Morgan's relationship with him.

I can't let that happen, even though I'm not looking forward, not even a little bit, to what's about to happen between me and this young woman. I never have any doubts about how good I am at my job.

It's just that there are days when I don't like doing it.

This is about to be one of them.

Brooke Milligan is young, beautiful, clearly intelligent, dressed chastely in a white dress, clearly made up far better than I am this morning, and here to tell one story:

How Morgan Carson, only seventeen at the time, was madly in love with my client.

"I was the only one she confided in," Brooke says. "But

once she did, I got such a bad feeling that I tried every possible way I could think of to talk her out of it."

She shakes her head. "She didn't know anything about boys, much less men."

I see Brooke Milligan pause now and take a sip of water from the glass next to her.

"This is all so awful..."

"Do you need a moment, Brooke?" Welsh says.

"I'm okay." She smiles weakly. "Even though I'm not really okay."

"You're doing fine," Welsh says. "Now, when you say you tried to talk her out of it, was it because you thought her relationship with the defendant was wrong, because of how much older he is and how young she was?"

"All of that, and more," Brooke says. "But it didn't matter what I thought. It was as if she had decided that after having been a good girl her whole life, she wanted to be a wild child."

She puts air quotes around "good girl."

"Could you please give this court a bit more context about what you mean by good girl?" Welsh asks.

She knows exactly what she means. So do I. And now the jury is about to know.

Brooke Milligan stares directly at Rob Jacobson as she says, "My friend Morgan was a virgin until he came into her life."

There are times when a quiet courtroom can become suddenly and deafeningly loud. This is one of them.

I am looking at the jury as I get to my feet, knowing that no objection is going to change the fact that the word—"virgin"—has landed in their box as if it exploded there.

"Objection," I say, trying to sound as if I'm lodging the most obvious objection in the world. "Hearsay."

"Sustained," Judge Horton says.

But it's too late for him to do me any good, either, because Brooke Milligan hasn't quite finished with her answer.

She turns to the judge then, looking fresh-faced and earnest and sincere almost to the extreme.

"It's the truth, Your Honor, even though it's not a pretty picture," she says. "About Morgan having been a virgin."

We understood you perfectly the first time.

Of course, she's right about it not being a very pretty picture.

Unfortunately, especially for Morgan, just not the whole picture.

SEVENTY-NINE

KATHERINE WELSH FINISHES UP with Brooke Milligan by asking her about the last time she spoke with Morgan Carson.

"The day he killed her," she says.

"Objection!"

"Sustained," Judge Horton says. To Brooke he says, "It's the jury's job to acquit or convict, young lady. Not yours."

"Sorry, Your Honor," she says.

"Please try not to let it happen again," Horton says.

"What I was trying to say was, it was the afternoon before the murders," she says. "And it was pretty important."

Welsh asks, "Important in what way?"

"She told me that she was going to tell him that she no longer wanted to see him, that she was breaking it off," Brooke says. "That her parents had just found out about their relationship, she didn't exactly know how, and that her dad said that if Mr. Jacobson ever came near her again, he—Mr. Carson—would kill him."

"Did she say anything else during that call?"

"She did," Brooke Milligan says.

"Please share with the jury what else she told you, if you would."

"Morgan said that she was more scared about what Mr. Jacobson might do than she was her father."

Katherine Welsh pauses, as if waiting for my objection.

But I let this go, because now it's go time for me.

Whether I like it or not.

"May I call you Brooke?" is my opening line.

"Please do."

"Well, then, good morning, Brooke."

"Good morning," she says, before sheepishly adding, "I guess."

"Like Ms. Welsh said, you're doing just fine, under what I'm sure couldn't possibly be more difficult circumstances for you."

"Thank you," she says. "And you're certainly right about that."

"It sounds as if you and Morgan really were besties," I say.

"We were."

"Close enough that she confided what can be a high school girl's biggest secret, about having finally done it, as we used to say when I was in high school back when dinosaurs roamed the earth. Is that correct?"

"It is," she says, nodding her head.

"So as far as you know, you were the only one who knew that she was indeed doing it, and with a much older man."

"If any of our other friends knew, they never mentioned it, and that was the type of thing they all would have mentioned," Brooke says.

"I'm just curious about something, since we're talking about secrets here," I continue. "Did you ever confide the same intimate details about yourself?"

"*Objection!*" Welsh says. "What Ms. Milligan may or may not have confided about her own life is irrelevant to these proceedings."

"Sustained," Horton says. "Let's see if we can stay in our lane today, Ms. Smith."

"Of course, Your Honor."

I walk all the way over to the witness stand and lean an elbow on the partition, smiling at her as I do.

"Being told something like that in confidence," I say, "I assume you didn't share what Morgan was doing—and with whom—with any of your other girlfriends."

"I would never."

"Did any of them confide to you about losing their virginity?"

I wait for an objection, but none is forthcoming, at least not for now.

"No," she says. "But I wasn't as close with any of them as I was with Morgan."

"So as far as you know, you were the only other person at Garden City High School who knew that Morgan Carson was having sex with Mr. Jacobson," I say.

"You'd have to ask our other friends but, like I said before, none of them brought it up, and I believe that it was something that a high school girl would bring up if she knew."

I nod.

"While Morgan's relationship with my client was going on," I say, "did you happen to have a boyfriend?"

"Objection."

She sounds almost exhausted just saying it. Like she's as tired as I am.

"Sustained," Judge Horton says. "Are we going anywhere interesting with this, Ms. Smith?"

"I believe you'll see when we get there."

"Please get there quickly."

"Have you yourself ever had a relationship with an older man, Brooke?" I ask.

"Objection!"

Horton puts up a hand. "I'll allow it," he says. "Speaks to both the victim's state of mind, and the witness's at the same time."

Brooke Milligan is looking past me, to Katherine Welsh. But Welsh can't help her right now because no one can.

Brooke turns to the judge. "Do I have to answer that?"

But Horton is looking at me. Occasionally there comes a moment when the person behind the bench has to trust the person in the arena, almost on faith.

I nod at him.

"Please answer the question," Horton says to her.

She tries to buy herself some time. "Could you repeat the question, please?" she says to me.

"Certainly," I say. "I just asked if you yourself had ever been involved with an older man, say the summer before school started that year."

"Yes," she says, her voice barely audible.

"While you were obviously the same age as Morgan?"

"Yes."

This is hardly more than a whisper.

"I'm not sure everybody could hear you, Brooke."

"Yes," she says.

"And could you tell us if that man is in this courtroom?"

She looks down at the hands in her lap, then back up at me. "Yes," she says.

"Could you point him out for the jury, please."

She waits as long as she possibly can, as if there is some way for her to run out the clock on this line of questioning, before she points directly at Rob Jacobson.

EIGHTY

A MURMUR RUNS THROUGH the jury box, and through the spectators behind me, like a low rumble of thunder.

It's several seconds before I'm speaking again, but I know it seems like much longer in Judge Horton's courtroom, and probably feels like an eternity, or two, to Brooke Milligan, who in this moment looks heartbroken.

I'm thinking, *You're not the only one, kid.*

"You had him first, didn't you?" I ask Brooke Milligan, thinking all over again how happy I am that Jimmy Cunniff had actually done his deep dive, even before we got our shitheel client to admit that Morgan Carson wasn't his first conquest at Garden City High, back when he'd briefly opened a Nassau County office for his real estate business.

Brooke Milligan is staring now at him, with a look I couldn't possibly begin to properly describe or comprehend, not sure whether it is sadness or anger or even shame.

"Did Morgan know?"

"Yes," she says. "But she didn't care. She was crazy for him. Like, literally."

"But the fact is, he basically dumped you for your best friend, Morgan, didn't he?"

She's shouting now, maybe because now everyone knows *her* secrets.

"Yes!"

I keep my foot on the gas.

"And isn't the real reason you came here today, Brooke, because at long last, you saw a chance to get even with him for doing that to you?" I say. "Humiliating you that way?"

"Objection!" Katherine Welsh says.

Now she's the one who has raised her own voice.

"I'm not only objecting to that question, I'm objecting to this entire line of questioning, which has only served to put a cooperating witness into the line of fire," Welsh says. "And embarrass her."

"Sustained," Judge Horton says, before telling the jury to ignore my last comment, and that it is being stricken from the record.

"I respectfully withdraw that last question, Your Honor," I tell him.

"Too late," Horton says, disgustedly. "You are completely out of order, Ms. Smith."

"I'm sorry," I say.

But I'm not looking at the judge.

I'm looking directly at Brooke Milligan.

EIGHTY-ONE

KATHERINE WELSH TRIES TO clean things up as best she can once I sit down, leading Brooke Milligan into answers about how revenge had nothing to do with this, how she was just looking out for a friend.

Brooke says, "It was like he had her under some kind of spell." Then she pauses and exhales and says, "I knew the feeling, at least until I came to my senses."

But I can see in Welsh's body language, because if you do this long enough you have to be able to read the room, that she knows the damage has been done. She was blindsided by a prior relationship between her witness and my client that she clearly had known nothing about. Maybe her own investigator hadn't gone as deep as Jimmy had, or simply hadn't asked the right questions, or enough of them.

I know the jury isn't going to stop thinking of him as a predator, for having had sex with a seventeen-year-old virgin, whether that age was legal in the great state of New York or not. Now, because of Brooke Milligan's testimony, he was a predator times two.

I've at least limited my own damage, to my very own client, as best I could, as much as I absolutely hate the way I just did it. Whether the jury members will believe that Morgan Carson feared, maybe even for her life, the consequences of breaking it off with Rob Jacobson is another matter entirely.

In the afternoon session, Welsh calls a couple of witnesses who testify to having also seen my client with Lily Carson in the weeks leading up to the murders, just to add more spice to the sauce. The last is a woman named Julie Barry, who's attractive enough that she gets me wondering how, if Rob Jacobson spent so much time in Garden City during the period in question, he missed hitting on her.

Maybe if he'd known her back in high school, the way he'd known Lily Carson, she would have had more appeal for the sonofabitch.

By now I have given up on trying to understand his obsession with mothers and daughters, and all other women who somehow ended up under the spell Brooke Milligan described, including my own sister. But I just keep telling myself—or perhaps rationalizing with myself—that he isn't going to be judged here on being a serial man-whore, just a serial killer.

Katherine Welsh waits until the end of her questioning of Julie Barry to ask if she was aware that Lily Carson had accused Rob Jacobson of sexually assaulting her after being his prom date in another lifetime for both of them.

"I frankly had no idea about that," Julie Barry says. "She just said they'd dated briefly and that it had ended rather badly. She tried to convince me that he had changed, despite their history." She looks over at Rob Jacobson. "Obviously he hadn't."

"Objection," I say, not even bothering to get up.

"Sustained," Judge Horton says.

"Your witness," Katherine Welsh says.

"Yes," I say, keeping my voice low as I pass her table, speaking loud enough that only she can hear. "She certainly is."

"Ms. Barry," I begin, "did you find it at all surprising that Lily had reconnected with an old high school flame, even after she told you that their prior relationship had ended badly?"

"Surprising?" she says. "I really didn't, to tell you the truth."

I smile. "Always a good thing."

"High school has always been complicated for high school girls," she continues. "I know it was for me. I just assumed that she still had feelings for him."

"But this was more than just an old feeling coming on strong, wasn't it?" I smile again. "Truth be told."

"I'm not sure what you're asking me."

"The question," I say, "is when did you become aware that Lily was having an affair with my client?"

Her eyes narrow. "You mean when he was having a sexual relationship with her *daughter*?"

She steps as hard as she can on the word "daughter."

"That's changing the subject, isn't it?" I ask.

"Is it?"

I knew the risks of this line of questioning before I got out of my chair, but in moments like these, it always comes down to risk and reward, the same old tightrope. But I feel as if the reward is going to be worth it.

"Respectfully," I say, "I wasn't asking about my client's relationship with Lily's daughter. I was asking about his relationship with Lily."

"I knew they were having an affair, yes," she says. "Exactly when I knew, I can't say."

"But you did know she was cheating on her husband."

Julie Barry doesn't immediately respond, but shifts just slightly in her chair.

"It's a pretty simple question," I say, "but I'm happy to repeat it."

"I knew, okay? I *knew*," she says. "But I want it made clear that it is not my intent, even as I'm doing my best to answer your questions honestly, to dishonor my friend's memory."

"I completely understand," I say, trying to make my tone sound reassuring. "And if you weren't under oath, and if my client wasn't on trial for murder, I happily *would* change the subject. But he is on trial for murder. So I can't. And we can't."

She briefly tents her fingers underneath her chin, almost as if giving herself a moment to regroup.

"It was well known in our circle that even while living in the same house, Lily and Hank had been living separate lives for some time," she says. "Another way of putting it is that it wasn't a very well-kept secret that both of them saw other people from time to time."

I nod.

"Other people," I say.

"Yes."

"So in addition to my client, there were other men in Lily Carson's life, weren't there?"

She shifts again in her seat. "I tried not to judge," she says. "But yes."

"Then let me ask you this," I say. "Are any of those other men with whom Lily Carson was sleeping around on trial for her murder?"

Wait for it, I think.

Three . . . two . . .

"Objection!" Katherine Welsh says. "That is a ridiculous question, even for opposing counsel. For whom, I have to admit, I now set a pretty low bar."

"Sustained," Judge Horton says. "Let me put this in language I'm sure you'll understand, Ms. Smith: Cut the crap."

Whoa.

"I withdraw the question," I say, "and have nothing further for this witness at this time."

"Redirect," Welsh says, almost before the words are out of my mouth.

"If it would please the court, Your Honor, I am requesting that your deputy be so kind as to read back the parts of Mr. Salzman's previous testimony about the DNA found at the crime scene," Welsh says to Judge Horton.

Horton nods. The deputy, a woman, types furiously away at her laptop, before looking back up and nodding at the judge.

It hasn't taken Katherine Welsh long to adjust to what I just did to another one of her witnesses, and on the fly, but she has.

She really is very good.

But I already knew that.

And I was setting a very high bar for her.

The deputy, a woman, begins reading the relevant testimony about the DNA, and where it was found near the bodies, with about as much inflection as if she were reading a grocery list.

When she's finished, Katherine Welsh walks over to the witness stand.

"Now Ms. Barry," she asks, "did you hear anything from the man who collected scientific evidence the night Lily Carson and her family were murdered in cold blood about finding DNA that *didn't* belong to the defendant?"

"I don't think anybody heard that," Julie Barry says.

"So the only man with whom your friend Lily Carson was involved who left DNA behind at the Carson home *was* the defendant."

"Objection," I say, not expecting to do much more than slow Katherine Welsh's roll. "Was there a question in there, Your Honor?"

Katherine Welsh turns and gives me a withering glance. "I frankly didn't think I needed one."

"Well, I've got one for you, Madam District Attorney," I say, knowing I am way out of line, but wanting to get in one last shot. "Didn't you mean to say DNA that someone *planted* at the Carson home that night?"

Welsh objects, the judge sustains, it's all by the numbers from there until Judge Horton says that court is adjourned until tomorrow morning.

"And by the way? The jury will ignore Ms. Smith's last comment," Horton says, getting in one last shot of his own.

Then he pounds his gavel so hard it sounds like a gun going off.

We all rise, and then he's gone, but not before the last big sound in Judge Michael Horton's courtroom is him slamming the door behind him.

I turn to Norma Banks.

"You think it was something I said?"

"I'd tell you that you need to do a better job of getting on his good side, missy," she says, "except that it's been my experience that once he puts that robe on, he really doesn't have one."

I turn to my right and see Thomas McGoey shaking his head.

"You," he says, "are a very bad girl."

"Thank you."

"I didn't mean it as a compliment," McGoey says.

EIGHTY-TWO

I'VE GOTTEN OFF THE Long Island Expressway and am in Manorville making my way across Route 111, the connecting road to 27 East, when Danny Esposito calls.

"Where you at?" he asks, and I tell him that I've just passed the McDonald's on 111, but withstood temptation and kept driving.

"Glad I caught you when I did," he says. "You're gonna want to make a stop in Southampton, which is where I happen to be at."

"This doesn't sound remotely good."

"It's not," he says. "Your good friend Allen Reese? Somebody put one in his forehead and one in the chest, and not too long ago, according to the ME."

In the moment, my brain flashes right back to the woman at the flower shop in Bridgehampton having been murdered the same way, execution style.

"Not only did somebody shoot him," Esposito says, "it looks like they did some job on his left hand before they did. Like they took a hammer to it."

"Sounds as if Mr. Reese owed somebody money."

"You think?"

I've already made the left off 111 and am now on the divided highway headed east, driving fast, though fast is a

257

relative concept on this stretch of 27. I tell Danny Esposito I'm probably twenty minutes out and ask if Jimmy knows.

Esposito says he called him first, adding that it was a cop thing.

"I was a cop."

"Ish," he says.

"Watch it," I say, and then ask who found the body.

"That's the weird part. The cops found him. The killer used Reese's landline to call them."

"You've got to be kidding."

"I wish," Esposito says. "You throw in the guy's hand, and the whole thing brings, like, a whole new dimension to breaking news."

"What did he say to the cops? The killer, I mean."

"He said, and I quote, 'You ought to head over to Allen Reese's house,'" Esposito tells me. "Then he said, 'Mr. Reese had an accident.'"

EIGHTY-THREE

ROBBY SASSOON HAS DECIDED to treat himself to a night at the Topping Rose House in Bridgehampton, and a meal at the Jean-Georges restaurant there.

The high-end inn, serving farm-to-table food, was originally owned by a famous New York City chef named Tom Colicchio. Though Colicchio sold the place a few years ago, Robby knows from experience that the quality remains at the superb level he requires when celebrating a job well done.

Now, before heading downstairs to dinner, he sits in his suite, following the reports about Allen Reese, well-known Hamptons real estate tycoon, shot to death in his own home, the lurid coverage making anybody reading it think that an oceanfront home in Southampton is suddenly less safe than if Reese had lived in the old South Bronx.

Robby was in no mood for any further lying from Reese today, or even tedious begging for his life once Reese realized why Robby had returned. Robby had been watching the house for several hours and had determined that Reese was alone. Finally, Robby came in through the unlocked patio door, found Reese in his study watching CNBC, put the first bullet in his forehead, then another in the chest.

He then used Reese's own phone—a nice touch, he thinks, almost whimsical—to call the Southampton police.

Now he's smiling as he moves from website to website, pleased with how they all quoted him correctly.

Pity that no one will ever know who the clever bastard really is.

His cell phone, turned up loud, is playing "No Good Deed," from *Wicked,* one of his favorite shows, when Sonny Blum calls, forcing him to pause the song.

"The assbird try to give you some bullshit about the money?" Blum asks.

"He didn't get the chance," Robby says. "We both know that once he got this far behind, he wasn't going to pay. He could've put his hands on the money, but he elected not to. He's supposed to have been such a smart businessman and didn't understand the cost of doing business with us."

"I gotta admit, I got a kick out of you calling it in," Blum says.

"You have to keep things fresh in my line of work," he says, "so you don't get stale."

Blum chuckles. "You really are a funny bastard."

There's a pause.

"I forgot to ask you," Robby says. "How'd your meet with Cunniff go?"

"I'll know if I got through to him when I see if he and the lawyer are still trying to fuck with me."

"And if they continue to do that?"

"*You'll* know what to do."

Robby feels a smile slowly crossing his lips. "Send me into the game, coach," he says.

When Blum ends the call, Robby hits Play, and now he's singing along.

"*One more disaster, I can add to my generous supply . . .*"

Robby opens up the menu they've left in the room, just to see if they've added anything since the last time he was here, when he spent the night after Bobby Salvatore's unfortunate and untimely demise.

He is smiling again when he sees that the butternut minestrone is still listed with the appetizers, he's been thinking about it almost since he put the second bullet into Allen Reese. Then his voice is rising suddenly, like he's playing to the balcony at the Gershwin, almost like he's singing for his supper.

"Let his blood leave no stain . . ."

Well, Robby thinks, *impossible to have everything.*

He walks over to the minibar now and pours himself a glass of Scotch.

Mr. Reese had an accident.

And people keep saying irony is dead.

EIGHTY-FOUR

JIMMY AND ESPOSITO AND I eventually decide that there is nothing further for us to do, or learn, at Allen Reese's home, and leave things in the capable hands of the Southampton police.

We decide to stay in Southampton for burgers and beers at Fellingham's, a sports bar and grill tucked away on Cameron Street, in the center of town.

Chief Carlos Quintero, a rising star in local law enforcement, destined for bigger things, walks me to my car.

"You have any dealings with Reese?" he asks.

"Just once," I say. "I crashed one of his parties."

"You know anything about him that I might find productive?"

"Bobby Salvatore was a friend of his, I know that."

"Friend," Quintero says, "or foe?"

"Bobby was in Sonny Blum's crew," Quintero continues. "But you knew that, didn't you?"

"I have a lot of interests."

"So I've been told. From what *I* know, Bobby did a little bit of this and a little bit of that," Chief Quintero says. "I'm wondering who might be doing what my old man used to call Sonny's button work."

"Jimmy met a young guy who's an up-and-comer as a

bookie," I say. "But from the way he described him, he's not your shooter."

"You think this was over a debt?"

"Don't you?"

"You think Sonny had this done?"

"With gusto," I say. "Same as with the flower lady, if you ask me."

"*Mucho gusto,*" Carlos Quintero says.

"Have it your way."

"You hear anything, you call me," he says.

"Yes sir!" I say, snapping off a salute.

"Okay, now beat it," he says.

Half an hour later, Jimmy and Esposito and I are tearing through cheeseburgers as good as they've always been at Fellingham's. It's a lot like Jimmy's bar, a neighborhood place that has survived what I call the fancification of the Hamptons, and one I'm certain would survive a nuclear attack.

One more time it's Jane and the boys. With me happily being one of the guys.

"I want to remind you," Jimmy says, "not that you need reminding, that it's not our responsibility to tie Sonny to Reese's murder." He nods at Esposito. "It's his."

"And I want to remind *you,*" Danny Esposito says, "that my role in this is to be a team player with the various branches of the local police. Because, as I'm sure you both know, there's no *i* in team."

"But there is one in Esposito," I point out.

"You sure it's only one?" Jimmy says.

"Nice to know that your new buddy, Mr. Blum, is still a stone-cold killer," I say, "whoever he had get this done. And about the guy alerting the cops? What's next, live streaming when somebody else who didn't pay is getting capped?"

"Capped," Esposito says to Jimmy. "She keeps trying to convince me how much of a cop she was."

"If Sonny's going out, he's going out in style," Jimmy says. "But I gotta say, I still don't see him as being the one who had the Carsons done."

For a change I'm cleaning my plate, not just the burger but the fries. And for this one night, the cold draught beer is going down fine, too.

"I actually never saw him on that either," I say. "For whatever reason, Sonny treats Rob Jacobson like there's some kind of force field around him. So I can't think of a single reason why he'd go out of his way to set him up on a triple homicide, then wait this long for the evidence to finally come into play."

"So why are you so fixed on making Sonny part of this trial?" Esposito asks.

"Because I need somebody," I say.

"Somebody?" Esposito says.

"Somebody else who could have done it. Or had it done. If Sonny is still killing people who don't pay their debts, he could have killed Hank Carson for not paying. And then things got out of hand."

Esposito grins. "So if I have this straight, you want to frame Sonny Blum for something you really don't think he did, the way somebody framed Rob Jacobson for something you say *he* didn't do."

"Pretty much."

"Cool," Esposito says. "Are you sure you don't want to go out with me?"

"Yes."

He shrugs. "I just feel as if I have to circle back on that from time to time."

"But Blum told me Carson paid," Jimmy says.

"Yes, he did," I say. "And if he's lying about that, well, golly, it's probably the first time that old dirtbag has ever lied about anything ever."

I push my plate, with most of my fries gone and only a quarter of my burger still on it, toward Jimmy now.

"This looks like some kind of half-assed bribe," he says.

"It is," I say. "I want you to reach out to Sonny and tell him you may have something for him."

"But I don't."

"So you'll be the one telling the first lie of *your* whole life! If you can reach him, tell him you need to meet."

"Then what?"

"Then slap him with that subpoena you've been carrying around and tell him he's been fucking served."

"Here's one last thing I need to remind you about," Jimmy says. "He says that if you even try to drag him into court he'll kill us both."

"Tell him to take a ticket," I say, and wave at our waiter and tell him we want another round.

Jimmy turns to Danny Esposito.

"She does talk a good game, doesn't she?"

"I really do think I love her," Esposito says.

"Get in line," Jimmy says.

EIGHTY-FIVE

BEN IS WAITING FOR me at my house when I get back from Fellingham's, where the last thing I told Jimmy was not to do anything crazy with Sonny Blum.

"*Now* you tell me not to go crazy?" he said. "That ship sailed a long time ago."

Ben has already walked and fed Rip and is watching a Knicks preseason game on television, a glass of red wine in his hand. He is one of those Knicks fans who keeps convincing himself that this is going to be their year. I keep telling him that I'm pretty sure there are meds he can take for that.

"Not human meds," he says.

From the couch he smiles at me and says, "And how was your day, dear?"

I ask if he has heard about Allen Reese, and he says he has, he got an alert on his phone.

"You want to talk about that?" he asks.

"Eventually," I say. "But there's something else I've been waiting to tell you, but I wanted to wait until we were together."

"Oh, shit," he says. "You're breaking up with me."

"Nah," I say, tossing my bag on the side table. "I've got too much time invested in you at this point."

"That's very practical of you," he says, then pats the couch as a way of telling me to come sit next to him.

I do, close enough to him that Rip can't even think about trying to insinuate himself between us.

"Okay," he says, as we turn slightly to face each other. "What's your big news?"

I take a deep breath.

"The big news of the day is that the tumor got smaller."

He tilts his head just slightly to the side, and his eyes get bigger. Or maybe deeper.

"Would you mind terribly much repeating that?"

I do, then say, "I didn't want to tell you over the phone."

He takes a great, big deep breath now. And for a moment, I think I might see tears forming in the amazing eyes of the normally implacable and unflappable Dr. Ben Kalinsky.

But I'll never know if he's about to cry or not, and neither will he, because then he's kissing me, like it's our first over-heated kiss all over again. Like we really are back to acting like teenagers in the front seat of a parked car.

When we come up for air, he says, "We need to celebrate."

"I really don't feel like drinking wine," I say.

"Who said anything about effing wine?"

He's up and gone before I'm even awake, on his way to surgery.

By the time the sun is all the way up, I am on the back patio, having walked and fed Rip and made a cup of coffee for myself and eating the Goldberg's flagel I've defrosted and toasted and slathered in cream cheese.

I see the hummingbird then.

They're supposed to be gone by now.

They're always gone before October and I know that. But every year, every single one, I stubbornly keep the feeder full of sugar water, checking it every morning in the hope that I haven't said good-bye to this year's hummingbirds for good.

And now here, out of nowhere, is my stray.

The color is a dull shade of green, telling me it's a female.

She looks beautiful to me, hovering in the air, staring at me, as if to say, *What are you looking at?*

I stare back, not moving a muscle for fear of scaring her off, unspeakably happy in this moment.

She's still here and so am I.

I watch her until she's at the feeder. When she's finished there, she's gone, disappearing into the rest of the morning, or maybe for good.

I tell myself that even if she is gone for now, I'll see her in the spring.

When I still plan to be here.

I get up and walk back into the house, smiling.

Taking another win.

Trying to convince myself that maybe I'm on a roll.

EIGHTY-SIX

HE IS SEATED AT the butcher block table, the table a little too rustic for his more refined tastes, drinking coffee that he's just made, when Paul Harrington comes walking into his own kitchen, wearing slippers and loose pajama bottoms and an open robe that's seen far better days, the way Harrington himself has.

Robby Sassoon sees that Harrington is also wearing a faded NYU T-shirt that once was probably a much deeper shade of purple.

If Harrington is surprised to see him sitting in his kitchen at six thirty in the morning, he hides it fairly well, even though Robby knows he's rocked Harrington before he's even fully awake.

They're all tough guys until they're not.

Mostly Paul Harrington just looks old, and tired, as if he hasn't slept well, if at all. But a lifetime living on the margins, and pretending to be something you're not, will do that to you.

"Okay, what are you doing here?" Harrington asks.

"I was about to ask you the same thing," Robby says, then points to the Keurig machine on the counter. "Coffee?" he says.

"I can get it," Harrington says.

He walks over, takes out the pod Robby left in the holder,

replaces it with a pod of his own, and hits the button, studying the machine pouring the coffee now as if it's the most fascinating thing he's going to encounter all day.

When the coffee is made he spoons far too much sugar in it and sits down across the table from Robby.

"We had an understanding," Robby says.

"I'm going," Harrington says.

"You were supposed to be gone already," Robby says. "Out of the country."

"She wasn't supposed to call me for a couple more days," Harrington says. "It's not my fault she moved me up at the last second. I had some things."

He offers Robby a smile made out of nothing. "Please don't shoot up my house again," he says. "I mean, what the fuck. We're on the same team here."

"But there's a difference," Robby says. "Only one of us is careless."

Harrington rubs a nervous hand over the white stubble of his beard. Being unshaven just makes him look older, the way it makes Sonny look older when he's the one wandering around the house in what looks like a thrift-shop robe. But the difference between the two old men, Sonny Blum and Paul Harrington, is that Harrington is the one with his balls in a vise.

Robby watches Harrington stare out his patio door to surprisingly lush gardens in his backyard.

"For the last time, Sonny's got no problem with me," Paul Harrington says.

Robby absently pulls on his earring. "You know how he gets," Robby says. "Anxious might be the best way to describe it, as the years pile up on him."

What was the line from *Pippin*?

I believe if I refuse to grow old, I can stay young until I die.

"He doesn't need to be anxious about me," Harrington says. "I'm on an afternoon flight from Kennedy to Saint Kitts. I'm not coming back anytime soon, maybe not ever."

He sips some coffee. Robby does the same. Harrington is still looking out at his flowers.

"Was it you who did Reese?" Harrington asks, not even turning his head.

"Is that a serious question?"

"No," Harrington says, "and I guess I don't have to ask about the flower girl over in Bridgehampton, either."

"You don't," Robby says. "We're all pulling on the same rope, right?"

Now Harrington turns to look at him. "I've done everything Sonny wants," he says, "for a very long time."

"Well," Robby says, smiling at him, "nearly everything."

"You can't possibly think I was going to show up at that courthouse this morning," Harrington says. "Give me more credit than that. They're sending a cop to pick me up, but I'll already be gone."

"What happens when they issue a warrant?" Robby says.

"Does them no good if they can't find me," Harrington says.

He sips some coffee. "And just so you know? I could have handled anything that bitch lawyer Smith threw at me even if I did end up on the stand."

"But now she's not going to get the chance, is she?" Robby says.

"By tonight," Harrington says, "I'll be sipping a drink with an umbrella in it and looking for some age-appropriate companionship."

"Who's taking you to the airport?"

"Sonny's limousine. Picking me up in about an hour. Which is more than an hour before my escort is scheduled to show up."

He gives Robby a much longer look, as if trying to read him, like trying to solve a puzzle.

"I'm sorry you had to waste a trip here," Harrington says.

"It's like I was trying to say before," Robby Sassoon says,

walking over to the sink and rinsing his mug. "The older Sonny gets, the more of a worrier he becomes."

Then he says to Harrington, "Mind if I make myself more coffee."

Harrington doesn't even turn around, just jerks a thumb over his shoulder.

"You obviously know where everything is," Harrington says.

He doesn't see Robby smiling.

"So I do," he says.

EIGHTY-SEVEN

KATHERINE WELSH AND JUDGE Michael Horton and I are in Horton's chambers. It is now nine thirty. The trial was supposed to have resumed a half-hour ago.

This is a smaller trial, but every bit as intense. We are all here because Welsh has announced to the judge and to me a couple of hours ago that she wants to move up the testimony of Paul Harrington, which would be the same Paul Harrington, former commander of detectives at the 24th Precinct in the city, who was arrested and later released for ordering a hit on Jimmy Cunniff and me.

So now, in chambers, I've been afforded my last chance at convincing the judge that Welsh shouldn't be allowed to call Harrington at all.

"I frankly don't understand why you're so dead set against this," Welsh says to me. "We both know Harrington has prior history with your client that I believe is relevant to these proceedings."

"Oh, bullshit, Katherine," I snap. "What you want is to get him on the stand and then have him accidentally blurt out that he thinks my client has been shooting people since he was a teenager, starting with his own father. Who are we kidding here?"

"I'm just looking for context," Welsh says, "that is probative, not prejudicial."

"Yeah," I say. "Probative like a trip to my ob-gyn."

"Ms. Smith," Judge Horton says. "You seem to have forgotten I'm still here. And can hear you."

"Harrington tried to kill me!"

"Allegedly," Welsh says calmly.

"Allegedly my ass," I say. "I know he did it, Jimmy Cunniff knows he did it, whether that case stuck or not. And if you're calling Harrington, you know full well that he believes Rob Jacobson shot his father and probably the old man's girlfriend, and you're just dying to get him to put that into the record."

"Now you're just speculating," Welsh says.

"Oh for fuck's sake," I say. "That's not speculation. It's just more bullshit and you know it."

"Whatever you think of him, Paul Harrington was once a decorated New York City policeman," Welsh says, "one who was on the job when Robinson Jacobson and Carey Watson died, whether you like it or not."

"I wasn't aware that they were giving out medals in those days for being in Sonny Blum's pocket."

Welsh shoots me a smile dipped in acid.

"Now there's your speculation right there," she says.

I look over at Horton. We all know it's getting late, but he seems to still be enjoying this—as a spectator and not the one who will eventually adjudicate this matter.

"Seriously, Katherine?" I say. "Why do you think Harrington ended up at Riverhead Correctional? Because he heard there were reasonable room rates there now that summer is over?"

"We are both aware, Jane," Welsh says, "that Harrington is a free man, one on his way to this courthouse shortly, because so much of what got him thrown in jail was classic fruit-of-the-poison tree. Which made it a classically bad arrest. If you really want to talk about bullshit."

"And then he got lawyered out of jail by that weasel Gabe Dees," I say. "Who because of what you must think is one of life's crazy coincidences, happens to be Sonny Blum's lawyer, too."

"Which, sadly, Ms. Smith, is irrelevant to this conversation," Judge Horton says. "A conversation we now need to wrap up."

He leans back in his chair. He isn't wearing his robe yet, just a white shirt and tie and cardigan sweater. Now Horton clasps his hands in front of him and says, "Ms. Welsh, I believe Mr. Harrington is second on your list for today. I am going to allow you to call him, as originally planned. But I am warning you here and now to choose your words carefully, and make it clear to your witness that he is to do the same thing. Is that understood?"

"Perfectly, Your Honor."

Horton stands now, unbuttons his sweater, and removes his robe from where it's hanging on a coatrack.

"Anything you'd like to add, Ms. Smith?"

I am already up and out of my chair.

"Just that I'll see you both in court," I say.

I am down the hall a few minutes later with Rob Jacobson and Thomas McGoey and Norma Banks, explaining to them that as hard as I just fought to keep Paul Harrington out of the courtroom, some good could come from him being in that chair, because it will give me a chance to bury him, when we hear a sharp rap on the door.

Katherine Welsh comes walking into the conference room then. I'm about to jokingly ask if she misses me already, before noticing how ashen-faced she is.

I haven't seen Katherine Welsh rattled by much of anything so far in this trial, but she is clearly rattled now.

"You no longer have to concern yourself with Paul Harrington," she says.

"He didn't show up?"

"He killed himself," she says.

EIGHTY-EIGHT

JUDGE HORTON CANCELS COURT for the day.

Danny Esposito tells me on the phone that he's called ahead to Chief Carlos Quintero to tell him that Katherine Welsh and I are both on our way to Water Mill, and that the district attorney from Nassau County has requested that until we arrive Quintero not remove anything in Paul Harrington's home.

Including Paul Harrington.

"Carlos told me it's his crime scene," Esposito tells me. "I told him that Judge Horton might not see it that way."

"You really think Harrington killed himself?" I ask Esposito.

"He left a note," Esposito says.

"Handwritten?"

"Short and sweet," Esposito says. "Carlos says it's the same scrawl as from a grocery list they found on the kitchen table where they found him."

"He wrote out a grocery list before he shot himself in the head?" I ask.

Danny Esposito says, "Maybe he didn't want to go on an empty stomach."

Katherine Welsh and I, even traveling in our own cars, arrive only a few minutes apart in front of Harrington's house, parking up the block from the emergency and police vehicles, one of them driven by the Nassau County Police Department detective Welsh dispatched to Water Mill to escort Harrington to the courthouse.

"You didn't trust Harrington to drive himself?" I ask her as we walk toward the house together.

"I know you think he was hot to tell his story," she says. "But the closer we got to him actually doing that, the more I started to worry about him. Even though he's an ex-cop, he asked what would happen if he changed his mind and didn't show. I told him we'd issue a warrant and arrest him all over again."

"You really are a hard-ass," I say.

"All that time in the gym," she says.

Danny Esposito tells us he's volunteered to pitch in and canvass the neighborhood. So he heads across the street as Welsh and I are handed gloves and blue crime-scene booties by one of Carlos Quintero's guys stationed outside the house. I'm struck by the fact that the color of the booties seems to match Katherine Welsh's dress almost perfectly, as if somehow the universe is accessorizing just for her.

Paul Harrington is slumped in a chair at his kitchen table. He's wearing a robe and pajamas and slippers and what I recognize as an NYU T-shirt. There is a mass of dried blood on the right side of his face, caked around the bullet hole there. His eyes are closed. Blood has dripped down on his robe, and there are spots of it on the floor, near what I recognize instantly as a Glock 19, the service weapon I saw on Harrington at Jimmy's bar.

I stare at him and imagine this as part of the trail of blood that has been following me around since I first decided to represent Rob Jacobson.

Carlos Quintero shows us the note on the butcher-block table.

Just two words.

Judgement day

By now Jimmy Cunniff is inside the house, and has taken his place next to me.

"Judgement with an *e*," he says. "Isn't that the way the English spell it?"

He never ceases to amaze me with things he knows that I'd never think he knew.

"Or it can be spelled that way in a legal context," Welsh says.

She turns to Carlos Quintero and says, "You believe it's a match? The handwriting?"

He walks her over to the table where the grocery list is.

"My wife calls it cop cursive," Quintero says. "We'll have to have it analyzed by an expert, of course. But to the naked eye, yeah."

Welsh looks at me. "Do you think he suddenly got guilty enough about all the things you say he's done and did this to himself?"

"Pardon my French, Katherine, but fuck no," I say. "I do, however, think somebody may have staged this whole thing to make it look like he did."

"A guy who thought he was above the law suddenly handing himself a death sentence?" Jimmy says. "Somebody might be trying to sell that here. But, sorry, I ain't buying."

"He wasn't the type to commit suicide," I say.

"There's a type?" Welsh asks.

"Ones who think the Grim Reaper will never find them," I say. "And would never punch their own ticket in a million years."

Jimmy moves closer to the body, staring down at it.

"Or not," he says.

EIGHTY-NINE

DANNY ESPOSITO SAYS HE'S heading back to his office and will check in with Jimmy and me later. Katherine Welsh is still inside the house. Jimmy and I are standing on Harrington's front lawn, waiting while the techs from the mobile crime labs are swabbing Harrington's gun with their nitric acid solution, and checking his hand for gunpowder residue.

It's nearly forty-five minutes later when Carlos Quintero comes out to tell us that there was indeed GSR on Harrington's right hand, as they suspected there would be, and that by now they pulled a single bullet out of the kitchen wall.

In addition, they said, the only set of fingerprints on the handle of the Glock belonged to Harrington.

Jimmy says, "Anything to indicate that some bastard who knew what he was doing could have wiped it?"

"Without wiping away Harrington's prints?" Quintero asks. "How would that work?"

"Somebody who wanted to make a murder look like a suicide, somebody who Harrington probably knew, could have come up from behind him, pulled the trigger, wiped the gun, put it back in his hand and then fired it again," Jimmy says.

"Sure, and maybe it was the second shooter from the Kennedy assassination," Chief Carlos Quintero says, "even though he'd have to be really, really old at this point."

"I'm telling you, this guy didn't kill himself," Jimmy says.

"Then where's the other bullet, if it happened anything like you say it did?" Quintero says.

"A pro would know how to fire it into something, collect it, and leave with the evidence," I add.

"You got any proof to back that up?" Quintero says.

"None," I say.

I see Katherine Welsh walking out the front door then, motioning for me to walk with her up the block to where she had parked her car.

"You're convinced he was murdered," she says when I get with her.

"I am."

"With nothing to go on."

"Maybe less than nothing," I say. "But as a good Catholic girl, I was taught that faith is believing in what you can't see."

"Catholic maybe," she says. "Not so sure on the good part."

"It comes and goes," I tell her.

She stops and gives me a long look, almost as if she's telling me to cut the shit.

"Who wouldn't have wanted Paul Harrington to testify today?" she asks finally. "And might have been willing to have him killed to stop him from doing that?"

"Do you even have to ask?" I say.

NINETY

I'VE MADE A TENTATIVE plan with Ben Kalinsky for a nice, quiet dinner for two.

But after I get home and take Rip for a long beach walk, I call Ben to tell him that I am totally deep-fried by the events of the day and am begging off.

"Plus," I tell him, "I need to start resting up for all the big things I have planned for your birthday this weekend."

"How big," he says.

"Isn't that your job, big boy?" I ask.

We both laugh. Even when I am as tired as I am tonight, and feeling more punk than I have since Sam Wylie gave me the good news about the tumor, Dr. Ben lifts my spirits and eases my soul.

But my stomach is feeling jumpy again, so dinner for me is a couple of scrambled eggs and dry toast. When I've finished and cleaned up, I once again try to call Claire Jacobson. She is a recent addition to Katherine Welsh's witness list, having waived spousal privilege, and I've left her several phone messages these past few days because I want to ask her why.

She hasn't returned my calls, though, or the ones her husband has placed to her. On top of that, Jimmy has driven a couple of times over the past week to the big house she once shared with Rob, only to discover that her blue Bentley was never in the driveway. He got the vibe that the place is unoccupied.

Claire Jacobson has assured me, on multiple occasions, that she still loves her husband, even with the way he has humiliated her in every possible public way. But by now my experience with Mrs. Jacobson is that I trust her just slightly more than I do her husband.

Tonight I leave another message, asking her to please call me as soon as possible, that I really do need to talk to her before she is scheduled to appear in court in two days.

I am back into the kitchen, fixing myself a cup of Yogi bedtime tea that Sam Wylie has convinced me to try, when I hear my phone from where I left it in the living room.

I run for it hoping it's Claire, just because I don't want to be surprised by what she might say under oath, it being a long-established fact that I despise surprises in court.

But it isn't Claire Jacobson calling me.

It is my ex-husband, Martin.

Always a joy.

"I'm in trouble," Martin Elian says before I can even say hello.

"In that case, Martin," I say, "you have probably reached this number in error."

"Believe me," he says, "if there was anybody else I could have called, I would."

"I love you," I say. "I do. But it's been so long since I believed, well, it's almost as if that never happened in the first place."

"Listen to me! It's serious this time!"

"It always is serious," I tell him, keeping my own voice calm. "But I've had an especially long day, one that has included the death of somebody who was scheduled to testify in my trial today. So I am about to go to bed and hope tomorrow will be better. And whatever your trouble is, I urge you to do the same."

"I need to see you," he says.

"Where are you?"

"The restaurant."

"You want to drive all the way out here tonight? Not happening."

I hear traffic sounds at his end.

"Jane, listen to me! I am in fear of my life!"

His language, even in two languages, French and English, has always been dramatic, and occasionally overwrought. *In fear of my life.* Who talks like that?

He does.

"Is this about gambling, Martin?"

There is a pause.

"Yes."

"How much this time?"

"Too much," he says.

The traffic sounds become more muted now, as if he's moved into an alley, or away from the street.

"It's worse than it's ever been before," he continues. His voice, something I once thought was so much of his charm, because of the accent, sounds like a band about to snap. "Even signing over the paper on the restaurant might not be enough to get me out from under this time."

Again, I keep my voice calm. "You promised the last time I loaned you money that it would be the last time I loaned you money," I say.

Once a conversation like this would make me angry. Or annoyed. Now it just fills me with sadness, and even pity. He's tried Gamblers Anonymous in the past, but it's never stuck, maybe because his addiction is even more powerful than he's able to comprehend.

What does make me sad is him still thinking I can be the one to fix him, even though we both know I can't. I do love him, despite everything. And have tried.

And failed, repeatedly.

I've known only winning in my career as a trial attorney. The opposite is true with him.

"Get help," I say. "Find a GA meeting tonight, there's always one going on somewhere in the city."

"I need *your* help!" he says.

"I'm sorry, Martin. I truly am, because as much as you've hurt me, and you've hurt me a lot, I truly do care about you."

I hear him rattle off something in French then, something that used to happen all the time when we were still together, and having another argument, either about his gambling or the other women.

When he finally stops, I say, "Can I ask to whom you owe the money this time?"

Another pause. This one is longer than the first, punctuated by another blast of a car horn.

"Sonny Blum," he says.

NINETY-ONE

Jimmy

JANE CALLED LAST NIGHT to tell him about her ex-husband—someone Jimmy has always considered to be a French lounge lizard even if he happens to own the lounge—being in deep with Sonny Blum.

"At this point," Jimmy told her, "maybe it would be easier keeping a list of who *doesn't* owe Sonny."

"I'd just prefer he doesn't add Martin's name to a different kind of list," she said.

"The one with the dead people on it."

"Yeah," Jane said. "That one."

"Listen," Jimmy told her. "He's your ex, not your kid. He needs to figure this shit out for himself, like a big boy."

Then Jimmy told her that against his better judgment, he would see what he could do about keeping Sonny Blum off Martin's back, at least for the time being.

"Now that I think of it," Jimmy said, "I might even have a way of making your boy useful, if I can keep him alive."

"He's hardly my boy," she said.

"Figure of speech."

Jimmy leaves at four thirty in the morning, knowing it's the only sure bet to beat rush hour traffic into Manhattan. He texted Jed Bernstein before going to bed, telling him they needed to meet for coffee, as early as Bernstein could manage.

285

Bernstein texted back right away.

What if I don't want to?

Jimmy wasted no time with his own response.

Wasn't a request

This time Bernstein's reply took longer, as if maybe he had to check his schedule.

9 a.m. Astor Court. At the St. Regis.

Jimmy told him he knew where the freaking Astor Court was and would see him there.

Now Jimmy is seated across from Bernstein in one of the most ornate breakfast places in town, muraled ceilings and low-hanging crystal chandeliers and $225 eggs Benedict, if you like your eggs Benedict with caviar. Both Jimmy and Bernstein are wearing blue blazers. Jimmy assumes that Bernstein's is more expensive, unless Bernstein got his at Jos. A. Bank, too.

"You ever run into any of your bookie friends here?" Jimmy asks.

"I'm not a bookie," Bernstein says.

"Sure," Jimmy says.

"Believe what you want to believe."

"I am curious about something, though," Jimmy says. "What's the next step up the ladder in Sonny's operation — Shylock?"

Bernstein sips some of the oolong tea he'd made a big production of ordering.

"Is that meant to be an ethnic insult?" he says.

"Literary," Jimmy says. *Merchant of Venice.*"

Bernstein raises an eyebrow. "Wow. A literary former flatfoot."

"Now who's doing the insulting?"

Bernstein sips more tea. Jimmy watches him do it, thinking the guy is as neat with his mannerisms as he is with his clothes.

"You must want something from me," Bernstein says, "or we wouldn't be here."

"I need to have another meeting with Sonny," Jimmy says. "He can pick the time and the place. He can even stop by my house and surprise me, the way he did last time."

"Very generous of you," Bernstein says. "But I can't make that happen."

"Can't?" Jimmy says. "Or won't even make the ask?"

"Both," Jed Bernstein says.

"Sonny told me he thinks we can help each other," Jimmy says. "And I've come up with some information that he's going to see as helpful."

"Pass it along to me and I'll pass it along to him."

"Not happening," Jimmy says.

Bernstein grins. "Because you can't, or you won't?"

"Both," Jimmy says. "But what I can share with you is this: If Sonny finds out this information didn't get to him because of you?" Jimmy shrugs. "Well, at that point I wouldn't want to *be* you."

Bernstein looks down at the menu in front of him. If he's shocked by the price of the eggs Benedict, he manages to hide it.

He looks back at Jimmy and says, "I'll see what I can do."

"Do it quickly," Jimmy says.

"And you could have done all this with a phone call," Bernstein says, "instead of driving all the way in here."

"I like looking people in the eye," Jimmy says. "It's a cop thing."

"Happy for you."

"There is one other thing you can pass along to Sonny for me," Jimmy says.

"And what's that?"

"I want you to tell him that what happened to the real estate guy, and to that flower lady in Bridgehampton, can't happen to Jane Smith's ex-husband."

"I'm sure I have no idea what you're talking about."

Jimmy smiles across the table at him. "See there, that's why I like to look people in the eye, so I can decide for myself when they're full of shit."

Bernstein gives Jimmy a bored look.

Jimmy thinks: *How many fake tough guys like this have I met in my life?*

"Happy for you," Bernstein says again. "Truly."

Jimmy says, "Tell Sonny that if anything happens to Martin Elian, he and I are going to have a problem."

Bernstein laughs. "You think you're going to scare off Sonny Blum?"

"You think Sonny scares me?"

"Maybe not the old man himself," Jed Bernstein says. "But there's a guy who works for him who ought to scare the piss out of you."

NINETY-TWO

JUDGE HORTON IS WELL aware that neither Katherine Welsh nor I considered Paul Harrington a crucial witness. But he was still a material witness in a murder trial, and his death—and the trial—have been front-page news even in the city tabloids.

So Horton informs me by phone early this morning that he's hitting the pause button on the trial for one more day, as if another day off will allow everyone involved, including him, to regroup.

"Just to lower the temperature," he says.

"If you can do that, Your Honor," I say, "you ought to take a crack at global warming next."

A few hours later I am having lunch with my sister, Brigid, and Dr. Sam Wylie at a table tucked into the far corner of the front room at Bobby Van's in Bridgehampton. Brigid is the one who has invited Sam. When I asked her why, she said she would explain when we got to Van's.

Brigid seems even more defeated than usual today, as low a bar as that is after the way the last year or so has gone for her. Cancer. A ruined marriage. And a relationship with Rob Jacobson that might be the most self-destructive thing she has ever done.

Another low bar, of course.

We order iced teas and various salads on the menu. After

our drinks are brought to the table, Brigid says, "I want you to know that I was with Rob last night."

"Gee," I say. "What's the good news, sis?"

"That *is* good news for you," she says. "And even better news, at least where you're concerned, is that he no longer wants to see me."

Sam is between us, saying nothing, just watching my sister and me as if she's watching us bat a tennis ball back and forth across a net.

"I was under the impression that you had *already* stopped seeing him after he beat you up," I say. "Silly me."

I hear a brief, sharp intake of breath from Sam Wylie.

"He didn't beat me up!" Brigid says. "Things got a little rough, was all."

"A man getting a *little* rough with a woman is like a woman being a little pregnant," I tell my sister. "In my book, there is no such thing."

"Whatever," she says rather wearily. "We're over, which means you're finally getting what you want."

"Am I allowed to ask why?"

Brigid turns to Sam Wylie. "You tell her."

"Tell me what?" I ask Sam. "Are you now doubling as a couples' counselor?"

"Brigid's cancer is back," Sam says.

NINETY-THREE

SAM TRIES TO GIVE me the medical explanation of what is happening with Brigid and why.

I don't hear very much after "Stage 4."

But Sam keeps going, talking about an advanced stage of the cancer that started in Brigid's lymph nodes. The doctors at the Meier Clinic and her oncologists here believed they had it under control after chemotherapy, and that she was in remission.

Only now, according to Sam Wylie, the cancer has spread to her lungs.

Stage 4. Advanced lymphoma. Pick your poison.

Literally.

Brigid stands suddenly, saying she doesn't want to be here any longer, she's already heard this once. I watch my sister make her way through the lunch crowd, not looking back until she's out the door and out on Main Street.

"Is it terminal?" I ask Sam. "And please don't tell me we're all terminal, I'm in no mood to play that particular game today."

"I'm not going to lie to you, Jane," Sam says. "This is bad."

"How bad?" I shake my head, almost in disbelief. "Are you telling me that I have a better shot at beating this than she does? Goddamn, Sam, she was supposed to be in remission."

"We've had this conversation about cancer before," she says.

"No one is ever really in the clear, no matter how much you love them. But in my opinion? Yes, you do have a much better shot of beating your cancer at this point than she does hers."

I feel the air come out of me and then my throat closes, as if it's just slammed shut.

And then I am looking all the way across the front room at Van's, across the busy, noisy lunch crowd, and see Brigid standing at the window, her nose pressed against it, like she's staring in at a normal world that doesn't include her and might never again.

Before she walks away.

I want to run after her, except I don't know what I'd say.

"This is so not fair," I say to Dr. Sam Wylie.

"I run into a lot of that in my line of work," she says.

NINETY-FOUR

THE NEXT MORNING ROB Jacobson and I, just the two of us, are sitting in our usual conference room down the hall from the courtroom. I have already prepared myself on the ride here from Amagansett for an extremely long day in court, mostly because I know what Katherine Welsh has in store for us:

A parade of Garden City cops who will slow-walk the jury through everything they encountered when they arrived at the crime scene the night of the shootings, complete with grisly crime-scene photos. After she's done with them, she plans to call an audiovisual expert who will use computer-generated animation—based on the findings of all those cops—to show how they believe the events of that night unfolded, beginning with the killer shooting Hank Carson on the first floor of the house before proceeding upstairs to where he found Lily and Morgan Carson in their respective bedrooms.

Jimmy or I have already interviewed these same cops. So I know they're certain the shooter used a suppressor, which is why the neighbors didn't hear anything, and why the cops believe neither Lily nor Morgan knew that Hank Carson was already dead as the shooter made his way up the stairs and finished his work.

I've already objected to the use of the animation, even

knowing there is absolutely no chance, none, that Judge Horton won't allow it. The truth is, I've used animation like this myself in the past, knowing what a powerful evidentiary tool animation like this can be.

All the jury will be seeing in Katherine Welsh's little movie is an avatar moving from room to room and doing the shooting. But I know she'll do everything in her power to make those twelve people see Rob Jacobson moving from room to room and firing his weapon. And I'll do everything in my power to distract them.

For now, Rob Jacobson and I are seated across from each other. He keeps looking up at the wall clock behind me, waiting for the moment when the two of us will make the walk down the hallway a few minutes before nine o'clock.

From the time I walked into the room, I haven't said anything to him.

"You have that look," he says finally, unable to wait for me to break the silence between us.

"And what look would that be?"

"The one that makes me feel like I've stepped in it all over again."

I notice, and not for the first time, that he's managed to maintain his summer tan. I assume that he's got a tanning machine tucked away somewhere in his rental home. But what his bronzing can't hide is his weight loss, the way the skin is starting to sag below his chin, the general strain on his face, despite an almost relentless effort on his part to appear—especially with me—as cocky and as sure of himself as ever.

If I didn't know any better, I'd think that he's the one who's sick.

"I had lunch with my sister yesterday," I tell him.

"Oh, so that's it." He nods. "She told you I don't want to see her anymore."

Now I'm the one nodding, a little too vigorously. "Yeah,

Rob, she was so upset at you kicking her out of your bed that she almost forgot to mention that she's dying."

I am fighting to maintain my composure. But by now I have learned, the hard way, that restraining myself from losing my temper in his presence—or hauling off and slugging him again—isn't the real battle for me. The real battle continues to be convincing myself that as much of a guttersnipe—one of my mother's favorite words—as he is, he's not a monster.

"You really should be thanking me," he says.

I turn and look at the clock. Still ten minutes before we need to leave.

I take a deep breath, let it out slowly, then repeat the process, like I'm back at yoga.

"Thanking you for what, exactly?" I ask.

"You wanted me out of her life and now I'm officially out of her life."

"Brigid is dying," I say quietly.

"Listen, I know she's dying, okay?" he says. "And I feel badly about that, I do, whether you want to believe me or not. But it's not as if I don't have my own problems."

I lean an elbow on the table and cup my chin in my hand, as if fascinated by him. Just because I so often am.

"And so, what, you don't have the time or the energy for a dying friend?" I ask.

"I know you're being sarcastic," he says. "But I really don't have it right now, as a matter of fact."

"The time or the energy?" I say. "Or maybe just the humanity?"

He says, "By now you should know me well enough to know that I really don't have it in me to deal with a dying chick, even if she is your sister."

I do push my chair back now, and stand, and see him flinching as I reach for the bag I'd set down next to me on the table. Then walk around the table and around him to the door.

"You know you're the one I really want in my bed," he says.

I stop, my hand on the doorknob. I turn around. He turns around in his chair to face me.

"I'd have to be dead already," I say.

I smile and shrug.

"But who knows, Rob? Maybe you're into that, too."

NINETY-FIVE

IT WAS A LONG day in Judge Michael Horton's courtroom that has felt more like a long night, meaning the night the Carsons died.

Katherine Welsh has artfully put the cops on the stand and then led them and the computer expert through the events of that bloody night, in the same artful way she keeps bringing the whole thing back to Rob Jacobson's DNA every chance she gets.

It finally reached the point where I thought that if these three words — "the defendant's DNA" — were the trigger for a drinking game, we'd all leave Judge Horton's courtroom drunker than St. Patrick's Day.

I offered as many objections as I could along the way, especially during the animated video, trying to slow her roll, but realized the entire time that my client and I were the ones getting rolled today, something I warned him in advance was about to happen.

In normal circumstances, my only immediate goal once this day in court had mercifully ended at five o'clock would be getting home, getting in a long beach walk with Rip no matter what the hour, followed by an even longer hot bath, followed by rice and beans from Fondita that I've been saving as comfort food.

But these are certainly not normal circumstances, which

is why instead of being back in my own home, I'm in Claire Jacobson's, in the living room of the big house in Sagaponack, uninvited and unannounced, after her husband told me she is back in town, listening to her explain to me, chapter and verse, why she wants to testify in her husband's defense, even though she'll be called to the stand by Katherine Welsh and not me.

"Let me help you," she says.

"No," I say.

I tell her I'd use stronger language, but that I'm a lady.

"Since when?" Claire Jacobson asks.

She is dressed as if on her way out to dinner, and not just for rice and beans from Fondita:

Black minidress with three-quarter sleeves that I am almost positive I eyeballed recently at Giorgio Armani in the city. Low heels the same color as the dress. Pearls. Her hair looks freshly done.

No wedding ring.

"I don't mean to sound presumptuous," I tell her, "but are you heading out on a date?"

"Of course you mean to sound presumptuous," she says. "It's kind of your thing, isn't it? Or at least one of them."

"You haven't returned any of my calls," I say.

"Kind of *my* thing," she says. "Not returning your calls. And as for your question: It's none of your goddamn business where I've been."

I'm seated on the couch. She's still standing and pacing, occasionally checking the phone in her hand.

"I *am* going out, as a matter of fact," she says. "Not that *that* is any of your goddamn business."

"I need to know why you are willing to waive spousal privilege and testify for the prosecution," I say.

"Because despite everything, I still love my husband," she says, "and have never believed he is capable of murder. I believe I can convince the jury of that."

"Or," I say, "you're as good a liar as he is and since you can't murder *him* for the way he's humiliated you, you want to get on the stand and do everything possible to bury the sonofabitch."

She doesn't so much smile as bare her teeth. "I guess you'll just have to wait to find out, won't you?"

"Don't do this, Claire," I say. "Because if Katherine Welsh gets you on the stand, the one who's going to get buried is you. Trust me."

"See, that's the thing," she says. "I'm asking you to trust *me*."

I shake my head. "You need to sit this out," I tell her. "By *not* sitting in that chair. You need to call Welsh and tell her that you've changed your mind on spousal privilege. Once you do, she can't compel you to testify."

"You don't understand," she says. "I'm the one who went to her."

I touch a finger to my ear, as if I hadn't heard her correctly.

"You," I say. "Went to her."

"I thought it would be more powerful if I were her witness, and not yours," she says. "It's brilliant, actually."

"Yeah," I say, "if it's an episode of *Law & Order*. But it's not."

"I'm doing this."

"What you're doing is walking into a trap."

She shakes her head now. "I know what I'm doing," she says. "Now please go. I really do have plans, and my dinner companion will be arriving soon. And please note, for the record, that I said companion, and not date."

"Claire," I say. "I couldn't begin to unpack your relationship with your husband. Or his with you. I have more than enough trouble understanding my own relationship with him. But you cannot do this. *Can not*. Whether you sincerely want to help him or not."

"For the last time," she says. "Trust me."

"You know who I trust?" I say. *"Me."*

"You don't know what I'm going to tell her."

"Okay," I say. "You got me. What *are* you going to tell her?"

"That I was with Rob the night of those murders," she says.

NINETY-SIX

AFTER LYING TO MY face, Claire looks down and checks her phone again.

"But we both know you weren't with him," I say.

"Ms. Welsh doesn't know that," Claire says.

"You think she doesn't?" I say. "You think she won't go into your phone records and know exactly where you were that night? Or go into the computer of your Bentley? All you will be doing, whatever your motivation is, is opening yourself up to a perjury rap."

"I'm willing to risk it."

She checks her phone again.

"The minute you say you were with him," I tell her, "Katherine Welsh will be waving the photograph of your husband in the vicinity of the Carson house the night of the murders."

"Rob told me that you told him that the photograph was altered."

"Thinking it and proving it are two entirely different matters," I say. "But I am pleased to discover that you and Rob have been consulting on my case."

"You mean as opposed to his case?" she asks.

"You know what I mean."

"Me testifying as one of Ms. Welsh's witnesses was his idea, actually."

I close my eyes, feeling a sudden ache behind them. Or maybe just feeling as if I'm still in court, the long day still not over.

"Is Katherine Welsh aware that you plan to provide an alibi for Rob?"

"She is," Claire Jacobson says. Another cat smile. "I was trying to be honest with her about my dishonesty."

"I hate to break this to you, Claire," I say. "But I'm an officer of the court. I can't knowingly allow you to commit a crime."

"What crime is that?"

"Perjury!"

"Prove it," she says.

The doorbell rings then.

"That must be Robby," she says, heading for the door.

"You're having dinner with your husband?" I ask.

"No," she says, over her shoulder.

Then she is opening the door and escorting the good-looking, dark-haired man in a dark tailored suit and earring, a man I think I vaguely recognize, toward where I am sitting in the living room.

"Jane," she says, "I'd like you to meet my friend Robby Sassoon."

NINETY-SEVEN

Jimmy

JIMMY IS BACK IN Sag Harbor when Jed Bernstein calls and gives him an address in Barnes Landing, an almost secret section of Amagansett, on Gardiners Bay. Jimmy knows the area, knows how the most expensive houses there overlook the small beach and the bay beyond. Almost like a gated community without the gates.

"It's one of Sonny's many safe houses," Bernstein says.

"Safe for whom?" Jimmy asks.

"Not you if you were lying to me about why you wanted to see him," Bernstein says. "So you better not be screwing around here."

Bernstein gives Jimmy a time then, tells him to come alone, reminds him again not to screw around, even though that is exactly what Jimmy Cunniff plans to do tonight.

It takes him about forty minutes to drive over from the bar, but he gets there right on time, nine o'clock. He knows enough to leave his gun and his phone in the car. He is wearing a windbreaker, jeans, old sneakers, and a Yankee cap that has more years on it than the sneakers, one he bought on the last night the Yankees played a game at the old Yankee Stadium. God, he loved that place. The new one, on the north side of 161st, reminds him more of a giant outdoor shopping mall with a baseball diamond in place of fancy chain stores.

Blum's house is a classic Hamptons saltbox, positioned

high up and well back from the road and in line with a terrific bay view.

Two of Blum's foot soldiers, built like jeeps, are waiting for Jimmy by the front door. Jimmy puts his hands high, almost in surrender, as he approaches them, lets them pat him down.

"Clearly not your first rodeo," one of them says.

"Is there really such a thing as a first rodeo?" Jimmy asks.

Sonny Blum is wearing the same jacket he wore to Jimmy's house, and the same pants, with what appear to be the same stains on them. He is in the kind of leather BarcaLounger from which Jimmy's old man used to watch baseball; only his looks a lot newer and more expensive than the one Jimmy remembers from the apartment in the Bronx.

Blum points to the couch.

"Sit," he says. Then with a trembling hand he points at Jimmy's Yankee hat. "You still root for them?"

"You can take the boy out of the Bronx," Jimmy says.

"I'm so old I remember when they used to make the World Series every year," Blum says. "No shit, can you even remember the last time they made it?"

"Vaguely."

Blum says, "I'd offer you a drink but you're not staying."

"Glad we cleared that up."

"So what's so important you needed this sit-down?"

"I think I'm pretty close to figuring out who killed the Carsons," Jimmy says.

"Talk to me."

Jimmy has rehearsed his answer on the way over here and delivers it now, telling Blum that from everything he knows, it can only be Jacobson's son, Eric. Or Edmund McKenzie, once Rob Jacobson's asshole buddy in high school. Or maybe even both. For all the tap dancing he's doing, this part is true. Or it *might* be true. Because the more Jimmy thinks about it, the more he keeps coming back to the two of them, just because they're the two who seem to hate Jacobson the most.

Jimmy doesn't have any new information, or real proof, at least not yet. But the old man sitting across from him doesn't know that.

"Can you nail this down?" Blum says when Jimmy finishes.

"Soon."

"You know, I could just have them both killed and tell myself that was God's way of sorting all of this shit out."

"You want to know what went down," Jimmy says. "I *need* to know. Let me handle this."

"Don't bother me again until you have."

Jimmy nods. "Ask you something before I go?" he says to Blum.

"You can ask," Blum says. "Don't mean you get an answer."

Jimmy says, "Why do you care so much whether Jacobson goes down for this or not? You ever plan to explain that to me?"

"Maybe someday," Blum says. "Just not tonight."

"Did Bernstein tell you about leaving my partner's ex-husband alone?"

Blum tries to laugh, but it turns into coughing.

"When Pierre pays up, then I'll leave him alone," Blum says.

"Martin."

"Who gives a shit?"

"Well," Jimmy says, "I had to try."

"You tried," Blum says. "Now get lost."

"Just one last thing," Jimmy says.

He takes off his Yankee cap and reaches for the subpoena on top of his head and walks across the room and hands it to Blum.

"You've been served," Jimmy says.

Blum looks at the paper in his hand, the gray skin suddenly turning red, then up at Jimmy. In that moment, Jimmy sees the killer in Sonny Blum, in total.

"You're a dead man," Blum says.

"Maybe someday," Jimmy says. "Just not tonight."

NINETY-EIGHT

KATHERINE WELSH RESTS HER case on Friday.

She was planning to conclude by calling Claire Jacobson but is denied the opportunity. For once, almost like an early Christmas miracle, both Claire and her husband listen to me, and are finally persuaded about the risks of her appearing as a witness for the prosecution, and the potential damage to our case.

Before we leave the courthouse, Jacobson asks if I'm still planning to call Sonny Blum as my first witness on Monday morning. Neither Jimmy nor I had told Jacobson about Jimmy handing Blum his subpoena, but Sonny did, apparently both colorfully and profanely.

"I'm telling you," Rob Jacobson says now. "This is a really bad idea."

"Not your call," I say.

"You still work for me."

"Yeah, but it's like they say in sports, Rob," I say. "This is *my* house."

He finally gives up when Thomas McGoey tells him I'm right, and how important it is to establish that Hank Carson had bet, and bet big, with Sonny Blum, whether or not Blum tried to tell Jimmy that Carson paid up before he died.

Finally, Jimmy and Norma both announce that the

meeting's over, telling me to get the hell out of here, get in my car, go have dinner with my boyfriend.

Jimmy walks me out to the hall.

"I have to make one quick stop first," I tell him.

I tell him where.

"What the hell for?" he asks. "You lose a bet?"

"Maybe I'm looking at it as penance for my sins," I say.

"With just one stop?" Jimmy asks. "I need a place like that."

Katherine Welsh has authorized a Garden City police captain to let me in to the Carson house.

"Why are you doing this?" Welsh had asked before I left the courthouse.

"Because whether or not you believe this, Katherine," I said, "we want the same thing from this trial."

"And what's that?"

"Justice for the Carsons."

"Even if your client is found guilty?" she asked.

"Even if."

She gave me a long look.

"Maybe I misjudged you," Welsh said.

"Guilty," I said.

Once we arrive, I thank the cop and promise that I'll deliver the key to Katherine Welsh when court resumes on Monday.

Now, at long last, I am standing in the front hall and frozen in place where they found Hank Carson's body, almost the exact spot from what I saw in the animated video.

Only this isn't animation. This is where it all happened that night. Scene of a bloody and brutal crime. Crimes, plural. There have been other times over the past several months when I've intended to come here. But I never did.

I have been present at more crime scenes in my life than I care to remember, and often on the night of or day of, both as a cop and as an attorney. Over the course of Rob Jacobson's first trial, I paid multiple visits to the rented house where the Gates family had been gunned down, copycat style.

Now here I am at the house once lived in by the Carsons of Garden City. I called Ben Kalinsky on the way over and told him I was going to be late for dinner, and why.

"I was wondering when you were going to finally check that box," Ben said, and told me to do what I have to do and he'll see me when he sees me.

I walk through the lower level before reluctantly heading upstairs, moving as slowly as if I were wearing leg-irons, making my way to the bedrooms where the bodies of Lily and Morgan Carson were found that night.

I do not linger in Morgan Carson's room, not wanting to spend much time—not wanting to spend any time at all, really—surrounded in there by all the girl's things, also frozen in place, and time.

The longer I stay here, the easier it is for my mind to wander to the extremely dark place where I can see her in a bed like hers with Rob Jacobson. It's a visual that only makes me wonder, all over again, what the hell *I* am doing here, in this case and in this house, looking around at stuffed animals that Morgan Carson had kept into her teenaged years, one of the walls dominated by an honest-to-God poster of Taylor Swift.

I think back to my conversation with Katherine Welsh about justice for these three people, and especially for this girl who never got the chance to become a woman, at least not in more important ways than the only one Rob Jacobson cared about. And as I stand here, surrounded by her things, I know I don't just want justice.

I want the truth, even if it turns out that my client committed this truly hideous crime.

In the end, this isn't about him. It's about Hank Carson and his wife.

And his daughter.

About the girl.

When I leave her room, I then walk down the hallway to what had clearly been Hank Carson's study, it taking hardly any imagination to picture him in here and with the door shut and talking furtively on the phone with whichever of Sonny Blum's bookies he was placing a bet or two or ten with at the time, in his own extremely dark place.

Sonny did in fact tell Jimmy that Hank had paid up before he died, and that whatever it was that got him killed, it wasn't that he was still in the hole.

But there is a part of me, a big part, that will believe Sonny Blum only when hell freezes over, presumably with him in it.

It is suffocatingly quiet, and sad, in this house, the air thick and heavy, causing me to wonder when the last time was that anybody opened a window, allowing maybe even the ghosts to breathe.

I finally walk back down the hall, past the bedrooms, and am at the top of the stairs when I see Eric Jacobson and Edmund McKenzie in the front hall now, standing in front of the open door, staring up at me.

NINETY-NINE

MY BAG IS IN my car. My gun is in my bag. It seemed crazy to think I might need it once I was alone inside the house. But now I have company, two men who I believe are certifiable, on a good day.

"Long time no see," Eric Jacobson says pleasantly.

"Not nearly long enough," I say. "So speak for yourself."

I haven't moved from the top of the stairs. I feel a breeze coming in through the front door.

There is a smirk from McKenzie that reminds me of the one I see all the time from Rob Jacobson, as if they've been practicing the look on each other since high school, or just in the mirror.

"You know, I've always gotten turned on when chicks talked down to me," he says. He shrugs. "Even when it's like the little balcony scene we've got going here."

"You two followed me here from the courthouse?" I ask.

"So we did," Eric Jacobson says.

"Why?"

He shrugs. "Thought it might be fun."

They have moved across the hall so now they're standing in front of the bottom step.

"I didn't see either of you at the trial," I say.

I am wondering how this will play out when I am ready to leave. But it appears we're not there yet.

"Come on, trials are boring as shit," McKenzie says. Shrugs again. "Unless you're the one actually *on* trial."

"What do you want?" I ask.

"Just to catch up," Eric Jacobson says.

"I'm still sick, the two of you are still punks, your dad is still up for murder," I say to Eric. "There. We're caught up."

"Now she's really making me hot," McKenzie says.

"What do you two really want?" I ask.

"What we want," Eric Jacobson says, "is to deliver a message."

"A message," I say.

"As sick as you are, Jane, it would be hazardous to your health for you to make the same mistake with us you're about to make with Sonny Blum," Eric says. "Or even try."

"Wait," I say. "You still think you can threaten me, Junior?"

I know how much Eric hates being called that. He gives a quick shake to his shoulders and I worry that his next move might be charging up the stairs.

"Think of it more as a warning," Eric says. "The only way you're ever going to see us in that courtroom is if we do decide to come inside."

"Got it," I say.

"Does that mean we won't get called?" he says.

"Well, not unless I want to," I say.

"You never learn," Eric says.

"My dad used to call me a spunky lass."

"It'll be hard to find us again after today," Edmund McKenzie says, "just so you know."

"Jimmy Cunniff is a lot better at finding people than they are at not being found," I say. "Long-established fact."

"Before we go, though," Eric Jacobson says, "how about we all go upstairs and have some real fun?"

"Now you are scaring me," I say. "Just not the way you think."

"You're a lot tougher when you've got a gun in your hand," Eric Jacobson says.

"You know, Junior, you're right," I say. "But there are occasions when I don't need one."

"Like when I'm the one with the gun in his hand," Jimmy Cunniff says from behind them.

ONE HUNDRED

"SO JIMMY SNUCK IN behind them with a gun?"
Thomas McGoey says.

He has driven over from Quogue to talk about the beginning of our case tomorrow. Really, he wants to know how I'm going after Sonny Blum, our first witness.

But he also wants to know about the scene at the Carson house on Friday afternoon with Eric Jacobson and Edmund McKenzie.

"It was a very Jimmy thing to do," I tell McGoey.

McGoey is shaking his head. "And I thought I was badass," he says. "I'm not even in the same league as the two of you."

"Eric tried to act cool about the whole thing," I say. "He said to Jimmy, 'You know you're not going to shoot us.' And Jimmy said, 'Don't tempt me,' and told them to get lost."

"They followed you and he followed them?" McGoey says.

"He was in his car in the parking lot and saw them pull out after me," I say. "But then he likes to say how sometimes being a good investigator just means hanging around and waiting for something interesting to develop."

"And they just left?"

"They did," I say. "But Jimmy yelled after them that he'd see them real soon."

"You think he can find them if we want to call them?"

I say, "It will be a lot less difficult now that he planted a tracking device on McKenzie's car, over the right front tire."

McGoey is shaking his head again, admiringly. "Badass."

I have been feeling punk all weekend. But I power through our meeting. Before McGoey leaves he says, "You've got to make sure that you don't make it look like elder abuse with our friend Sonny."

"He's a killer," I say.

"But he's not on trial," McGoey says.

"You sure about that?" I say innocently.

When he's gone, I am feeling well enough to take Rip to the beach, knowing I first have to make a stop at Rob Jacobson's house, where he wants to take one more swing at changing my mind about putting Sonny Blum on the stand. And about something else.

"For the last time, put me on the stand," he says when I get there.

"For the last time, no," I say.

"I can win over the babes on the jury," he says.

"Keep telling yourself that," I say. "Now let's change the subject."

"Sonny is blaming me for this," Rob says.

"Good to know that the two of you are staying in touch."

"I told Sonny I didn't think I could change your mind."

"My sincerest apologies."

"So when I did tell him that," Rob continues, "he said to make sure to tell you that you have now been warned for the last time."

So a weekend that began with a threat from Eric Jacobson is now ending with one from Sonny Blum. I remember a line from "Send in the Clowns" then:

Isn't it bliss?

Jacobson offers to walk me to my car. I tell him not to bother. I drive Rip and me to Indian Wells, where we happily discover that the wind has mostly died down tonight, despite this morning's severe passing storm. But its aftermath, big, loud, crashing waves, are wonderful to see and hear.

You've been warned for the last time.

Being such a cultured girl, and not just with music, I fell asleep the other night rewatching *Braveheart,* long enough to hear my favorite line from the movie: "Everybody dies, but not everybody really lives." Something like that. I smile thinking about it now. That was when Mel Gibson was still Mel Gibson, still cute and sexy as hell even with his face painted like he was at a college basketball game.

Rip and I walk the beach and I feel the salt air in my face, not whipping at me the way it sometimes can, more gentle tonight.

I suddenly feel the best I have all weekend.

Maybe because I'm here.

Still effing here.

The wind is slowly picking up, Rip and I walking right into it for another hundred yards or so before I plan to turn around. And I am thinking about the effing trial again, even in what has always been my safe place, my best place, not even remotely surprised that it's followed me here.

I know Katherine Welsh's case is stronger, knew that going in, know it tonight on the eve of presenting my own case. But I felt that same way about Kevin Ahearn, the Suffolk County DA, before Rob Jacobson's first trial.

Now I'm in the barrel again, in what might be my last trial.

The thought stops me cold.

I turn and stare out at the ocean, a sight that really has always made me feel in total contact with my soul.

Is this my last trial?

Maybe.

But if it is, I don't plan on leaving anything in the locker room, something our hockey coach at Boston College used to tell us was the worst penalty a player could commit.

"You do that," she always said, "you're on your way to losing the game before it even starts."

I hated losing then, I hate it even more now.

Starting with cancer.

I start running now, yelling over my shoulder at Rip to catch me if he can, not feeling weak or sick. Or terminal. Not tonight, and not tomorrow morning.

Back in the house, I take Rip into the kitchen and give him treats, more than I usually give him after a beach walk, but I can spoil my own damn dog if I want to, it's the same for him as for me.

You only live once.

I treat myself to a glass of wine, taking it into the living room and setting it on the coffee table and putting my feet up next to it.

Then my phone is playing the BC fight song, the one that would always play when we skated out onto the ice.

It is a London number, one I recognize as belonging to my friend Fiona, who beat cancer when hers was supposed to have been much further along than mine.

She is the cool English chick I met on my first trip to the Meier Clinic. When I said good-bye to her that time, I thought we were saying good-bye for the last time. But it turned out she was back when I was back and we met again. I was out for a walk one afternoon and there she was. I thought I was seeing a ghost, but she was very much alive, and in remission.

We promised each other we would stay in touch, but haven't since she was back in England and I was back here.

It's not her voice at the other end of the line.

"Is this Jane?" a male voice says when I answer.

"Yes. Who's this?"

"This is Jeremy. Fiona's husband."

I suddenly feel as if my soul is leaving my body.

"She died a few hours ago," he says.

ONE HUNDRED ONE

"YOU LOOK LIKE SHIT," Norma Banks says to me the next morning when she's waiting for me in the park across the street from the courthouse.

"Don't sugarcoat it," I say. "Give it to me straight."

"I know you've heard me say that to you before," Norma says.

"Not something a girl forgets," I say, "whether she's got cancer or not."

"Did you get any sleep?" Norma asks. "Because you look like you didn't. How many times do I have to tell you that you need your sleep?"

"How many times do I have to tell you that you're not my mother."

"Am now," Norma says. "Battlefield commission, like they used to say during the war."

I grin at her. "Which war?"

Then I admit to her that I hardly slept at all, and explain why I couldn't after the call from London. I relate the conversation I had with Fiona's husband, how she suddenly went into a downward spiral and there wasn't even time to get her back to the Meier Clinic, it was too late and she was too far gone.

Norma says, "I'm sorry about your friend. You know I am, because she was your friend. But just because it happened that way for her doesn't mean it's going to happen that way for you."

"I kept telling myself, after the last time I saw her and she'd given me her good news, that if she could beat it, so could I, Norma. Like it was some sort of sign."

"And nothing changes with you because of the way it happened with her."

We are about to cross the street when a limousine pulls up and Sonny Blum gets out of it.

"Holy crap," Norma says as Blum begins to shuffle toward the entrance, helped by two bruisers in dark suits on either side of him. "He looks as if he's on his way to the chair."

"He is," I say.

I tell her to pick up the pace, I'm due in the judge's chambers.

ONE HUNDRED TWO

SONNY BLUM WEARS A royal-blue sport jacket that appears to be a couple of sizes too big for him. Underneath is a black polo shirt buttoned to the collar.

"Thrift shop chic," Norma Banks whispers to me after Blum has been sworn in.

I get up from my table when I'm ready to begin, walk toward him, stopping about six feet away.

He is staring at the jury box.

"Good morning!" I say brightly.

He seems startled by my voice as he turns to face me.

"Hi?" he asks tentatively, as if wary I might make a sudden move.

"My name is Jane Smith," I say. "I am the attorney for the defendant, Mr. Jacobson."

"Hi," he says again.

"Could you state your name for the court?"

"What?"

"Your name, sir."

"Sonny," he says.

"Your full name, please."

"Sanford Blum. But my friends call me Sonny."

"And what is your occupation, Mr. Blum?"

"Excuse me?"

"What do you do for a living?"

The question seems to confuse him. At least he wants to act as if it has. But then this is all an act.

"I'm retired," he says after a long pause. Then he smiles and turns back to the jury. "But you know what they say about being retired. You can never take a day off."

"Good one, Mr. Blum. But would you mind telling the jury what your occupation was before retirement became your everyday job?"

"Waste management," he says.

"Waste management," I say, my voice in a lilt, as if I've found that information fascinating.

I nod at him and smile.

"But that's not your occupation according to the federal government, isn't that correct?"

"The government?" he asks, looking even more confused now, almost as if wondering where he is. I find myself wondering how much he has practiced this routine at home, in front of his lawyer and his boys.

"Yes, sir, the United States government," I say. "Because it is their studied opinion that your life's calling involved loan-sharking, racketeering, and bookmaking. And, honestly, Mr. Blum, that's the short list."

I leave him to ponder that as I walk back to my table, pull a thick sheaf of papers out of my bag, and hold them up for Sonny and the jury and everybody else in the room to see.

"Mr. Blum, I am holding in my hands just some of the documents involving court cases against you over the years, which I would be happy to submit into evidence," I continue.

Another smile, this one smaller than before, plays across Blum's face.

"Am I on trial?" he says.

"Oh, my, no," I tell him. "I'm not here to convict you of past crimes, real or imagined. Just to establish that you're a career hoodlum."

"Objection!" Katherine Welsh says, up on her feet now. "Is

there a point to all this, Your Honor, other than Ms. Smith insulting her own witness?"

"Sustained," Judge Horton says. "Ms. Smith, you have established the witness's bona fides, shall we say. Now we need to work on the relevance of this line of questioning."

"Of course," I say. "Totally understood."

I theatrically toss the papers on my table.

"Let's move on, Mr. Blum," I say. "Did you know the deceased, Hank Carson?"

"Who?"

"One of the three people my client is accused of murdering," I say, "along with Mr. Carson's wife and daughter."

"Can't say I had the pleasure," Blum says. "But sometimes I can't even remember things I think I can still remember." He puts out his hands, helplessly. "You know what they say? Getting old isn't for sissies."

"Did Hank Carson owe you gambling money at the time of his death?"

"Like some bet him and me made?" he asks. "Why would I bet with somebody I don't know?"

"Despite what you say is your inability to remember things, Mr. Blum, isn't it true that Hank Carson was a million dollars in debt to you at the time of his death?"

"I don't know what you're talking about."

"Are you sure about that?" I ask.

I am walking now, across to where the clerk of the court is sitting, and reach for the plastic case with an old-fashioned compact disc inside.

"Your Honor," I say, "as both you and Ms. Welsh know, this disc was already entered into evidence, before court began today, as Exhibit DX-1. And I would now like the court's permission to play its contents on the large screen I'm going to ask the clerk to wheel out here, so the jury can see."

"The court has already acknowledged that you can play it, Ms. Smith," Judge Horton says.

"I just wanted it on the record, sir."

I turn to Katherine Welsh. "Does esteemed counsel have any objections?"

"You and I both know they've already been lodged in chambers," Welsh says, clearly resigned to what she knows is about to happen, unable to stop it.

The screen is wheeled to the center of the room. The clerk inserts the DVD into the laptop in front of her.

"May I?" I say to the clerk.

She nods.

Then I hit Play.

ONE HUNDRED THREE

IT TAKES A FEW seconds for the technology to kick in.

But then, in front of Katherine Welsh and Judge Michael Horton and the jury and maybe even God Herself, an image of Sonny Blum appears on the big screen, remarkably clear, reclining in the BarcaLounger in the living room of his safe house in Barnes Landing, one that pretty much turned out to be the opposite of safe for him.

This is the video that Jimmy had made with the tiny 1080P HD recorder, almost invisible to the naked eye, that a local seamstress in Sag Harbor had carefully sewn into the interlocking NY of Jimmy's Yankee cap—the camera he used to record his conversation with Blum the night he served Blum with his subpoena, in another small miracle of technology.

It was the recorder he'd tested out at the bar with his bartender Kenny before heading over to Gardiners Bay.

"Just out of curiosity," we hear Jimmy saying now, *"how much did the late Mr. Carson owe you?"*

Blum: *"A million, give or take a few thousand."*

Jimmy: *"Lot of money."*

Blum: *"He's lucky something unfortunate didn't happen to him sooner."*

Now I make a big show of leaning over and hitting Pause on the clerk's laptop, freezing the image of Sanford (Sonny) Blum.

"Could you possibly be referring to something unfortunate like his whole family being shot in cold blood, Mr. Blum?"

Blum is shaking his head, furiously, eyes closed.

"I got nothing to do with that," he says.

But when he opens his eyes, he suddenly looks very present, and alert. And angry. They all get mad when they get caught.

"But after the testimony you just gave about not knowing Mr. Carson and about your career in waste management, why in the world would you expect anybody in this courtroom, starting with the jury, to believe a word that's coming out of your mouth?" I ask.

And then Sonny Blum is halfway out of his chair, pointing to where Jimmy Cunniff is seated behind my table.

"I told that bum that Carson paid!" he bellows. "It's on the tape!"

I walk over and now I'm just a couple of feet away from Sonny Blum. We're practically eye to eye.

"Then I guess my last question for you goes something like this, Mr. Blum," I say. "Can you prove that?"

I lean closer to him.

"Perhaps with some kind of video evidence?" I ask him.

Then I walk away from him, jerking a thumb over my shoulder and saying to Judge Horton, "I'm done with *that* bum."

ONE HUNDRED FOUR

IT'S A SPECIAL NIGHT and so Robby Sassoon has decided to treat himself to the Broadway revival of *Merrily We Roll Along* that he's been wanting to see before its closing, his problem being that work kept getting in the way.

It's a Sondheim production that got no respect when originally staged back in the 1980s, closing after just sixteen performances, Robby knows. He has always been steeped in the history of Broadway, even before he could afford Broadway.

Now he's delighted to discover that the revival has lived up to its notices with the small cast that includes the actor Daniel Radcliffe, who as a boy played Harry Potter in the movies.

Not the only wizard in the house tonight. Robby smiles to himself.

The show is everything he heard it would be and everything he hoped it would be, all the way to the closing number, "Our Time," when they all sing, "Something is stirring..." before working their way to the song's big, rousing finish, repeating the same lyrics over and over again:

"Me and you... me and you... me and you."

He can't get those lyrics out of his head even when he is out on 44th Street, knowing he can take his time before he begins to make his way uptown.

"Me and you," Robby sings softly to himself.

A familiar feeling is stirring inside him.

★ ★ ★

He stops for dinner at Becco, a simple and unassuming restaurant in the theater district, for two of his favorite dishes, the polenta appetizer, one listed as Polenta con Speck, and the Parmigiana di Vitello. He even allows himself a single glass of Antinori Tignanello cabernet, not worried about it dulling his senses, rather than enhancing them. The wine is also one of his favorites, and expensive.

So am I.

When his entrée arrives at his table, Robby neatly tucks his cloth napkin into his collar, not wanting any of the sauce from the veal dish to end up on the front of his white shirt.

Robby doesn't want it to look like blood.

The aesthetics would be all wrong.

In the end, he decides to skip dessert. It's getting late, close to midnight. He hails a cab, gets out a couple of blocks from his destination, walking the rest of the way until he is finally walking down a narrow alley, past the trash cans, to the back of the building.

No security cameras back here. None in the back of the place. Robby has checked.

Robby knows the man will be here. As sloppy as the man is with so many areas of his life, starting with the gambling, he is a creature of habit, as Robby is. So this is another night when the man is the last one here, the only light once Robby is inside coming from the office near the kitchen.

Jane Smith's ex-husband, the owner of Café Martin, doesn't hear Robby come in, doesn't see him until Robby is standing in the doorway to the office, gun pointed at him.

"Good evening, Martin," Robby says.

ONE HUNDRED FIVE

COURT ADJOURNED BEFORE KATHERINE Welsh could even begin her cross-examination of Sonny Blum, because Blum had suddenly clutched his chest and fallen forward out of his chair and started yelling, in a choked voice, that he was having a heart attack.

Playing a confused old man while I was questioning hadn't done the job for him, so then he dialed it up, rather convincingly, I thought, even though I would have bet all the money Rob Jacobson was paying me that he was faking the whole thing like a champion.

But a doctor was summoned and Blum was wheeled out of the room and into the waiting ambulance and taken to NYU Langone Hospital–Long Island. Judge Michael Horton said we would resume in the morning. If Mr. Blum was still hospitalized, Horton said, I could call the next witness on my list.

There was no reason to tell Judge Michael Horton this, but I was happy—thrilled, really—to get out of there, mostly because I was starting to feel almost as sick as Sonny Blum had wanted us to think he was when he went into his flop.

I don't tell anybody on my team how lousy I'm feeling. Just the usual and relentless and oppressive bullshit. My next appointment with my oncologist isn't scheduled until the trial is over, which I've told Dr. Gellis could be as soon as a couple of weeks.

Maybe less.

I keep telling Jimmy Cunniff, even on my bad days, that we're too close to the end now, that I'm going to see this through even if it kills me.

Every time I do, he replies the same way: "There has to be a better way of you saying that."

He said it to me again today, right before we walked into the courtroom, and I suddenly turned around and kissed him.

"How many times do I have to tell you not to be gross," Jimmy said.

When I'm finally home, I tell myself I'm not dying tonight, even though I feel as if I might be. Usually I manage to walk Rip, even if it's just a short one around the neighborhood, when I get back from court. Occasionally, I wait to do it until I've had dinner.

But there is no dinner for me tonight, even though the nausea has finally dissipated.

Ben calls around seven and asks how I'm doing.

"Lousy," I say, telling the truth for a change.

"You want me to come over and look in on the patient?"

I tell him that's sweet of him, but no.

"Are you feeling lousy enough that one of us should call Sam Wylie?" he asks.

"No," I say. "For now, I'm going to take one glass of wine and call her in the morning."

"Is wine a good idea?"

"Is it ever really a bad one?" I say, then tell him I love him, and that I will check in with *him* in the morning.

I only make it through half a glass of chardonnay before I go straight to bed. It is one of the rare occasions when I am asleep almost immediately, dreaming about being on a walk with Fiona Mills, not surrounded by the mountains near the Meier Clinic, but on the beach here...

I am awakened by the ping that says I have an incoming text message.

It's been sent by an unknown number.

You were warned

The second message comes in about thirty seconds behind the first.

This one is a photograph.

A photograph that makes me stare with horror at the phone in my hand, the glow from the screen providing the only real, and eerie, light in my bedroom.

It is my ex-husband Martin, on his back, on what I'm certain is the floor of his restaurant kitchen, eyes wide open, a bullet hole in the middle of his forehead and what looks like another in the middle of his chest, blood everywhere, on his face and white shirt and the floor around his body.

I scream then.

Loud enough to get Rip barking his head off.

Just not loud enough in this case to wake the dead.

ONE HUNDRED SIX

JIMMY DRIVES US TO the city.

Even though the last thing I want is to have my phone back in my hand, I briefly use it to text Katherine Welsh, wanting to get that out of the way now, telling her what's happened. Despite the hour, she texts me back almost immediately, telling me she'll contact Judge Horton and request the trial be pushed back another day, and for me to do what I need to do.

But she sends one more text before she's done.

Who would do something like this?

I shoot her a short reply.

Sonny Blum would

"I should have done more to help him," I say to Jimmy from the passenger seat.

We're off the FDR by now and making our way across Manhattan to the West Side.

"He knew who he was dealing with," Jimmy says.

"So do we."

"Three people, at least three that we know of, have died in the past couple of weeks because they were betting with Sonny," Jimmy says. "So the guardrails are clearly off with that crazy old fuck."

"When were they ever on?" I ask him.

Jimmy told me when he picked me up that he'd just called NYU Langone Hospital–Long Island and that Blum had left without being released. So he's gone, just not the way we both want him to be, and neither of us thinks he's coming back anytime soon, if ever.

When we get to Café Martin, the crime scene unit's van is still in front, along with three cruisers. It's three in the morning by now, but there are still onlookers on all sides of the yellow tape, with others watching from across the street, where I used to stand and look across at the front window of Café Martin, occasionally catching a glimpse of my ex-husband.

This is the big, bad city, of course, the one that never sleeps, especially when there's a show like this, even in the middle of the night.

Detective Craig Jackson, Jimmy's friend, the one who Jimmy says looks more than a little like Samuel L., is waiting for us on the sidewalk, Jimmy having called him when we were off the highway to tell him we were close.

I've known Jackson a long time, if not as long or as well as Jimmy has. He hugs me and says, "Sorry, Janie."

"Me, too," I say.

"Nothing taken," Jackson says. "We already talked to the manager, people hardly ever pay cash, so there was really nothing to steal. This looks like a hit, all day and all night."

"Only because it is," I say.

Jackson says, "I understand you've had a couple like this out east recently."

Jimmy nods. "Both clients of Sonny Blum's, the way Jane's ex was. He'd already been threatened once by one of Sonny's goons about payments past due."

"You happen to know which goon?" Jackson asks.

"I should have asked," I say. "But I never did."

"You think there's any way to connect the three murders?" Jackson says.

"Sure," Jimmy says. "When rats fly."

"Front door was locked," Jackson says. "Shooter must've come through the back."

He turns to face me. "Body's already gone, Janie. But you want to go inside, anyway, have a look around?"

"No," I say.

Thinking again about all the times I was drawn here, knowing I was acting crazy but knowing that Martin was inside, even after he'd hurt me the way he had.

I tell Craig Jackson now about Rob Jacobson's conversation with Sonny, Rob passing on Sonny's message that I had now been warned. Then I take out my phone and show him the first text, the one that says the same goddamn thing. Jackson takes my phone, uses it to send the text, and the photograph of Martin, to his own phone.

"One to the head, one to the chest," Jackson says, staring at my screen.

"We saw," Jimmy says.

"Whoever Sonny's guy is, he's very predictable," I say.

We all stand there on the sidewalk in silence now, in the reflection of the flashing lights of the cruisers. I'm still not quite sure why I'm here. I knew the body would be long gone by the time Jimmy and I arrived. But somehow I had to be here for Martin, even though I was too late.

"There's one more thing," Jackson says. "Like the cherry on top of the ice cream."

He takes his phone back out and shows me the screenshot he found when he opened the laptop on Martin's desk.

The image is the online preview of what I'm sure is going to be the front page of *Newsday*'s print edition, probably on the trucks already.

It features a picture of Sonny Blum on the witness stand and me in front of him, pointing a finger like I'm pointing a gun at him.

The headline reads this way:

MOB SCENE

ONE HUNDRED SEVEN

NEITHER ONE OF US is even considering sleep when we get back out to Long Island, so instead of my house Jimmy drives me to his bar, unlocks the front door, and makes coffee for the two of us.

"You need full-time security," he says.

"No," I say, "*you* do. And maybe Ben. Or even Rip the dog. For reasons only Sonny knows, and maybe God Herself, Sonny wants Rob Jacobson to beat this rap. And he knows I'm still his best option to make that happen. The old bastard wants to torture me, not kill me."

"Whoever this shooter is," Jimmy says, "he's very good."

"And has done everything except hire a skywriter to let us know it's the same guy doing all these killings."

"Maybe he killed those two families for Sonny, too."

"But why?" I ask.

"Like he ever needs a reason," Jimmy says.

He tells me he could take a walk over to Jack's and get us muffins.

I tell him I'm fine.

"Like hell you are,"

"I feel responsible," I say. "So shoot *me*."

"Cut the shit," Jimmy says. "This was as inevitable as the freaking tide."

"I should have taken Martin more seriously."

"You didn't take him seriously all the other times he was in over his head and he came to you for money," Jimmy says. "Nobody shot him those times."

He walks over and pours himself more coffee and comes back.

"This was payback for you putting Sonny on the stand, pure and simple," Jimmy says. "It's *The Untouchables,* for chrissakes. You send one of theirs to the hospital, they send one of yours to the morgue."

"I'm worried about you," I say.

"I can take care of myself."

"You think you could find Sonny again if you had to?"

Jimmy grins. "Not in this life and not in the next one, either, that's for shit sure."

Jimmy says he can have some of his boys watch Ben without him knowing it and do it on Rob Jacobson's dime. We know we don't have to worry about Brigid, at least for the time being. She's already back at the Meier Clinic, having been flown there by Jacobson, who explained the gesture by saying that he wanted to show that he did have feelings for her.

"And not just in my pants," Rob Jacobson added, just so I wouldn't forget who I was talking to, as if I ever could. In this life or the next one.

When we've finished with coffee, and Main Street is starting to come alive outside Jimmy's front window, he drives me home.

Danny Esposito is sitting on my front steps when we get there, a tall to-go coffee from Brent's in one hand, his phone in the other.

As we get closer to him, I see a thick, padded envelope next to him on the step.

"Brought you something," Esposito says. "And sorry about your husband."

"Ex," I say. "How'd you know we'd be here?"

He grins. "I'm an ace detective," he says. "Plus, I hacked into your phone."

"Isn't that against the law?"

"Not if you do it right," he says.

He picks up the envelope now.

"You're welcome," Danny Esposito says. "I didn't even make you two wait until Christmas."

There's a yearbook inside. Garden City High.

"All the time we've spent combing Morgan Carson's social media, looking for anything that might help us," he says. "And it turns out all we needed was in here the whole time. Old school. *Her* school."

He's bookmarked the page he wants me to see. It's Morgan's personal yearbook page. More heartbreaking images from her too-short life. Her on Halloween, dressed like Taylor Swift. Her in her track uniform, arms up as she crosses a finish line, huge smile on her face. Prom picture. Her in a bikini on the beach.

"This," Danny Esposito says, his finger on the photo at the bottom of the page.

It's Morgan at a football game, probably a Garden City High game, with some girlfriends, all of them mugging for the camera. All of them looking heartbreakingly young.

"What am I supposed to be looking at?" I ask.

"Two rows behind her," Esposito says.

And there it is.

Or, more accurately, there *he* is.

"Well, I'll be damned," I say, and hand the yearbook to Jimmy.

Seated two rows behind Morgan Carson is Eric Jacobson.

JANE SMITH.

FOR THE DEFENSE.

ONE HUNDRED EIGHT

WITH SONNY BLUM OUT of play, I call Steve Salzman, the learned young crime scene evidence technician, back to the stand, first thing the next morning.

"I have only a few more questions, Mr. Salzman," I say in opening. "And I apologize in advance, because these are questions I should have asked when you first testified."

This is a lie, of course. But I'm not the one under oath.

These are questions I've been saving.

"Still happy to be of assistance," he says.

"I'm sure you are," I say. "Now, if you don't mind, could you once again take us through where you found the DNA evidence, hair and skin and whatnot, that allegedly belongs to my client."

"*Objection!*" Katherine Welsh says, cutting me off right there. "Counsel is completely aware that there is no such thing as *alleged* DNA. We've gone over this. That the trace evidence found at the murder scene comes from the defendant wasn't in dispute the first time Mr. Salzman testified, isn't in dispute today, will never *be* in dispute."

"Sustained," Judge Horton says.

"With all due respect, Your Honor," I say. "Aren't we really splitting hairs here?"

I turn long enough to give Katherine Welsh a quick wink. "Hair," I say. "See what I did there?"

Horton pounds his gavel.

"Ms. Smith," he says. "For the last time, let's dispense with what you obviously think are humorous asides."

"Sorry, Your Honor." I turn back to Salzman. "We were discussing DNA," I say.

He takes us all through it again, what he found in the front hall, in Lily Carson's bedroom, in Morgan's.

"Anywhere else besides those three areas?" I ask.

"No," he says.

"So if I understand what you're telling us, Mr. Salzman," I continue, "you only recovered my client's DNA near where the bodies were found?"

"Yes, that's correct."

"Did you swab all the other surfaces of the Carson home?"

He hesitates.

Because he now knows what I've known all along about his work from that night.

"No," he says finally.

"Mr. Salzman," I continue, "how many murder scenes have you been present for in your career as a crime scene tech, whether as troubling or grotesque as this one or not?"

Salzman hesitates again, shifts slightly in his chair, gives a quick roll to his neck.

"This was my first," he says. "Of any kind."

"And by the time you did arrive there, as part of the second wave of respondents, that house must have been crawling with cops," I say.

"It was."

"Did they tell you to sweep all the other rooms in the house?"

"There was so much going on."

"I'm sure there was," I say, almost as if trying to be helpful.

Salzman swallows. I see a light sheen of sweat forming over his bald head.

"They told me to focus on the bodies," he says. He pauses,

and looks over to Katherine Welsh, as if looking to her for help. But none is forthcoming. Her witness is on his own. "There was so much blood," he says in a small voice.

"Totally understand," I say. "I'm a former cop, and have seen bad things, too. But just for the sake of this conversation, about this particular crime scene, let me ask you this: If you were looking to manipulate a murder scene, wouldn't you sprinkle DNA, almost like pixie dust, *only* in the immediate vicinity of the bodies?"

"Objection," Welsh says. "Ms. Smith once again leading a witness into a familiar fever dream."

"Overruled," Horton says, surprising both Katherine Welsh and me. "I'll allow it."

"I mean," Steve Salzman says, "I guess it's possible, if you look at it that way."

"And the best kind of DNA evidence, as I understand it, is the kind that shows hardly any indication of deterioration, which you've already testified yours didn't," I say, trying to sound smarter about science than I really am. "I mean, as opposed to more organic material."

"Again," Salzman says, almost reluctantly, "if that's your hypothesis, I guess so, yes."

"You *guess*?" I say. "Mr. Salzman, that's exactly how Cooper framed Bruce Willis in *Red*!"

The sound of Judge Horton's gavel and Katherine Welsh's objection fill the courtroom at almost the exact same moment.

"The next time I am forced to warn you about asides like that, Ms. Smith," Horton says, "I will hold you in contempt."

I nod, walk back toward Salzman one last time, as if Horton has just sent me to my room.

"So you didn't sweep all the rooms of the house, and you *only* found evidence near the bodies," I say.

"No," he says. "Or maybe I should say yes."

"No further questions for this witness," I say.

Katherine Welsh is already out of her chair and walking toward the guy who'd been her witness and turned out to be mine instead, looking to clean up the mess this tech just made, because sometimes that's all you can do, no matter which side of the aisle you're on.

As I pass her, I whisper, "That guy did frame Bruce. *Big time.*"

ONE HUNDRED NINE

I CALL MY NEXT witness, a retired police captain who is, next to Jimmy Cunniff, the smartest and best cop I've ever known. A friend of my father's when we lived in Patchogue, he now runs a private security firm in Manorville and has helped me out on other trials.

John Kyle looks younger than I know he is, more like an army general than a retired cop. Tall, bald, cobalt-blue eyes, ramrod perfect posture, even sitting down. Even in civilian clothes, he somehow seems to be in uniform. I half expect the members of the jury to sit up a little straighter once he's been sworn in.

Addressing him as Captain Kyle, I lead him into a brief history of his career. Then I get right to it, having already asked the clerk to put up the time-stamped photograph that Katherine Welsh has long since introduced into evidence, the one of Rob Jacobson walking down the Carsons' street the night of the murders.

"Captain Kyle," I say, "in your professional opinion, should the jury automatically assume that this photograph was actually taken on the night in question?"

"*Could* it have been?" he says. "Certainly. But that hardly means it's conclusive that it was."

"Please explain, sir."

Kyle says, "There are multiple photo editing programs now

available for digital pictures. Anybody has the ability to add them to their computers and devices. If you want a picture to appear to have been taken on a specific time and day, you could theoretically use any picture from your own files, change it by zooming in a little closer on it, then save it in its new form."

"So this new picture could have been created—I put quotes around 'created'—to show the desired date and time. In this case, the date and time shown on our screen?"

I walk over to the time stamp, which I asked the clerk in advance to highlight.

"If you had the phone used to take the picture," Captain Kyle continues, "you could set it in a savvy way that wouldn't be obvious but would stand up to even intense forensic examination."

"Is there any other way to falsify what is essentially supposed to be a moment frozen in time?" I ask him.

He nods, and grins. "There are other ways, actually, including nefarious ones."

I grin back at him. "Nefarious, sir?"

"Dishonest would be another way of putting it."

"Perhaps the kind of savvy and dishonest person looking to frame an innocent man?" I ask.

"Objection, Your Honor!" Welsh snaps. "I'm sorry, is this Ms. Smith questioning this witness, or her offering yet another preview, if an unsubstantiated one, of her summation?"

"Sustained," Judge Horton says. "Ms. Smith, you have made this same point on countless occasions throughout this proceeding. Ms. Welsh is right, in this instance: Save the editorializing for the summation, one I'm sure we all look forward to."

"I apologize profusely, Your Honor."

Profusely and insincerely.

To Captain John Kyle I say, "Please elaborate for the court the ways a dishonest person could alter a photograph like this one."

"You simply change the date and time on a cell phone or digital camera after you've unchecked your update tab," he says. "That alone will make the cell phone appear to have taken a picture on a particular date and time when it was, in fact, *not* taken at that time."

"That will be all, Captain," I say. "And thank you."

He's not quite finished, as it turns out. John Kyle isn't just not an ex-cop. He's a rigidly honest ex-cop.

"I'm not saying that's what happened with this particular photograph," he says. "But it absolutely could have happened." He shrugs. "I hope I haven't sounded too obtuse."

"Not obtuse at all, sir," I say. "Because when it comes to the *alleged*" — I give Katherine Welsh a quick look as I step hard on that word — "authenticity of what was presented as such a damning piece of evidence, you're really only talking about one important thing here."

I turn to fully face the jury.

"Reasonable doubt," I say.

Other than "Not guilty," the two most beautiful words in the English language.

ONE HUNDRED TEN

JUDGE HORTON ANNOUNCES A longer-than-usual lunch break—no explanation—so Norma Banks and I are having lunch at the Chefs Corner Café on Mineola Boulevard.

I order a salad. Norma orders a cheeseburger with bacon and sides of both onion rings and fries.

"Don't judge," she says when the food arrives.

"Hey," I say. "Whatever you're doing is working for you. And, let's face it, I'd make a lousy judge, anyway."

"How are you feeling, by the way?"

"In general, or today?"

"Today."

"I've had better todays, frankly."

"You need more color in that face," Norma says.

"Maybe we can stop and pick some up on the way back," I say. "I think we passed a CVS."

I'm having an iced tea. She's having a milkshake. Now she's just taunting me.

"How do you think I did this morning?" I ask.

"You did swell," she says. "But it doesn't matter."

She says it casually, as if she's just asked me to pass the ketchup.

"What's that supposed to mean?"

"Don't get me wrong, kid," she says. "You're good. I've

been at this a long time and you're as good as I've ever seen. But you need to know you're gonna lose this time."

"That does it," I say. "You're buying lunch."

"You want me to lie to you?"

"Maybe just a little."

She seems to inhale a French fry without even chewing it.

"I've been reading juries since before you were born," Norma Banks says. "It's part of my job, and I've got a gift for it. And these people think he did it, with all the head fakes you threw at them this morning about DNA and the time stamps and the rest of your bullshit."

My salad remains untouched in front of me. It's probably because I've quickly lost what little appetite I had when we sat down.

"So what would you suggest I do about that?" I ask her.

"Listen," she says. "I know how much you want an acquittal. The only one who wants one more is your sleazebag client."

I tell her what I told Katherine Welsh.

"What I want," I say, "is justice."

"For him?"

I shake my head.

"For them."

"Look me in the eye and tell me something," she says. "You still believe he didn't do it? And not because you need to believe it. Because in your heart you really do."

"So help me God," I say.

Like she's just sworn me in.

"Then you and your buddy need to find out who really did it before it's too late," she says.

It isn't that I'm suddenly feeling sick to my stomach. It's not that, I know that feeling, I've been living with it, off and on, for a while. This is different. I read somewhere once where this old football player was trying to define choking in sports, and finally just said it really was nothing more than a cold rush of shit to the heart.

344

I don't believe I'm choking away this case.

But sitting here across from Norma Banks in the diner, I feel as if I'm the one experiencing the cold rush of shit to the heart.

"Tell me what I need to do," I say, too loudly, to the woman who's become my surrogate mother, knowing it sounds as if I'm making a cry for help.

"I know what you need to do," a man says.

I look up and see Rob Jacobson standing over our table, neither Norma nor I having noticed him when he walked in.

"Put me on the stand," he says.

And in the next moment I hear myself say, "Okay."

ONE HUNDRED ELEVEN

I SPEND THE REST of the afternoon session questioning a couple of forensic experts I've used in the past.

I know I can't make the DNA belonging to Rob Jacobson disappear completely, as much of a magician as I consider myself. But I continue to throw as much shade on it as humanly possible, the way I did with the photograph of Rob Jacobson in the Carsons' neighborhood that night. If I haven't made the time stamp on that baby disappear, I've caused it to fade enough so as to be nearly invisible to the naked eye.

That's the way I see it, anyway.

Then as soon as Judge Horton announces we're adjourned, I'm back in the conference room with everybody on the team—except Jimmy, who has a meeting with Danny Esposito—to discuss the decision to put Rob Jacobson on the stand.

When everybody's seated, I say to Rob Jacobson, "I've had all afternoon to think about it, and I've changed my mind. I'm not putting you on the stand."

"Sorry, but it's not your call," he says. "It's mine, honey. And I don't need your permission to do it."

Honey.

"As long as I'm your lawyer you do need my permission, actually," I say.

"Am I allowed to ask what made you change your mind?" he asks.

I take a deep, calming breath, knowing it's probably a waste of time. But I give it a shot.

"It's my job to give you the best goddamn defense I can," I say. My voice is rising and I don't care if they can hear me in the goddamn hall. "I did it once, and against all *possible* odds might be about to do it again, unless you try to blow yourself up, which is what you'll be doing if you get on the stand. So, yeah, Rob, I changed my mind. What can I tell you? I'm a girl."

"You know, I wonder about that sometimes," he says.

Norma Banks leans over and says, "Are you looking to get slapped, sonny?"

"You've got it all wrong, grandma," Jacobson says. "Some of the women I screw like it rough. Not me." He gives me a quick look and says, "You can ask Janie's sister."

I'm the one who wants to slap him now. But before I can, Norma gets up and walks around the table and heads for the door. As she passes Rob she raises her hand just enough to make him flinch.

"You really are a bitch," she says to him.

The room is silent for a moment after she's gone.

Finally, McGoey says, "You don't want to do this, Rob."

"Listen, I know how risky it is," Rob Jacobson says. "But I've always been a risk taker."

"You mean other than with underaged girls?" I ask.

Jacobson's eyes narrow to slits as he turns to face me. The room has now officially turned into a hockey fight.

"You can follow grandma right out the door if you want," he says. "I'm not taking any shit from you either, Thomas."

"Listen to Jane," McGoey says.

"No, you listen to me," Jacobson snaps at McGoey. "Janie here wouldn't even have considered this if she didn't think our case is going into the shitter."

He turns back to me. "You're not saying anything because you know I'm right."

"It had to happen eventually," I say.

McGoey extends his hands toward both of us, as if stopping traffic. "We need to take the temperature down," he says.

"Listen, if either of you is worried about me handling that bitch DA, don't," he says.

I stare down at my hands, as if I'm addressing them. Or am I just trying to keep them where they are.

"She will eat you alive," I say.

"Why?" Jacobson says. "Because she's another woman who thinks she's smarter than me?"

"Well, for starters, yeah," I say.

I am still managing to keep myself under control. But barely. I can feel the heat rising in me, ready to explode. Mount Saint Jane.

"Just listen to me for once," Jacobson says. "So maybe I might not be able to charm the pants off the esteemed Ms. Welsh. I'll concede that. But I sure as hell can do it with the women on that jury." The smirk is back, just like that, not that it's ever very far away. "And maybe a few of the guys, too. You might not believe this, but dudes dig me, too."

My father made me learn the Serenity Prayer after he finally stopped drinking and joined AA. I can hear him reciting it to me inside my head now, from what feels like a hundred years ago.

Give me the serenity to accept the things I cannot change . . .

Jacobson lays his palms flat on the table, making me think he's finished his dumb-assed presentation.

"So are we done here?" I ask.

"Not quite," he says, then adds, "I've been saving the best for last."

He pauses, but only briefly.

"You're not going to be the one questioning me, Janie," he says. "Thomas is. And I'll tell you why before you even ask: Knowing Thomas, it won't bother him nearly as much as it would bother you when I get up there and lie my ass off."

I sit there in a kind of stunned silence. I thought I was beyond being surprised by him. Wrong again.

"Aren't you going to say anything?"

"Just this one thing you've heard before," I say, my voice still sounding relatively calm, but knowing that the explosion is here. "But something about which I am now as serious as cancer."

I get up now and walk around the table and get so close to him our noses are nearly touching, and my voice explodes out of me, nearly knocking him back over in his chair.

"*I fucking quit.*"

ONE HUNDRED TWELVE

STILL ON FIRE, I walk out and down the hall and blow past Judge Michael Horton's assistant so quickly there's no attempt made to stop me, and I give one firm rap on his door and walk right in on him without being announced.

"Pardon the interruption," I say.

I expect him to be angry with me, as he so frequently is in his courtroom. He's dressed in an old-fashioned cardigan sweater with pockets on the sides; he's clearly getting ready to leave. But instead of chastising me, he surprises me with a wide grin.

Pardon the Interruption? Horton says. "I love that show."

I know he's talking about an ESPN show, one I've occasionally watched myself. But I'm not here to kick around the sports issues of the day.

"You seem upset, Ms. Smith," he says.

"No shit, Your Honor," I say, "with all due respect, of course. I only need a couple of minutes of your time."

"That's all you're getting," he says. "Mrs. Horton has promised to hand me a martini, perfectly chilled, when I walk through the door." He cocks his head slightly. "A martini I richly deserve after today's antics."

"I'm withdrawing as Rob Jacobson's counsel," I say, then add, "effective immediately."

He sits back down behind his desk, briefly closes his eyes, opens them.

"May I ask why?"

I imagine in this moment that he's slipped his robe back on and slipped right back into character, if reluctantly.

I tell him about the conversation I've just had with my team and with my client in the conference room, excluding the part where Rob Jacobson has promised to flat-out lie on the stand. I'm unwilling to breach privilege, even with this client, honoring my profession even though it means protecting him.

Horton gives me a long look and says, "There's not a chance in hell that I'm allowing this." His eyes narrow. "No shit."

"Your Honor, I can't in good conscience continue to defend him under these circumstances."

"You mean because he wants to break up with you?" Horton says. "Get over it."

"No," I say. "It's because I'm charged with giving him the best defense possible, and he's about to make it *im*possible for me to do that."

"Thomas McGoey is an accomplished trial attorney."

"He doesn't know this man the way I do!" I'm shouting again, just like that. So I take a deep breath and sit down in one of the chairs across from his desk, doing that before I fall down, I am suddenly that exhausted, by just about everything.

"And yet," Horton says placidly, "you have now represented this man in two murder trials for which, I am guessing, you didn't hire yourself."

"Things have changed," I say. "There's simply too much conflict for me to live with."

"Get over that, too," Horton says. The smile has disappeared that quickly. "We both know you're not a quitter and never have been and never will be."

"I know," I say quietly, getting myself under control, aware that yelling at this man will get me about as far as it just did with Rob Jacobson. "I *know*. That's why it was so difficult for me to come in here and even make this request."

"And even if you really wanted to quit, which I believe you don't, there aren't enough grounds or enough conflict for me to consider this request," Horton continues. "Is there some ethical issue I should know about?"

It won't bother Thomas nearly as much as it would bother you when I get up there and lie my ass off.

"Not that I'm at liberty to share," I say.

"Then we're done here," he says. "And let me just add that you're too good a lawyer to have thought even for a New York minute that I was going to open the door even a crack for a mistrial at this stage of the game," he says.

He comes around the desk, reaches down to help me out of my chair without being asked, begins to walk me to his door.

"And if you ever mention quitting to me again I will hold you in contempt," he says.

And in that moment, I shrug off Michael Horton and step back and look at him and say, "Do it."

"What did you say?"

"Do it," I say.

"You're on very thin ice here, Ms. Smith."

"Deal with it," I say. "I've been living on thin ice for a while."

Then I tell him what I just told my client, minus the language, not sure if he can cite me for contempt right here.

"I quit," I say, and walk out of his chambers.

ONE HUNDRED THIRTEEN

Jimmy

JIMMY CUNNIFF IS STANDING with Danny Esposito in the living room of the Carson house, listening as Esposito continues to complain about having to drive from East Farmingdale to be here, and for what?

"You're aware that this is a complete waste of my time, right?" Esposito says. "And I'm gonna admit something to you, even as long as I've been at this kind of work: There's something about this place that gives me the creeps."

"Poor baby," Jimmy says.

"Tell me again what we're doing here, just so I have it clear."

"We're here doing our goddamn jobs, hotshot," Jimmy says.

"Hey, relax," Esposito says, making a calming gesture with his hands. "I'm as frustrated by this whole thing as you are."

Jimmy gives him a long look. "No you're not," he says quietly, "unless you've got a partner with cancer you haven't mentioned."

"You're gonna play that card?" Esposito says. "Seriously?" But he manages a grin. "Because if you are, that's it, you win."

Esposito is in the same uniform he almost always wears: bomber jacket, jeans, boots, shades. Still going through life needing a haircut and a shave, even though it's always just a trim with both.

"Are we looking for anything in particular?" he asks.

"Yeah," Jimmy says. "Something everybody else missed."

"Well, okay then, since you put it like that," Danny Esposito says. "Finding shit everybody else has missed is one of my specialties. Some might even call it a gift."

"You really are a cocky bastard, aren't you?" Jimmy asks.

"Why do you think we get along so well?"

Jimmy turns and sees Esposito giving him another crooked grin, as if to say he's also going through life knowing shit that nobody else does. Jimmy has met a lot of young hotshots like him. But he keeps finding out this one is special, Esposito having just proved it again by discovering Eric Jacobson in Morgan Carson's yearbook. Not that he's going to admit that to him now.

When Jimmy asked Esposito to meet him at the house, he explained that they now had to treat this like a whole new ball game because of the yearbook picture, that Eric Jacobson had to have been stalking the Carson girl, in plain sight, even getting as close as sitting right behind her at a high school football game.

"Doesn't mean he had anything to do with killing her," Esposito says.

"Doesn't mean he didn't," Jimmy says. "And doesn't mean either one of us is going to start believing in coincidence at this late date."

"Still would be one giant leap for mankind to go from that to him framing his asshole father for murder," Esposito says.

"We needed to come over here and feel this place," Jimmy says.

"Now you're going all touchy-feely on me?"

"You know exactly what I mean," Jimmy says. "Just being here a few minutes the other day when the Jacobson kid and McKenzie ambushed Jane, got me pissed off all over again about what happened here."

No grin from Esposito now.

"I hear you," he says. "And just standing here makes me feel the same way."

"Stick with me, kid," Jimmy says. "You'll learn a lot."

"Fuck off," Esposito says, and they both laugh, the sound much too loud in the quiet of the Carson house.

Jimmy says he'll take the upstairs. But all he finds up here isn't more anger, it's the sadness Jane described after being in Morgan Carson's room. And for some reason, one he isn't sure he understands, Jimmy is just as sad in the main bedroom, where they found the mother, Lily, that night. Lily Carson: who, when she was her daughter's age, had been Rob Jacobson's prom date.

Now Jacobson stands accused of murdering her, and Jimmy is goddamn sure he'll never be as convinced of his innocence as Jane is.

When they meet again downstairs, Esposito says, "You find anything of interest?"

Jimmy shakes his head.

"You want to switch, and you look around down here and I'll go back up there?"

Jimmy is still shaking his head. "Other people miss shit," he says. "We don't."

"So we done here?"

"Not quite," Jimmy says. "Let's take a walk around the property."

"For the exercise, Batman?"

"Because I still feel like there's something *we're* missing," Jimmy says.

"Another feeling?"

"Go ahead and kid," Jimmy says. "But yeah."

"Those feelings ever wrong?"

"Hardly ever."

They head outside and separate again, Jimmy going right, Esposito going left. They've both noticed the Ring doorbell camera over the front door and know from the police reports that there are three others on the house, one on the right side, one on the left, one over the back door. All had been deactivated, they learned from the Garden City cops, on the night of the murders.

"Paranoid much, Hank?" Esposito says.

"And in the end," Jimmy says, "all the security in the world did him no freaking good."

"Guns win again," Esposito says. "Amazing how often it works out that way."

They are standing in the middle of the back patio. The lawn that stretches out in front of them looks perfectly manicured, which means someone is attending to it, maybe the bank that now holds the paper on the house and is getting ready to sell it as soon as the trial ends. Did the killer come through the door here, or the one in front, or even through a window? They'll probably never know.

Jimmy notices the hummingbird feeder, full of rust now, but still hanging from the sturdy branch of a small tree on the other side of a low brick wall.

He thinks: *What is it with women and these damn twitchy birds?*

Suddenly, though, he is staring at the feeder, as if he's being pulled toward it by some kind of weird magnetic force, no birds in sight; Jimmy knows from Jane that they're supposed to have migrated south for the winter, Jane sounding as sad when she told him this as if Rip the dog had run away.

Jesus Christ, he thinks.

The old altar boy in him has him bowing his head, even though he hasn't said the Lord's name out loud.

He walks toward the feeder, until he is right in front of it, now frozen in place, eyes fixed on the feeder.

"Well, I'll be damned," he says softly.

Esposito walks over now. "What?" he asks.

Jimmy reaches over and puts his finger on a small camera set into the top of the feeder, almost invisible against the black paint, as small as the camera he sewed into his Yankee cap.

"This is what," Jimmy says, pointing.

Esposito leans closer. "I had a girlfriend had one of these," he says. "You can take pictures of the birds with this thing."

"Maybe not just birds," Jimmy Cunniff says.

ONE HUNDRED FOURTEEN

IT TAKES JIMMY AND Esposito all of the next day to find what they hoped they might find, if they finally did catch a break.

The separate company that Hank Carson had hired to install the camera in the feeder—called WeSeeU, an out-fit neither Jimmy nor Esposito has ever heard of—wouldn't even talk to them until Danny got a court order. Once he did, they checked back on Hank Carson's account and told them that the camera was still operational on the date in question, the night the murders at the Carson home had been committed, the battery not dying until a month or so later.

But whatever footage there was, from that night and the time leading up to it, was stored on Hank Carson's iCloud.

Jimmy and Esposito have set up shop at Jimmy's house by now. Court wasn't in session today because Katherine Welsh requested an additional twenty-four hours—and perhaps more than that—to prepare for cross-examining Rob Jacobson once Thomas McGoey finishes with him.

Welsh doesn't know that Jane has quit the case. Apparently, the judge hasn't said anything to Welsh, because he thinks Jane will change her mind. It just says to Jimmy that Judge Michael Horton hasn't been paying close enough attention to the action.

Jimmy and Danny Esposito are seated side-by-side at Jimmy's kitchen table now, both of them staring at the screen of Jimmy's laptop. It turns out that Carson, paranoid to the end, had separate iCloud accounts, too.

They don't have a password for the one where the feeder video is stored.

"So how do we get in?" Jimmy asks. "And good luck trying to get a court order that Apple ever gives a shit about when someone is trying to storm the privacy barricade."

"You forget something," Danny Esposito says. "I already hacked into Jane's phone as a way of keeping track of her."

"Another gift?" Jimmy asks.

"Bet your ass," Esposito says.

"You figure out a way in and I might kiss you," Jimmy says.

"Wait," Esposito says, "that's your idea of a pep talk?"

It takes a couple more hours, but eventually they gain access to Carson's files. At one point Esposito says, "Check this out," touching his index finger to the screen.

"All I'm seeing is numbers," Jimmy says.

"This is a bank account I bet even the lovely Mrs. Carson didn't know existed," Esposito says. "It turns out that old Hank did pay Sonny back before he died."

Esposito needs more time to sort through Carson's files and all their various hidey-holes, a lot of them containing very detailed accounts of what a shitty gambler he'd been, Esposito bitching every time he would end up going down another rabbit hole.

Finally, Danny Esposito says, "Now *I'll* be damned."

Both of their noses are nearly touching the screen. They turn to look at each other, then back at the screen, and the images on it. Two men, captured on the camera from the bird feeder, walking in through the back door of the Carson house, guns out. The time stamp lines up perfectly with the evening of the murders. And this time stamp, they both know, is real.

Jimmy puts up his hand and Esposito gives him a soft high-five.

"Gotcha," Jimmy says to the images of Eric Jacobson and Edmund McKenzie on the screen in front of them.

ONE HUNDRED FIFTEEN

THE BIG-ASSED HOUSE, OVERLOOKING Mecox Bay in Water Mill, is only a few miles from where Paul Harrington, once the head dirty cop of Sonny Blum's squad of dirty cops, lived and died.

By now Jimmy and Esposito have called Jane to tell her what they've got and who they've got and where they're going, before heading to the Southampton Town Police to pick up an arrest warrant.

"This one we do by the book," Esposito says. "This arrest ain't getting tossed the way Harrington's was."

"Gee, I sure hope they don't resist," Jimmy says from the passenger seat.

"Wouldn't that be a crying fucking shame?" Danny Esposito says.

Jimmy smiles to himself. This is what it was like in the old days, with his partner Mickey Dunne, sitting in the front seat of the car and closing in on something big.

Looking to close something, period.

There is one car parked in the driveway, the one with the tracking device that led them straight here.

They drive a quarter mile or so up the street and park, then walk back to the house. By now they both have their guns out.

"You think they'll be armed?" Esposito says, sounding almost hopeful.

"Probably," Jimmy Cunniff says quietly. "Armed and stupid."

Jimmy says he'll go around to the back. He tries the back door and finds it unlocked. As he eases himself into the kitchen, he hears rock music coming from the front of the house.

Jimmy keeps his Glock out in front of him as he silently makes his way through the kitchen and into a small dining room, betting on it being just the two of them inside.

He stops before he gets to the open door at the far end of the dining room and sees the two of them, facing each other on matching couches, a giant bottle of Tito's vodka on the coffee table between them, the bottle set in a crystal ice bucket. Nothing but the best for these rich assholes.

Jimmy feels his heart beating so loudly inside his chest he's afraid they might hear it from the living room, even over the music coming out of the speakers.

It is at this moment that Danny Esposito comes through the front door and appears in the foyer, his own Glock pointed straight at them.

"Eric Jacobson and Edmund McKenzie," he announces, "you are both under arrest for the murders of Hank Carson, Lily Carson, and Morgan Carson." He pauses just long enough for them to process that before he adds, "You worthless sacks of shit."

McKenzie doesn't move right away. Neither does Jacobson.

"You're the sack of shit if you don't have a warrant," McKenzie says.

He even takes a sip of vodka.

"Don't say another word," Eric Jacobson says to McKenzie. "Not another fucking word."

"You don't tell me what to do," McKenzie says.

Then, to Esposito, McKenzie says, "What, you think you got proof?"

Esposito grins his crooked grin.

"I got the two of you on the one camera you didn't disable that night, asshole," Danny Esposito says.

Jimmy moves in from the dining room, behind them and out of their range of vision, without announcing himself, gun steady in front of him.

Armed and stupid.

He's got his eyes on McKenzie, but that's not what distracts him now, and distracts Danny Esposito.

It's Eric Jacobson standing suddenly, putting his hands out as if for them to be cuffed, saying, "Let's get this shit over with."

As he does, McKenzie quickly leans over and reaches for a gun that Jimmy hasn't spotted near the ice bucket, and neither did Esposito. McKenzie grabs the gun and rolls forward, trying to get underneath the coffee table, before firing off two shots at Danny Esposito, the first one blowing a hole into a painting behind him. The second hits the ceiling.

"Fuck you!" Edmund McKenzie yells as he comes up and aims at Danny again.

Jimmy and Danny both fire on McKenzie before he can get off another shot; the simultaneous gunshots sound like a single bomb going off. Eric Jacobson dives for cover. The bullets hit McKenzie center mass, like two bullets grouped neatly inside the bull's-eye of a target at the Maidstone Gun Club.

Like Jimmy and Danny are competing with each other, the way Jimmy and Jane do.

Jimmy fires again, hitting McKenzie again, pretty much in the same grouping, firing the last shot for the Carsons.

Maybe for the kid most of all.

On this night the blood, a lot of blood, on him and on the expensive carpet and on the couch, belongs to Edmund McKenzie.

They hear Eric Jacobson say, "I want a lawyer."

"The best one's taken," Jimmy says as Esposito leans over

to cuff him. "Pity." Eric Jacobson remains prone on the carpet, hands behind his back.

Jimmy goes over and kneels next to McKenzie, who he can see is dying.

Just not yet.

And, as it turns out, still in love with the sound of his own voice.

ONE HUNDRED SIXTEEN

Sonny Blum

ROBBY SASSOON IS SITTING with Sonny Blum in the den of Sonny's home in Port Washington, one of his many. Robby has been called here by the old man. Sonny already knows about the shootout in Water Mill.

"If they finally lock the Jacobson kid up at the jail in Riverhead," Blum says, "maybe he can get some kind of family discount."

Blum knows what he knows, as he tells Robby, because he has a cop in Southampton on his payroll, the same way he has cops on his payroll just about everywhere.

Robby jumped at the chance to have a face-to-face with the boss. Maybe this is how he's going to be told about his next assignment. He's assuming it has to be Jane Smith, or her investigator.

Or both.

He and Blum both have glasses of whiskey in their hands. It's late, but they have been talking for a while. It's not often that Sonny Blum gets to confide in somebody like this.

"I've always been a big-picture guy," Blum says now. "Not so much of a detail guy. But then, I got guys like you to handle details, which means doing their fucking jobs the way I want them done."

They both drink. It's a warm night, but Blum still has a fire going.

"What I've always known, though, as a big-picture guy," Blum continues, "is the power of information. You hear people talk about information being power all the time. But, see, with me it was always information *and* power. It's why I started putting all those cops on scholarship, way back. Joe Champi. Anthony Licata. You ever hear of them?"

Robby nods.

"I had them on the payroll at the start, along with their boss, Harrington," Blum says. "The one you just capped."

Robby smiles. "He never saw it coming."

"Sometimes that's the best way, am I right?" Blum says, and starts laughing, until the laughter dissolves into a coughing fit.

There's a glass of water next to the whiskey. He drinks some of that and the coughing eventually stops.

"It all started around the same time, me owning these cops and owning Jacobson and McKenzie after the two of them got high one day, high as a kite in high *school,* and shot Jacobson's old man and his girlfriend," Blum says. "My cops show up and they collect all the evidence, and they immediately know they've got these kids by the balls. So I've got two rich kids. I've got McKenzie's old man, too. And from that moment on, just with Jacobson's money and the money from McKenzie's old man, it's like they're a main branch of the Bank of Sonny Blum. How'd that old song go? I felt rich as Rockefeller."

Robby smiles and raises his glass, in admiration. "Nice work if you can get it."

Blum drinks more whiskey now. "And the money has been flowing, from the Jacobson family and the McKenzie family, ever since."

"Sounds like a sweetheart deal," Robby says.

"But then this Rob Jacobson, as much of a dumb-ass as he is when it comes to women, turns out to be a smart bastard," Blum says. "And when he's old enough, he cuts himself a side deal with Joe Champi. Used to call him his Uncle Joe. At which point Joe is double-dipping out of the same pot. And unfortunately, what Joe is selling is proof of me doing all kinds of things—including the kind of shit you do for me—that would put me away for about two hundred years."

"How come you didn't have me take him out?" Robby says.

"Jacobson?"

"Yes, sir."

"Because he made it clear that he had it set up so's if anything like that ever happened to him, the shit he had on me would go to the cops and to the feds," Blum says. "So now Rob Jacobson and me, we had each other by the balls."

"So how come you didn't have me take out Champi?"

"I was about to," he says, "except the lawyer lady took him out first."

Blum pauses as if he just remembered something and says, "You still seeing Jacobson's wife, by the way?"

"Sadly, no," Robby says. "But I've got to tell you, Mr. Blum, it was fun while it lasted."

"No shit," Sonny Blum says. "The pictures you took of the two of you? I sent them to Jacobson. Just to remind him I can get to him anytime I want and anyway I want if he ever tries to screw me over."

He finishes his drink.

"I hate loose ends," Blum says.

He stands now. It's late and he's tired. Getting old truly is for shit. How can you be this old with a fire going?

He notices Sassoon's glass is empty, too.

"Is it time for me to take out Smith and Cunniff, Mr. Blum?" Robby asks. "I assume that was one of the reasons you wanted to see me tonight. You've already told me I'll have to get that done at one point or another."

Blum nods. "It's time," he says, then points to Sassoon's own empty glass. "One more for the road?"

"Why not?" Robby Sassoon says.

The old man takes a long time getting out of his chair, shuffles across the room, takes Sassoon's glass out of his hand as he heads for the bar behind him.

"You really are good at what you do," Sonny says.

"Well, thank you, sir."

"Too good," Blum says, before he takes the gun out of his pocket and blows the back of Robby Sassoon's head off, the sound like a cannon going off in his den, able to back up quickly enough that the blood doesn't get on him, not that he would care much either way.

He watches Sassoon slump to the side, hit man who just got hit, almost like poetic justice, blood pouring out of the head wound, what's left of him slowly sliding out of the chair and onto the floor.

Sonny Blum looks down at the body. It's time for a new rug in here, anyway.

ONE HUNDRED SEVENTEEN

JIMMY AND BEN AND Danny Esposito and I are celebrating the next night at Jimmy's bar. Thomas McGoey is there, too, along with Norma Banks, who already might be the most overserved person in the place.

I have even allowed myself a second glass of wine.

McGoey is the last to get here, having just arrived from the courthouse, the charges against Rob Jacobson having been officially dropped a few hours ago, not just because of the video from the bird feeder, but because of what turned out to be the late Edmund McKenzie's rambling deathbed confession, recorded from the floor of the house in Water Mill, on Danny Esposito's phone, before McKenzie was DOA at Southampton Hospital.

Judge Horton was persuaded. So was Katherine Welsh.

Just like that, it was over. I didn't make the trip to Mineola, mostly because I don't want to be part of another photo op with Rob Jacobson for as long as I live.

Even if I somehow manage to live.

"Who's going to represent Eric?" I ask McGoey. "Rob mention anything to you about that?"

McGoey doesn't answer right away, somehow managing to look everywhere in Jimmy's bar except at me.

"Don't you tell me this, McGoey," I say. "Do *not* tell me this. Or you may be out of this bar."

"I haven't officially told him yes," McGoey says.

"If you didn't say no, you know you've already decided to do it."

"His dad is going to pay my fee," McGoey says. "The full boat."

"Now you've really got to be shitting me," I say. "After he and McKenzie tried to set him up for murder *twice*?"

"Rob says he feels guilty that his own son could hate him even more than Rob hated his own father," McGoey says.

McKenzie told Jimmy and Danny Esposito a lot before he died. Jimmy says it was clear even to McKenzie that the ambulance probably wasn't going to get to him in time, as much as both Jimmy and Esposito tried to stop the bleeding, not wanting to lose him.

Once Eric Jacobson was on his way to the Southampton police station, McKenzie confessed that he and Eric had been planning the Carson murders for a long time. Eric had somehow found out Rob Jacobson was doing yet another mother-daughter act, this time with Rob's old prom date; Eric knew the act very well because there had been multiple occasions when Rob Jacobson had taken girls away from his own son.

Jimmy asked McKenzie which one of them knew enough about DNA to arrange the frame-up. Jimmy forgot that McKenzie had once told him what a science whiz he was before he dropped out of Princeton.

I could have been on one of those CSI shows.

Eric had been the one who helped harvest his father's DNA. It had taken time, and a lot of secret visits to the house in Sagaponack. But he'd managed.

Jane watched the video of McKenzie from Esposito's phone. Twice. When Jimmy asked why they had framed Rob and then waited to do anything about it, McKenzie, even starting to fade, actually choked out a laugh before croaking, "Because we both liked it so much, we wanted to do it again."

Then they knew that Rob Jacobson's DNA would be in the system once they'd done a less elaborate frame on the Gates murders. After that, they were prepared to sit back with their popcorn and watch the movie play out, even if they had to sit through the same movie twice.

"It must've been when they started to worry that you might get him off that they tried to kill both of us," Jimmy says.

"They both hated Rob that much," I say, almost in wonder.

Jimmy says, "McKenzie just hated him longer."

Then Jimmy tells me something we both heard on the tape.

"And if you got him acquitted again, they were just gonna kill him this time," Jimmy says. "And then probably us."

He raises his glass of Scotch.

"But they were just the latest to find out how hard we are to kill, Janie," he says.

I raise my own glass, clink it gently against his, and then smile at my partner.

"And they might have gotten away with it," I say, "if it hadn't been for the hummingbirds."

We drink to hummingbirds then.

It's the last thing I remember before I wake up in the ambulance, sure I'm dying.

ONE HUNDRED EIGHTEEN

WHEN I OPEN MY eyes, Jimmy Cunniff is sitting next to my bed.

"Hi," he says.

He puts up his hand, in a small, almost sheepish wave.

"Hi," I say.

Groggy as I am, I look around and can see I'm in a hospital room.

"How long was I out?" I ask.

"Since last night," he says.

I can see I'm hooked up to an IV and to a heart monitor that is hopefully doing efficient, heart-monitoring things.

"I remember being in the ambulance," I say. "And then nothing after that."

"I was there with you, till you went out again," he says. "Ben and me. I had to practically pull a gun on them to let us ride with you."

I slowly lift my hand, the one with the IV port attached to it, the same kind they used on me for chemo. My arm feels so heavy, like I'm trying to lift up the back of my car.

"What happened to me?" I ask.

From the other side of the room, I now hear the voice of Dr. Sam Wylie.

"A whole bunch of bad shit," she says, "all at once."

She comes around my bed now and stands behind Jimmy.

"Is that your professional opinion, doctor?" I ask her.

She smiles.

"Not exactly as I was taught in med school," she says. "But I gotta say, pal, in this case it's *accurate* as shit."

The room goes silent then, except for the monitor. I hear the PA system outside in the hallway, a nurse being summoned to one of the rooms on my floor. The ping of an elevator bell. Hospital sounds. Again. I've spent too much time in hospitals lately, in two countries.

Now I am back.

It never ends.

But I knew that before ending up here again.

"Is this about my cancer?" I ask Sam Wylie finally.

"Yes and no," she says.

ONE HUNDRED NINETEEN

DR. BEN KALINSKY COMES into the room, having gone to get coffee for him and for Jimmy. He leans over and kisses me on the forehead, pulls up a chair next to Jimmy, and takes my free hand in his.

"But I *am* back from the abyss?" I ask Sam Wylie.

She looks fabulous, as always, in a navy dress. She's even wearing pearls.

"Back from the abyss yet again," she says.

She does her best then to simplify what I generally refer to as her doctor hooptedoodle. The first time I used the expression, she told me in her smart-ass way that it actually came from a John Steinbeck book. She even told me what book. *Sweet Thursday.*

The things you remember.

Sam tells me that fainting the way I did at Jimmy's bar was the culmination of what she says was a perfect medical storm: the drugs in my system, fatigue, dehydration yet again, hypertension, dangerously low blood pressure, and the thing that she said was like a lit fuse for all the rest of it, anemia.

"Are there any boxes that I didn't check?" I ask when she's finished.

"Yeah," Sam Wylie says. "A broken fucking leg."

She further explains that the IV to which I'm attached

has been pumping me with a cocktail of vitamins, minerals, antioxidants, and fluids ever since I was admitted last night.

"So maybe drinking wine wasn't the best idea I've had lately?"

Sam smiles again. "Yeah, but ask yourself something, Jane," she says. "When has an extra glass of wine ever been a good idea for you?"

"So, I'm not dying."

"Not today."

"So when can I get out of here?"

Ben squeezes my hand. "Asks Miss Impatient," he says.

"Just a bad patient, if you ask me," Jimmy says.

"Look who's talking," I say.

"Mike Gellis is on his way," Sam says.

My oncologist.

"Since you were already so nice to come to the hospital," she continues, "Mike doesn't see any reason to wait until next week to do more imaging on the tumor."

"Hey, I'm fine with waiting," I say.

Ben turns to look up at Sam. "What can I tell you?" he says to her. "The impatience comes and goes."

"Oh, trust me," she says. "I know."

"I just want to go home and see my dog," I say. "Who's looking after him, by the way?"

"Kenny," Jimmy says. "World-class bartender and world-class friend to dogs. It's people he's not very good with. Even *for* a bartender."

"So we're going to find out if the tumor has grown or shrunk since the last imaging?" I ask Sam.

"Quickly," she says.

"And if it has shrunk a little more?"

"Then we throw another party," she says. "Just without the extra glass of wine."

I know the drill by now. "CT scan?" I ask.

She nods.

Now the only thing I can hear in the hospital room is the beating of my own heart. I look over and see a little jump in the needle on the monitor.

I want the tests and I don't.

"What if it *has* grown?" I say finally.

"Shut it," Sam Wylie says.

ONE HUNDRED TWENTY

THEY DECIDE TO KEEP me another night at Southampton Hospital.

Sam Wylie says it's strictly precautionary. I tell her before she leaves that I'm sorry, but I have to call BS on that. When you are living with cancer, when that's your reality and your world, you don't think any part of the process is precautionary. If your life were a movie, you'd be sure that in the very next scene somebody would be coming through the door with a gun.

"Dr. Gellis wants to wait until tomorrow and back up the CT scan with an MRI," Sam says.

"Why does he want an MRI, too?"

"Because he wants to be sure," she says.

"Of what?"

"Of all the things we need to be sure of before we tell you where we are," she says, and promises me that they will fast-track the results as soon as the tests are finished in the morning, or several people at Southampton Hospital will be ripped a new one.

I tell her what I always tell my sister, Brigid, whom I spoke to from Switzerland a few hours ago, where she's hooked up to her own machines, and undergoing more tests of her own, because we're both a couple of lucky ducks.

"And people think you're the nice one," I say to Sam Wylie.

She gives me a kiss of her own on the forehead then and leaves me with Ben.

When it's just the two of us I say, "I'm scared about tomorrow."

"I know."

If his chair were any closer, he'd be in the bed with me.

Neither one of us speaks then, for several minutes. He just sits there and holds my hand and seems content to do it all night. Somehow this good man has made me more comfortable with unspoken thoughts, and silences like this, than I've ever been in my life, with anyone.

"At least you're done with Rob Jacobson," he says eventually. "That has to make you feel like you've been given a brand-new lease on life."

"Hardly," I say. "But at least we know what happened to the Carsons. And to the Gateses. And I have some sort of understanding why those two sociopaths *made* it happen." I turn my head so I'm looking directly at him. "But is that justice?"

"Maybe on that one," he says, "you need to do that thing you're always talking about."

"Which thing is that?"

"Let God sort the rest of it out."

I am able to manage a smile. Not much of one. I can only imagine what I look like at this point. But I can still feel the smile.

And somehow manage to feel safe.

"I've sort of been busy asking Her to do that for me the last couple of days," I say. "Not to keep making this all about me."

"Hey, kid," he says. He gets out of his chair and kisses me lightly on the lips. "As far as I'm concerned, it's *only* about you."

Before cancer the end of a trial had always felt like crossing the finish line, like finishing some sort of marathon no matter how long the trial had lasted. And before Rob Jacobson—a different kind of malignancy—came into my life, the end of a trial had been cause for celebration, for Jimmy and for me.

Just not now.

After what feels like hours, I can feel myself starting to fall asleep, the pill they gave me finally starting to work, feeling as if I'm waiting for another verdict to be handed down.

I pray then.

And tonight don't dream about anything at all.

ONE HUNDRED TWENTY-ONE

I TAKE MY RIDE through both machines first thing the next morning, the MRI taking longer than the CT scan, as I knew it would.

Then I go back to my room and shower and dress and do a little bit of makeup work, as much for me as for Ben Kalinsky. And maybe even for the fabulous Sam Wylie.

Then I wait.

There's always more waiting.

Ben and Jimmy come back into the room after I'm dressed and ready to get out of here and get home and see Rip the dog. And hopefully, by the grace of God Herself, get on with the rest of my very long life.

We all wait for two more hours, during which I feel, truly, as if time has stopped, and the waiting just might kill me before cancer ever does.

"This can't possibly be good," I say. "How can it possibly be good if it's taking this long?"

"Still a bad patient," Jimmy says, doing everything he possibly can to lighten the mood.

"Might be the worst I've ever encountered," Dr. Ben Kalinsky says, "at least among humans."

"This isn't funny," I say.

"We know," Ben says quietly.

By now I know my vitals are back to normal. My blood pressure is all the way normal again. My anemia has been addressed; otherwise, the nurse tells me, they wouldn't even be thinking about releasing me.

And yet with all that, I feel as if I might pass out all over again. If hypotension was a contributing factor to my fainting spell and going down for the count at Jimmy's bar, as Sam told me it was, this now feels like tension on steroids.

At last, a little before one o'clock, there is a knock on the door and Sam Wylie and Dr. Mike Gellis come walking into my room.

As they enter, I realize I have backed myself into a corner of the room without even realizing I've done that.

"Gee," I say, just to say something to alleviate the tension, at least for me, "that didn't take long."

"We wanted to be sure before we talked to you," Sam Wylie says.

"Sure," I say. "You guys are doctors. You're not like lawyers." I laugh nervously. "You can't make things up."

She smiles. "Let somebody else talk for a change."

"I'll shut it now," I say.

Ben comes over and stands next to me and takes my hand. Jimmy is on the other side of me.

"When we looked at the CT scan, we thought there had to be some kind of mistake," Mike Gellis says. "But then the MRI confirmed it."

I look across the room and see Sam Wylie start to cry.

"Tell me, Sam," I say.

She takes a deep breath and keeps crying.

"The tumor is gone," she says.

I feel all the air go out of my body.

The best I can do in the moment is this: "Gone where?"

And the esteemed Dr. Michael Gellis, whom I have never

heard ever utter anything resembling a bad word, smiles and says, "Beats the shit out of me."

Then I am crying, and starting to slide down the wall, until Jimmy and Dr. Ben Kalinsky each grab an arm to catch me.

"We got you," Jimmy Cunniff says, and then I can see that he's crying, too.

ONE HUNDRED TWENTY-TWO

IT IS TWO DAYS later.

By now I feel as if I could pass a spot quiz about the spontaneous regression of tumors, and how the body can sometimes trigger its own response against specific antigens on the surface of cells, in combination with the drugs and the treatment a patient has received. The patient being me, in this case, and the chemo treatments I had already received, and most recently the antibody drug conjugants I received at the Meier Clinic.

"In the end," Dr. Sam Wylie told me, "what just happened to you is difficult to quantify."

Then she hugged me and said, "The best way for me to explain it in a way you can understand is that sometimes all the shit you've been taking actually works."

On this particular morning Dr. Ben Kalinsky is in surgery. But we are planning dinner tonight, our first night out since I got my news at the hospital, at Page in Sag Harbor. We may even show up early for a drink at Jimmy's.

Eric Jacobson was arraigned this morning at the same courthouse in Mineola where his father had been on trial for murders that Eric and Edmund McKenzie had committed, out of hate and madness.

Thomas McGoey, bless his heart, was at Eric's side for the arraignment.

When Thomas started to speak to reporters outside the courthouse, I dove across my couch for the remote and shut off the TV in my living room.

"Best defense his daddy can buy," I say to Jimmy Cunniff.

"Well," Jimmy says, "*almost* the best."

Then we put Rip into Jimmy's car and drive to Indian Wells Beach, where I plan to think about living and not dying, for a change.

It is an almost perfect autumn morning, the sun high in the sky. Jimmy keeps throwing a tennis ball for Rip to chase down.

"I keep forgetting to ask," Jimmy says. "How's Brigid doing, really?"

We've decided to walk all the way to Atlantic Avenue Beach. It's that kind of morning, and there's nowhere else we need to be except here, and nowhere else we want to be.

"They tell me at the Meier Clinic that they are, quote, guardedly optimistic, end quote," I say. "That would be wildly optimistic anywhere else."

I take a turn throwing the ball, mostly to show Jimmy I still have the arm, after everything.

"But," I add, "they plan to keep her there for a couple more weeks, at least."

"Which keeps her from rushing back into Rob Jacobson's arms for a couple more weeks," Jimmy says.

"She will do that when she does come back over my extremely healthy body," I say.

"Have you talked to him yet?" Jimmy asks.

"He keeps trying," I say. "And I keep *not* taking his calls."

"Has he tried to stop by?"

I smile at Jimmy. "He's not an idiot. He knows I'm still armed."

We stop now and stare out at the water, calm on this

morning and beautiful and endless. Rip plops down, panting, in the sand.

"You got any immediate plans," Jimmy asks, "other than dinner with your boyfriend tonight?"

"A lot of nothing," I say, "followed by more nothing."

"I hate to point this out," he says, "but doing nothing has never been one of your strong suits."

He is wearing his Yankees cap, just without the camera sewn into the front today.

"Even an old dog can learn new tricks," I say. "Isn't that right, Rip?"

We start walking back to the car.

"There is *one* thing I'm thinking about doing," I tell Jimmy. "If you can keep a secret."

"Always."

"I might just up and ask Ben to marry me," I say.

"For real?"

We've stopped again before heading up to the parking lot.

"I'm not there yet," I tell him. "But feel like I might be getting there."

Jimmy puts his arms around me and pulls me tight to him.

"Can I be maid of honor?" he asks.

When we get back to the house, Jimmy comes in for one fast cup of coffee before he heads back home.

I take my own coffee mug with me out to the back patio and find myself standing in front of my hummingbird feeder, already thinking about buying a new one for next spring, maybe one with a camera attached to it.

I am still putting sugar water in it, even though the birds are gone until then.

I start to turn and head back into the house when I see a flash of color out of the corner of my eye.

The lone hummingbird is back.

There is no way she should still be here, not at this time of year. She shouldn't have still been here the last time I saw her.

And yet here she is.

But she's not here to drink.

She just hovers there, looking straight at me.

Almost as if making sure I'm the one who's still here.

Then she flies off.

ONE HUNDRED TWENTY-THREE

ROB JACOBSON IS STANDING at one of the main bedroom's floor-to-ceiling windows, back in his own house in Sagaponack, looking out across the backyard and the dunes to the Atlantic.

As always, Rob Jacobson doesn't so much appreciate the view as he does that it is *his* view.

"Well," Claire Jacobson says from the bed behind him, "that was even rougher than I remember, mister. You even left some bruises."

"Not the first time," he says without turning, seeing the waves begin to build in the distance. "And they've always healed in the past, haven't they?"

"Come back to bed," she says. "Says a glutton for punishment."

"Not what I was hearing a few minutes ago."

He continues to stare at the water. Jane was always telling him how the ocean filled her with a sense of peace. But Rob just doesn't get it.

"Well," she says, "you won again, didn't you?"

"I always win," he says.

He opens the French doors to let in the breeze.

It's back to being all mine, he gloats.

Knowing him, he's already thinking about going out

tonight, hitting a couple of the kids' bars, having some fun. Meeting someone new.

"Eric still won't see me," she says. "I keep trying. But that lawyer you hired, McGoey, keeps giving me the same message."

"To leave him alone," Rob Jacobson says. "The way he says we always did. When I did get in to see him at the jail, for about a minute, I thought he might want to talk. But only long enough so he could tell me to fuck off to my face."

"But you're going to pay McGoey's fee anyway?" Claire asks.

"What can I tell you, honey," he says. "I know from experience what it's like to hate your father that much."

He turns finally and walks back toward the bed. She has covered herself up with a sheet. She really is very attractive, and still has some body on her, for a woman her age.

"I still hate you sometimes," she says. "But I have missed you."

"Have you?" he says. "Because my friend Sonny Blum shared some photos with me the other day."

He reaches over and picks up his phone from where he left it, on the nightstand on what he still considers his side of the goddamn bed.

He scrolls through photos until he comes to the ones of Claire in bed with Robby Sassoon.

Rob Jacobson hands his wife the phone.

"How *much* did you miss me, exactly?" he asks.

Before she can even reply, he slaps her hard across her face, knocking her to the side and nearly all the way out of the bed.

Claire Jacobson screams then, right before he slaps her again, harder this time.

Then he is climbing on top of her.

But she fights him as he tries to pin her arms, and manages to roll out from underneath him, pushing herself back toward the ornate headboard that has made it all the way out here from the town house in Manhattan.

He crawls toward her, but not quickly enough, because then Claire Jacobson is reaching under her pillow and coming up with the gun she keeps there.

He laughs, even with the gun pointed straight at him.

"Really?" he says, but stopping where he is. "Who the fuck in this family *isn't* a shooter?"

"Really," Claire says, and then shoots him in the middle of the chest, and then again, and keeps firing until the gun is empty and the shock is gone from his face.

And the smirk, at long last.

She calmly watches as his body slides off the bed to the floor.

Then she is the one reaching for her own phone, on the nightstand closest to her.

The number is on speed dial.

Jane Smith picks up on the first ring.

"I just killed Rob," Claire Jacobson says. "I'm going to need a lawyer."

ABOUT THE AUTHORS

JAMES PATTERSON is one of the best-known and biggest-selling writers of all time. Among his creations are some of the world's most popular series, including Alex Cross, the Women's Murder Club, Michael Bennett and the Private novels. He has written many other number one bestsellers including collaborations with President Bill Clinton, Dolly Parton and Michael Crichton, stand-alone thrillers and non-fiction. James has donated millions in grants to independent bookshops and has been the most borrowed adult author in UK libraries for the past fourteen years in a row. He lives in Florida with his family.

MIKE LUPICA has been inducted into the National Sports Media Hall of Fame. He is an award-winning columnist for the *New York Daily News* and has written seventeen *New York Times* bestsellers.

Also By James Patterson

ALEX CROSS NOVELS

Along Came a Spider • Kiss the Girls • Jack and Jill • Cat and Mouse • Pop Goes the Weasel • Roses are Red • Violets are Blue • Four Blind Mice • The Big Bad Wolf • London Bridges • Mary, Mary • Cross • Double Cross • Cross Country • Alex Cross's Trial (*with Richard DiLallo*) • I, Alex Cross • Cross Fire • Kill Alex Cross • Merry Christmas, Alex Cross • Alex Cross, Run • Cross My Heart • Hope to Die • Cross Justice • Cross the Line • The People vs. Alex Cross • Target: Alex Cross • Criss Cross • Deadly Cross • Fear No Evil • Triple Cross • Alex Cross Must Die • The House of Cross

THE WOMEN'S MURDER CLUB SERIES

1st to Die (*with Andrew Gross*) • 2nd Chance (*with Andrew Gross*) • 3rd Degree (*with Andrew Gross*) • 4th of July (*with Maxine Paetro*) • The 5th Horseman (*with Maxine Paetro*) • The 6th Target (*with Maxine Paetro*) • 7th Heaven (*with Maxine Paetro*) • 8th Confession (*with Maxine Paetro*) • 9th Judgement (*with Maxine Paetro*) • 10th Anniversary (*with Maxine Paetro*) • 11th Hour (*with Maxine Paetro*) • 12th of Never (*with Maxine Paetro*) • Unlucky 13 (*with Maxine Paetro*) • 14th Deadly Sin (*with Maxine Paetro*) • 15th Affair (*with Maxine Paetro*) • 16th Seduction (*with Maxine Paetro*) • 17th Suspect (*with Maxine Paetro*) • 18th Abduction (*with Maxine Paetro*) • 19th Christmas (*with Maxine Paetro*) • 20th Victim (*with Maxine Paetro*) • 21st Birthday (*with Maxine Paetro*) • 22 Seconds (*with Maxine Paetro*) • 23rd Midnight (*with Maxine Paetro*) • The 24th Hour (*with Maxine Paetro*) • 25 Alive (*with Maxine Paetro*)

DETECTIVE MICHAEL BENNETT SERIES

Step on a Crack (*with Michael Ledwidge*) • Run for Your Life (*with Michael Ledwidge*) • Worst Case (*with Michael Ledwidge*) • Tick Tock (*with Michael Ledwidge*) • I, Michael Bennett (*with Michael Ledwidge*) • Gone (*with Michael Ledwidge*) • Burn (*with Michael Ledwidge*) • Alert (*with Michael Ledwidge*) • Bullseye (*with Michael Ledwidge*) • Haunted (*with James O. Born*) • Ambush (*with James O. Born*) • Blindside (*with James O. Born*) • The Russian (*with James O. Born*) • Shattered (*with James O. Born*) • Obsessed (*with James O. Born*) • Crosshairs (*with James O. Born*) • Paranoia (*with James O. Born*)

PRIVATE NOVELS

Private (*with Maxine Paetro*) • Private London (*with Mark Pearson*) • Private Games (*with Mark Sullivan*) • Private: No. 1 Suspect (*with Maxine*

Paetro) • Private Berlin (*with Mark Sullivan*) • Private Down Under
(*with Michael White*) • Private L.A. (*with Mark Sullivan*) • Private India
(*with Ashwin Sanghi*) • Private Vegas (*with Maxine Paetro*) • Private Sydney
(*with Kathryn Fox*) • Private Paris (*with Mark Sullivan*) • The Games (*with
Mark Sullivan*) • Private Delhi (*with Ashwin Sanghi*) • Private Princess
(*with Rees Jones*) • Private Moscow (*with Adam Hamdy*) • Private Rogue
(*with Adam Hamdy*) • Private Beijing (*with Adam Hamdy*) • Private
Rome (*with Adam Hamdy*) • Private Monaco (*with Adam Hamdy*)

NYPD RED SERIES

NYPD Red (*with Marshall Karp*) • NYPD Red 2 (*with Marshall
Karp*) • NYPD Red 3 (*with Marshall Karp*) • NYPD Red 4 (*with
Marshall Karp*) • NYPD Red 5 (*with Marshall Karp*) • NYPD
Red 6 (*with Marshall Karp*)

DETECTIVE HARRIET BLUE SERIES

Never Never (*with Candice Fox*) • Fifty Fifty (*with Candice
Fox*) • Liar Liar (*with Candice Fox*) • Hush Hush (*with Candice Fox*)

INSTINCT SERIES

Instinct (*with Howard Roughan, previously published as
Murder Games*) • Killer Instinct (*with Howard Roughan*) • Steal
(*with Howard Roughan*)

THE BLACK BOOK SERIES

The Black Book (*with David Ellis*) • The Red Book (*with
David Ellis*) • Escape (*with David Ellis*)

TEXAS RANGER SERIES

Texas Ranger (*with Andrew Bourelle*) • Texas Outlaw (*with
Andrew Bourelle*) • The Texas Murders (*with Andrew Bourelle*)

STAND-ALONE THRILLERS

The Thomas Berryman Number • Hide and Seek • Black Market • The
Midnight Club • Honeymoon (*with Howard Roughan*) • Sail (*with
Howard Roughan*) • Swimsuit (*with Maxine Paetro*) • Don't Blink (*with
Howard Roughan*) • Postcard Killers (*with Liza Marklund*) • Toys
(*with Neil McMahon*) • Now You See Her (*with Michael Ledwidge*) • Kill
Me If You Can (*with Marshall Karp*) • Guilty Wives (*with David Ellis*) • Zoo
(*with Michael Ledwidge*) • Second Honeymoon (*with Howard*

Roughan) • Mistress (*with David Ellis*) • Invisible (*with David Ellis*) • Truth or Die (*with Howard Roughan*) • Murder House (*with David Ellis*) • The Store (*with Richard DiLallo*) • The President is Missing (*with Bill Clinton*) • Revenge (*with Andrew Holmes*) • Juror No. 3 (*with Nancy Allen*) • The First Lady (*with Brendan DuBois*) • The Chef (*with Max DiLallo*) • Out of Sight (*with Brendan DuBois*) • Unsolved (*with David Ellis*) • The Inn (*with Candice Fox*) • Lost (*with James O. Born*) • The Summer House (*with Brendan DuBois*) • 1st Case (*with Chris Tebbetts*) • Cajun Justice (*with Tucker Axum*) • The Midwife Murders (*with Richard DiLallo*) • The Coast-to-Coast Murders (*with J.D. Barker*) • Three Women Disappear (*with Shan Serafin*) • The President's Daughter (*with Bill Clinton*) • The Shadow (*with Brian Sitts*) • The Noise (*with J.D. Barker*) • 2 Sisters Detective Agency (*with Candice Fox*) • Jailhouse Lawyer (*with Nancy Allen*) • The Horsewoman (*with Mike Lupica*) • Run Rose Run (*with Dolly Parton*) • Death of the Black Widow (*with J.D. Barker*) • The Ninth Month (*with Richard DiLallo*) • The Girl in the Castle (*with Emily Raymond*) • Blowback (*with Brendan DuBois*) • The Twelve Topsy-Turvy, Very Messy Days of Christmas (*with Tad Safran*) • The Perfect Assassin (*with Brian Sitts*) • House of Wolves (*with Mike Lupica*) • Countdown (*with Brendan DuBois*) • Cross Down (*with Brendan DuBois*) • Circle of Death (*with Brian Sitts*) • Lion & Lamb (with *Duane Swierczynski*) • 12 Months to Live (*with Mike Lupica*) • Holmes, Margaret and Poe (*with Brian Sitts*) • The No. 1 Lawyer (*with Nancy Allen*) • Eruption (*with Michael Crichton*) • The Murder Inn (*with Candice Fox*) • Confessions of the Dead (*with J.D. Barker*) • 8 Months Left (*with Mike Lupica*) • Lies He Told Me (*with David Ellis*) • Murder Island (*with Brian Sitts*) • Raised By Wolves (*with Emily Raymond*) • Holmes is Missing (*with Brian Sitts*) • 2 Sisters Murder Investigations (*with Candice Fox*)

NON-FICTION

Torn Apart (*with Hal and Cory Friedman*) • The Murder of King Tut (*with Martin Dugard*) • All-American Murder (*with Alex Abramovich and Mike Harvkey*) • The Kennedy Curse (*with Cynthia Fagen*) • The Last Days of John Lennon (*with Casey Sherman and Dave Wedge*) • Walk in My Combat Boots (*with Matt Eversmann and Chris Mooney*) • ER Nurses (*with Matt Eversmann*) • James Patterson by James Patterson: The Stories of My Life • Diana, William and Harry (*with Chris Mooney*) • American Cops (*with Matt Eversmann*) • What Really Happens in Vegas (*with Mark Seal*) • The Secret Lives of Booksellers and Librarians (*with Matt Eversmann*) • Tiger, Tiger • American Heroes (*with Matt Eversmann*)

MURDER IS FOREVER TRUE CRIME

Murder, Interrupted (*with Alex Abramovich and Christopher Charles*) • Home Sweet Murder (*with Andrew Bourelle and Scott Slaven*) • Murder Beyond the Grave (*with Andrew*

Bourelle and Christopher Charles) • Murder Thy Neighbour *(with Andrew Bourelle and Max DiLallo)* • Murder of Innocence *(with Max DiLallo and Andrew Bourelle)* • Till Murder Do Us Part *(with Andrew Bourelle and Max DiLallo)*

COLLECTIONS

Triple Threat *(with Max DiLallo and Andrew Bourelle)* • Kill or Be Killed *(with Maxine Paetro, Rees Jones, Shan Serafin and Emily Raymond)* • The Moores are Missing *(with Loren D. Estleman, Sam Hawken and Ed Chatterton)* • The Family Lawyer *(with Robert Rotstein, Christopher Charles and Rachel Howzell Hall)* • Murder in Paradise *(with Doug Allyn, Connor Hyde and Duane Swierczynski)* • The House Next Door *(with Susan DiLallo, Max DiLallo and Brendan DuBois)* • 13-Minute Murder *(with Shan Serafin, Christopher Farnsworth and Scott Slaven)* • The River Murders *(with James O. Born)* • The Palm Beach Murders *(with James O. Born, Duane Swierczynski and Tim Arnold)* • Paris Detective • 3 Days to Live • 23 ½ Lies *(with Maxine Paetro)*

For more information about James Patterson's novels, visit www.penguin.co.uk.